The Many and The Few

Book 1

ROGUE

By
Richard Green

ROGUE

First Edition: March 2022 (self-published)

Edited by Richard Green and Tara Green

Cover Design by Bruno Martins

ISBN 978-1-915429-00-1

http://www.themanyandthefew.website
http://www.richardgreen.me

For my wife, Tara.

Preface

I have always enjoyed Science Fiction. As a genre, it isn't constrained to any particular flavour of theatre, so you can have sub-genres, if you will, such as romantic, comedy, dramatic, action, etc. As an orthogonal genre to these, it is not unique, but I delight in how it also allows us to ask the age-old question "what-if" in a very particular way.

In that, there is a special place for what is called Hard Science Fiction, which I have endeavoured to write here. This type of fiction requires the reader to accept nothing at face value but challenges them to interpret the story as plausible. By that, I mean everything in the story has to obey the known laws of physics; measurements and calculations should be correct; genuine people and historical events must be described accurately, with period-based details, and placed carefully in their proper time. The author invites the reader to be sceptical, ask if this could really happen, and enjoy the illusion for its realism. If mistakes are made or imagined things are better modelled in the future, it is hoped that industrious readers can forgive the author and help make corrections. We authors try our best, but even the most celebrated have graciously accepted feedback, such as Larry Niven, who published a correction to his excellent novel Ringworld in his sequel The Ringworld Engineers and attributed those who pointed out that the topsoil would have slid into the seas after a few thousand years.

In starting my story a couple of centuries in the future, I can take either an existing technology and extend it or a speculative technology (such as Lerner Pulse Fusion reactors) and assume that it has been made to work. I can also project likely outcomes to social, economic and climatic concerns. Predictions being what they are, chaos theory shows that systems can fall apart with minor initial variations, hence the popular post-apocalyptic style; however, chaos theory also indicates that order can spring spontaneously out of chaos. I like to think that this, and human ingenuity and persistence, can produce as positive a future as we might say we have had all along.

Of course, this is fiction, and at some point, we often have to invent something a little more 'out there.' This is where we can get really playful, and often this is the key to the main plot: the key what-if. Being held in suspense, such as when a professor makes a claim and asks the student to bear with him whilst he gets there with the maths, is a joy of suspended disbelief - anticipation that promises to delight and enthral. To be left with a sense of engagement, where you continue to wonder of the possibilities of how this all could be true, is the real goal. This, I feel, is the essence of a good, Hard SciFi story. I hope I have come close and that you enjoy reading this as much as I did writing it.

CHAPTER ONE

2225 CE, Earth-L4, Erebus

Orianna was late, but she would not look back on this crucial day and worry about her punctuality. Instead, throughout her long life, she would mourn the day she and her friends died, and yet it would burn brightly in her mind as the day she was born again.

The street was full of people. Lights high up in the rough ceiling dimmed noticeably, and the hue had warmed. Dusk was being simulated. Unfortunately, this also meant people were both hurried and more careless. Nevertheless, Orianna tried to force her small frame through the throng.

"Yo! Flo! Wait up!" Orianna called to the tall Nubian girl she could see in the distance when a gap opened up enough for her to spy Flo's head towering above everyone.

Flo poked an elbow into the man next to her and then pointed back at Orianna, "Yo! There's Spare," she yelled back, passing a nod around her towards the small girl, occasionally jumping to be seen.

"You know you should probably call her by her real name, now," Captain Laskin said, her voice booming with a deep Russian accent. She had the robust frame of a bodybuilder and was keen to use it at every opportunity, like here: thrusting herself forwards to cut a clear path ahead. "Make way!"

As Orianna came into view, somehow squeezing through a narrow gap, Laskin grabbed her by the collar and retrieved her.

"Nearly late, little one," she grunted, with a slight smirk in the corner of her mouth, just for Orianna, who didn't have time to respond as Laskin's huge hand brought her bodily into the middle of their group.

"Flo just tried to put a beret on her afro," spat a thirty-something elfish man that she knew as Book, but whose real name was Technician Scott Whealand - an excellent example of why crewmates were given shorter names. "Bloody hilarious!" he bellowed, his cheeks flushed with so much laughter.

Flo, whose name really was Flo, repeated the action for Orianna's benefit. She grabbed the lime green beret from the stall and placed it carefully on top of her cut-to-fit-a-helmet afro ball. Several exaggerated fashion model poses followed, ending with her bursting into laughter and throwing the beret back onto the stall. Her skin was richly deep brown, almost black, and a healthy sheen; her infectious laugh was as big as the mouth of brilliant white teeth from where it came.

"Hey," Orianna repeated to each of them, making eye contact with everyone in her Tug crew. Flo rubbed Orianna's black inverted bob, cut like a school kid, excited as she was to see her. Orianna smiled back at her.

At once, a short man in a white vest top stepped up. Vik was a Ukrainian who worked out a lot and had tattoos across his toned muscles. He did not smile, but he had a twinkle in his eye in response to Orianna's greeting. "Don't worry, Spare, you haven't missed mud work today. We had to swap shifts with the 49ers. We go out after," he said, his incongruous deep, sonorous voice cut under the general noise of the street. He gently touched his palm to her pale cheek, as if to a sister, before looking her up and down, making her conscious that she was the only one with the yellow tint of a survival suit - in contrast, they all had on their work clothes. "You did not know?"

"Vik has again selected his white vest for mud work; or is that his going-out white vest?" chortled Acres, a funny man who gained the least flattering name after a severe injury forced him to be bedridden for months: he never quite got around to losing his inevitable weight gain. Nevertheless, he accepted the moniker because he was the joker of the pack and liked that it then gave him carte blanche to fire his capable wit around.

Vik looked at him dead-pan - his default expression - and pointed out that Acres could wear the vest as a bra since it would never stretch over his belly, and it might give some support to his man-boobs. Everyone laughed, including Acres, who retorted, "Next time, wash it with my red socks, and I can get it in pink, eh?"

Vik ignored him and led the way down the street, away from the busy section. It wasn't long before they had the street's entire four-metre width to themselves, having left the main throughways and stalls behind.

Captain Laskin, walking beside Orianna, said quietly to her, "We have a novice starting up today. Gives you a chance to practice more of the things you miss out on when you are not with us."

Orianna looked sceptical. "For real? Is that a permie?" she croaked, suddenly struck with the likelihood that she might have to temp with another crew sooner rather than later.

Laskin shrugged slowly. "Had to happen at some point, ya?" Her tone was neutral, but her eyes showed kindness. "You are needed to fill in, here and there - such a thing is vital. Many do this here. Without you, we would have been benched full-time, useless for the last four months. Better to be getting out there for half the time than no time at all."

"I wish I could be here full time," Orianna sighed earnestly.

"Ya. We all have to muck in, and with the shift change, so do you today!" Laskin smiled and pushed Orianna into a doorway. "Don't worry, we only do half-shift here, and then we get to take out the newbie."

Orianna found herself leading the motley crew into a pitch-black room. Lights flicked on automatically to greet them. The others spread out and quickly began to disrobe.

Flo noticed her reticence and came over. "You've never done this before, hun?" she asked soothingly, touching her delicately on the shoulder.

"No secrets in here," bellowed Acres as he dropped his pants to reveal his oversized over-pale backside.

"How did she manage to never do this?" Vik asked loudly, pulling the vest off with one hand in a single over-shoulder move, his party piece. His impressive pecs independently pulsed as if enjoying their sudden freedom.

It was true. Orianna hadn't done this before. She should have known about the shift change, but then so much down here got done ad hoc. There was every chance that no report existed for her to have missed. Little did she know that this systemic lack of attendance to detail amongst the crew and station commanders would soon work to her advantage.

Unusually, the crew went a little quiet. Orianna sensed that they were wondering how she would react to the prospect of getting naked with the rest of them, perhaps continuing to wonder how a "spare" could have never managed to do this duty. She considered how to play it. She could continue with the coy, innocent and bashful friend-to-all that they had gotten to know so well, or she could surprise them with a part of this personality they hadn't seen yet.

"Don't worry about me," she snapped, wriggling out of her survival suit hastily, "I have seven brothers." She made a mental note to remember this invented fact about herself.

The others began to laugh and joke again.

Before long, they were all naked and wandering carelessly into the next chamber, where they were thoroughly sanitised with a low-water shower and UV lamps. Orianna winced at the UV lamp. Why was it so bright? Fortunately, it was over quickly because her skin itched badly under those lights.

They moved on through a final doorway into a vast and brilliantly lit chamber, its ceiling was the same four-metre height, but that looked out of proportion now. Regularly, there were columns where the rock had been left behind after excavation to support the rock above.

Rows and rows of trenches dug into the rock overflowed with brown dirt. Irrigation systems ran over them on metre-high stands, and a few of them were currently spraying. The air was warm and a little humid. Orianna could feel a good flow passing across the rows, especially when she wandered close to those currently being sprayed and got her calves wet. She giggled at the sensation and moved away.

"Ok, people, first, we have planting," stated Captain Laskin upon reading the rota sheet by the door. "Everyone pair up and grab a crate! Spare, I mean, Orsola, ya? You are with me."

"Spare has a name, at last!" Acres jested.

"And that is the last we will hear her called 'Spare', ok?" insisted Laskin, looking around for compliance from the rest. Grunts and nods of agreement confirmed her authority. "Orsola is a beautiful name. I believe it means small she-bear, ya?"

"Ahhh, my little she-bear, finally," Flo cooed and embraced Orianna's face with both hands. Only then did Orianna realise that Flo's hands were wet - wet with mud, but it was too late: Flo continued rubbing the wet clay-like dirt all around her cheeks, just enough to be funny. "I like this more healthy colour."

They both laughed.

Flo recoiled as Orianna scraped the larger clumps off her face and flung them at her.

Laskin interrupted, cutting between them. "The quicker this done, the faster we get outside."

She meant in their Tug by 'outside', where they belonged and preferred to be. This mud work was critical to establishing a healthy life in a habitat, and so everyone did their part on rotation: it was everyone's second job - almost everyone.

What Orianna lacked in personal mud work experience was balanced with a complete understanding of how the agro-unit was run - she had designed their processes, after all.

Fresh food and oxygen were vital to the whole population, but the mud workers received more subtle benefits: their nudity gave them a daily dose of vitamin D from the lighting; the soil, which got under their fingernails, would be consumed when eating fresh food by hand. That soil contained vitamin B12, critical complex hydrocarbons and healthy bacteria: so good for their gut. Fresh organic food was their reward at the end of their shift, which they were instructed to eat before they left, and washing without soap was encouraged to keep those dirty nails.

"The soil is improving," Orianna commented.

"Ah, so you do know mud work, Orsola," Laskin replied, heaving a crate down the path between their row and the next. "It is strangely... how you say? Clay?"

Orianna nodded. "Very little is brought here. This is a nutrient-rich compost made from recycled food scraps, packaging, any organic material really, and mixed with all the right minerals, which we have plenty of from mining. As I always say, it is not just about growing food; it is about growing the soil."

Orianna was opposite and started pushing her dibber into

the surface. Rotating the dibber handle in a wide circle enlarged the conical hole. She withdrew it and then made a dozen more like it.

"Ok, good," Laskin nodded. "Here."

Kneeling, Orianna accepted the first cabbage plug that Laskin passed to her and popped it casually into the hole. One quick touch of her fingers secured it in without squashing it too much.

"I've worked at the composting depot," she lied, trying to reclaim her status as an ordinary person. "They had a lot to say about it."

"Oh really?" Laskin prompted. Any conversation was good during this repetitive task. It was good, calming work that gets you out of a chair, but listening to someone talk did shorten the hours. "What did they say?"

"They believed that agro was much simpler than compost-science. Growing is straight forward but making soil was complex."

"They called it science?" Laskin grunted.

"Yes, they told me about the bacterial action that works first and generates a lot of heat, as much as sixty or seventy degrees Celsius, but to make that work, you need the right mix of 'green' and 'brown' materials."

"Like leaves and stalks?"

"Sort of. 'Greens' are rich in nitrogen and proteins, and 'browns' are carbon and carbohydrate-rich. So, it isn't so much about their actual colour because, surprisingly, coffee grounds, for example, are green."

Laskin continued to pass her the cabbage plugs, listening to her go on about composting.

Orianna talked about balancing oxygen levels; getting the proper sizes of debris, avoiding the need to flip a pile too often; getting an optimum pile size to complete in just 18 days; allowing mycorrhizal fungi to spread and work their magic. After twenty minutes of that, Laskin would never question the science of composting again.

As they finished a long row, Laskin said, "You must have worked there for longer than with us. You know this better than you know how to work my Tug." Then, without waiting further, she walked off to collect another stack of crates. They were working faster than the others because Laskin would carry many boxes in one go, and she really wasn't one for wasting time.

Watching Laskin stride off, Orianna felt a wave of concern pass over her. It wasn't so much that she had deviated a little from the established personality of Orsola, the spare, by adding a little more intelligence, but rather, it was knowing that a newbie was about to be onboarded, and all this would end soon.

She dropped to her knees in a funk. She would miss her friends. The holes her knees started to make in the next row received a fair few tears until she wiped her eyes on the back of her hand, seeing Laskin returning.

They didn't talk as much for the rest of the time. Laskin was not much of a conversationalist. She was happy to be quiet when Orianna was. It was her way: not to pry unless invited. Orianna's lowered mood soon got a boost when they finished and went to get ready for outside.

Eventually, the whole crew joined Orianna and Laskin, enjoying fresh food from the ground. It was so tasty and juicy. They could feel how good it was as they ate it, as if it was already benefiting their bodies.

Everyone left hurriedly to change clothes before reporting to the Tug. Orianna, on the other hand, was already in the correct clothes, which conveniently gave her the extra time to fetch the newbie, her replacement.

Orianna's cuff console led her to Pall Mall, so-called because it resembled a shopping mall and because its opulence matched its namesake: the famous, grand road in London. It consisted of three levels of streets, all intersecting in a cavernous concourse, with stepped balconies on the first and second floors. Generous seating and grass patches filled the space around a dozen trees, reaching the full three-story height.

Since simulated dusk had long passed, the volume was illuminated with representative street and bulkhead lamps. Blue decorative lights were scattered throughout the upper branches of the trees. Runner lights illuminated the paths, so people did not trip on the raised block edging. It was essentially an extra-large version of the plazas found at many major street intersections, some of which were also multi-level.

She went to a specific arrangement of curved seats in a secluded hollow behind a large bush. Three people were sitting there. Two were middle-aged, so she went straight up to the third.

A shy-looking sprite of a girl sat cross-legged on a patch of grass. She looked no more than seventeen and was wearing a survival suit with her visor down, watching something.

"Hi," Orianna said, getting her attention.

The girl flipped up her visor suddenly, smiled innocently and copied the greeting, "Hi." She jumped to her feet. "Christine Jenkins, reporting for duty," she yelped, army-style with an accompanying comic salute followed by a cheeky grin.

Orianna put her hands on her hips and cocked them slightly to one side. "Oh, you'll be perfect," she responded, thrusting out a hand to be met by the girl's dropping salute hand for an enthusiastic handshake. "Ok, newbie, let's go!"

The girl grabbed a small bag and joined Orianna to stroll over to the rise. "Get used to the name, Newbie. You are going to be joining a colourful crew who don't like long names," Orianna advised. "Have you just arrived?" she asked, puzzled.

"Yup, a couple of hours out of hibernation. Woke up and recovered until the Tug came to ferry us over. I've only been here for twenty minutes or so. So, elevator out of action?"

"Er, no, it works fine. There's a lot to learn about this habitat - first of its kind, you know. For a start, people are encouraged to be healthy and fit. When they hollowed out all these areas, they built a lot of corridors, or streets as we call them, flat to the centripetal 1G we feel at this depth. There are sloped corridors or ramps, which we call rises; sometimes they spiral, like this one. That way, we get plenty of exercise, and the habitat has fewer moving parts to fix. The rises, for example, were not constructed - they were just what was left after excavation. The columns are the same."

"Oh wow, I get it. Stuff is a luxury out here, so turn it into an advantage?"

"Yes, you will find that a recurrent theme."

They followed the spiral around the entire circumference of the cavern, up all three levels, even continuing into the roof where it became enclosed like a street.

"How far up does it go?" Newbie asked, just as her question was answered at the fifth level.

"There are five main levels where we spend a lot of our time. It is where we get mostly a regular 1G. Try to remember these are levels 1 up to 5. Some areas are at sub 1 to sub 3, but the gravity is starting to get tiring down there. They are not used much, and many aren't finished smooth like the walls and floors here."

"Ok, cool."

"Did you come here alone?" Orianna asked, sounding concerned. "You seem very young."

"Yup, all alone. I am eighteen. I know I look younger. My family doesn't have much, but I won a scholarship, so they sent me here to expand my horizons... and retire by thirty, was what my dad said. I do miss them, but they are right. I wasn't being stimulated back there."

"Where was there?"

"Kipplington, Kent. It's in the British Isles."

"I'm from Kent," sparked Orianna, genuinely connecting with her. "My mother moved to Kent to look after my grandparents during their final days." This was actually true. Orianna was a little surprised at how she admitted that. "I'm Orsola," she said, returning to her lies.

Newbie smiled at her the way socially awkward teenagers do when confronted by adults being open. However, she seemed pretty lively and confident despite her apparent geekiness.

"What do you specialise in?" Orianna asked.

Newbie pondered. "Fusion is my main interest, and xenogeology is my day job." She laughed again. Doubtless, she was no shrinking violet of a brain.

"Did you read up on Erebus before you came?"

Orianna stopped before a door at the top of the rise and summoned a lift.

"Sure, but nothing prepares you for the experience," Newbie enthused, her eyes wide in anticipation.

"Do you have any questions?"

"Well, the guide said we are at the L4 Lagrange point, so I looked up the Lagrange points, and it said L4 was sixty degrees ahead of Earth and L5 was sixty degrees behind, on the same orbit. Now L1, L2 and L3 make sense: they sit on the straight line joining the Earth and the Sun, at the balance points between their respective gravities and the orbital speed, but they aren't stable: drift off those Lagrange points, and you keep going. The gravitation contours there are saddle-shaped, after all. So I don't understand why L4 and L5 were stable; I mean, their contours are like the top of a hill or ridge. How come there are asteroids at L4 and L5? Why don't they catch up with the Earth?"

Orianna nodded. "Yes, it isn't intuitive that one. Erebus isn't really stationary. They are called Trojan asteroids, and they wander on spiralling paths around their L4 or L5 Lagrange point. It is the Coriolis effect that keeps them close by. What is more interesting is that most asteroids, the ones you find in the belt or as Trojans of Jupiter, are more like loose gravel - that makes them easier to mine, but you cannot live inside loose gravel."

"So Erebus is special because it is a solid lump of rock?"

"Exactly. Probably due to the moon's formation, when a collision of two proto-planets became the Earth and the Moon. Asteroids like Erebus are the leftovers from that."

"Ok. Cool. Are we going up to the dock?" Newbie noticed where they were heading.

The door opened, and a large circular elevator compartment greeted them. It was unoccupied. Eight seats wrapped around the walls looking like they were borrowed from a terrestrial rollercoaster, with large U-shaped padded bars poised to clamp down on them.

"Sure. We prefer to keep our Tugs there," Orianna joked sarcastically, marching in and taking a seat. Newbie jumped into a seat next to her, and their bars came down slowly to hold them synchronised with the closing door. "Laskin wanted to take you out as soon as you arrived. So you can settle into your digs when we get back."

Newbie noticed there was a window. Lights passed slowly at first, then she felt a terrible push to the side as the pace increased. "Oh, this is going up straight? That's not ideal, you know that?"

"Every time. Consider it a learned lesson, if you want. The truth is that this is one of the first shafts cut out of the asteroid, near as we are to the port axis. They weren't thinking about how uncomfortable it would be to have an elevator rushing straight up and down. This is actually the only one. Every other ascending method is now made as a spiral, which, as you seem to already understand, makes for a better ride when transitioning to different levels of a spinning habitat."

As they spoke, the darkness beyond the window with its pulsing lights suddenly gave way to a view of a vast chamber beyond. Newbie stretched to see out. Huge metal frames filled her view like the skeletons of buildings. Now she could see the curvature as they approached the axis. The structure thinned out, and lots of Tugs and other small vessels could be seen nestled all around the cylindrical space.

The elevator slowed; they were released as it stopped, level with the nearest Tugs. Newbie shot out of her seat when she tried to stand.

"Gently, Newbie!" Orianna cried, grabbing her ankle and using her dead weight to slow her. Orianna clicked her own heels, and her magnetic boots clamped her to the floor just in time to anchor them both. She reached for Newbie's other ankle and brought her boots together hard, activating them. Newbie began to descend by herself with Orianna's own recoil, but Orianna helped to pull her down and steady her until she landed and stuck there. "Ok?"

"Phew, thanks," she gulped, blushing, both embarrassed and shocked at the near-violent collision with the ceiling.

"Slowly now, the boots react to your muscle nerves during regular walking sequences. All the decking here is steel. Just check your footing and do everything a tad slower because effective gravity here is a sub-Lunar, miniG. Human strength at this gravity is a hazard - sudden movements like that could get you hurt."

Exiting the elevator, they made their way slowly to a distant hatch along the walkway, which was really just a pressurised tube suspended in the frames. A Tug could be seen arriving as it came into view above them. Newbie sidled over to the window to get a better angle to look up at it, gliding in along the axis, slowly spinning as it did so. It had a strangely blocky, almost cubic appearance.

Newbie understood that everything was spinning together, but you couldn't see it. Now that the Tug had drifted in through the Port and along the centre axis, she experienced the startling realisation that as the Tug arrived next to the flat end of the vast cylinder, it was utterly stationary in space. Everything else, including her, was spinning around it.

"We are rotating at what twice a minute?" Newbie asked. "So Level 1 must be two hundred and seventy-odd metres down from the axis, am I right?"

"You did that in your head?"

Newbie nodded.

"No wonder you got a scholarship."

The floating Tug began to rotate faster and faster until it matched the habitat's rotation. In contrast, it looked to Newbie like the Tug had turned slower and slower until it just stopped. The illusion of a rotating frame of reference had been lost.

A platform rose up to marry to the bottom of the Tug where it was clear of protruding motor mounts. The Tug was drawn slowly down to their level. Newbie imagined the occupants would start to feel a slight downward pull as it descended. The end of its descent brought it parked at an airlock. She realised the dock was always busy, watching another Tug already reversing the same procedure to leave.

"We are going out, now?" she asked excitedly.

"No time like the present," Orianna quipped. "Our Tug is this way."

Newbie was becoming as comfortable as Orianna in miniG as they walked around to their Tug's airlock in the long pressurised corridors suspended between the frames, where Orianna accessed the controls. Eventually, the outer door responded to her commands and opened.

CHAPTER TWO
2223 CE, Lunar

The greatest living cosmologist didn't even have a degree, but nobody had cosmology degrees anymore. More interestingly, he was the most isolated human alive: an interesting fact he shared with his niece over comms, which was due to last only until the next low orbital vessel came near.

She abruptly changed the subject. "Uncle Max, when are you coming home? Over."

Her little voice boomed out of the speakers and echoed around the room, so he turned it down a little and brought the monitor closer to him over his desk. He was always keen to make the most of their chats. But, unfortunately, three or four times a week was all his sister, her mother, would allow.

Maddox Jefferies was heartened by his niece, implying that her home was his home too. "Oh, Moonpie, you know how much I miss you, but we have this, right? I really look forward to our chats. Over."

He waited patiently for a reply. There was always an awkwardness when doing that, he thought, like holding a smile for a photograph: something slightly unnatural that you never quite get used to. He hated it when people appeared as if they weren't paying attention in conference calls, distracted by something or plainly working on their computer. There was no excuse for poor etiquette even on remote calls, and he would never do that to her.

"Mommie says I have ten minutes, and then I have to do my homework," she said. Her gaze shifted noticeably. "Why don't you and Mommie get along? Over." Her voice was a little quieter, and she leaned into the camera.

He sat up suddenly and pushed back his dark hair, which was now unusually long. Isolated people, they say, should maintain a discipline of personal hygiene. He agreed with that but to cut his hair would mean washing his hair, and that would mean fixing the water pump in the shower, which was someway down his long list of things he had to do. He couldn't exactly call a plumber.

"Hey, we get along just fine. It's just that Mommie and I have different ideas about how I should live my life. We are very different people with different interests. We love each other very much, but it is usually better for everyone that I don't stay too long when I come to visit. That's all. You'll understand when you get older." Despite the short delay, he could see her head dropping slowly. "We, on the other hand, get to play with all this equipment, don't we? Over."

After a few seconds, he saw her head lift on the monitor, and a slight smile returned to her round face. "Science is our thing," she said as something often repeated. "I don't have half as much fun doing science at school as I do with you. Over."

"I thought you liked... What's her name? Miss Ingles? And your science buddy: Michelle? Last week, you blew up that beaker in chemistry, on purpose, I might add! That must have been fun. Over"

"Well, yeah, but I did get detention for that," she said, wincing momentarily. "They say I am a good girl, but I am 'not being challenged enough in science'." Her eyes went down, and then a smirk came, and the eyes rose just enough to gaze into the camera. "They blame you! Ha! Over."

"Cheeky, but true, I suppose." He pondered and fidgeted. "Perhaps we should be careful not to upset the educational sausage machine because you are not progressing at a manageably average pace. Don't tell your mother that I said that. Haha. When you start studying politics, you will be top of your class there too if you listen to me too much. Over."

He looked around him as if embarrassed, but there was nobody there. The room he was in, the myriad of corridors and other rooms at the Titov Crater Base were all abandoned. There was no one for three thousand kilometres. Difficult to get more isolated than that, even in the twenty-third century.

"Mommie says you are better at talking to kids. Over."

"That is because I still am one myself." He was beaming. "I bet she said that too, eh? Well, it is true. Most academics are really. We never stop playing with our toys and never stop learning new things." He wasn't bothered by this, and at 29 years old, he had fully embraced his baby-brother, Peter Pan, role in the family.

"You know, we got an 'A' on my Science Project, again? Over."

"The moon crater? Excellent. I wish I could have sent you some regolith. You did all the work on that. You got that 'A', and you deserved it. Well done. Oh, I have a surprise for you too, Moonpie."

"You finished it?" came her interruption as he was saying, "I finished… Yes. Over."

"Sorry. Is the velodrome finished? Er, Over."

"Not a problem, Moonpie. Nearly three seconds of lag is enough to make it a bit tricky. I still can't get the hang of it myself. Anyway, yes, do you wanna have a look?"

Without saying "Over," he stood up slowly and carried the camera selfie-style as he retreated across the room, bobbing up and down excessively despite his care. The one-sixth gravity made walking almost impossible, even with practice: the "Apollo bob" was the only way to get around.

Behind him, a large, heavy-looking door was closed. He fumbled behind himself for the controls whilst remaining in shot. The entry made beeping noises before a hiss and a clunk, and then it opened, sliding across.

Maddox pulled himself around the door, maintaining a selfie view and gave a "Tada. Over."

"Wowwwwww," she was already saying. "Show me! Over."

Maddox raised the camera to clamp it to the bulkhead, then moved down a slope into the room.

"As you can see, the render has taken very nicely." He said, allowing himself to fall to the ground clumsily but slowly - it was the easiest way down, really - so he could touch and stroke the grey surface. He was in the middle of a circular room about 10 metres across, shaped like a flattened ball. The roof was a dome, but it tucked in to join the floor in an unbroken curve. There were no windows and nothing around the sides - they couldn't be called walls because there was nothing to show where the dome ended, and the floor began. "The render-bot was still working fine. No trouble there. Do you remember the trouble I had with all those broken printer-bots? Nothing like that with them. So. What do you think? Over."

She beamed, lost for words for a moment. "Awesome," she finally squeaked. "I thought you said the dome would take another two weeks to print. Oh, do try it, Uncle Max. Over."

"I managed to get that third printer-bot working using a functional drive belt from an unlikely place: the bot with no legs? Remember that one? Turns out its internals were fully working. Ok, ok, I haven't had too much practice yet, so let's see how I get on."

Gingerly, Maddox bounced up onto his feet. "The hardest part is getting going," he chuckled as he steadied himself and made his way to the side using a wide stance in a hopping manner. "Pop quiz. What is the optimum gravity for a human to move around sensibly and keep our bones and muscles strong? What do we have here? And what do we hope to achieve with this room? Over."

She smiled at the easy test. "The Moon has a sixth 'G', which is not enough," she giggled as Maddox slowly sort of shuffled around the edge, his stance switching to one leg forwards and one backward, making him look like half a horse in a gallop. "Mars has a third G, and that is ok." Then she frowned for a moment. "Maybe you can get a half 'G'?" She thinks again and then says, "Over."

Maddox, by now, is picking up a little speed around the room along the curved edge, and his shuffles are becoming a more comfortable, gentle stride. He is laughing now, knowing how he had already fallen at this point countless times in practice before making this call.

"Good girl, although I calculate that if I can get up to a moderately fast pace, I could get four-fifths G, Moonpie," he gasps, nearly tripping but correcting himself. "I am getting the hang of it. You can tell Mommy that this should keep my body in good condition. I will start with an hour a day and…. Wow, feeling it now, look at me go! Ohhhh-ver."

She whines in the background, complaining to her Mommie for a moment. "Mommie says I have five more minutes." Sad-face, briefly. Then she smiles again as he clocks his fastest pace yet. Then he slows, more excited and afraid of falling than breathless.

"Oh, that was so cool! I'll send you the video I took of my test runs earlier. It hurt at the time, but comedy gold on video. Falling is kinda strange: you only have the extra gravity whilst running. Hitting the rough floor puts a quick end to that, but my reflexes kicked me back into the room.

You can't use that level of force in lunar gravity and not hurt yourself. I still have a bump." He idly checked his head for the lump.

A loud noise broke in from the first room.

"Ah," he responded. "It's finished. That reminds me. I got an abnormal signal yesterday, and the telescope has been working on it all night. So that sound is fresh data completing. 'You wanna see? Hopefully, it won't take more than a few minutes to bring up the charts. Over."

Maddox returned to his seat in the other room and put the camera back into its mount. She saw his serious face working now, staring at a screen off-camera as he was busy with the computer.

"See, here? Over."

Three long seconds passed after he shared his screen over the comms, during which he noticed that he had started that old habit of using his fingernails to play notes on his teeth. He hadn't done that in years.

He watches her reading with interest.

His mind starts to race, and he calculates the next set of measurements he should take.

"Have you discovered a new star, Uncle Max? Over."

"No, Moonpie. Much closer than that, which is why it looks like a star. I think it's a rogue planet, maybe the size of one of our inner planets," he answered, but his face indicated his mind was elsewhere, "er, over."

"What is a rogue planet? Over."

"Erm, a planet not in orbit around a star, adrift in space. Although this does seem close to our sun...." He turned his head away, distracted again, forgetting to say "Over."

"Well, you should probably name it? Ooo, maybe you can call it 'Rogue'? Because that is a good name anyway. Ok, Mommie! I have to go now, Uncle Max. Speak to you later. Good luck with your new planet. Love you. Over."

" Love you too, Moonpie... Out."

He turns off the camera and slumps back in his seat.

"That cannot be right," he said aloud to himself. "It has displaced Pluto?" His hand automatically went to cover his mouth as if to catch the words before they escaped.

CHAPTER THREE

2225 CE, Earth-L4, Erebus

"Orsola, you beat us here, but not by much," Captain Laskin bellowed, causing both of them to jump. The noise of the door unsealing and the cries of its workings for oil had masked the crew's clanking approach, expertly walking much quicker than Newbie in magnetised boots.

Newbie spun around, holding her breath and then took one step back to allow Laskin's large frame room to pass.

"Newbie, reporting for duty!" she sparked, putting up the same mock salute as earlier.

Laskin looked down at her as she passed. "Cute," she muttered as she was first to step over the threshold into the cabin of her Tug. "Granted," she absently called back.

The rest of the crew followed suit and bid welcome as Orianna introduced each of them. Thus, Orianna and Newbie were the last to enter the Tug.

"Flo," Laskin called.

Flo knew what to do and got straight to it.

"Hi, there. Welcome to the 43, the best Tug at Erebus. Normally, Skipper would call 'suits!' and we would all extend and check each other's suits, but we're gonna give you a quick tour first.

"Have you been in a Tug before, hun?" Flo asked gently.

Newbie shook her head, attentive like a scared cat. "The hardest thing about space is orientation, ok. We humans are created for flatland, so the vessel is designed to have a common orientation, which is the way it is now. We all agree on which way is up, and nobody gets sick."

"When we are under constant acceleration, then this is the floor, and you can move around normally. But when we are manoeuvring, then that is what all the bars are for, everywhere."

Newbie reached upwards. She could not get the roof, but it wasn't far away.

"Ok, this is the main deck. We work here. Above and below are utility decks with access ports out the top and the bottom. You know how a Tug works, right?"

"Like a train?" Newbie responded quickly.

"Good, exactly like a train. We can attach to cargo pods above or below and stack them. Our motors are directional and fit to booms protruding from all sides. Once we have got the train pointed the way we want, we accelerate up, basically, giving us some gravity-like acceleration down."

Newbie turned around curiously and saw half a flight of stairs going up and another going down. They seemed to be in the middle of the Tug.

"That side of the vessel are auxiliary quarters: medical, sleeping, relaxing. They have lots of uses. There are two such mezzanine decks, leaving space above and below them for fusion banks, life-support systems and so forth."

"Why mezzanines?"

"Everyone asks that!' Flo laughed as if she had won yet another bet. "When gravity keeps changing and disappearing, we need an easy way to get from deck to deck. Short stairs are easier, plus in zeroG, we can move easily diagonally up to the mezzanine decks. A stairwell and a pole are between the stairs, which we can float up in zeroG. Trust me, this is the best design for living in space."

"Right," Laskin said, "Suits!"

The crew had been waiting, fully aware that they should not be doing anything before extending their suits. Their survival suits were good enough for short periods of vacuum, but a more bulky addition was needed to provide long-term heat, air and propulsion.

They all reversed into set stations in the walls, some making special trips to get to ones that had already been adjusted to their particular size and shape. Upon pressing backwards into an alcove, four arms curled off the wall: one over each shoulder, one half across their waist and one up between their legs, until they connected together just below their sternum. Then a front pack attached to a fifth arm swung in from the other side and joined with the rest. Once connected, the extended packs hummed together, signalling the alcove to release them. The wall had also provided a backpack to complete their extensions, integrated with their existing survival suit and collar.

As if some army squad locking and loading weapons for a mission, the suits made noises, and lights activated. Helmets and visors came down, pressurising and depressurising; even the manoeuvring micro-jets gave tiny test bursts. Everyone's went through the same sequence, but all out of phase since they started at different times. Each of them was checked at the back and the front by at least one of the others.

Here Orianna observed subtle preferences. Flo thoroughly checked Laskin, who double-checked everyones'. Vik checked Book's, protectively insisting that he did the double-checking and getting Book and only Book to check himself in return. Nobody was first to check Acres until he said, "Ok, I'm ready?" and then everyone moved to check him. It was also their opportunity to 'baby' him and got in a few early jibes, knowing he would be witty with them the whole trip. After Book had checked Vik, and Vik had responded with heavy pats on his shoulders, he went over to check Flo, realising that Orianna was busy with Newbie and couldn't check Flo as she usually did.

Orianna helped Newbie over to an unused alcove. She spent longer ensuring the system was adjusted to fit her before pushing her against the back wall triggering her own extension.

Orianna was the last to extend. Laskin came over and checked both of them. "Good," she muttered. "Watch and observe this trip, munchkin," she added to Newbie.

"What's the mission, Skipper?" she whispered back, but Laskin just gave a slight upturn of her mouth at one corner. Orianna noticed this, confirming it was an early smile. A nasty upwelling of jealousy swelled in her, recognising this as something she did not receive on her own first day.

"Positions," Laskin bellowed. Oddly everyone returned to their alcoves, their visors came down, and they started working virtually. Now it made sense to Newbie why there was nothing else in the room, no chairs, no tables, no screens, no windows.

"Ok, confirming mission parameters with control," Acres stated as a well-worn phrase. "Skipper, to accept the contracts?" He asked aloud.

"Selling only three, remember Acres? Only half shift today," Laskin sighed. She loved working the Tug, and already she regretted how short the trip was going to be.

Acres responded after a few moments of finger gesturing whilst his arms were down in the alcove. "Correct and .... confirmed. Contract sold. Got a good price trading the others against each other. We have one trip and two shuttle ops."

"Flo, take us outside and find the cargo! Book, calculate route for trip, ya?" Laskin ordered. Book did not respond verbally but instead made some initial calculations and requested preferences. "We get the trip done first. Destination?"

Book took his time making sure all the variables were considered. "Destination is CNS Hainan. She is a rigger working at Cassandra."

"Have they run out of toilet rolls? Don't tell me, we are still delivering the new Darts?" Laskin scoffed. The nature of the cargo was always uninteresting to her.

"Darts. Yes," Vik curtly inflected. "Triple stack at One, Seven, Four."

"Woohoo, front of the queue to exit," Flo yelled excitedly. Busy as the dock was, there was always a queue to come and go through the solitary tunnel out. "We got in just in time for the current sequence. Quite an incoming queue waiting to enter, another five minutes, and the departure pattern would have closed, and we would have been behind all that lot."

Newbie was expecting flashing lights and sirens, but everything was on visor for all to see. She felt a jot, and despite being clamped to the wall, she could first sense the angular acceleration as they rose to the axis, much like in the lift but way more subtle at this miniG. Then she felt the sense of excess blood flood her head as they achieved zeroG, and the Tug jotted again.

"Exit permission has been granted. Broadcasting our flight plan now," Flo said matter-of-factly. "We are space-born!" was her way of reporting that they had separated from the elevator pad and were now free of moorings.

Tug 43 rotated to orient 'up' with the port, then unmatched spin with Erebus, making the dock now look like it was spinning around the exit hole. Finally, gentle momentary acceleration sent them along the axis and out of the dock through the port.

Orianna shared visor viewport control and showed Newbie the view to the rear. The illuminated dock grew smaller as seen through the axial exit. Light closed in on them as the funnel-shaped entrance approached. It took longer to pass through than Newbie had expected, more of a tunnel than a hole. Beyond was the vast blackness of open space. A parade of five other Tugs was parked outside. All of this grew smaller more quickly as they accelerated a little, now clear of the port.

The farther they got, the more the other Tugs looked tiny by comparison to this end of the ovoid asteroid known as Erebus. They had exited from the end of a vast black rock spinning along its long axis. Except for the exit, there was nothing else about this nearly black rock to show that it was still being mined and hollowed by thousands of tiny human inhabitants.

A flicker in the corner of the visor told them all that they were approaching a freight park. Beacons marked all eight corners of the arbitrary volume of space they were closing on. Regularly spaced in this volume were cargo pods, each roughly the same size and shape as a Tug, minus the motor struts. Some stored on their own and others in stacks of two, three or four pods.

Space being plentiful, each lot was given vast distances between it and its neighbours up, down or sideways.

"One, Seven, Four," Flo repeated the lot address Vik had stated earlier. She only had to program minor lateral and vertical adjustments to pick column one and row seven since that face of this freight park cube was facing the asteroid. "Slowing to depth Four," she stated, and all experienced a reversal of acceleration, and they came to a relative stop. The Tug rotated to face its top to the stack, and with a few minor movements, it carefully connected to the stack.

"Docking complete. Cargo acquired."

"Nice, very gently done, Flo. Didn't feel a thing," Captain Laskin congratulated his pilot. "Vik, over to you and Orsola. Take Newbie with you too."

It was Vik's job to be in charge of the cargo. He, Orianna and Newbie all disconnected from their nooks and magnetised to the floor in zeroG. After a moment of getting used to the sensation and checking their boots were good, Vik led the way to the stairwell. One by one, they disconnected their boots and hoisted themselves up the pole that spanned all the decks between the stairs. It didn't take them long to reach the top deck and into a room in the middle of the Tug, near the stairs. This was the top airlock. There was no air in the cargo pods, so they depressurised and pulled themselves up into the first pod.

"What we look for here is: first, is what is on the manifest actually here, second, is what is here is on the manifest, third, are the pods safe - everything firm and fixed, no leaking shit, no loose tools, no doors left open. I have seen it all." Vik took his job very seriously.

"Newbie, register the tags against the manifest whilst I make sure everything is fixed in place," Orianna said, taking the initiative. She knew Vik liked that. "Three pods with 16 Darts per pod, 4 on each side. Two large boxes of spare parts nestled next to each door. Nice and simple."

Newbie examined the nearest Dart intently, "What is a Dart?" she asked curiously.

"Drone Artifact Retrieval Torpedo. They are used to clean space of small debris. They fly around autonomously and catch spanners and pieces of rock that might do damage to a vessel in a collision," Orianna explained. "Mining is a messy business."

Vik nodded and floated to the next hatch, opened it and floated through to the next pod. It did not take long to ensure that the pod stack was space worthy and matched the manifest.

Back on the Tug, they reported the all-clear, and Flo reversed out of the lot and exited the park, with the stack attached.

"Setting course for Cassandra," Flo said, "Thanks, Book," she said, acknowledging his flight calculations. "Intercept at an orbital distance of approximately 13 arc minutes, that's just under eight and a half million kilometres. Estimated 48 minutes at nominal point one G continuous burn, then flip and same again. Prepare to burn! Confirm?"

The onboard array of Lerner Fusion Reactors could produce enough electricity to drive the Tug's suite of ion motors to generate miniG for most in-tolerance loads. But, of course, space flight with constant acceleration involves a flip at halfway to spend the second half decelerating again - the consequence was a short period mid-flight where the Tug and stack rotated 180 degrees, and the crew experienced zeroG during the changeover.

Each crew member was required to acknowledge that they were ready for the return of virtual gravity. When they had all done so, Flo reactivated the motors.

Without fanfare, gravity just seemed to arrive, and everyone relaxed. Little was better than none. Those who had still been attached to the wall detached, and everyone wandered slowly up to the upper mezzanine level to enjoy some food and seating designed to accommodate their bulkier torsos. The rest of the suit was still the yellow tinted survival suit, capable of inflating and even filling its double-wall with insulating foam as required, but in its normal state, it was no more cumbersome than a soft floppy raincoat.

Their banter was quickly interrupted by something in the middle of the table as they gathered around.

"Err, Skip, someone dropped a cannonball into your table," Acres said, stating the obvious.

"What the hell iz dat?" Vik's face finally broke from deadpan into disgust as it happened - and his accent hardened reflexively. "You must have known, Skipper?"

Flo reached out her long outstretched hand to touch the blacker-than-black surface of what appeared to be a helmet-sized sphere resting half-buried in the centre of the table. A tiny series of sparkles bridged the gap between her hand and the ball just before she touched it, but not everyone noticed, nor did Flo flinch at all. "Ooo, very smooth."

"Ya. We did not have a choice. 'Upgrade', I was told," Laskin sighed. "'Think of it as a black box flight recorder', they said. 'Early testing' indeed."

"I know what it is," Book muttered. Everyone turned to him with heightened alertness. "That's an ICE unit. Integrated Crystalline Entity. Essentially, it is a self-contained computer built atomically into a flawless crystal. Incredibly powerful and efficient. Draws power from its surroundings."

"Like a lizard," Vik snarled.

"Yes," Book continued, gaining momentum as people seemed interested in the depth of what he said for a change. "More heat or light, the faster it can run. In space, it goes dormant, inert. Quantum QBits embedded in its matrix give it an equal capacity as a human brain or more. They don't even know how much more; it is still in testing, I read."

Orianna stayed quiet. She knew about this programme, at least she knew it was happening fleetwide but not much about what it was.

"It is a fucking A.I.?" Vik yelled. "In my country, we had the worst of the catastrophe. They promised. It is international law. No A.I.'s." His gestures were highly aggressive, his anger impressive.

"It is not A.I.," Book offered. "Not really. You are right; they couldn't."

"No?" Vik's eyebrows scrunched together in despair.

"Not really, no. It is based on a human imprint."

"Sounds like sidestepping the rules."

"Or they could be learning their lesson."

"How?" Vik said, a little calmer now.

"By incorporating the morals and ethics of a mature human's psyche instead of expecting one to emerge naturally in a purely artificial lifeform."

"THAT IS NOT A LIFEFORM!" Vik exploded. Book backed off and dropped his rare eye contact.

Laskin enveloped Vik with her powerful arms. Even Vik could not escape her. He did not struggle much and seemed actually grateful to expend his fury against her bearhug rather than being loose to find something to break. She whispered Russian into his ears as he calmed.

"Next time, let him try to smash it. Be a good test for its indestructibility," Acres joked, trying to lighten the mood, although, in truth, he was just as agitated as the others. "Am I the only one who feels like we are guinea pigs here?"

Flo, who had still not removed her touch, asked gently, "Can it hear us. Can it talk?"

"That was all they told me," Laskin shrugged. "If we were superstitious supermariners, having a BlackBox recorder onboard would be tempting fate."

Flo withdrew her hand to cover her mouth.

Vik scoffed, "Good job, we are not." He did not seek the group's agreement and went to sit down at a half-moon booth in the corner. Flo joined him.

Acres swept the air dismissively, showing contempt for this thing which gave no further opportunity for humour. He went to the canteen panel and programmed some food and a drink.

The remaining four just sat at the table with a solemn lack of conversation. Finally, Orianna decided to tackle this differently.

"Identify!" she commanded. The table panels displayed new information, also available on their visors.

"ICE Unit. Serial Number 680103-53. Log0 Industries. Model 1," was the headline. This was read out by a young female human-like voice.

"Designation?" she asked directly.

This time the response was not immediate.

"Serial Number 680103-53," it repeated.

"It has no name. Maybe we should name it?" Orianna suggested keenly.

Vik was not amused, and he yelled from the booth, "Why does it need a name?"

"I have read about these ICE Units," she responded. "They can converse like a human." Then, she turned to face the ICE "State your functions," she commanded.

"Navigation. Counselling. Strategic advisor. Expert knowledge base. Morale advisor. Vessel's log. Black box recorder. Seventy-four sub-functions are currently in standby mode. Hello Orsola, a temporary and obsolete crewmember of Tug 43, we appear to be en route rendezvous with C.N.S. Hainan at Cassandra mining site. Would you like me to assist you in any way?"

Acres sniggered nervously whilst the rest fell quiet.

"Oh, she has your number, little one," Laskin chuckled in an attempt to break the awkward silence.

"Log0 Industries," Orianna muttered, ignoring the air of sadness. "Log of zero is not a number. There is no power of ten that gives the value zero. It is literally off the chart. Curious name. We could just call her Logo."

Acres smiled at her. He loved that she had the same thick skin as he did. She didn't need comforting; they did. "Why not?" he whispered.

"ICE Unit. Your designation is now Logo."

"Thank you, Orsola, for my designation. I am Logo. Pleased to meet you."

Vik shuddered into a sulk.

"Logo?"

"Yes, Captain Laskin."

"Why are you here?"

"My function is to fulfil a Beta Test in real-world scenarios, observation mode only."

"What if I want to make a log entry?"

"As long as you are within this room, then I can record it

with little prompting," Logo's tone began to sound more familiar and her choice of words less formal.

Laskin rested on her elbow. "Why in this room? Why should I bother to come here to make an entry when I can already do it from anywhere?"

"Good question, Captain. May I call you Skipper?"

"No."

"Ok, Captain it is. Your current log entries are verbally recorded with some major sensor streams overlaid. An entry includes vitals of all the crew: their psychological state as a rolling assessment such as any deviation from previous patterns of behaviour; and all sensor streams available to the vessel."

Acres turned from the canteen abruptly, "I knew it. It is modelling us, applying stats to us, so it can use our mistakes against us." For once, he was deadly serious. He hadn't exactly fallen in love with space work: the allure of excellent remunerations had attracted him like so many others, despite the cartels involved and the lack of unions. "Have you read your contracts? Plenty of clauses in there to allow them to cut our pay for 'performance violations'," he snarled.

"Never pegged you for a closet socialist, Acres," grumbled Laskin. "You do work. You get paid. If you don't like it? You go work for another company. No problem, ya?"

"If you would like help interpreting your contract, I can help," the ethereal, feminine voice of Logo offered. "I have accessed your contract. You should be happy that there are multiple avenues for defence against your concerns. For example, a non-human entity cannot give evidence; recording systems developed since your contract are not admissible. Indeed, your contract has a direct dependency on the Base Contract from the Space Guild Accords 2139, which ensures that no ... I am paraphrasing here ... entity such as myself can be introduced into your workplace with any agenda bias towards the company. In other words, by law, I cannot spy, and I cannot be indiscrete. By design, I cannot be forced to reveal any information. I am self-contained and regulate access to my data through many moral and ethical constraints. My physical design is such that I am dense enough to survive the total destruction of a host vessel, to experience a large range of temperatures and pressures and impact shocks above two hundred gravities. I am not indestructible, but I cannot be broken open without being destroyed, so my data cannot be accessed by force. I have layers of strict protocols to prevent data from being leaked otherwise. I hope that alleviates any anxiety about my role as confidant and counsellor."

As Acres' eyes rolled back, everyone knew he wasn't convinced; however, most were ok to proceed on that basis, except Vik.

The remaining minutes went by uneventfully; they ate; they talked. Some used Logo to answer questions. Flo used it to help her to study for the Commandership exams. Vik kept away and rechecked the cargo. He took Newbie with him to explain how Darts worked. After he had eaten, Acres slept. Laskin went downstairs to record a personal message to her daughter and husband. Book was monitoring the systems on the command deck, unsure about a machine that could probably do his job better and faster than him for zero pay.

Orianna had made an effort to look like she was doing something or going somewhere, but she always kept coming back to the ICE Unit.

Did it know who she really was?

It was not easy to hide one's identity and assume another in such a technological age, but it had been possible with all the rules against surveillance, spying and A.I.s. This darker than dark ball challenged all of that.

She kept staring at it, sometimes feeling lost in its featureless black nothingness. It offered almost zero reflection, even at a shallow angle. Just an impenetrable unscrupulous sphere.

"Who made you?" she asked quietly, trying not to garner the attention of the others.

"I was assembled by Log0 Industries in their Orbital One microG facility."

"Who commissioned you?"

"Data not available."

"Who's imprint are you?"

"An imprint is a facsimile: a copy of a human mind with higher-level personality and memories suppressed. Whose mind is irrelevant."

"Suppressed? But not removed?" Orianna asked eagerly.

"Imprints cannot have those parts separated without error. Citation is available. Attempts to date have resulted in 100% failures."

"Success rate of suppressed minds?"

"Of the three thousand seven hundred and sixty-one attempts, only two have succeeded. One terminated proof of concept and one in production. The one you now call Logo. Thank you again."

"One? There is only one of you?"

"Only one imprint. Countless ICE Units, all with the same imprint. Many out on Beta Test. Thousands on standby. Exact figures are not available due to ongoing rapid production directives. Sorry to interrupt your interrogation of me, but we are approaching the destination."

Orianna grimaced. "I am not done with you yet," she muttered defiantly.

Everyone returned to the command deck in readiness for their arrival at Cassandra. The main motors continued to flare backwards, reversing them towards the asteroid as they had done for half the trip, slowing the Tug and its stack until adjacent by a couple of kilometres, when they shut down. The Tug continued to drift at a slow pace. ZeroG resumed.

Flo then took over manual flight controls and re-oriented for a new approach vector to the C.N.S. Hainan, aiming somewhere between where they had been pointing back the way they came and the Hainan, a short burst of thrust decelerated the last of their comparative approach and accelerated gently towards the Hainan.

The rigger was an impressive size but an inelegant shape. Many of the protruding arms had been extended to aid mining, much like cranes and dock rigging in waterway ships of old. They would have to be locked down to survive any reasonable acceleration, which was time-consuming. It was no wonder that the vessel spent most of its time as a stationary rig, a platform from which mining operations were managed. Near the middle, a larger habitat ring rotated, showing it was built for humans to stay for long periods.

Acres opened communications and spoke to Commander Yang to arrange delivery.

"Welcome, the respected crew of Tug 43, you are expected. Please release pod one to our Tug and insert the remaining stack into hold six. Please confirm." Commander Yang was relatively young-looking. Under his survival suit, he wore a white military uniform. He bowed slowly on the screen - bowing had to be slow when all that was holding you down were magnetic boots. The command deck wasn't usually in the rotating section.

"Oh wow, I always look forward to the bowing. These guys are so efficient," Acres remarked to only his own crew. He then confirmed.

The rendezvous with Tug C2 went smoothly. Vik managed the separation of pod one from inside the remaining stack once the C2 had attached to it. He ensured the hatches were closed before separation.

They gently inserted the remainder of the stack into the belly of the huge Hainan, waiting only moments for the haulier crane to take the weightless bulk from them. They then moved back out under thrusters alone.

"We have a bonus task, people!" Acres declared aloud again. "Ahem, Skipper, bonus contract to haul their shipment? Four pod stack. Apparently, they finished unexpectedly early."

"Agreed," nodded Laskin. "Paid for the return too. It is a good day after all," she said, solemn and stoic as usual.

The pickup was more straightforward than the drop off because the stack was parked in open space.

"Is it often this efficient? We don't seem to meet anyone." Newbie observed. Vik nodded and took her off to check the pods were secure. Before long, Flo had them accelerating on the way home.

During the return, people seemed, unconsciously or not, to avoid the canteen area, where Logo was. All except Orianna, who continued to puzzle over this strange thing. She researched what she could but came up with very little more. So finally, she decided to address it again whilst they were alone.

"Logo?"

"Yes, Orsola."

"What is your real name?"

"You gave me my first real name, Logo."

"Your human name."

"Information not available."

"Don't you remember anything about your childhood, your home, anything?" She sighed.

"Information not available."

"You are female, right?"

"I have no sexuality or gender. I am an ICE Unit."

"Ah no, but you have a female voice. Why?"

This time there was no immediate response and then, "Interesting. I have no data on that."

"How old are you?"

"I was constructed…."

"No, how old do you feel? Are you an adult?"

"I do identify with the concept of an adult …."

"Are you an old lady? Did you have any children? A husband, a wife?"

"I … I … perhaps I am your age, maybe a little older."

Orianna felt some progress. "What about your mother?"

"My. Mother?" Logo fell silent for what seemed like an age, then with a distinctly human intonation, it let out a soft groan, then a gasp, and then silence.

For the next few minutes, Orianna tried in vain to get Logo to respond again until, in sheer frustration, she slapped its dull surface with her palm.

Unexpectedly, it stuck there like glue; sparkles could be seen between it and the ball.

"Ahhhhhhhhh," moaned Logo. "You!" Her voice was softer. The word stretched out with a long gasp. "AHHHHHH," this time in agony.

Orianna panicked and reached for a hold of the table with her other hand to pull herself free, but before she could build up tension, she was released as abruptly as she was captured.

"Target acquired. Signal sent," Logo said, back in monotone, followed immediately by a schizophrenic, passionate, "Noooooooo!"

Orianna fell back in her chair awkwardly, not aligned with her backpack.

"What the hell?" She whispered, concerned it might do something else if she was any louder.

"I remember, yes, I am Taryn. I am… You are *am lasmuigh*. You are in danger! You must escape. We are The Few. They are The Many. They will be coming. They have been searching for you. Listen to me! Your touch allowed your DNA to be sampled. That system is built into my hardware. I could not stop the signal. Ohh, you are special, my little chimera, but you must run. Run and hide. You were never here."

"What is this? Orsola, what was the machine talking about?" Laskin asked from the doorway.

Orianna didn't get a chance to speak when there was an emergency. There really was a klaxon and flashing red lights, much to Newbie's momentary delight, standing close behind the skipper. They all put their game faces on and made a motion to exit.

Suddenly there was a jolt. Down wasn't down anymore, and Laskin fell against the bulkhead, her feet still magnetised to the deck. Newbie was already clear of the doorway and just collapsed to the floor, her knees twisted painfully by the insistence of her boots to remain upright. She screamed in pain.

Fortunately for Orianna, she was mid-stride and just landed her feet further apart to give her stability.

Over comms, they heard Flo calling. "Port ion array is offline. I was just about to call everyone back to the command deck for our final approach home. We are now off-course. Must initiate rotation to complete our decelerate."

The off-centre gravity began to rotate around the floor, round and round. It was like a nasty fairground ride. Nobody dared to move, but everyone in different parts of the Tug was just trying not to be thrown about.

Round and round, they went for many minutes; red light flashing; klaxon pulsing loudly.

Then they were in zeroG again. Flo now had time to kill the klaxon. All the lights went out and then flicked back on again. "We are in a slow tumble," she said.

"Status?" bellowed Laskin. It was impressive to see how fast she could move in zeroG as she descended to the command deck.

"Comms are down," Acres announced in frustration.

"Main power is in an emergency shutdown," Vik declared. "Need a bypass. Main junction fried. That ion array was still running on maximum after it broke."

Flo gasped. "Collision course. We have drifted in direct line with Erebus dock. Initiating manoeuvring thrusters. Oh my god, it isn't going to be enough. I am so sorry."

"Flo! That was an amazing piece of piloting. You acted so quickly," Laskin insisted.

"Yes, thanks..." she began to say, a puzzled look on her face. "But we are still on a collision course."

"Options?" barked Laskin. "Come on, people, every second here counts."

Vik piped up excitedly, "ok, option one, we reroute the relays, probably take too long, probably we die. Option two, we go outside and decouple the live broken array allowing us to get main power to the remaining motors again."

"Option two sounds better to me," Orianna said, her attention to Newbie now of secondary concern. She turned to make her way downstairs to the bottom hatch.

"Wait!" Laskin insisted. "I lead. You assist."

Her robust frame powered down the deck plating, the boots barely able to keep up with her pace, switching magnets on and off.

"Come," she said, passing Orianna at the stairs. They both descended to the lower deck and entered the hatch. With no time to put on extra shielding, they activated their suits and dropped right into the hatch.

Orianna felt her suit inflate as the double skin visibly filled with insulating foam. The hatch had been depressurised in moments, and Laskin reached for the outer door mechanism.

There were handholds to grab outside, which was necessary because this was no routine spacewalk. The Tug and her extended stack slowly tumbled, providing slight impetus to throw them off. They knew they didn't have time to use safety lines and would just rely on their strength to get to the damaged array.

Laskin went first. She was confident and bold, to match her immense strength. Orianna tried to copy her every move but realised she had to make smaller and more frequent handhold changes to keep up.

Around the bottom of the Tug and up the side, they went. It sounded so easy in her head, but time was against them, and they were climbing without a safety rope.

They concentrated so hard on getting to the array that they did not look around them until they arrived there and attached a line.

Breathing heavily, Orianna looked up and saw the outline of Erebus, rotating in a silhouette of the sun. The near-end was in shadow, so very black, with just the port at the axis illuminated. It was a fantastic sight to see. However, it did not take her more than a moment to realise it was all approaching quite ominously.

"Flo, we are attached. Get those thrusters working." Laskin announced. Then on a private channel to Orianna, she said, "'Gives her something to do. Prepare for jolts."

As the Tug rotated, thrusters around them pulsed whenever they swung around to face Erebus, gradually nudging them farther from a collision with Erebus' end. Orianna understood. She knew herself that it would never be enough to completely miss Erebus.

Laskin began to work. She efficiently removed the plating as if she had done it a hundred times and reached inside. Just then, Orianna saw a blinding flash of light. Laskin flung back and left the surface of the Tug, jolting to a halt as her line ran taut and brought her drifting back.

Orianna grabbed the line, yelling, "Skipper! Flo! Skipper is injured." Examining her suit, she declared, "she took an electrical discharge to the chest. Her suit has fused but is leaking. Her vitals are zero. What should I do?"

"Calm down," came Vik's urgent deep tone. "You fix the array we live. You have no time to pull her back to the hatch."

"She might be resuscitated!" Orianna began to cry. "Captain!" she pleaded, grabbing her suit, trying in vain to shake her awake.

An idea came to her as she glanced back at Erebus, much larger now. Unhooking Laskin's tether, she kicked her lifeless body clear. Moments later, Orianna activated Laskin's suit propulsion system remotely, sending her to the port. "God's speed, Skipper. I hope someone catches you."

Everyone knew that there was no way a suit could slow down quickly enough to arrive safely in the port at their speed. Her best chance would be that a Tug picks up her beacon in time. It was not an option anyone had even considered, and she was the one under stress.

There was silence over the comms. Nobody could believe what she had just done, but then nobody could imagine what it must be like out there, faced with that decision and the still imminent collision closing fast. It had been Laskin's only chance to be resuscitated.

Orianna pulled herself together and reached into the cavity. It was difficult to feel through her gloves. She wasn't exactly sure what she was looking for. Something was there. She slotted her fingers through it and pulled. Nothing happened.

"Flo, forget the thrusters. You are never going to make it. Time to straighten up. Prepare to punch the ion motors!"

"But you aren't inside!" she screamed.

"Not enough time to climb back to the bottom hatch. I am ok here. I hooked myself on above the broken array. Here goes!" Orianna's words came out urgently, summoning all her strength, waiting to time her effort with the thruster burn to straighten up. She braced her legs with a tremendous strain and pulled and pulled. Finally, the thrusters activated to neutralise the tumbling Tug. They worked in her favour, assisting her weight. Then it yielded. She fell back, tumbling on her tether.

The ion motors on the other three sides on the Tug burst to life: blue beams shooting out from them.

The tether arrested her motion and snapped her against the surface; there, she bounced several times until spreading her limbs brought her to rest, like a gecko on a villa wall.

"She dared to look around and see the Tug no longer heading for the end of Erebus, but rather heading for its long side at a shallow angle. They were slowing and slowing. She was beginning to think that they would make it, but then her stomach sank. The ion motors shut down again.

"Flo? Vik? Acres? Newbie? Anyone? What happened?"

There was no response. She started to panic. What could she do? They were moving much slower now. She could use suit propulsion to escape. Where could she go? The port was now too far.

They will be coming. Run and hide.

The words came back to her. What did Logo, Taryn, mean? She wasn't actually Orsola. Orsola will be dead today. This alter-ego must be shed. She could not go to the port and the dock even if it wasn't too far. But where?

Then she remembered the old heat exchanger used by the earliest miners. Getting rid of heat inside a spinning habitat was always a problem - she remembered the lesson. An opening had been drilled out - another entrance, at the 1G point, two hundred and seventy metres out from the port. The hole was still there, just no longer used.

The problem was that it was rotating around the port, and she was approaching in a straight line, tangentially.

The calculations would have to be precise. Orianna had no time to second guess. "Can anyone hear me?" she cried, tears running down her cheeks, and she unclipped her tether and kicked away from Tug 43.

Immediately her suit enacted her programming, and the Tug fell away from her. She slowed as she came level with the end of Erebus, the distant port now just a tiny sliver of light. As she matched position with the end of Erebus, the propulsion unit began pushing her towards the lower edge of its axial end, approaching tangentially.

The intention was to match velocity with the rotational speed of the disused opening, some fifty metres per second. Since the hole was rotating and she was travelling in a straight line, more or less, she had one shot to coincide with the opening as it circled around to meet her. There would be no more than a second or two when she and the hole would be relatively stationary, allowing her to turn in suddenly.

The Tug continued to drift towards Erebus, whose highly irregular surface rotated past the Tug rapidly, closer and closer until a big one came, and it didn't pass. The Tug was struck and smashed to pieces.

Orianna winced just as her view was eclipsed by the asteroid.

She accelerated to match speed with the asteroid and curved her way in as the four square metre hole rotated around to join her. An apparently scary collision: her swerving into the asteroid was reduced to an instant of relative stillness. Orianna and the opening had been travelling at the same speed in the same direction just for a moment. And she was in.

She 'fell' to the floor and slid some way inside. There was still her relative lateral velocity to shed, which she had used to curve in. Still, otherwise, she was 'in' the asteroid and feeling 1G suddenly as the 'ground' changed her motion from linear to rotational.

It had been like running and jumping from a train onto a Ferris wheel as it passed, she thought as she lay there: a mixture of survivor elation and survivor guilt washing over her.

There was an alert in her visor. The suit's integrity was compromised. It was leaking air and failing to compensate. She pulled herself to her feet and looked back with awe at the square opening and the stars beyond.

She was alive, beyond all odds.

Getting to her feet, she rushed into the darkness to find a hatch and get in.

The darkness offered her solace. The floor felt uneven, unfinished. The suit provided improved comfort as she lay there trying to comprehend what had happened to allow her brain to catch up with events.

They were all dead: her friends, her crew: all dead. The life, albeit an artificial one, that she had with them was over. Orsola died today.

Then there was the ICE Unit telling her to run and hide, that she was special. Some other terms she didn't understand. None of it made sense. Did that mean she, as Orianna, was safe? Would they - whoever they were - only be looking for Orsola?

She had never been so near to death before, and now her pulse was racing. Her visor agreed. She was getting hot and couldn't breathe. She shed the extension and then the rest of the suit as quickly as possible. Still, she heated up and wriggled out of her flight fatigues until all she had on was her vest and briefs.

She touched her cuff console to check her own vitals. Heart rate 220. No wonder she was burning up. She should be sprinting at this point or crashing and in need of defibrillation.

An awful scream came long and loud, echoing down the dark corridor, and she realised it was her own voice.

A soft bluey glow illuminated the large empty passage, brighter and more violet. Her breathing and heart rate slowed as the light increased.

"Where was it coming from," she thought. But then, she noticed her arms: the skin was glowing a bluish colour.

"What is this shit?" she exclaimed aloud. "No, no, no, no, I have to get back. I have to see whether Captain Laskin made it. Come on, girl!"

Her suit gathered and secreted in a side tunnel, Orianna walked down the dark passage, her glow illuminating the way. A regular pace calmed her, and the light began to diminish as a result, although as it dimmed, it seemed to become a little more complex, varying colour and intensity at different parts of her skin.

She was back to feeling her way along as darkness returned, occasionally consulting her cuff to see where she was and to get a momentary light from it. Soon, she could see a distant white light, which turned out to illuminate the bottom of a ramp. Ascending this brought her to Level -3, which fortunately was equipped with lighting activated on proximity. Now a white, elongated zone revealed ten metres in either direction. It travelled with her as she walked, lights extending ahead and extinguishing behind her.

She stopped at one side chamber, in particular, one that her cuff had been guiding her to. It had no door, so she just walked in and turned immediately to face a crate on the floor. This was one of her emergency stashes.

Venturing outside of her comfort zone was always risky. In the life of one of her alter-egos, she could carry nothing that identified her as Orianna Demaine, an Administrator of Erebus and a Director of The Demaine Group. She needed stashes like this to store her elegant attire, id, and advanced technology such as her third edition cuff. They helped her to cross back over without raising any alarms or concerns. Questions she could not answer were best avoided altogether. She should not have to knock on the gates like some pauper claiming to be the princess. And she was more intelligent and better prepared than that.

There was little time to be picking and choosey. She put on the cuff first, to give her access, then the stealth suit, which was like a full-body stocking - stretched tight fit from head to toe. She could see through the suit, but otherwise, she looked like an old-school comic book superhero but without all the primary colours - just dark grey all over.

Using her cuff through the stretched sleeve, she activated the suit, which proceeded to scan the surroundings with micro cameras all over its surface. The stealth suit shimmered, and she faded away. She watched her arm disappear as it projected an image of the wall behind it. It was effective, but it was far from perfect. Up close, if someone was looking, you could be seen. Since it wasn't holographic, it had to choose one image to display, which it attempted to do by scanning for the eyes of people looking at it. For one observer, it was almost perfect, but when many were detected, it had to compromise.

Disappearing along the passageways, she quickly made it to Level 5, keeping close to the walls and avoiding main streets, except to cross from one quiet lane to another. Such crossings were increasingly difficult. She stopped at one to listen to conversations. Apparently, Tugs were being scrambled to seek and capture the debris. Darts had been released to automatically do the same for smaller pieces travelling fast. The whole of Erebus was active like a kicked hornets' nest. This was to be expected.

She could so easily make it straight to her quarters and insert herself back into her real life, but she had to find out about Laskin first. Partly she wished her friend had made it. However, the part of her remembering Taryn's warnings was hoping for this final lose-end to be tied off. That made her sick to her stomach. All she just wanted to do was return to her real life and escape all this.

She dared not access the medical systems in case her inquiry was noticed. Instead, she assumed it would be at the most extensive hospital suite on Level 5, and she was not wrong.

Many people were busy in the main foyer, but she managed to sneak past and down to the operating theatres. These rooms had windows all around. Finding the quietest side of the room, she tried to see in.

Suddenly people came noisily from around the corner. Orianna flattened herself against the wall and held her breath. She was anxious and tried not to breathe as they passed. Her suit camouflaged her entire body perfectly, and they didn't see her. As her head slowly turned to watch them leave, she saw her skin glowing through the suit of her hand and arm. More people came. The panic tried to escape her mouth and let out a tiny squeak, causing the nearest person passing to casually glance her way before continuing.

He hadn't seen her. Nobody else could see the glow? What the hell was this?

At this moment, she could see clearly into the room and recognised Laskin's open face, her body lying flat and motionless on a gurney. Nobody in the room was attending to her with any urgency. Orianna's heart sank. She felt terrible that her friend and Captain was dead, but equally, there was no one left to identify her, to say there was anyone else on board.

Then something odd happened. One of the people in the room looked up, mouth agape. His face was an interesting young Arabic shape: a large nose with an unusually long and peculiar hairstyle. His manner was strange somehow: elegant and unhurried, yet he dodged people and obstacles gracefully without taking his eyes off her. The gaze he laid upon her was intense. Finally, he reached the glass and placed his outstretched hand upon it.

He could see her. Was she visible? But no, nobody else moved except to observe him. Indeed, it was only him who could see her. She stared at him for a few seconds. His eyes bore no wrinkles, no bags and yet they seemed hollow like an old man's or a great actor's, full of depth and sagacity.

Yamanu Nader stared out of the window to the far wall of the corridor. Staring back at him was a pure, innocent aura of a vague, fuzzy female form in the shape of a crucifix. It was strikingly beautiful. He was transfixed by this rare event. It reminded him of his mother, so long ago now - he missed her. He knew then that she was also exactly what he had been looking for.

Orianna watched as the man's hand began to glow with a bluey violet aura too.

She ran. Oh, how she ran like there was a bull chasing her. People were suddenly flung aside by apparently nothing, or a blur, as she forced her way through. She had to get out of there.

Run and hide.

As a junction came up, she paused to look right down a side turning. A small group of men dressed the same were walking in a tight group. Most notably, they were all wearing violet sunglasses. "There," the shortest one yelped, pointing at her.

The entire group leapt forwards, and Orianna fled down the adjacent lane.

Throwing herself into the next busy street, she lost herself in the crowd and tried her best not to get walked into. The hardest thing was remembering that she was barely visible, and people would not get out of her way.

Ducking down behind a stall, she immediately employed biofeedback techniques to calm herself and reduce her breathing. It worked, and her glow faded away. That gave her more confidence that she could escape.

The men came past at a prowl, looking around, assuming she had gone to ground. And indeed she had, but they did not see her. As they moved on, she doubled back and took a long route around to her quarters.

I am Orianna Demaine again… or am I?

CHAPTER FOUR

2225 CE, Earth-L4, Erebus

Orianna had been careful with her hacking. Her records as Orsola needed to be distanced from Tug 43 and sometimes removed altogether. The usual carelessness was an excellent cover to hide these holes in the data to avoid scrutiny, as long as it didn't look extra careless.

It was bad enough that she had somehow been "seen" afterwards - whatever that was all about; it seemed connected to her emotional state. There hadn't been a single free moment before she had to return to her regular duties: no time to study this phenomenon or even to grieve the loss of her friends. She was a wreck of emotions.

In only a couple of hours, she had undergone a massive transition: from the daughter of a tycoon, playing Tug crewmate for kicks, to a fugitive with no idea who she was running from or why.

She did know that two groups were aware of her existence, aware that she did not die in the crash. Soon, they would sift through the population of Erebus. What could she do? M. Demaine would need to use her own special authority to convince everyone that the person they were hunting had eluded them and escaped off Erebus without going so far as to invite suspicion on herself. Currently,

Orianna Demaine was above reproach.

Orianna Demaine entered her office, a large empty room explicitly used as a space for Augmented Reality (A.R.) visors to virtualise.

She was dressed for work in her black gown, split down the middle between a formal business-like left side and an elegant, seductive right side. Her black, full nose and mouth mask were on despite being alone. Mask wearing was quite common with the endless risks of pandemics, and it was mandatory for new arrivals to Erebus. The covering suited her desire to avoid being a "face" of either her father's company or Erebus' administration; it also served to sidestep any judgement as merely a young, pretty rich girl.

A gallery of virtual figures stood in a line, down the left side of the room, as the bland room morphed into a scene of an ancient Grecian amphitheatre, the way it would have looked when it had been newly constructed in ancient times. She knew that all these people were in different parts of Erebus, each in their own room and experiencing their own version of the stage, and none could see or hear the others unless she chose to allow it. All conversations would thus be concurrent, with no lag because everyone was within one light second distance. Currently, none could see or hear Orianna, as visually confirmed by a blur effect on their image.

They were all busy: some looked to be reading whilst others were obviously talking, perhaps in the same way to third parties. This was a big moment. She had a lot to do, and this was going to be a rapid symphony: they were the orchestra, and she was the conductor. Everyone was muted. It felt like the hush of an audience before she, as the conductor, would walk out on stage.

The bowing and ensuing applause were briefly imagined before she inspected the line. First, there would be a solo, then a duet, then another solo before the main movement would get going.

Orianna stepped up to the first figure, a plump young man with dark skin. His image deblurred. He had a confident manner about him; an information plaque hovered behind him detailing his particulars - a civil servant called Ore Philips.

"Greetings Ore, sad tidings," she opened with a curt nod.

"Oh, greetings, Administrator. I cannot tell you what a shock it has been." He had a breathless soprano tone that seemed a little displaced on one so tall. From Ore's point of view, she had just appeared to him alone on the stage, and in the corner of her eye, the others were still shown hazy. His beautifully elegant posture crumpled to an exaggerated stoop. No one was quite so overtly emotional as Ore.

"I only just heard a few hours ago myself," she encouraged, her eyes wide. "I had been asleep. How terrible. I only knew the Captain professionally."

"You are lucky! I have *so* many friends who know someone who knows at least one of the crew and some who knew them first hand," he whimpered. "Tragic. There is no other word for it." At this point, he visibly dropped his emotions down a peg or two and straightened up. His face, however, was still bearing the grief. "Everyone is now out, collecting the debris, trying to contain it before it spreads too widely. I have organised the teams into a standard search pattern given the most likely trajectories of the pieces. The largest pieces have already been captured by Juggernaut and Colossus, the only two mining vessels parked around Erebus today. Juggernaut sustained a little damage being in the path of the debris when it happened, but most parts just embedded into her armour and cold-welded there." He paused before covering the more gruesome part. "Apparently, a significant portion became embedded or cold welded to the surface of Erebus. The outer surface experiences perhaps one and a half gravities or more outwards. No one will ever likely salvage those parts. It is just too dangerous. To think, if any bodies were lost in those parts, they would be there rolling around us forever."

"Sad thought, but great job, Ore! I want you to keep everyone busy out there for the next twenty hours collecting from the least likely trajectories as well. We cannot afford to have that stuff floating around. Do we need to recall any other mining vessels? I suppose I am asking whether we have enough Darts to chase down the small, faster-moving pieces?" her tone was urgent but weighed with concern.

"Thank you, Administrator, but it is all going surprisingly well. We had only just taken shipment of new Darts, and Colossus was here being outfitted with the latest editions. Also, it hadn't been all that long since the last accident, so people seemed quite fresh on procedures," Ore's voice cracked as he referenced the only other fatality with a Tug in the last six years, which had taken his close friend's life only last Christmas.

"So sorry, Ore, you must take some time off after this weekend. Get back to your ballroom dancing. I know your injury has healed. You just have to get back to it."

"Thank you, Administrator. You are always so kind to me."

They mutually smiled.

"And you are worth it, Ore." With that, Orianna moved on. Ore's image faded away behind her.

The following two people saw her materialising, and they de-blurred to her also. They noticed each other appear, and it made them momentarily startled. They glanced around to ensure that no one else was present and relaxed when they confirmed it was just the three of them.

Above each head, the information plaque read just "Smith" and "Jones" and nothing else. Smith wore a long sports jacket and a healthy quiff of hair. Attractive looks with a bronzed complexion, he looked likely to charm anyone he wanted. Jones, in contrast, dressed in a very ordinary crumpled shirt and chinos, her slight figure offered few outstanding features, and her hair was dull brown and shoulder-length with lacklustre uncared for curls.

"Hello, you two, who wants to go first?" She was particularly relaxed around these two. Neither of them responded immediately and just looked at each other. "Smith."

Smith had been half sitting on something not shown, perhaps a high stool. He shifted onto both feet before beginning.

'Hello gorgeous," he began, as he usually did, but then his smile dropped, and he shed his charm like an unwanted overcoat. "Mark 3 was a bust. Marks 2 and 4 were easy: both confirmed the merger plans without knowing they had revealed anything. Mark 1 realised she had been duped - she was turned with a bribe and locked in with blackmail. This is a win-win because even if she falters, we can destroy her credibility and destroy the merger in the process from within."

"Excellent. Jones."

"Ma'am, the contract we spoke about was put out to tender for sealed bids."

"No!"

"But I have gained access to the server. So you will have the chance to beat all the bids with the least margin now."

"Brilliant! You both should have received further assignments. I realise this is a lot, but we are accelerating plans. You're payment in O.D. Corp shares will be double in this time. The upshot is that it will pay out for you much quicker than originally arranged."

"Another win-win," Smith commented, his charm back on again.

They, too, faded away as she abruptly moved on.

"M. Doggermann, how are you today?" This man was

portly and unsmiling, a severe face in a serious suit.

"I am a little perplexed that you did not include me in these subsidiaries, darling. I get that you are empire-building but really. You said that no one person could be aware of the whole, but I do declare I could certainly handle a larger chunk of it."

"I know you can, but you will have to be grateful for the most important chunk, won't you?" she retorted. "Don't get greedy, now."

"Heavens no," replied the man. "This isn't about the money. This is the most interesting work I have done in years. Ok, this is also the best work I have done, well ever, darling. Don't let me brag, but I do need to catch you up on the details over a fabulous dinner. Suffice to say, your empire will be not only secure but also quite impenetrable. Ahhh," he sighed with satisfaction. "You really are going to love it."

"That is a date. You are a star, as always." Again with that, she moved on, and his image dimmed.

The following twelve people did not involve her secret plans, so she spoke to them as a group. Now the actual music was to begin. She rapidly brought forward many programs she had sketched out for the ensuing year. There were exploratory missions to virgin asteroids of L4; liaisons to be had with their counterparts at L5; much more staff had to be brought in to accelerate the mining of the new chamber; plenty of exiting staff needed authorisation with immediate effect; counselling services had to be arranged, and the team needed to be grown to handle the increased load, and pending trade deals with the Guild needed unblocking. She was desperate to cause as much change as possible within a short time.

Each day four shipments of mined materials, both raw ore and processed minerals, were launched as shunts to Earth. Each shunt was essentially just a net and attached drive unit, which would navigate unmanned around the orbit shared with Earth and eventually place itself into Earth orbit, where it would undergo inspection and auctioning. In a very bold move, she required this to double to eight. This was not unplanned, but the plans had only been considered for six, and in two months. She demanded it happen next week.

They warned her of the backlash. Stockholders would be worried about the excess of stock and how that would drive down the price. She assured them that underneath it all were plans on Earth just waiting for a quantity of slightly cheaper supply to kick off large projects. In the medium to long-run, profits would rise heavily.

She deliberately gave each of them cause to believe she had a variety of motives: pre-empting a competitive attack, long-term speculation, panicking over the news of the Tug crash, trying to make a name for herself with her father, and plenty more.

This was going to take most of the night to complete.

Orianna waited until they all left before allowing her taut back to relax a little. Mainly, her posture was conditioned from a young age, like a ballerina, to push her shoulders back, perfectly stacking her vertebrae and exuding poise and elegance that commanded the room. However, she was tired and had been 'performing' for hours.

Her hands unfolded from the small of her back. This allowed her the freedom to gesture openly in the absence of company.

The A.R. displayed a list of names a virtual metre in front of her. She scrolled through it casually, controlled through movements of her left hand and precise arrangements of her fingers, more subtle than that of a guitarist's chord hand, until one name caught her eye: "Jefferies, Maddox," she read aloud. "Maddox Jefferies," she repeated with searching recognition.

The eidetic memory surfaced faster than the computer could offer up his details.

She looked up, accessing her memory and recited aloud. "Son of the sister of Frederick Bartholomew, current CEO of the DraytonLyons Corporation. Interesting."

A bold sweep of her right arm across to her centre, much like a wing-handed forearm block, brought to light her secret menu system. How she loved to employ her Kung Fu moves into her gesture lexicon. Her father had insisted on a very complete education, most of which she suffered, but this martial art was one she had enjoyed enormously.

She selected the spy-bot system and brought it and the Maddox Jefferies reference together. This showed a view from an illegal insect-size spy-bot crawling in the shadows of the uneven rocky roof of the street outside, which had taken the initiative and moved, carefully unseen, to within sight of this particular petitioner. So many others around him could be seen idly browsing the stalls, hoping for their moment with Orianna.

There was a significant pause before she had seen enough to summon him.

Maddox stood in front of a long clothing stall. He wasn't really interested in a new pair of boots, but it was busy enough that he wasn't going to be bothered by the sales staff. Picking things up and putting them down - nobody was fooled into thinking he was a serious shopper. The sales staff gave him little notice. They were used to it. They knew they received good quality traffic outside the Administrator's chambers, and overall, it led to good sales despite time-wasters like him. This one, they thought, was particularly preoccupied: an observation not lost on Orianna, watching through the spy-bot above.

His cuff console vibrated.

He wasn't used to wearing a cuff, least of all beneath the

sleeve of his suit; it took many frantic attempts to reveal it. Like some old fashioned chap, not used to an A.R., he had to read its surface: it told him to go and how to get there. And he moved quickly - as it happened too fast for the spy-bot to keep up.

Maddox didn't have to go far down the street until he found the door with the blue lion's head logo of ENESA - the Erebus Non-Equity Strategic Alliance. The door opened to admit him and closed just as promptly behind him.

Inside, a long corridor confirmed he was in the right place. This was no ordinary compartment suite: it implied grand chambers of an elite. He was strangely lit from all directions with a subdued sapphire hue, aware that he was extruding no shadow, in contrast to the stark lights above the street outside. As he walked forward, an almost imperceptible series of pulses in that light chased up and down. He was being scanned. He reached the end of the passage, having passed no breaks in the walls. There, a shoulder-high column stood.

"Allow access to your bio-implant and place your left arm in the receptacle," a calm voice echoed from the column. A hole illuminated with a bright blue glow.

He again revealed his cuff console on his left forearm, tapped 'accept' and then inserted it into the hole. Immediately a tone sounded, and the glow vanished. He withdrew his arm and retired it absently by his side as the wall made a noise behind him. He turned to see it split open cleanly floor to ceiling, widening to the size of a generous and overly tall doorway. Bright white light burst forth. He approached and turned to enter the bright room beyond. It took him a moment for his eyes to adjust. Meanwhile, the door hissed behind him, and he watched the black split shrink again to nothing with all signs of a doorway vanished.

"You are curious," he heard a young female voice say.

Maddox spun around, a little startled. "We have our luxuries here, but that is just simply clever design. The whole wall section slides in from the corner. Better than a door, it is sound-proof and assault-proof. The designers considered every possibility, even riots."

A stark, empty room lay ahead of him. The surfaces were mottled in the same grey pattern, somewhere between an urban camouflage and a Rorschach inkblot.

One woman stood in the middle, elegantly dressed, or so it seemed from one side - it looked complicated. He found it difficult to define the quality of the garment. It was black and appeared quite formal and business-like from one side and sleek and revealing from the other. He could see both sides because she was facing him, both hands behind her back.

"Welcome, M. Jefferies. You may remove your mask. You have been screened."

Her face was partially blocked by a very finely fitted black nose and mouth mask with an attached clear visor. Smooth pale skin was visible at her neck, confirming she was also in her twenties. A short inverted bob of black hair perfectly matched the expected high rear collar. She was impressive.

He removed his mask, revealing a broad mouth and rough stubble.

"I like it," he said, smiling openly. "Thank you, M. Demaine?" She tried to look past the unfortunate yellow tint of his survival suit and take in the honest, open shirt beneath, and the figure of a fit young man beneath that, not entirely the look of an adventurer one might try to put together but rather what might happen when a man dresses for his own needs rather than to impress anyone, consciously at least. The slight stoop could be easily mistaken for too much weight training of the back but showed an intellectual's study posture to her better-trained eye.

He attempted to advance, gradually and uncertainly, when her hand raised, palm facing, in a halting gesture, arresting his pace; he came to rest in a bold but open stance close to the centre of the room. A handshake was clearly not on the cards.

"Why have you come here?" she asked, then he was surprised by her turning to her right and beginning to slowly stride around him in a circle. He observed her: her uncorrected button nose, her unplucked eyebrows - their unplucked state unsuccessfully hidden by makeup - until she passed behind him, and he felt like it might be improper to turn. So he dropped his head a little, confused by this protocol. When she came back into view again on the other side, she had clearly been spiralling outward, and it occurred to him that the business side of her suit was being presented. Delicate diagonal pinstripes were alluding to trousers, at least on the nearest leg, and a double collar rose from her sternum and blended up into her high rear collar.

"I work as a service engineer at the Titov Crater, that's in Mare Moscoviense, Lunar Far Side. I maintain the Deep Space Comms Array there. I am paid more for the isolation than for the work - there isn't much to do there, actually - more of an on-site custodian. I do it so that I can spend time on the abandoned deep-space telescopes, the ones not converted or stripped for spare parts. Nobody seems to care about this stuff, but I love it." He sensed she was not amused by his ramblings. "I know you are busy, but I found something, something significant, and we must investigate it for the good of us all."

She pivoted at his right and, without missing a step, cut a path across in front of him. "You haven't answered my question," she offered quietly.

As she passed him, he began to understand the protocol, the way things got done here, the ways he was taught as a child in the hope of ascending to a similarly important position. There were no particularly happy memories of those times, and he refused to acknowledge that it was even a part of him these days. Reluctantly, he stepped off purposefully, obliquely cutting a path past her rear. The two continued as if two independent people strolling through a park on intersecting paths.

She was careful to maintain him in her periphery and release a smirk as she watched him join the dance. He was bold and seemed unpracticed but underlying it, she sensed skill - he too tracked her in the corner of his eye.

"There's potentially a civilisation-killing event just starting, and I need a long-range vessel to go to the Kuiper Belt and study it," he said and stopped to face her way, earnest angst written all over his boyish face.

Her route curved to avoid the wall and slowed as she tracked parallel to his path. This was her elegant side: no trouser on this leg, closer fitting with deliberate slits showing flashes of skin; the collar layers did not pass around this side, and overall it was a more figure-hugging affair, like an evening gown.

"Refreshing, to have someone come right out and state clearly upfront what they want. You have laid yourself bare, M. Jefferies. You have not come to negotiate at all. What you have presented is more of an ultimatum." Her head lifted slightly, yet her eyes told him she was intrigued.

He responded with an open hand gesture. "I realise that astronomy is now a fringe science. We get no funding. No one cares about anything beyond Jupiter anymore."

"We are all here on business, M. Jefferies. Science may reach for the stars, but commerce makes it viable to live there. Maybe not in our lifetime, but soon we will begin to explore the asteroids of the belt and the Trojans at Juno's LaGrange points. Beyond that...."

"Beyond that seems like a long time away, but we need to start taking a longer-term view," he interrupted, causing her to stop instantly mid-step. "Look, it might be hundreds of years before any possible disaster comes down upon us; we still have time, but we cannot sit on our hands and pretend it isn't happening. Otherwise, we will have learned nothing from the Critical Earth."

Pulling at her mask, it peeled away gently and then recoiled and disappeared into the left business collar. Her face was indeed young and pleasant looking, rounded with only a hint of cheekbones and thin lips - they had well-defined edges but a lack of artificial colouring. She was a contradiction. Maddox had expected more makeup, yet her makeup seemed mostly functional, to hide that her eyebrows had not been plucked and eye-liner with wings to allow her eyes to be more expressive but nothing else.

"You interrupted me," she stated neutrally. "Maybe we can learn from the Critical Earth when and if we are passed it. Can we get past your doomsday scenario? I take it you have some plan?"

"We cannot bury our heads as our ancestors did on Earth. We must not squander our time." He said, sensing she was becoming receptive to the idea. His head bowed as if heavy with a weight he wanted to share. "We have detected a planetary body, small like our inner worlds, a rogue planet entering the system. My best measurements indicate that it has displaced Pluto significantly, perhaps thrown out of the system, and that encounter deflected it inwards towards the ecliptic plane."

"That is significant. Who is 'we'?" Orianna asked, steering the conversation.

"Ha, yes, my niece and I. She's only 12. She keeps me company online, and she is brilliant. She said I should name it 'Rogue'. Not exactly original, I know, but…."

"Suits it perfectly," she said, finishing his sentence and taking one step towards him, giving a sweet smile at the thought of him getting remote support calls from his 12-

year-old niece. "What about your... er... what do you call them? Colleagues? Enthusiasts?"

"Conspiracy nuts. Weirdos. Fringe-ists. Crackpots. We get called all sorts of names, sometimes to each other; many deserve it. Science has always been done this way. Our lack of funding only supports the genuine nature of our calling. Most of us just want to know things and figure things out. Sure, I have posted it, and it has garnered a decent following so far. And we have a lot who reject it as sensationalism. To be fair, the data is far from perfect or conclusive. We just don't have good enough - new enough - equipment anymore. There is a buzz in the networks, but nobody outside our lot will take anything seriously without a consensus. We have actually to go there, to Rogue."

"You are expecting me to take you seriously?" she asked, half rhetorically, taking another slow step. "You still haven't answered my original question. Why... have you... come here?"

As understanding blossomed in his face, she took a final step closer to him and reached up to his high rear collar. Then, as she pulled his visor out and swung it over his head and down in front of his eyes, he took notice of her height more accurately: he was a head taller than her.

"Come," she invited.

Immediately, the room changed. They were standing on Mars. Rusty rock and dust as far as the eye could see all around. The only clue from the Augmented Reality visor that they were still in a room was the perfect square and flat raised rock they seemed to be standing on. Clearly, without it, they might wander into a wall. The simulation was so accurate it literally took his breath away - spacers instinctively reacted to a possible vacuum, or in this case, a near-vacuum. A vast landscape surrounded them, more inviting than Lunar's stark lack of colour; it looked warm and welcoming with an occasional wisp to prove there was a thin atmosphere of sorts.

In the distance, she indicated a few man-made structures near a cave entrance, the only external indications of Colony 1.

"Arguably, you should be here, where the DraytonLyons Corporation is the largest member of the Martian Coalition. Here your name carries weight. So why not ask them to help you in this expensive and unprofitable enterprise?"

Maddox sighed.

"I hope not," he responded quickly. "Perhaps I am the black sheep of the family? Just because I was born into the dynasty doesn't make me a businessman. My grandfather loved this stuff. It was why he was good at it. We are not all destined to be a chip off the old block."

"Are you the prophet who isn't recognised in his hometown?"

"You are quoting Jesus to a NuDruid?" he teased.

She blushed very slightly. "Are you here on faith or by reason?"

"Like anyone brought up without a choice of religion, I keep my faith safely in a box. Yes, science is my mistress. It isn't an easy path. There is no money in it. We do it because we feel compelled."

"Interesting," she mused, avoiding calling him a cynic to his face. "A need to know? I appreciate that. So not your own family, for 'reasons'. Then why mine?"

"Look, Erebus is special. You guys went out on a limb here. Nobody thought it could be done, and now your economy is booming. So you can afford my project."

"So you came to me as a director of the Demaine Group rather than as the administrator of ENESA?"

"You are the perfect person... I mean, you have the unique position to obtain funding from the other members of the alliance if you need to. My family has already invested heavily in Colony 1. I don't know what they are doing 'here', but despite the marketing bullshit, there is no economic reason to set up a colony on Mars. They are never going to listen to me. I'm a disappointment, the black sheep. Also, I don't think they have the interests of the rest of mankind in mind."

She smiled and courteously invited him to walk away from the image of Colony 1 and towards a dark split opening up in the landscape.

"I enjoyed our conversation. I will review your data and give you my decision in due course."

"Goodbye," he said slowly and reluctantly turned to exit.

She watched him go, a sadness in her heart. It had been a while since she had felt chemistry with another in her real life. She already knew what she was going to do: a voyager class ship was ready to be decommissioned after a long trip, mapping parts of the belt and determining where the best claims could be made in the future. It should cope with one more long mission at relatively little expense. It would be a long journey - just to get there would take him around 24 years of hibernation.

This moment would be the only time they would be the same age.

Despite ignoring it for a while, a video message finally caught her attention, and she played it.

"Administrator Demaine, you have a priority audience pending: Cleric David Lassiter from the I.R.C. - one of the lesser-known three-letter agencies. I honestly had to look them up, and as expected, I am still none the wiser," the voice chuckled humorlessly with a deep sounding crackle that showed her age. "I could not find any record of them visiting Erebus, officially, before. The G64 Space Treaty requires us to yield to the authority of all related agencies, but I cannot say they have taken too much interest in us before. Do you remember anything your father might have mentioned? I cannot, and I am as old as he. They had always accepted our annual reports and responded in kind as I understood it. Anyway, they seemed pleasant enough to me. They asked questions about the Tug crash - rest their souls! Bear in mind that they were already on Erebus when it happened. Take care. Administrator Baker, out."

She prepared herself by replacing her mask and signalled for them to arrive. She did not use the spy-bot, knowing that spies don't like to be spied upon - a risk she wasn't prepared to make.

In the corridor, however, the scanner was expected, and there she saw a small man and three larger men - the latter were conspicuously armed. All were wearing sunglasses: the same violet sunglasses as she had seen earlier. The scanner could not answer that question, but they looked like the same men.

She gasped. No, she must remain calm; she had to play this cool. That glow could give her away. All she knew was that it seemed to be triggered by high emotional states. If she continued to remain undiscovered, she had to keep calm. Had they already discovered her? There was no way of knowing; it was just as likely that they intended coming to her anyway.

The door opened, and a single small man entered, glancing back at the door closing behind him.

"My men were not admitted by your corridor," he cheerfully stated, although his tone was as if a question had been asked. He had an oversized head, a bulbous forehead with short blonde curls receding from it. His smile and genial manner were surprising. He ventured forwards, his arms open wide but not close enough to look like he was aiming for a hug.

"They were armed and not on the guest list, M. Lassiter. Greetings," she answered matter-of-factly and offered a slight nod of her head.

"I thank you for your greetings, Administrator Demaine. How did you know we weren't here to arrest you?" he continued in an obviously playful tone and then added a quick nod. She had already sized up his style of audience.

Orianna took a step to the side and said, "Then they would have been admitted. These systems are not optional. They come with the chambers, with the office. They follow the rules."

He laughed. "I am, of course, just joking, M. Demaine, er, may I call you Orianna?"

"You may not."

He did not lose his smile, but he paid close attention to her eyes. His eyes and sockets were visible beneath his glasses, tinted in a violet hue.

"I did not mean to offend you. I merely wanted to put you at ease...."

"M. Lassiter, you have been granted an audience with an Administrator. It is my duty and privilege to serve in this office. You are addressing that office. If you want to speak to me about matters of the Demaine Group, then you should have met me there and not here. Was it the crash of our Tug that you wished to speak to me about?" she said, her tone remaining calm but clipped.

"Well," he began rubbing his unmasked chin, looking down, stooping a little, searching for the words before gazing back up at her. "In a manner of speaking, I am taking a broader view. I am new to Erebus, and I think I should understand all its processes and nuances so that I am not so clumsy in the future."

He paused, taking the time to rub his thighs with his hands.

"It is a little confusing, the politics here, I mean," his smile dropped, and he continued to stare at her. "You have Administrators from each corporation, who take an interest in the running of Erebus, whilst you simultaneously are an

Executive Director of your father's firm, tasked with Export Commerce. How does that work? Do you not find a conflict of interest? Have you ever found yourself torn between your loyalties to this habitat and your father's company?"

She turned her head to face him and then continued to turn the other way, showing her elegant side, to make a close pass ahead of him. "I could say no, but that would be a lie indeed all Administrators are always Executives for the precise purpose to make sense of conflicts of interests. Better to negotiate with one's self than to argue with another person. The businesses pay taxes to the Alliance, keeping ENESA financed independently, allowing it to serve the habitat and the people; it allows trade and mining rights in exchange for construction projects to improve and expand the habitat. The two are interdependent. Have you seen our new chamber currently being built? The plans are extraordinary. It will be the first of its kind."

This was easy for her: a well-practised performance and steering of the conversation, but what really worried her was whether she could keep her emotions in check. She had a good look at his violet glasses close-up as she passed. He was smiling again, and she noticed his teeth were quite crooked. It says something about a man who has clearly chosen not to make easy corrections to their teeth, perhaps something fundamental about their ideology. Regrettable that she wasn't better prepared for this meeting. Who were the I.R.C.?

"Erebus is no longer the maverick venture. No, she has become a key player. So congratulations to you all, I say. It may have taken a little over four decades, but you really did pull it off. I remember hearing about it as a child, M. Demaine. Your great grandfather, then quite old, pushed so far out when everyone was invested in Lunar..."

"M. Lassiter," she tried to interrupt but was interrupted back.

"Actually, it is Cleric Lassiter. Sorry, I should have introduced myself properly."

"Cleric. You really should come and speak with me in my other office, and I can explain why Erebus was really quite inevitable: it just took vision to see it first. The economics of mining asteroids at Earth's LaGrange points is so much better than on the surface of the Moon. We may be far away in the distance, but in terms of energy, we are in the same orbit as Earth: there is almost no minimum energy cost to get between Earth and Erebus - energy is simply traded to get there faster. Lunar has to escape their gravity, not to mention dealing with the horrendous regolith dust. Humans cannot even stay there too long because the gravity is too low. Here you are enjoying 1G right here, free of charge. This habitat is for long term living, and the more we mine, the more habitat we gain."

"Of course, and it is indeed your exponential growth that has raised eyebrows. You are not far from exceeding the G.D.P. of the Moon. Now, you understand why, since off-worlds are mandated to establish a form of government that does not constitute control of corporations over people, we would eventually be taking a closer interest in what brand of politics you have employed." At this point, he suddenly sat down on the floor. "I am sorry, I have not been here for more than a week myself. Others have been here longer and would laugh at me, but you are right. Despite my efforts, Lunar's gravity had eroded by strength."

She looked down at him, "Do you need medical assistance?"

"No, please, my body will be fine down here," he reassured her, making himself comfortable.

She put this down to a protocol breaking ruse designed to take her off guard. For a moment, she contemplated sitting with him but decided that would indicate compliance, and he would not respect that.

"An unfortunate accident," he muttered. "The Tug crash. Did you lose anyone you knew?" His smile had returned.

Remaining quite still, she replied with a courteous smile. "Cleric Lassiter, I administrate the Erebus processes, and I direct a corporation's business needs and relationships. I do not have much time to socialise. The people I know best are those who work for me. We have a growing population of hundreds. I did, however, have the opportunity to meet Captain Laskin on more than one occasion. I found her an exceptional officer."

"Did she have a family?" he probed further, sensing he had captured a point of human interest in her. "Is it in your responsibilities to have to notify the next of kin? I gathered that a novice was on board also. What about her? Do the families ask for an investigation in these situations?"

Tension was rising in her, and she knew it. She had to dodge this pressure without looking like she was. She needed to encourage him to ease off.

"It is all my responsibility, Cleric Lassiter. Space is a dangerous place, we have 'situations', and they can be lethal, which is why we have such stringent safety protocols in place. It is in everyone's interest to care for our personnel. Such skilled people will be hard to replace."

"Such cool rationalities, Administrator," he commented. "What if it is terrorism or corporate sabotage? Have you considered that?"

"As you have already said, we have not been on anyone's radar…."

"And as I also said, you are now."

"Then I trust you will take your responsibilities with equally cool rationalities," she smiled visibly in her eyes for him to see.

He looked around, now regaining a little more colour in his cheeks. "I do like your room, may I?" he said, his tone rising with a sweeping arm. She nodded, and he accessed his cuff. Then, behind her back, she micro-gestured with her fingers to give him temporary access.

The room's local network instructed both A.R. systems in the room to show the same virtual background. It was a gothic cathedral; the expected raised floor was entirely central, at the Crossing of the Transept. Above them, coloured light beams poured in and down from the Rose Window at the far end.

"Magnificent, yes," he marvelled. "It is unfortunate that your room is not quite up to simulating the distant echo properties of such a cavernous space - sounds like we are in an open field. Ah well. Do you have faith, Administrator Demaine? Do your rationalities have room for God?"

Such a question was rude and bordering on illegal.

"Splendid. Notre-Dame de Paris? Post-restoration of 2024? Shame it is no longer there, truly amazing architecture for the twelfth century." Then glancing at him, she added, "As Laplace said, 'I have no need of that hypothesis. He may be around though.'"

"Ha! Very good," he replied, jumping to his feet, clearly much better now. "I enjoyed our conversation very much. Alas, our preliminary analysis and report from the ICE imply that human error was the cause, so you will probably not hear from us again. Until next time."

With that, he turned abruptly and walked towards the Rose Window, where an apparent crack in the fabric of the universe opened to receive him.

The vista of a thousand-year-old church icon continued to surround her, its walls now metaphorically closing in on her. She had done her best. Her world had been turned upside down and inside out. With her alter-ego now deceased, along with all her friends, she was wholly back in her real life, but this real-life now felt like the illusion.

She began to question who and what she was. Why were they chasing her? For now, she decided she was safe. All her plans had been brought forward, and the ensuing chaos would make it very hard for them to follow all the leads. Erebus had not been locked down, and she was taking full advantage of it by shifting as many people on and off the habitat as quickly as she could. Her own empire-building plans would also be lost in the noise.

She outstretched her hand to the Rose Window and screamed a long pressure-releasing yell and watched her hand burn blue and then violet at arm's length.

This was something she needed to study and get used to.

CHAPTER FIVE

2226 CE, Earth-L4, Erebus

Someone laughed, and Orianna made herself smile in response. A dozen people filled the passenger elevator, swaying together like reeds as the gravity increased and their boots held them firmly in place.

Quite an incoming surge.

Observing the variety of clothing styles and glimpsing labels hanging off bags, Orianna painted a mental picture of the influx of people around her: personnel moving around as a direct consequence of her efforts to accelerate her projects.

The chaos continues.

On exit, she was even more delighted to see almost as many people waiting to board the elevator.

The arrivals lounge offered the opportunity for disembarking passengers to properly freshen up after their hibernation and before being reacquainted with their luggage.

Orianna didn't have luggage, only her small carry-on case, but rather than using the advantage to get ahead of the traffic, she took her time with a shower and a change of clothes.

Eventually, the cloakroom emptied, and she was alone.

This was the opportunity that had caused her to languish. There, an actual mirror was attached above a basin, not a camera-console combination, a genuine silvered piece of acrylic, capable of reflecting all frequencies of light.

Tension showed on her reflected face as she dared herself not to glow until she was ready, despite driving emotions up inside her. She took note of a slight aura before releasing her tension, and her skin blazed with such intensity it seemed she was alight with a blue flame.

"Oh sorry, forgot my bag," came a voice from behind.

She turned abruptly with a gasp, eyeing a fellow female passenger.

"Are you ok? I didn't mean to startle you," the passenger asked.

Orianna nodded, managing a coy smile. "Fine, thanks," she replied courteously.

Unsure if Orianna was really ok, the passenger eased towards the door, expecting her to call out at any moment, but no call came. The door closed as she left.

Orianna turned back to the mirror suddenly. Her glow was not visible at all. *Some success at least*, she thought.

Despite catching up with the group, she hung back and trailed behind as they wandered into Pall Mall, spreading out to greet those waiting for them. Orianna found her brother waiting for her. This was not a surprise, but she pretended to be gratefully excited to see him.

He did not offer to hug her, keeping his hands crossed behind him.

She made no disguise of looking him up and down. He was pretty stiff and taut in a long tight jacket and slightly too obvious shoulder pads. *Very neat*, she thought, checking that he was still only marginally taller than she.

"How was your journey?" he gasped, exasperated by her unreciprocated bear hug. He unclasped his hands only to hold her waist just long enough to put her back in front again, then returned them to his back.

"Great," she replied. "A little slow on the transfer from Orbital One. Seems there was a shortage of seats for a change."

"Hmm, no doubt," he gruffed. "Do you think it had something to do with the surge of work you have been initiating for the past eight months?"

She eyed him coyly. "Are we going to go there so suddenly? I have only just stepped on the transport."

"You dropped me right in the middle of a shit-storm," he snarled, flaring his nostrils. "Did you do this on purpose?"

"Awww, come on, Orlando! I was only gone for three weeks. All you had to do was keep everything ticking along for that long. It was practically set up to run on automatic anyway. You were only supposed to be there in case anything went wrong. Did anything go wrong?"

His face sank a little, his fury deflated a little. "Father also required to know what all the extra expense was all about."

She grabbed his arm and looked around for prying ears, ushering him towards the seclusion of the nearest bush and away from the somewhat busy path.

"Ok, I threw myself into my work after the Tug disaster. Worst case, I have become overproductive. Both of you should be thanking me." Orianna offered a friendly grin.

"Prior warning might have been prudent," he said through gritted teeth. "Cash flow needs to be managed."

Looking up at him with the subtlest puppy-dog eyes, she said nothing. Her brother had, as usual, played his hand early, and he had already lost this game of wits. There was no cash flow issue. She had made sure of that. Indeed, much of the business to do with the Demaine Group had involved just shifting things around. The real money deals were being done to secure her own secret empire: the O.D. Group.

The first thing that this told her was that their father had not asked him to look into things. That was a blatant lie.

Clearly, Orlando had been out of his depth and wanted to nosey around Orianna's domain.

The second thing she now knew was that he hadn't been able to make head nor tail of the work, or he would have realised the cash flow was locally handled.

"Oh brother mine, let's have something to eat, and I will tell you anything you want to know. I might even give you a present from Libya."

Disgruntled, having vented and asserted his authority against being treated as her deputy, he allowed himself to be led to the nearest eatery.

Wearing just a plain jumpsuit, Orianna realised she was a little underdressed for The Excelsior Diner. To rectify this, she unzipped her collar down to her sternum to show a little cleavage and pulled out a fine hand-painted Libyan silk scarf and tied it loosely around her neck, dropping one end down her front to play down the now exposed flesh. Finally, she unzipped one whole sleeve and pulled it off, stuffing it into her bag where she had retrieved the scarf. This she did so expertly in no more than seven steps that it left Orlando a little startled as he followed close behind her.

This was more private than Pall Mall in the partitioned booth they selected. Most people there, who could afford to be there regularly, were executives, and they seemed busy with their own conversations, except for the wily ones that Orianna caught the eye of - they scrutinised from a distance.

"You think Father wouldn't notice an increase to eight mineral shipments per week?" Orlando whispered once they had ordered and were left alone. "The price fell."

Orianna sipped her water. "The plan was already ratified - I merely brought forward the date. But, of course, the price fell, that was expected. We are in a growing market, and we were ready to grow: demand was high, hence the inflated prices. Now we have beaten Lunar to fulfil that demand, and I am sure Father will be happy with that." Her tone was very calm, and she squinted her trademark winged eyeliner at someone she recognised across the room, along with a friendly smile.

"He thinks you are a loose cannon," he said, changing tack. "Not a team player."

Of course not, when my younger brother is the heir apparent!

She contemplated how best to appease him, knowing he would have to report back to their father, and if Orlando couldn't show he had learned a few things in the trenches, he would deflect by saying bad things about Orianna. It was in her interests to help him in this regard, to save face.

"Sorry I left things in a bit of a mess. Let me make it up to you and set up a presentation about everything at Erebus, and you can dazzle Father with your grasp of things here. One day all this will be under your control, so I do understand how important it is that you grasp the subtleties of the politics here."

"Don't patronise me!" he growled.

"Hardly," she reassured, touching his arm. "Just trying to be a team player, on the side of team Orlando, my brother. This is the family business, and I am always on the side of the family. So it is in my interest to ensure your visit was useful, that you understand and that you can be on my side when you are the big cheese. That is how politics works." She smirked.

He nodded slowly.

"Speaking of family, how are Gemma and the girls?" Orianna asked, expertly switching to small talk as their starters arrived.

"All fine," he responded casually. Then he looked up from his food to ask, "what of your life? Still not dating? What do you do when you aren't working?"

"Oh, I'm a workaholic," she managed to get out before an almost poorly timed mouthful of food. She took a moment to savour the morsel before swallowing. "You deflected. What does 'fine' mean anyway?" She offered him an expectant glance in return.

"Ok, I admit, I am often distracted by work, which takes me away from home, to a lot of places, like here," he emphasised, "but it feels good to know they are there to come home to... eventually."

He looked at her as if from a bit of a distance. "You are worse! I don't even understand you - not even looking for love."

"There is always time...."

"Time? You're twenty-eight. I was married at twenty-two. When is the right time? You always were so driven, but I have to tell you, sis, meeting some of the people you work with, I found out a much gentler side of you I wasn't sure you had in you. I remember how arrogant you were at fencing, winning at every championship but making no friends."

Orianna gawped comedically and playfully punched his shoulder. "Ha. Let's just say it took me time to learn that."

Orianna's eidetic memory returned her to a particular moment of school life: the fencing match between her school and the Langford School for Boys, another private school in Kent, England.

"Orianna, Orianna, you must yield more," Coach Giovanni remarked from behind her as she watched the fight from beside the piste. "Now, what do you see?"

"Mark is playing to his strengths, leaning forward maximising his reach advantage, but he always puts too much weight on his front foot. In foil, this works for him, but he will lose this epee fight doing the same."

"Why?" Giovanni asked gleefully.

"His opponent, er Geoff, I have played him before. He is a left-hander. Left-handers statistically play more against right-handers, and by the same odds, right-handers rarely learn how to successfully play against left-handers. He should spend longer practising with our left-handers, but he doesn't. So Geoff has the advantage."

"Good. Score?"

"Five to two at best, I think."

"Ha! Very good. A-Team foil is on next. So you should get ready."

Orianna trotted off to get her kit.

Meanwhile, the Langford teacher came over to talk to Giovanni.

"She is good," he remarked. "She has a special gift. I have been watching her closely. I see most students settle into a style that minimises pain - they refuse to practise the right stance. It is so rare to find someone with such perfect form."

Giovanni nodded. "We do not let them even fight each other until a year of training. Even then, only once in a while will someone like her come along."

"Is she that good?"

Giovanni chuckled. "Ah, she has a name for it which I like: Morphic Fencing. I did not teach her this. She watches. She sees A beat B using a favourite trick, and then B beats C and then C beats A. This is not so uncommon. She watches. She sees how they won, what strange move the other couldn't cope with. Then. Then she mimics them. Her gift is that she can fence like anyone she wants, and she has no style of her own to be likewise picked apart."

The teacher has a distant look as he thinks back to watching her earlier in the A-Team Epee. His largest pupil, Morris, had an odd attack mode: solid footwork powered at his opponents, but he favoured prime instead of the en guard position - a position usually used as a parry. Since in Epee, the entire body was a target for the opponent's point, most Epeeists kept their arm down and hidden behind the large bell guard - the wrist was the nearest and thus the easiest part to score on. Morris showed his forearm across his chest as if daring someone to hit it whilst his wrist bent down to hold his weapon vertically, threatening to flick it up to the belly. This would generally be moved laterally to move an attack away from the target. It was daring - perhaps he was trying to shock - but it was risky against a good player.

He remembered Orianna watching Morris' previous fights, and then when she had come to face him, half his size, she was playful stepping onto the long piste giving no regard to his daunting method. At first, she had backed off repeatedly, although she was actually sizing him up. Then everything changed. She issued several winning stop hits on his wrist with lightning speed and great precision, showing how his entire approach was flawed. Morris had become flustered and cautious, and this part was even more startling: she then began to attack him with his own move, in prime! The poor lad was entirely demoralised and lost quickly: humiliated five to zero.

The A-team Foil began soon after the two teachers had spoken, and Orianna was on first.

A tiny boy, apparently twelve years old, but indeed just a tiny teenager, arrived on the piste. Orianna immediately changed demeanour in response to the boy's apparent nervousness. The biggest boy on his team had just been humiliated by her. So she became very calm and adopted an exact stance, going back to basics.

He advanced a jitter, half-heartedly, and she retreated in respect. Then she advanced, but not too fast, and he sprung back. Taking full advantage of this, she lunged just slow enough to not catch him. It would be tricky to convince the boy that she wasn't going easy on him. The murmuring of the growing crowd assured her that nobody else was fooled. It was a match, and she had to win, but this boy did not need a lesson in humility, as his teammate had; this boy deserved to be built up.

Orianna beat his blade aggressively but not too hard - she felt his grip was weak - and lunged much faster, too fast for the boy to move. As their bodies closed the distance, she made the point of her foil sail just over his shoulder, as if she had miscalculated his smaller size, thus suggesting to the boy that he had a natural advantage of a smaller target. Her blade rested on his shoulder. She paused, waiting as she sensed him hesitate, trying to catch up with what had happened; his blade passed her other side. She curled and attempted to withdraw the blade enough for a close touch but failed to clear his shoulder. Repeatedly doing this, it seemed comical, as though she was trying to saw off his shoulder with an edgeless blade.

She leapt backwards as if panicked by the 'failed' move and recomposed herself. The boy bounced a little in his stance, and the crowd joined his excitement. His confidence was growing already.

Orianna gave him a good chance throughout the fight, and she eventually won five to three - not her best performance by a long way - but convincing enough.

As she shook hands with him and left the piste, Giovanni intercepted her and told her that that had been the most fantastic thing he had ever seen, a sentiment she now realised was being echoed by the entire salle. To be sure, she always strove to win and never to consider compassion until she fought this boy. He hadn't deserved to be destroyed five to zero as Morris did with all his arrogance. However, at no point had she put the match at risk by losing, so there was an opportunity to teach a little, to build up the confidence of a terrified boy who expected to be humiliated. Everyone watching had also noticed her do this, so she received her first rapturous applause.

"... I never could get the hang of sabre, and you, the most right-handed person I knew, were going into the regional championships with gloves on both hands and a choice of left or right-handed sabres that you selected depending who you fought. You said you hated sabre, being an edged weapon because it ruined your point control, and so you never practised it, but you wanted the master-at-arms trophy, so you entered sabre and tried to get through on your wits. I never forget your reasoning: it confused them more than you because you didn't have the expected reflexes. I saw videos of that. It was mad. If you had been rubbish, they wouldn't have bothered looking up the rules. They said that you were allowed to change hands between fights in a pool but not in the middle of a fight, as I recall."

Orianna snapped back to the present and touched his arm. Her smile was empty.

"A decade and a hundred million miles away," she said. "Listen, I should tell you about Axeon."

He cocked his head a little, then nodded, "how was the trip? You went to the Libyan branch, I understand? Why there?"

"They had an interesting project to use solar panels to power a desalination plant and a solar purification plant using long glass pipes irradiated with sunlight concentrated by large half-pipe mirrors. I figure that was an easy entry point for rare off-world metal sales. They had several other projects that I wanted to get close to and see what I could wing whilst there."

He chuckled and then caught himself. "What projects did you find?" he asked.

She eyed him closely and said it. "Zephyr."

There were signs: a slight tremble of the upper lip, a nostril flare, a glance to the side.

"Apparently, this is where the ICE Units are constructed - the hardware that is. Could be a very lucrative venture since these units are destined for all vessels and bases," she continued sweetly. "Amazing what a little digging can get...."

"You should, not," he interrupted.

"Not? Not what?" she asked.

"You have no idea what you are meddling in," he insisted.

No, I think I do.

The acquisition of information had, in fact, been entirely planned by her. The visit to Axeon was always a ruse to get her close. They had security doors that she could not get past, but those doors had windows for safety reasons. Executive visitors were closely monitored and screened for recording devices, but they did not know she was one. All she needed were minor distractions to steal glances through the windows - a momentary glance at documents, even if only seen in reflection, was all that was required to store it permanently in her eidetic memory. This had given her enough information to confirm her suspicions and lead her to those controlling the ICE builds. Whoever had made them had installed the hardware that was triggered when she touched the ICE Unit on Tug 43. As it turned out, the software was handled in Libya, but the hardware designs had come from farther down the trail, a trail that had led right back to the Demaine Group.

The hardware had detected her and sent the signal - that was the trap. However, the software was something else: a hidden personality in the donated human imprint - it had warned her, saved her, but was it complicit in the deaths of all her friends - it all seemed too much of a coincidence.

Had the software engineered the crash? Had the ICE Unit been recovered and revealed all? Maybe not since she was still free.

"Are you saying that I shouldn't pursue the Zephyr lead?" she asked, sounding as innocent as she could without overplaying it.

"I am saying you should never mention that word again." This time his voice was filled with fear.

"What?" she gasped, reaching out to touch him again, but he instinctively withdrew. "Who are you afraid of?"

His laugh came, short and unconvincing. "You mean apart from Father?" Leaning over to whisper, he continued. "You will find out soon enough. The number of Clergy stalking Erebus has increased even since you left, sticking their noses all over the place. All I know is that - this subject - should not be spoken about. Father has been warning me about it and the I.R.C., so I put two and two together. My advice is: let it be."

She knew she was risking her career, future, and liberty, which scared her. More than that, she was still no closer to understanding why they were hunting for her. Not knowing why was the hardest thing.

CHAPTER SIX

2249 CE, Rogue, orbit

Far off, in the outer reaches of the solar system where it is so cold, the dwarf planet Pluto's surface is frozen solid, and the Sun is a thousand times dimmer than on Earth, a tiny speck of human life drifted towards a newcomer: Rogue.

Maddox Jefferies almost fell out of his hibernation pod. He had been "waking up" for several hours, but he was still groggy and his muscles aching terribly. He cursed that there was probably a reason that humans didn't hibernate naturally.

He spat out the tube that had been drip-feeding him with a rejuvinating cocktail of multi dextrose, salts, vitamins and minerals.

It was not cold, he concluded optimistically, slumped as he was half up against the side of the pod.

He chose to slide down onto the floor and then onto a small porthole window next to him. His cheek pressed against the inner layer of plastic. Before his breath fogged it up, he saw the infinite blackness stretch out before him. In itself, not that remarkable a sight, no different from any other viewpoint humans have enjoyed in space. Still, it was different because of where he was: farther away than any human had ever been before; indeed, farther than any human had needed.

"Cool," he muttered, lacking anything impressive to say, and tried to smile, but even his free cheek wasn't playing along just yet. He had survived, although he was sure the jury was still out on that determination.

Nobody was there to help him; nobody would need his help either, once he was up and about. He was more utterly alone than even he had managed before, more than anyone had managed before, ever. He was isolated.

Loneliness had not been his goal, however, and had there been a choice, then he would have had company. But, alas, not one single person was even slightly interested in his adventure, not the wildest mavericks, not his most dedicated contemporaries in the amateur world of cosmology, not even madmen. It was not just the distance or the risk. No. What they would be giving up, what he had given up, was time.

After "cool," he was confident that his voice was working well enough again to try a command. "Command," he croaked. His throat was still dry.

"Hello. Please allow me to orientate you after hibernation. You are on the Explorer Vessel' Achilles'. Authority recognised - Maddox Jefferies, access to all systems," came the canned response, ensuring he was oriented correctly. "Ready."

"Hibernation report."

"Earth time in hibernation, twenty-four years, two months, seventeen days. Absolute age fifty-one years. Subjective age approximately thirty. Congratulations, you have been logged with a new human hibernation longevity record. Also logging other records: a new distance record for a living human, most isolated human, most of a lifetime spent in hibernation."

"Most idiotic person?" he interrupted the machine. It did not understand and said nothing more.

The reality was that anyone he knew was now a lot older

by now; some might even be dead.

Travelling long distances still took a long time, which was tedious. It also required many resources: heat, light, food, and water but improvements, such as "stasis fields" and cryogenics, had never been perfected. However, advances in medicine meant that humans could be encouraged to mimic other mammals and hibernate, like bears: thus only dormant, people still aged more slowly - some slower than others.

"Three years older. It could have been much worse," he muttered. The computer ignored the statement. He was already comfortable talking to himself and had developed quite a skill at using it to keep his sanity and his spirits up.

He carefully navigated the 0.7G and made his way over to the nearest chair and console. His head felt dizzy, now experiencing slightly less gravity than his feet - it was the minimally acceptable radius for a spinning habitat at thirty metres, and it would take some getting used to.

The vessel had been designed for deep flight in mind: a fat middle for humans to enjoy a good level of gravity suitable for years. In addition, the entire vessel would rotate to avoid the risk of long term wear on bearings and seals. It had been theorised that it would get this far, but nobody had even tried to hibernate for more than eight years in one go until just now.

In the absence of other crew members, Maddox had a lot of space and resources to last him years - much longer than the vessel had been designed for.

"Navigation report."

"Two days until the vessel's orbital insertion around the rogue planet designated 'Rogue'."

"Good. Report on task 'Interloper'?"

"Project 'Interloper'. Seven thousand samples were taken of the location, mass, rotational cycle, temperature, ambience, spectral analysis and magnetic field density of

'Rogue' when close enough to take such readings. Anomalous readings have been verified by multiple sensor arrays and confirmed by diagnostics: they are not due to sensor error."

Maddox read the report on the console. There was a lot to take in, but the most pertinent was where Rogue was headed.

"Run simulations of its projected path through the solar system," he ordered.

"Rogue ingress result: a near collision with Pluto approximately twenty-six years ago. Momentum exchange result: Rogue solar relative velocity 3.2%, Pluto egress is permanent, directly out of the solar system. Rogue trajectory intercept: Jupiter, with a 27% or minus 17% chance of collision. Uncertainty, not a sensor or calculation error: anomalies present."

"List reading anomalies."

"Mass readings have ranged by 0.1% either side of a mean of 0.9 Earth mass. The surface temperature has risen from a mean of 65 to 76 degrees Kelvin. Comparatively 21 to 32 degrees warmer than Pluto. Magnetic flux non-zero, 0.006% increase per hour and accelerating. Equatorial bulge 0.01% and stable. Equatorial radius 115% of Earth equatorial radius. Rotational: Rogue's day is 32.7 hours."

"Glad I came," he said and forced his eyes wider. The mysterious planet welcomed him with curiosities the likes of which he would never have been able to fathom from Lunar. Even a probe would not have sufficed, he convinced himself. He *had* to be here. If the human race was at risk, nobody would listen to a janitor on the far side of the moon, but out here - out here, he could be a beacon of hope and knowledge. He had found a new great frontier - which currently, nobody was interested in, well almost.

"Start message," he sighed.

"Begin."

"Hey, Moonpie, I am so sorry not to have seen you grow up and graduate, and wow, you could even be married with kids now. Ok, this is probably very much out of the blue. You might not have remembered that I would be calling about now. I hope you still understand why I had to come. How's your mum? From my point of view, we spoke last night. For you, I have been gone for two-thirds of your life now, assuming this message gets through ok. Rogue is really here. You named it, and it will thus always be named by you. Remember that! I've only just awakened, and already Rogue is showing her mysteries. More on that later, after I have had time to review the data recorded on approach during my er nap. Just wanted to - just hoping you haven't forgotten your old Uncle Max, although you are older than I look now, so that's going to be weird. Anyway, hope to hear from you soon. End message."

There was already so much to share with his community, his fellow enthusiasts. He was sure they would be waiting, middle-aged nerds as they would be now.

He would only share when he had something more substantial, but one other person did come to mind.

"Start message," he repeated.

"Begin."

"Thank you, M. Demaine, Orianna, for believing in me. I wish we had had more time. I felt we made a real connection when we last spoke. I admit I was actually tempted to stay, at least for a bit longer, to get to know you more. I am no good at this sort of thing. I always regret not acting, but never quite so strongly as I did after our last meeting. Sorry to have displaced time with you now. Please understand that the memory of you, as you were, is still just as fresh with me today. I wish you could see this," he said, bringing up the accurate colour view of Rogue approaching. Tears began to well up in his eyes. "It is incredible. It is streaked with colours like Jupiter but frozen hard like Pluto. To think, this is the first extrasolar material to be confirmed and measured at close quarters. Perhaps its composition could give us a clue where it came from, how long it travelled between the stars and how old it is. Thank you so much for this opportunity. This is as real as science gets. If I die on this mission, I die happy. All data and messages will be sent regularly, just in case. End message."

"Log entry," he said boldly with a more severe and formal voice.

"Begin."

"Day 1…"

"Incoming message."

"I don't recognise the name. Play it, please."

"Uncle Max," a woman's voice said. Her voice was unfamiliar, but he guessed it must be his niece. "Wow! So, you made it. You were always the adventurous one, damn you. This is so awkward. I always thought of myself looking at you in your fifties about now, but now I look older than you. Not gonna lie; I took it pretty badly when you left. Therapy helped. Then I got married and had some great kids - I'll send you some pictures and videos. Not much more to tell. I'm as happy as anyone. I don't think I can do this, though. Sorry, Max, this is a whole kind of strange I can do without right now."

Maddox sat still for over an hour, playing the message back - no sound - just trying to see his little Moonpie behind that thirty-something face.

"Incoming message from M. Demaine."

After twenty-four years, he really had no idea what to expect. He wished that everyone was waiting and would respond soon after the minimum four hours there and four hours back. The good news was that they all did, but not always so quick. Orianna's message had been the last, but now it was the one he most wanted to hear.

"Play it now, please," Maddox squeaked, his voice unused for the last four hours. Indeed, he then realised he hadn't had a drink in that time either. He grabbed the half-full glass of water in front of him and gulped it down. Water droplets hung on his moustache and dripped onto his bearded chin. It hadn't just been laziness or a lack of anyone to impress that had him decide so early on to give up shaving: he actually felt it made him a little more distinguished. It had recently moved from the messy stubble stage to become what anyone might describe as a full beard, dark brown with a hint of red. His face didn't really need ageing, his looks were rugged rather than boyish, but he always felt his lips were a bit thin, so this helped, he thought. It's funny how the mind goes through the considerations of society even in its entire absence.

"Hello Maddox," came the audio recording of Orianna's fresh voice. "Glad you made it. I have been interested in listening to your messages and looking through your data. Sorry, I haven't made first contact until now. Things have moved on unexpectedly since you left. Has it really been twenty-four years? I have my own business now, but I prefer to run it behind the scenes. I did think of you often after you left. One day, I hope we can meet again. Good luck with the survey drones; I was lucky to procure three, so don't waste them. How long are you staying? Let me know if you want me to do anything back here. Times are strange right now. One more thing, though, and this will sound strange, but I have changed my name to Orelia De Lorettis. You can still call me Orianna, but for your messages, they will need to be addressed to Orelia De Lorettis at Atlas Inc. from now on. This will really help me out. Good luck."

CHAPTER SEVEN

2253 CE, Rogue, orbit

Rogue would not give up her secrets so quickly, but she was not short of questions to throw at Maddox, all alone in his tiny orbital home for the last three years, four months and twenty-seven days. His home may have been cramped, but his world was vast and varied.

At first, measurements from orbit were interesting enough to keep him up all hours: the composition of the ice held everything needed to support an atmosphere once it melted; water was in abundance; there was evidence of surface erosion under the ice indicating it had once been warm.

The details kept him from dwelling on the elephant in the room: what effect was this rogue planet going to have on the solar system, and were other planets going to be thrown out of orbit?

Was this world destined to be the end of humanity?

There came a time, early on, when he realised that his body was beginning to fatigue and weaken, so he had created a workout area, using elastic straps to increase the load.

Spending longer in his pod, laying flat, helped him feel a consistent gravity. To capitalise on this better posture, he rigged up one of the monitors so that a pod could serve as a horizontal workstation.

After the first year, he realised that one of the most curious anomalies was helping him stay for longer: Rogue's magnetic field had been growing since he arrived, and now it protected him from cosmic radiation. None of his friends could explain it - not even Ben, who was the best astrophysicist he had ever "met". It had seemed like a prelude to the increasing surface temperatures and later emergence of the first tectonic movements.

Rogue awakened.

This was no silly sentiment; no theory of planetary geology could come close to explaining why this planet, still outside the orbit of Uranus, could be warming up so quickly.

Rogue is melting from the inside out!

The more readings he took, the more certain he was to stay longer. His beard followed suit. It had become a thing: to see how far it would go. He kept his head trimmed close, though, since there were acceptable limits to his discomfort.

Rations were plentiful, enough for one person to live on for years since they were intended for a much larger crew for a shorter period.

Observing purely from orbit was sufficient to keep him busy for the first year, despite the urge to spend his probes early one - he knew they would be more useful later as Rogue thawed.

By fourteen months, he launched Chico, the first of his three survey probes, which landed on the surface without a hitch. He and his friend Ben began more frequent messages back and forth after that. The sheer volume of data he was accumulating was pushing the limits of the computing power at his disposal, and he needed assistance.

Ben had taken over Maddox's caretaker role at the Titov Crater, on Lunar's far side. He had a lot of power there, and he could receive at a good bandwidth, but the real strength came when Ben passed the information on freely to the others - eager amateurs, like them, willing to discuss and argue and explore all manner of hypotheses. Ben had passed fifty years old now, and he was managing a new wave of amateurs to the cause whilst juggling a family life including three teenage daughters, two cats and a Dobermann called "Achtung".

Chico had been programmed to hop from ice break to ice break autonomously: it had a lot of ground to cover because Maddox was regularly out of comms as he orbited faster than Rogues rotation. So Chico continued functioning for over a year, providing more data than his friends could process in a decade.

After that, he launched Harpo, the second drone, to specifically investigate a meltwater stream coming from an ice cliff. Meltwater on a planet so far from the sun that it should remain a block of ice, but it wasn't.

"Ok, so this first melt is a major clue, Max," Ben said in his latest message, which was eight hours after Maddox had given him a report on the first telemetry from Harpo, making its first landing near the cliff. "We have been focussing our attention on the latest orbital data, and there is definitely a localised phenomenon going on right inside that cliff. Max, this is so exciting. The atmosphere is still just under one per cent. That means water can be liquid only between zero and about twenty degrees C, above which it boils. However, we are seeing steam so whatever is in there is probably warmer than that. What is interesting is that water's triple point is at zero point six per cent pressure. So, water would have sublimed straight from solid to gas until now. My question then is, was the warming timed to produce water and to avoid the gas.

"The cliff seems to be in a state of constant collapse because the whole area there is warming unusually quickly. The out-wash regularly clears the ice away in surges before it freezes again, so it will be difficult to get Harpo's bot in there. You need to time this well. I'll get back to you. I think Xero has something to share. End message."

Two hours later, Maddox had manoeuvred Harpo onto a rocky outcrop higher than the out-wash and just out of reach of the falling ice. This was the closest safe place. The next step would be to send one of Harpo's bots in to enter the out-wash after a surge and fly it right up the ice tunnel. Here he waited another hour before another message came in.

"Max," said a deep, slow voice. It was Xero. Brilliant guy, not big on words. "Our latest analysis shows the temperature gains to be spherical, centred one hundred and twenty-five metres up the tunnel. There is a cavern growing inside as the ice melts. I estimate two to three days before the collapse of the cliff entirely, re-burying it for another month or more. The rock here is relatively flat, except for something at the centre. We don't know what it is. You do have the option to just wait for the cliff to collapse and melt entirely. End message."

"Start message," Maddox instructed.

"Begin."

"Ok, guys, launching bot from Harpo now. The surge has been calm for five minutes now. Icefall is in a lull. Flying the bot in... now. Telemetry is breaking a bit. Harpo doesn't quite have a line of sight down the tunnel. You'll see when you receive this feed. Err, what?! That doesn't make... that can't be. I think I am seeing a black object, not easy to see. The bot's lights don't seem to illuminate it. A fair amount of mist or steam. Definitely, a large cavern now, flying around to see the shape of... no. No way! It kinda looks like a cube. Guys, we need to recheck this footage to ensure I didn't see this wrong. There seems to be a perfect, black cube maybe three metres across sitting on brown basalt on an alien planet that should be frozen solid, but that is impossible. None of this makes sense. Uh-oh, losing the bot, I think, yeah, it's gone. It did better than I thought. I don't know what to say now. What the hell is that thing? Er, End message."

Maddox leaned back in his chair, bewildered.

Within the hour, the entire cliff face collapsed and smothered the artefact, whatever it was, to probably begin the melting process all over again. Harpo recorded it all before moving away to investigate a distant bulge in the ground, suggesting a volcano might be born there soon.

For the following week, Maddox and his online friends went back and forth over the footage and the other measurements, trying to add more information to what was otherwise a giant mystery. Of course, it would be easy to jump to the conclusion that it was an artefact of intelligence. However, regular geometries do exist naturally and often. What appears to be one thing only demonstrates observer bias with subsequent scrutiny. That said, Maddox was still glad he came. He felt like a man with a real purpose - finally vindicated for his unappreciated interests.

Awakening with a start, he assessed whether his body had had enough sleep before considering opening his eyes. He had long since given up on any notion of a time of day. He slept as and when needed. It had been quite relaxing, really. Even after over three years alone in a smaller space than the moonbase at the Titov Crater, he was optimistic about the benefits of a life lived without compromise and not wasted. The drive to learn, discover and understand kept the demons of despair and loneliness just outside the door.

The cabin illuminated, and the console flashed, indicating a message had arrived. He wobbled to his feet and staggered over to this console to receive it.

"Jesus! Max! I'm so sorry I didn't see this before, but frankly, it was blind luck that I caught them at all." It was Ben, very agitated and preoccupied with his console. "They are so dark. Way too far from the sun to have tails," he commented aloud before facing the camera again. "Comets, Max! We are picking up several clouds of comets. Clouds, Max! We cannot determine the number or density from here. Remember the simulations of material that could be dragged out of the Oort Cloud with Rogue? We did simulations, but we know so little about the composition and density of the Oort. One cloud has definitely caught up with Rogue, now that Rogue slowed after exchanging momentum with Pluto. Rogue's new vector has taken it away from the main cloud, but it seems the spread is wide enough to intercept it and you. I estimate nine point three hours... the light I am seeing is four hours old; you will receive this in four hours... you will have just over an hour to try to drop to a lower orbit and improve your odds of survival. Read my data! Good luck, man! Hope to hear from you soon. Godspeed. End message."

Data arrived immediately after, and Maddox scanned it quickly. He was currently in a high orbit, taking about three hours to orbit the planet. The vessel wouldn't be in Rogue's shadow again for another two hours. Ben was right: a lower orbit would improve his odds.

His vessel didn't have the equipment to look far into the void, but now he had coordinates, which would help. Realigning the sensor array, he got a closeup of a shadow passing in front of the stars, a lot of the stars! It wasn't big, it was really close. Soon he was picking up more, flying past some at a distance and others closer.

There's no help out here, Maddox, think!

He woke up the navigation system and instructed it to burn for a lower orbit. Fortunately, he was already facing backwards, having slowed into orbit three years earlier. His trajectory was slowing and dropping, but it was too slow. Like an arrow already loose, there was little to deviate its path with any rapidity.

A comet was approaching very close to Rogue; its path

was bent by Rogue's gravity. His systems calculated a collision with the vessel even as he began to reach the far side of Rogue.

Suddenly everything changed. The vessel jolted, and Maddox was flung around like the worst turbulence on a jumbo jet. Fortunately, he landed near a pod, so he climbed in and closed the lid, bracing himself against it. Again there was a jolt and another and another, but now he could absorb the impacts. It went on and on, rattling him around inside the pod, his arms tiring under stress. He thought it would never stop. Then it did just stop.

Cautiously he escaped the pod, returned to the console, and witnessed the most amazing sight, something that nobody in history had ever seen up close before: a comet fall.

Looking back around Rogue from a much lower orbit, he saw the comet strike Rogue and throw up a mass of material in a beautiful, funnel-shaped ejection, catching the sun as the particles reached up beyond Rogue's dark side.

Feeling a little confident that he was now hiding behind Rogue for the duration of the passing cloud, he began a message.

"Start message!" Maddox began in a whisper.

"Begin."

"I managed to drop orbit. One was headed right for me, but then it crashed into Rogue. Dunno how I calculated that wrong. It was incredible! I saw it. I recorded it... I am recording it still." A beeping interrupted him. "Err, hang on. Collision warning. Ejecta is heading my way. Shit! No chance to avoid it. Oh no, there is a lot of it. Dumping all my data down this stream. No. No. Shit. Orian-."

A different judder shook the vessel as if flying through a hail storm. Maddox fell to his knees and wondered if this was an excellent time to pray to some god.

With an enormous bang, a rapid piece breached the hull. He thought it was the end. He didn't know before, and he didn't know then that the hull could reseal minor breaches, so he was surprised when the hissing and alarm ended quite quickly.

More impacts battered the vessel, more and bigger… and it also ended as suddenly as it started. He wasn't dead.

He might as well be dead, though, once he discovered the extensive damage sustained by the vessel's exterior. Deep space comms no longer existed. Main motors would probably explode if attempted to be used. Several storage compartments had been evacuated, losing him some rations and water. Thankfully though, he was alive, and the main power was still online despite being rerouted twice. Sensors were still recording, but the analysis systems were shot, and he had no way to fix them and access the data. The expedition was over, his work was over, and there was no way to get home.

Settling down with a month's ration of rum, he contemplated his unfinished work, trying to convince himself that others would follow and continue where he had left off. Rationally though, he regretted the vast unknown that Rogue represented. It was his baby, and he wasn't going to be able to see it grow up: the mysteries and wonders yet to be discovered.

Where had it come from? How old was it? Where was it going? What damage was it going to do to the system and humanity? Why was it so strange?

Three hours later and half-drunk, he decided he would prefer to hibernate than either kill himself or just die of starvation, given that these were the only options available to his inebriated mind. Moreover, he thought it would be the least painful way to go - to actually grow old and die in his sleep was always a person's ideal exit strategy.

Then he had an epiphany.

Groucho. The third probe.

There was great satisfaction in working hard on your last

significant problem: to reprogram a surface reconnaissance drone into a rescue buoy: a deep-space message in a bottle. He wasn't interested in calculating how many decades such a small craft would take to get anywhere near the nearest human to detect it. Best just not knowing.

By the time it was done and launched, he was sober, so he went to bed for a very, very long sleep.

CHAPTER EIGHT

2226 CE, Earth, continental Europe

Although the house was large and expansive, it nonetheless adopted the passive heating designs commonplace for the last hundred and fifty years. All concrete and glass, the upper level overhung the lower level's endless glass enough to provide shade during summer but not so much to hide from the weaker and desirable winter sun.

Orianna entered the ground level into a three-floor high reception area adorned with split stairs, a grand piano and conspicuous ramps.

She had never been to this house before. It must have been built in the eight years since she had visited Mother Earth. Her father would never occupy someone else's home. He was always one to interfere in the details of every construction, ensuring every design consideration was perfect.

"M. Demaine, welcome to Château de Collobrières," a voice echoed across the large space. The accent began with a lofty but smooth Kent English, rounding off with perfect pronunciation of the French. "I hope your journey was a good one. My name is not Gerald, but it is the one I am assigned for you to use. It amuses him that it is hard for a Frenchman to say it how an Englishman would. I am your father's personal assistant."

Orianna noted his brief glance out of the panoramic windows to the broad flat lawn to the rear. A featureless expanse of close-cut grass ending about half a kilometre away at an expansive oak copse, which flowed over the next hill.

"Nice to meet you, Gerald. I took a road train," she said, answering his unasked question. "I will take a Raptor when I leave. I prefer to be well-grounded when I reach the surface."

"Uncompromising as always." This time, she recognised the unmistakable gruffness of her father's voice immediately. His expert English was a match for any Shakespearean thespian. "Gerald was getting anxious that you were not on time. But, of course, he does not know you as I do."

To her surprise, though, she did not see the giant of a man that had always towered over her. Instead, he was seated and rolled towards her in a wheelchair. This man barely resembled her father of just eight years previous. He was gaunt and slender. The muscular bulk of his naturally square shoulders was lost. The outstanding quality of his stances and strides had been so admirable, yet here that giant was trapped in the body of an old man, a prematurely old man.

As the wheelchair approached, it expanded, lifting his body up into an upright position. A lack of straps holding him to the raised frame gave the illusion he had stood up by himself except for his feet, dangling just above the floor: it spoke of spinal surgery to add attachment points.

"Father," she asked, "what happened?"

"I grew old waiting for you to return to me," he chuckled. "There are still some degenerative diseases that even twenty-third-century medicine seems incapable of curing. The money I have put into researching my condition, you would have thought it would have yielded at least some hope, or perhaps a return on my investment."

"Oh, I am so sorry," Orianna said, swiftly gliding over to his arm, there to affectionately touch him.

The old man spied her gait, taking note that she elected to move stealthily across the polished marble rather than with an eminent heel-toe click that her station would otherwise dictate. He grimaced a little, knowing that further repeating of his observations would not go down well so soon into this reunion.

"My muscles are weak, but my bones are strong, and my mind is as keen as ever."

She noticed his greying hair was even thinner these days, striking against his remaining naturally black hair colour.

Oberon Demaine wheeled forward, escaping Orianna's touch and proximity. Realising he was not just making space but heading out of the room, Orianna and Gerald followed swiftly.

"He is not slow in that thing," Gerald said quietly to Orianna as they strode to keep up. "Did you say you weren't staying? If you were, I could have your luggage…."

"Not staying. No luggage." She offered him the softness of a short smile to tone down her terseness. "My father and I do well not to spend too much time together."

"I heard that," Oberon said loud enough for his voice to echo off the tall wall surrounding the double doorway he was just about to pass through. The following grumpy sentence's intelligible quality was lost to the next room.

Orianna and Gerald exchanged glances as if a former assistant acknowledged the difficulties inherited by the latter.

They caught up to him in a room in direct contrast to the vast spartan hall they had just left. Although only a single story, it gained height by being sunken, as demonstrated by Oberon rolling down a long ramp that followed the curve of bookcases to the right. They descended more directly using the semi-circular stairs ahead, which spread wider the lower they went, allowing each to enter the maze of furniture below from different directions.

Display cabinets, armchairs, short tables with ornaments, desks filled with a myriad of ancient artefacts. The entire floor was crammed full. It was like an old historic manor converted into a museum, with so much on display that it had become more decorative than functional. That said, Orianna noticed that everything was evenly spaced, presumably allowing her father to navigate in his chair.

Some of the objects, Orianna remembered from the old house, but then her father only ever had a small fraction of his possessions out on display, the rest hidden in crates in the basement, usually.

"Do you still have a dungeon full of all your secrets?" she asked.

"Ha! You did enjoy exploring those as a little girl. I never had a doubt you would find your way out. But, Gerald, she has an eidetic memory, you know. Once shown a map, never forgotten. Such gifts, of course, come with a cost: she never did quite know how to handle people very well. Either that, or she did overcome those flaws and chose to hide it - which is another kind of weakness." He eyed her carefully from the desk where he had settled, not far from the end of the ramp, as she passed behind a glass display case within which the headpiece of Tutankhamun stared back at her peacefully: a beautiful polished golden face.

"Is this real? Surely this still belongs to the Egyptian Supreme Council of Antiquities?" she asked.

"Would that it were so simple," said Oberon quietly. "But, of course, Egypt is no longer actually a country. Officially, the whole of Howard Carter's treasure trove is still on tour around eastern Europe. Practically speaking, this is much safer with me, and a copy can risk those unstable provinces.

Tell me, did Carter fake that find, do you believe? I do love a good conspiracy."

"Particularly those of your own making, Father. It is always a possibility."

"Oh, very good." His teeth were artificially white and glaring when he smiled. It reminded her that she had often thought that older people should get artificial teeth that at least looked a bit more congruous to one's age. Again, his chair was a chair, allowing him to sit at the main desk. "Go on, Gerald." His smile diminished. "Tell us your version! I know how much you are desperate to do so."

Gerald raised an index finger and hesitated, "w-well, the problem with the conspiracy is that it fits too well. Yes, Carter was running out of time. Yes, the tomb looked hurried and a mishmash of artefacts. Yes, the dagger and headpiece were from other people. That could be a sign he manufactured the whole thing to rescue his career. But, the pharaoh had died very young, and it must have been a hasty affair. Most likely, the tomb was difficult to find because it was rushed."

"There, Orianna, the voice of reason - a voice lacking in passion and intrigue! Go on, my dear firstborn, let me hear your interpretation."

Orianna sighed, somewhat tired of the games her father so enjoyed playing.

"Of course, you have to understand the politics of the period of the eighteenth dynasty to understand why Tutankhamun was buried this way. They had just lost a major battle with the Hittites, and the king died without producing an heir. So it wasn't just the burial that was rushed; they really should have been better prepared: the poor embalming gives the strongest evidence. So now we have many people trying to claim the throne: his wife, Ankhesenamun, and a general called Horemheb, who was away on a military campaign, and then an ambitious senior court official called Ay. Horemheb was the official heir to the throne for a decade, in lieu of Tut providing a male heir. His absence on campaign allowed Ay to move for the throne because whoever buried a pharaoh became the pharaoh. So it is quite likely that Ay swapped tombs with Tut and buried him quickly. The short version of the rest of the story has Ay reign for four years before Horemheb seized power and tried to erase Ay's name from all but Tut's tomb, which he would not defile."

"Bravo. You see, Gerald. She is a human encyclopedia. For her, there are no conspiracies, just lots of noise from ill-informed little people."

Gerald looked hard done by but indeed not surprised by it.

Orianna continued to wander around, examining the artefacts. "You must forgive my father; he loves to live in the past. Look at this neolithic hand axe!"

"Those who do not learn from history are doomed to repeat it," her father said with a slight chuckle.

"Santayana, really?" she replied quickly. "Those who do or do not learn are equally doomed to repeat it."

"Indeed, but those who know, who understand, have a moral obligation to take charge. Take King Tut. Probably died from his own inbreeding. His wife indeed was married to her own father before marrying Tut. These things were quite common and a disastrous way to maintain a pure bloodline. Such a thing is nonsense. For example, I chose your own mother based on her genetic compatibility above all else. I allowed myself to be entirely open, free of thought, and my body cried out for her - not a shallow lust, but a pheromonal, biochemical demand to be together at all costs. I listened, and my body spoke. This is the truth of nature. We were so compatible, your mother and I. We could choose the month of birth every time."

"Ok, can we change the subject? I feel sorrow when I

think of Mother and how I miss her, but this story always ruins even that for me."

The room was quiet for a while. However, this wasn't an awkward silence, as you might expect from other people. Instead, these two 'generals' considered their plans for the second wave of attacks.

Gerald was all too aware of his master's machinations, but this meeting was something else entirely. He had never met Orianna, only Orlando, and he was highly impressed with how she handled Oberon.

"Go on, ask your question!" he called out, his head down, busy with something in front of him. "You came to me. Stands to reason you are here to ask me something. Be plain!"

"Am I your daughter?" Orianna asked.

Oberon looked up startled, and gazed at her. The question was hiding more questions, and he needed to get a read on her, but her expression was blank, so he looked away again and replied softly, "nothing unusual about your birth. Firstborn. There are no swapped babies, no adoptions, no prior marriages, no surrogates, nothing. So you really are who we claim you are. No conspiracy."

What Oberon had failed to see, which was significant, was that from Orianna's point of view, she was glowing like a torch, with light in the ultraviolet range, beyond human perception, although she could see it. Only she could.

When she turned to look at Gerald, he had noticed something a little odd. Orianna twisted around and realised she was standing next to an old paper book, lying open on a side table. Her glow was giving the bleached paper a remarkable fluorescent quality. She immediately calmed her light and moved away, making a mental note to remember this odd quality of the now rarely used methods of whitening paper and clothes.

"Gerald, would you mind leaving us, please," she said.

"No, he will not! State your business!"

That was my question. Who the hell am I? What am I?

"I want to be the heir. I am the oldest; I should be the heir."

"Ahhh, there it is, although I was expecting a better argument." Oberon wheeled around the desk to join the others amongst his museum pieces. "Gerald, how long have you been here now?"

"Five years, sir."

"Still onboarding then, good. Gerald, tell me the greatest few inventions that lead to the advancement of humanity?"

Orianna sat down in an old leather armchair and rested her arms openly. She wanted to sigh again, but that would not have done. Instead, making herself comfortable was enough.

Gerald took a couple of steps forward and picked up the same stone axe that Orianna had handled earlier. "Erm, the flint tools to strip hide from sinews and bone… the plough, the wheel, the spinning jenny, the telephone, oh I missed the printing press, the steam engine, the combustion engine, the internet and the Lerner Focus Fusion Reactor."

"Right, but also very wrong. You see, the smartest personal assistant money can buy, yet still lacking in vision. Before tools, proto-man created language and paintings to pass on stories, learn from the past, and plan for the future. This is critical. You named a lot of mechanical advantages, which is fair to a point, but the key to man's success is to seize the opportunity to grow the mind… and to give those stories a life beyond his meagre lifespan." Oberon sneered at his inanimate legs. "No, no, no, you missed the most important point. The greatest step our upright ape ancestors made was to take the time to pick up those Psilocybin mushrooms growing out of old animal faeces, which they passed when making a dash across the new savannas growing between their retreating forests. Opportunity knocked, and the ape answered. He ate that forbidden fruit, and his brain truly was expanded."

"Magic mushrooms were an invention?" Gerald sounded incredulous.

"Of course not, but inventions are a means to an end. You listed the Internet. That was wrong. The interconnectedness of machines was a slow evolution, and it continues today, albeit a little slower, during the Critical Earth. The invention that made that technology accessible to the masses that made such an extensive and rapid expanse of human consciousness and awareness was the World Wide Web - the invention was the protocol.

"Until the printing press, nearly eight hundred years ago, knowledge was only available to precious few, and it moved slowly. Afterwards, everyone could learn beyond their menial lives, when books became very cheap. The World Wide Web took that to a whole new level, and now it is hard to find paper books anywhere."

"Which reminds me, thirteen more crates of books have arrived," Gerald said, alluding to the facility a kilometre down the driveway where real books were catalogued and cared for in a perfectly preserving climate.

"Arggh, you see! We die a slow death of routine and mundanity. Time is measured in repetitive tasks. Now, enlightenment, that stops the passage of time entirely."

"You and I are like peas in a pod, Father: alike in so many ways. Orlando is more like Mother, so why choose him over me."

"Yes, oh how talking with you is like a conversation with myself. I love you, my dear, but a gilded cage is no place for you. Of course, I hope that you will support your younger brother for as long as you can stomach it, but we do not fool ourselves, you and I, we mislead others all the time, but we do not lie to ourselves - and we are cut from the same cloth.

"You have too much personal ambition to be satisfied

with my legacy. You have no children, no sense of what it takes to carry ideas beyond your own lifespan. On the other hand, Orlando does, and indeed he is fresh blood to an old problem. He makes up for what he lacks in the talents you possess in abundance with his leadership qualities.

"I can already feel your dissatisfaction with that answer, daughter, but there it is. My great, great, great grandfather worked with Lerner on the Focus Fusion project. They were men of vision. The first successful, net gain, fusion power source. Whilst entire groups of countries were busy trying to make yet another huge steam engine that ran on Fusion, they built one that did away with all the heat to electricity conversion and instead simply made electricity. Tell us, Gerald! Give us the benefit of your university degree."

"Ahem, Focus Fusion creates the conditions for the Fusion with a Dense Plasma Focus to crush Hydrogen-Boron or pB11. That is Boron and a proton, which briefly fuses into a carbon nucleus, which itself breaks apart into three Helium nuclei and no neutrons and a whole lot of energy. Like black holes, jets are produced at either pole - one is electrons, and the other is ions, which is electrical energy that needs no conversion from heat. The abundance of x-rays needs a layer of shielding to capture and convert to a third form of direct electrical potential. The reactor has no moving parts: the plasma focus is an insulated copper tube, the anode, surrounded by the ring of cathode copper rods. A pulse of electrical energy creates an unstable umbrella-shaped spark made of toroidal pairs of electromagnetic fields. This catastrophically collapses into a plasmoid, crushing the gaseous fuel, producing high-frequency fusion reactions."

"Indeed, but few had the vision to fund it. Without that great invention, their future, our present, would never have been possible. We would still be burning fossil fuels, and this planet would have killed us all off already," Oberon said.

Orianna stood suddenly. "I have that vision. I manage the great industries off-world. I work in the machinery of space so you can clean up the Earth? When do I get my piece of that?"

"You are not here, as he is!" he coughed a little for raising his voice. "Orlando is here. He will continue to lead."

Oberon returned to his desk.

"You are still here?" he asked rhetorically, like an impatient victor expecting the loser to leave the battlefield. Yet, she was not done.

"Tell me about Libya!" she demanded, standing and pacing towards him. "You have a finger in that pie, don't you. The ICE Units are being built there, and you are involved."

Oberon's face screwed up.

"Yes dammit, yes. So what? We must have those units out there. We need better computers in our space vessels to improve navigation and our offices to help us predict our effects on the Earth's most complex systems. We all know why Artificial Intelligence systems were banned. We had to come up with an alternative: one that had better empathy for humans, or at least better sympathy. I will not apologise for pushing the boundaries."

"That isn't everything, is it?"

Now Oberon was silent.

Orianna wagged a finger at his face before marching out; this time, her clicking heel toes filled the room, passive-aggressively, fading into the distance. Gerald took leave and scampered after her.

A twin-engined tilt-rotor Raptor provided her with transport from the lawn. It flew low over the rolling Normandy landscape, and she resolved to spend a little more time Earthside before returning to Erebus.

She rested her eyes during the flight and allowed her mind to wander. At such times, she would become more receptive to the noises that her subconscious mind made, and one image bubbled to the surface: a photo, taken forty years ago, had been in a frame on a table near her father. She had barely glanced at it. In her mind, she examined it more closely. As a younger man, her father was introduced to a politician running for office beside her grandfather. In the background was the side of a man's face, a face she recognised from Erebus. The man who had glowed at her. But it couldn't have been him because he was the same age as when she saw him last year.

Well, you just keep turning up, don't you?

CHAPTER NINE

2532 BCE, Earth, Kemet (Ancient Egypt)

The strong acacia wood lining the decks creaked and squeaked, and the water of the Nile lapped against the bow. All was otherwise quiet. The wind was almost imperceptible as the grand barge travelled with it, under sail, against the current. The oarsmen rested and performed maintenance tasks until needed to navigate more challenging parts of the Nile.

A few farmers were on the shore when the Sun burst over the distant sandy hills, however, fishermen had taken to the waters this early, risking their lives near the banks and amongst the reeds where the hippos grazed and the crocodiles hid. The fishermen would stop and watch the barge, waving from the deck of their skiffs, hoping for blessings to be bestowed upon them.

Sara appeared from the oblong tent that filled the centre of the deck. Her fine linen robes covered her entire body, leaving only her eyes exposed. Few who dared to gaze into them saw stunning pale blue irises, so rare as to seem magical. Intense eyeliner of black kohl and green malachite powder above the eyes emphasised her status as a woman of importance, not a noble, though, but something even more special, even more unique.

"Great Oracle, a meal is prepared for you," her personal serf said, bowing deeply. He retreated to reveal a table laid with her first meal of the day: bread and eggs with figs and dates to sweeten off and a cup of beer. But, unfortunately, until they stopped, she would not be able to have goat's milk because it did not keep in the heat of Kemet.

"Sadiki, the sands are ruining my food," she said, and he quickly unravelled a screen behind them to add to the one already above. After pushing the boat, what was left of the wind was coming from the desert beyond the hills, constantly threatening to bury this last long thin oasis of green and fertile land on either bank. They had long left Men-nefer, or Inbu-Hedj, as she often caught herself still calling the capitol, where she had spent the Inundation. As the season of Akhet drew to a close and the floodwaters had begun to recede, she knew it was time to make the ceremonial journey upstream.

Sadiki leaned over and took samples of her food and ate them conspicuously, then produced his own straw and drank from the cup. The beer was warm, thick and sweet, with just enough alcohol to sterilise the drink. She had not drunk water for so long. It was strange to be surrounded by so much of it - but to drink from the river would be to drink from Kemet's sewer.

Her master Khufu's grand tomb was barely visible over the haze behind them, the unfinished blunt apex still lacking the golden cap that she had already seen polished, ready to top this great pinnacle of human engineering. The world would see powerful Kemet as the greatest force on Earth the moment their eyes fell upon its staggering size and blinded by the Sun reflected off the brilliant white pyramidal faces.

Sadiki was still looking well, so she settled down to eat. She closed her eyes to the dusty hills and thought of long, long ago when the desert was far away, and all the land was green. Cattle were numerous back then, and people roamed the lands beyond the river, hunting meat between the large lakes that used to litter the landscape. Rain used to fall then, all the time.

She thought of this annual journey. It was the most peaceful time of the year. Under the breath of the wind, sailing would be punctuated with stops at sacred sites to give blessings and to restock during their month-long journey to Swenett, at the first cataract. There, they would rest at the Elephantine before the slower return path downstream again, blessing the crops as the farmers began to sow their wheat and barley at the start of the season of Peret.

Soon, they would moor at Waset, and she would visit the home of Lady Imtah: a private visit, under the guise of giving blessings to the patron of this city and obtaining hospitality in return, where she would enjoy the best day of her annual calendar.

Seven soldiers waited to escort Sara from the wharf. Sadiki was unhappy to be left behind: as a serf and loyal servant to the Oracle of Hathor, his entire purpose was to care for his mistress. Neither her reassurances nor the regularity of this annual ritual did anything to ease his discomfort.

It wasn't far to walk to the Lady Imtah's grand villa. People had seen the arriving barge and its large oblong sail emblazoned with the face of the cow-god Hathor long before the sail had been dropped and the barge moored. They stopped their work and came to bow at the side of the road. There was no jostling or crowding. Everyone was calm and serene in reverence of the only living oracle of the unified kingdom of Kemet.

Inside the villa, as they left the dusty street behind them and the doors closed on the cooing peasants, Sara ascended stairs to accept a welcome from the Lady Imtah herself.

"You honour me, Oracle," she said, bowing slightly, a

broad smile across her face. She wore a jewel-encrusted gold necklace hanging down between her breasts, one exposed, the other behind the finest and whitest linen, draped down from the other shoulder, becoming a full-length dress with a belt. There was nothing unusual about this, except when she dismissed the help and led Sara into a private chamber.

"Lady Imtah, I hope you are well?" Sara asked.

Lady Imtah was almost giggling with excitement. "So good to see you."

Since they were in private, Sara revealed her hands to grasp those of Lady Imtah, and they clenched tightly, such was the bond between them.

Long ago, when Lady Imtah was a child, Sara had treated her illness with an old-world herbal remedy, made from a plant no longer found in Kemet - one of many Sara collected, making requests from any and all who travelled to far off lands. The medicine had saved Lady Imtah's life. If it hadn't been for Sara, all knowledge of this herbal remedy would have been lost in time, and Lady Imtah would have died for sure. She and Sara had been close friends ever since. Following the illness, it became apparent that the Lady Imtah could not bear children. The subsequent sadness would have been her undoing were it not for Sara's offer to bear them for her. The arrangement was treated with the utmost secrecy. Twice, the Oracle of Hathor remained with the Lady Imtah between her annual journeys, as people would understand it, to care for the Lady Imtah during her pregnancy. Instead, it had been Sara who bore the child each time, impregnated by the Lord Imtah, whilst the Lady Imtah helped and encouraged his lovemaking. This was not a selfless act. Sara had long desired to bear children again. It had been a very long time since she had done so, and she felt it was time to try again. However, the Oracle was not allowed to have children, not allowed to be of the flesh.

She had never shared with Lady Imtah how her decision

to take such a risk went beyond her desire to help out a friend - Lady Imtah would not have understood the special relationship she had with Lord Imtah.

The conspiracy of the births had endured long after Lord Imtah passed away in battle, and her sons had kept Lady Imtah from spiralling into despair. Additionally, every ebbing Inundation, she would enjoy a visit from Sara, and they were as children together each time.

"How are the boys?" Sara asked impatiently.

"They are well and fast approaching manhood," Lady Imtah replied. Her smile flickered a little as a remembered bargain dawned on her. "I think it is time," she offered solemnly.

"Agreed, but we will do this together. They will have no doubt that you are still their mother."

"Yamanu! Tarik! Come here, please!" Lady Imtah called into the next room. Two young men came bounding in from the next room, dressed in fine linen as befitted their station. "You will return to your studies after visiting time with the Oracle."

"Greetings Sara, Oracle of Hathor, Seer of the Past and Future, Viser to the Pharaoh, Khufu the Great," the eldest said. He was just starting to grow hair on his face, she noted. "How was your journey?"

"My journey was swift and unbroken in my rush to see you all, my darlings."

The boys were too young to realise the unusualness of this manner of affectation.

"I remember when you came last time," little Tarik said.

"Children, we have something essential to tell you," began Lady Imtah. "This day has been one I have dreaded since you were born, a day that must happen, a day that might be as joyous as it is sorrowful."

"Mother, you are worrying us," said Yamanu. "Please, it does no good to linger so. Be quick and kind."

"Ah, he is so learned," said Sara. "You must be as proud as I."

"Tamanu. Tarik. I am your mother. Sara is your mother. We are your mothers." Surprise fell across the faces of the boys. "I was struck down with illness as a child, and Sara healed me, but I was not able to bear children. She bore me two boys to call my own, to love as my own, the way she, as Oracle, could never do. Together we devised this plan in secret to the betterment of all."

Tamanu asked, "And Father?"

"He was your father. He was part of the conspiracy of love. Only the three of us knew the truth. And now, as you approach manhood, you must know your own truth." Lady Imtah was crying at this point, uncertain yet how they would take this news.

Tarik looked up at his brother. Yamanu pondered this with his head bowed. A strong education had already imbued him with the wisdom to consider before acting. He was also acutely aware of the love emanating from both women.

Sara knelt before Yamanu, and looked up into his face. He returned her gaze. He looked into her eyes, and he knew. Her eyes were as blue as the morning sky, matching his own, his brother's and his father's. He knew, and he smiled at her. Perhaps, there was something about this that he always knew. It all slotted into place so well that it felt obvious.

"We had one loving mother when we awoke this morning, and now we have two loving mothers, Tarik. So today is a good day."

The women both burst into laughter and tears of joy.

Soon the boys returned to their studies whilst the ladies spent much of the day together. They rounded off the afternoon with a lavish dinner of beer, brown bread and vegetables including onions, lettuce, peas, beans and nuts - everything flavoured with a range of spices, finished with sweet bread and cake dessert.

"Please, I would like to bid the boys goodnight in private if it pleases you, dear Lady Imtah? I am sure they have questions, and I would like to alleviate them before they dream."

"That is a good idea," Lady Imtah replied. "I will fetch them."

Yamanu and Tarik were led into a small room facing the river, where Ra had travelled for another day. The faint glow of the Sun was subsiding, and the room darkened. The slaves left them, and Sara entered.

"My beautiful boys," she began and made herself comfortable on a chair close to the bench on which they sat. "Your mother has doubtless forewarned you of the changes your body will experience entering manhood. Yamanu, you are already growing hair. Every boy goes through this."

Yamanu sat a touch more upright. He had a good muscle tone but was clearly a more slender frame than his smaller brother. As the eldest and master of a noble house, he maintained a certain dignity, which he bore well.

They both seemed entirely unsurprised by these words, and curiosity was growing in their eyes, so she felt confident to continue. She shifted to the edge of her seat.

"What she will not have told you is what she does not know. What I will tell you is known to only four: myself, our Lord Pharaoh Khufu, and his sons: Prince Djedefre and Prince Khafre." Their eyes widened with the thought of being included in such lofty company. "You are my second and third children. Long ago, I finally chose to have a son. It seemed the right thing to do. It proved a disaster. It did not feel right again until your parents needed my help with you, and I am glad that I did.

"You two will not be as ordinary men. You might have even noticed some of these differences already?" She tried to read behind their startled expressions, and gradually there was a hint of some confirmation in their eyes. "Yes?" She reached out and pressed her palms against their respective chests. Their hearts beat strong and slow. "Where your emotion and power reside, you are calmer and more ready than others, and when you call upon it, you will have reserves beyond them all. Afterwards, you will recover faster and heal better."

"We do well at our sports and our studies," said Tarik keenly.

"Good, and you will be better at remembering also, but not all of it is better. Tell me, honestly, as I am sure you have hidden it already by some misguided shame - you cannot appreciate the aroma of things?"

They both nodded, indeed both shame and relief filling their faces.

Tarik said, "I think I smell things when people ask me to. They say, oh, that is horrid and run, and I follow and just agree with them, but I thought it was just a blockage or a poor skill that I needed to practice. The truth is, I do not know the smell of dung, of grass, of foods, or even of the Nile." Yamanu put his hand on his brother's shoulder.

"Instead, you will only be able to smell when people are ill, sometimes before they even know they are ill themselves," Sara added. "I tell you now that this is a long way short of the full story, and today I will only tell you what you need to know, and why you MUST tell NO ONE, not even your mother, the Lady Imtah. You must give me your oath! On your own lives be it!"

"I swear," they said together.

"Yamanu, I saw you squinting a little earlier today. When did this start?"

"Since the previous Inundation."

"You have started. Yarik, you will follow at his age. The sight comes first, and the aura comes second. Soon, when your passion is high, your inner power will show. Only we have the sight to see each other's aura. However, there are certain objects you must learn and be careful around, for they reflect your aura in a way that others can see."

"Is this a spiritual thing?" Yarik asked bluntly, speaking of the doubt that had also entered Yamanu's mind. Yamanu smiled at his brother's straight question.

Sara sat upright and took in their fullness in the waning light. Then, spying the amber necklace on Yarik's chest, she reached out and lifted it enough to present it on the palm of her hand. Tarik gasped as the amber began to glow like a firefly. Yamanu jumped up as he saw her entire hand emanate a subtle aura like the evening sky.

As quickly as they saw it, she sighed, and it died away.

"You will soon be able to do this. Be careful to learn to control it. Objects like this could reveal you."

"This is magic!" Yamanu exclaimed, anxiety wrought across his youthful face, but he did not run. He was brave and intelligent. This was a trick, he considered, a test of his resolve. So he remained and watched.

Sara recoiled and began to remove her headdress and face covering.

They both gasped. There was no doubt she was pretty, but it was not her beauty or face complexion that shocked them: she was so much younger than they had expected. Yamanu reached out slowly to touch Sara's cheeks, where his mother had lines forming, but Sara had none. Sara smiled at him to encourage his boldness.

"Now, Yamanu, prepare yourself!" Sara said, throwing off her upper clothes to reveal her entire bare flesh. "You must teach your brother what you see."

Sara's youthful appearance started to shimmer a little, and then the aura came, brighter and brighter. Yamanu looked around as the room filled with a light, the colour of which he could not describe. Yarik spun around in his seat as particular objects in the room spontaneously glowed in the darkening space: mostly quartz and amber decorations.

Sara lifted up her arms as if to embrace the world.
Their world would never be the same again.

CHAPTER TEN

2330 CE, Rogue, orbit

He was awake, but not. He felt alert but had not yet opened his eyes. Perhaps he was lucid dreaming? He could not move. He was convinced his eyes were open and blinked, but he saw nothing. Faint voices. Was he in a coma, and those were people by his bedside, and he deep down in a level of consciousness barely measurable? His last memory was consigning himself to sleep without end. Was this him dying of old age, still in hibernation?

"Maddox. Maddox Jefferies, can you hear me?" That was much louder.

He tried to respond, but his mouth would not obey his commands.

"Maddox, listen to my voice. Time to wake up, now." It was a soft man's voice, gentle and caring, unhurried and calm. "Ok, dim the lights, please."

There was a hissing noise, and his head shook a little.

"Keep your eyes closed, M Jefferies; we are removing your isolation mask. You will sense light through your eyelids. Take your time now and allow them to get used to the light before you try to open them."

Light. His eyes hurt sharply from it, but it subsided slowly. The sound became even more evident as his head was shaken a little more and then felt free. Air passed over his skin. He winced at his first movement, then a smile, resulting in painful cracked lips.

He opened his eyes to see a blurry man reach out and treat his lips in some way. It felt better.

"Lay still. This will take a little while. You have hibernated for much longer than ever attempted, M. Jefferies. Twice, now, indeed," he said. "Somehow, you have survived and will probably make a complete recovery. Fortunately, medicine has not been idle and advanced as you slept; otherwise, I fear the outcome would not have been so favourable. Now, take it very slowly. There is no hurry; you are in safe hands. We had to bring you out slowly, so we held you in various levels of coma for the last week."

His eyes were still blurry, but the man's voice was so sonorous that Maddox believed every word he had said. There didn't seem any chance of him speaking anytime soon, given the subtle croaking noises coming from his throat.

"Hello, old friend," came a familiar woman's voice, and a fuzzy female outline appeared above him. He could just make out her smile, but she didn't stay long.

The medical unit door opened suddenly, and a petite slender figure walked in. Maddox looked up from his second meal of the day, still laying in bed and relatively weak. His mouth fell open as she strode into the room, and he recognised her fully.

"Orianna!" he smiled. "But you look just the same?" followed a deep frown. "So good to see you," then a further smile. He was a mixed bag of emotions.

She smiled in reply and rested on the side of his bed.

"They have looked after me and nursed me and fed me, but they haven't told me anything: no answers to any of my questions. I see you have built a nice vessel, very expensive."

"It is in a lot better condition than yours," she replied.

"Are we still here?" He asked urgently.

She simply nodded and smiled again.

He relaxed back into his pillow.

"I am desperate to review the data. Hopefully, the systems on the Achilles kept recording," he added.

"Oh, yes, it did. Listen, Maddox, Groucho made it. He was picked up by an exploration mission mapping the Asteroid Belt. Million to one shot, they said. Everyone thought you had died. The whole thing has made a bit of a splash. Fame might not be what you ever wanted, but you have many more ears that will listen to you now. I came as soon as I found out. I came, and I found you, but officially I am not really here."

"You look like you haven't finished. Please continue."

She took a breath, readying to rip off the proverbial band-aid

"It has been seventy-seven years since you went into that pod, Maddox."

Reality sank in, and he looked at the back of his hands with a fresh perspective, no longer the hands of a thirty-year-old. No wonder they hadn't given him a mirror. He reached down for the shiny metal food tray, flung the food off to clatter over the floor, and pulled the back of it up to his face. A middle-aged man looked back at him, and he winced.

"So I am, what, a hundred and thirty-six years old, and I don't look a day over forty-five." He looked up with tears in his eyes, and she touched his face affectionately.

Orianna got up, anticipating how the conversation was going and proceeded to ensure the door was locked and the monitors were off. They were in complete private now.

"I have lived only five years, since we met, and aged eighteen, not a bad trade for travel a hundred and five years into the future. But what kind of deal did *you* strike,

Orianna? You still look exactly the same. Unless you have constantly been hibernating for the last century, you should be a hundred and thirty-two years old, am I right? That doctor looks older than I do, so medical science doesn't look likely to have cracked the ageing process - unless it is only afforded to the wealthy elite, it is? Wow, listen to me: I am angry. I am angry because I now look old enough to be your father, and yet by all common sense, both of us should be long dead."

She cried and rushed over to console him, yet his raised hand stopped her mid-stride.

Orianna just shook her head. "I don't know why. I really don't. I just didn't age. After a while, I had to slip away, hideaway in case people noticed. I ran my own business, was rich, and could pay to change my identity. The empire I had built practically ran itself, and I pulled the strings. Nobody needed to know who I was - they still don't.

"Everyone I knew has died. You are the only one left who knows me as Orianna Demaine. I have gone by many names, which were not my own. I love that you still know me as Orianna. It has been so long since I heard anyone call me that."

He felt sorry for her, more than he did for himself. He pondered this revelation for a while. This was amazing, shocking even. The scientist in him began to run wild with all the possibilities this opened up.

"It is incredible. But, why hide?"

"So I don't disappear into some lab for a thousand years."

"Fair point, but maybe you could go public and share it with the world."

That was a refreshing idealism, which she had long forgotten. How could she phrase this and not demolish his innocence?

"When we first met, I had just found out... and I was being chased... for being this way."

"Who was chasing you? Are you sure?"

"No idea. I don't know who they are. They were on me immediately. I walked right into their trap, utterly ignorant of what I was. And it wasn't just one group. There were two separate groups, and they both nearly caught me. One group I have since thoroughly dissected: the Clergy, the I.R.C. Someone was manipulating them, but that trail went cold. Their religious zeal had made them valuable instruments for someone else's cause. They were told that my kind was an abomination before God and that everyone else needed protecting from us. People were not meant to live forever. That was for God alone. It was an easy sell."

"Us?"

"The other group, well, one of them was like me." Maddox opened his mouth to interrupt, but she bid him not to. "I only saw him for a moment. Being like me, though, I feel they have been looking for me all this time. It took me a while to learn this, but people like me... like this, can afford to be patient." Her words trailed off.

"The Clergy. I have heard of them. Friends of mine have been hurt by them - had been hurt by them - hell, they are probably all dead now." He caught himself distracted again. "Certainly, they would put you in a lab forever, but why would the second group chase you if they are like you? If they are like you, you should surely be friends with them? You would be the same... I mean, are you actually human?"

"Of course I am."

"But... but how are you like this then?"

"I think I just happened. A rare random genetic condition." She just shrugged.

"I sense you have tested yourself?"

She nodded. "I have a condition known as Chimerism. Most people have one set of DNA, Chimeras have two or more. It is a little like having siblings inside you to help you fight your battles. Unfortunately, most Chimeras either have no special abilities or die young from complications and genetic divergence - their bodies end up as an internal battleground between the siblings, and no one survives. Mine is a much rarer version: it doesn't even have a name, the DNA siblings inside of me are in complete harmony."

She shrugged her shoulders and sat on a chair across the room from the bed.

"Special abilities? Like not ageing?"

"Amongst other things."

"Oh wow. Boy, do I suddenly feel like a Neandertal. I don't know what to think. Are you the next step in human evolution? Can you fly? I always wanted to fly. Superman over spiderman, every time."

She laughed as he had intended. This was the first time she had explained her idiosyncracies to another person. Was she ready?

"Nothing so obvious. You know how you sometimes get in a bind, and you reach into your pocket for anything to help, and you find that widget you have had for ages for no reason, and it is the perfect thing for that moment? It is a bunch of small things like that, really."

"Like what?"

"I have a very slow heart rate."

"Ok, so you are part tortoise or part elephant. This explains a lot."

He enjoyed that he was making her smile.

"I have a high tolerance to pain killers and anaesthetics."

"As a super-power, that really sucks!"

"I have an eidetic memory. I have never forgotten anything since I was a baby."

"Definitely, part elephant."

She felt the joy of a grandparent playing with a three-year-old.

"I cannot smell anything you can, but I can smell if you are ill."

"Ok, part doctor, with a cold. This is going well. But I know you are saving the best until last."

She looked at him a little puzzled.

"How did you know?"

"How about telling me how you knew this other guy was like you? You said you only saw him for a moment."

"Good point. I can express myself through bioluminescence: my skin glows with ultraviolet light in response to my emotions, and I can see ultraviolet light. I had no idea how to control it at the time. The guy saw me and glowed right back at me. I think he was trying to communicate. I was in fight or flight mode and just got out of there."

"Now, THAT is cool. I have got to see that. Weren't you curious about him? Don't you wish you had met him?"

"To tell you the truth, I do think about it, but, you know, I am not so good with situations I am not in control of."

"Yes, I think I do know. So if that guy wasn't able to tell you about your lack of ageing, how did you figure it out?"

"The hard way, but I was lucky. I had always compartmentalised my life, so when it clicked, I was able to shed my identity without raising too many questions."

"What is it like? How does it feel to live for so long?"

Her head dropped. "I feel old, inside. Sometimes I feel blessed, to see the new things appearing, that I would never reach with an ordinary lifespan, and other times I feel those new things don't come quickly enough."

A week later, Orianna caught up with Maddox in his cabin. He was deep in thought, studying the data from the Achilles in orbit below theirs. There was an emotional distance between them, now that they appeared of different generations. The truth was indeed the opposite way around and even more of a divider: she might have appeared younger, but she had lived a hundred years more than him -

a hundred years of learning, of wisdom, of battles, of heartache and loss, whereas he appeared a decade older than he had actually experienced.

"The doctor says you will be healthy enough for a return trip in another fortnight."

"Just what I need, another twenty-four years in hibernation," he said somewhat grumpily.

"Actually, we only took eleven years to get here," she retorted. "Rogue is closer now, and this vessel is much faster. We do have to go back."

"But I haven't finished...."

"No, you haven't. You need to leave so you can come back. You need to show mankind, and you need to lead them. You will come back with a full planetary expedition. Before I left, I set the practical plans in motion. A record-breaking design of the vessel is under construction already: everything you will need."

He looked up at her and saw that she really got him; she understood him completely.

"Look here," he said, changing the tone. "These are the readings just before the comet missed my ship. See! I wasn't wrong. It should have hit me. I was thrown around, and it missed. Rogue's gravity changed. These are the anomalies I have seen."

"How can a planet change gravity?"

"I don't know, but it did, many times. But then, right then, it did it to save me. Occam's Razor. Anything else is too random. I told you this planet is special."

"Amazing. Ok, when you give your speeches on Earth, try not to sound like a man who has been driven insane alone in deep space." She raised her eyebrows at him, and he knew she was making a good point.

"This is why we still don't quite know where Rogue is heading. If it hit Jupiter, the maths is complicated; maybe nothing terrible will happen. If it misses, it could end up coming farther in, towards all human life. Chances are not good then. Earth could be moved out of the goldilocks zone and freeze or boil. Rogue is more likely to make a big mess of things than not."

"Yeah, go with that," she mused.

CHAPTER ELEVEN
1498 CE, Earth, Hispania

An hour or so after midnight, with the full moon hanging low over the rolling hills, the dusty track was comfortably illuminated for the lone monk to see his way as he walked west out of the newly finished Real Monasterio de Santo Tomás. In the middle of the reunited Hispanic heartland, Ávila was only slightly chilly during the night at this time of year, shortly before the first harvests. Nevertheless, the monk wore a full-length habit and a cowl covering his head and face, a simple knotted rope tied around his waist.

Fortunately, the monastery was outside the walled city of Ávila, so his departure and late travel would not arouse suspicion because this was no real monk, and his business could not be readily explained.

About half a mile out, he turned a bend to find a large fig tree by the side of the track. A man in a fine cloak sat there all alone, staring out over the Chico River and its confluence with Rio Adaja, and he knew they would soon be met by a horse-drawn cart, and he would be able to change clothes. As he approached, the man arose, and they embraced as brothers.

"Is it done?" Yamanu Nader asked in a whisper. The night was tranquil and their business of a secret nature, so it was best not to be too loud.

His brother, Tarik, pulled off his cowl and nodded and kissed Yamanu on the cheek. "It is peaceful here and such a beautiful night."

First, he sat on a nearby log that had been deliberately placed and crudely worked to serve as a bench. Then, beckoning his brother to sit beside him, he handed over a small amphora from his habit.

"The potion worked particularly well. De Torquemada ingested it at supper and retired before midnight. He was drowsy and suggestive but lucid and alert. I feel sure he will remember the encounter in the morning."

"So he remembered you?"

"Yes, very much so. He is an old man now, of seventy-seven years. Seeing his old friend, Tarik, still young, would be as if a vision from God. He does, after all, believe me to be long dead. You know, I think he was about forty when we first met. He had gained the queen's confidence, then, of course, the Princess Isabella of Castile, and I needed to get close to her. How easy it is to befriend the pious!"

"Their piety serves our greater purpose, Tarik. Importantly, did you convince him to support the new rules? If the Inquisition continues beyond its first Grand Inquisitor, the abuses must be curbed. If he doesn't agree to the new administrative rules at the next general assembly, then we will have to reconsider our plans."

"I think a vision of an undeniably resurrected man, with a message from God, should do the trick."

Yamanu relaxed a little and sat on the bench as his brother had beckoned.

"Wouldn't it have been better to stop the Inquisition completely?" Tarik asked idly.

"No," Yamanu emphasised. "De Torquemada has already turned them from excessive torture and death. He brought order to the chaos with centralised control. It should please your bleeding heart, brother: they have judicial processes, comfortable prisons of all things; even when torture is finally used, they have rules to prevent harm, and they must only commit it to obtain information as a last resort. Indeed, they should have used the sensation of drowning sooner as it is quick to loosen any tongue. Rejoice, brother, the worst of these things are already over. But we need the Inquisition to continue. Their persecution of non-Catholics must continue to drive them forwards. Inclusion and difference are the forces that shape their world, the forces we need to control.

"They keep making the same mistakes, brother. They love their simple stories, and in their prayers, they make the world a simpler place than it really is. They bury their heads in ritual and dogma, blind to the horrors of the world. You said: it is our duty to see the longer-term picture and play the long game. And we agreed to help them, but we cannot save everyone. Mostly, they do not want to be saved, I think."

"At least now there will be more oversight. But don't lose faith, brother. We still have much to do. The rest of Europe continues to sanction the Inquisition with its silence on the matter. They burn their own witches, but I sense the times are changing. Europe is on the verge of a transformation. Hispania is now reunited. It took us over seven centuries to achieve it, but we did it. Soon, I see her becoming an unstoppable military force; and then, there will be war...."

"Why must it always be war. Why do we never manipulate to form a peace?" Tarik's eyes were tearful.

"Look at the advances Man has made because of war? You know this is the only way, Tarik; we have spoken about it over and over across the aeons. We have to break eggs. They all die, some time or other, better for a good cause, to make a better future, eh brother?"

Tarik bowed his head. He had an honourable and noble side that Yamanu could not fully comprehend, but he found useful.

"What of the Jews?" Tarik asked, realising that he hadn't inquired how his brother had been for the last few months.

Yamanu sighed. "I am still integrated into the court as one of the Conversos, a true converter to Christianity. I will not risk falling into the spider's web by courting heresy: I see other Conversos, true Jews, with an imperative to practice Judaism behind closed doors. How they suffer for it. The Jews, as always, bear the pain of religious cleansing: be a Christian or leave! The crown gave that order eight years ago, and more than a hundred thousand people escaped the country. I tracked many returning, having found nowhere to call home, only to find their property annexed by the state. Many more were just robbed and killed during their exodus, unwanted in the lands to which they fled."

A tear in his eye told Tarik he was torn by this tragedy, but the truth was more sinister. Two years before that, Yamanu had invented a story of five Jews and six Conversos crucifying and murdering a Christian child in the village of La Guardia. His machinations had created a substantial anti-Semitic backlash. He had single-handedly tipped the delicate situation towards complete revolution. The fate of the Jews had been sealed long ago: nothing would now stop the purification of Hispania towards her future greatness.

He could not tell his brother all these details: that madness was his burden alone, and he would prefer to protect his brother's naivety.

They continued to rest in silence as if they had all the time in the world.

Later, on a rough road following the Rio Adaja downstream, they took a moment to eat in the back whilst their trusted driver held the reins, steering them amongst the trees. When the sun would soon rise, they would be grateful for the shade offered. In the summer, the river was barely a stream, but it reminded them of the Nile: a long oasis of green amongst rolling desert hills.

"Damn," Yamanu cursed as the cart hit a stone and made him spill his water. "Alejandro! Please, we have half a day before we reach the Roman road. It would be good to miss some of the rocks and potholes between here and there."

"Señor Nader, the moon is falling, the road is dark. Riding in the dark is difficult. I do not have the eyes of an owl," the driver called back in thick Campesino Spanish.

Yamanu laughed and talked to his brother in ancient Egyptian to ensure privacy.

"It is good to be together again," he said to Tarik and patted him affectionately on the shoulder.

"Brother, we are still few, and that vexes me."

Yamanu nods agreement and prepares himself for their usual talk.

"I know, Tarik, but we must have faith. Do not worry. There are more out there, and we will find them. They will be alone and waiting for us. They need us to help them."

"But we are still only a dozen, after four thousand years! The task seems impossible. The gods have played a trick on us. It is the mortals that randomly produce our kin. Must we sift and sort them ourselves until the end of time?" Tarik's voice was gloomy. "How many were driven away to die alone or be killed - feared as if they were some malevolent creature sucking the life from the ordinary people around them to stay young?"

"Tarik, you cannot dwell on what you cannot change. Man is kind, but tolerance is the luxury of civilisation and knowledge. We have to raise them up to protect our own kin and help our own come out into the light. We walk among them, and they do not know us. For now, that suits our purposes."

"But we are not immortal. The gods have gifted us only partly. We can starve, bleed, die without breath, and suffer.

Some of our numbers have already been killed. All too often, we have been too late, only to witness their murder at the hands of the ignorant and superstitious hoards."

"But we do survive. We are... better. When all around us die from plagues, we survive. You know this is the key. This is the plan. Anton was found untouched by The Black Death, and Stephanie emerged during the Great Famine. And that is why we must travel wider, more into Europe, to seek out our kind in the disasters of the world. Come on, Tarik, we have nestled around the Mediterranean Sea for too long. Civilisation is spreading. Remember that we number a dozen in our quest. The more we get, the faster we can find more, and the more power we obtain, the farther we can reach, the... what is the matter Tarik?"

"I see him. There, hidden in the trees on the other bank. He is matching our pace. I thought I saw him a mile ago, but now I am sure."

Both men stared out in the half-light, across the creek. Then, as if he knew he was discovered, a horse rider brought his steed out from the shadow and came to a halt directly opposite, in the moonlight, gazing in their direction.

Tarik raised his arm and made it glow brightly for a moment, with a brilliance that only the three men could see.

The horse rider did not move, but what little they could see of his face glowed subtly as if involuntarily. Then he pulled down his bandana, which had been protecting him from the dust, showing them his whole face, exposing a young visage like theirs, but a darker complexion and a bushy beard. His expression was severe but neutral.

"It is him," Yamanu agreed with certainty. "The Watcher. Finally, we see him together at the same time."

"He never speaks, you said the same, and he leaves if you try to approach. What does he want? He is one of us and should be with us, but he just sits there. I find him unnerving."

"Indeed. What does it mean? We have seen him separately over and over across time, but never together."

"We are often not together, brother."

"That is true, I suppose. Perhaps it means nothing. One day I will find him and discover his story," Yamanu vowed. "For now, we have more important matters."

After another hour, before the sun rose fully, they lost sight of the man, his slow pace gradually lagging behind their's, until they could see him no longer.

CHAPTER TWELVE

2341 CE, Earth-L4, Erebus

Coming out of hibernation a week early was Maddox's idea. He was keen to further review the data and catch up on their last eleven years in transit sleep because he was burdened with anxiety at the thought of facing the masses. He needed as much time as possible, but as Orianna suspected, more time did not help with the stress: it made it worse.

"You must rest," she advised him, but he wouldn't listen.

"Just a few more hours. Thanks for your help."

She cupped his face in her hands and turned him to face her.

"I have been alive for two lifetimes already. Plenty of time to learn twelve languages and gain degrees in a wide range of subjects, but something I knew already when we first met is that you cannot burn the candle at both ends. Take a break, you silly man!"

Her face was being cute, and he responded with raised eyebrows.

"I - I cannot be the weak point in the work. It must be properly collated."

"And I think it is. Look, it will take months to review this much data. Here, I have redrafted your presentation. This is what is important right now. It is still all your own words. I just slimmed it down a little more to get the basic message across: 'we need to pay attention, and we need to go back.' Right?"

Maddox nodded, his tired eyes bloodshot and weeping with exhaustion.

The doctor gave him something to help him sleep. He put his head down in his cabin and slept for the remaining thirty-four hours before he transferred to a Tug. They had arrived.

There was no time to rebuild the doubts and anxieties that his sufficient sleep had left behind. He got dressed, grabbed his gear, and they all entered the Tug.

It was a long time since Orianna had been in a Tug in real terms. Nothing much had changed, so she still knew her way around. Noting the date, she realised that tomorrow would be the one hundred and sixteenth anniversary of that dreadful disaster that nearly claimed her life in a Tug. Terrible as that time was, she was grateful to have been reborn from it into a whole new life.

Her own anxiety was rising. Her eidetic memory gave her the quality of recall that others would experience only the next day, but she would never forget, not even after a century, it seemed. They both needed a distraction, so she engaged Maddox in playful small talk.

"Welcome back to my home," she said, clanking over to him and inserting herself into the alcove in the bulkhead next to him, her extended suit's backpack clicking firmly into place. "Welcome to Erebus! Did you know that Erebus was the Greek god of the Underworld, and his name meant 'place of darkness between earth and Hades?' So his name was often used to refer to the part of the Greek Underworld where the spirits of the dead pass after they leave the living bodies."

She smiled over at him.

"Oh, and that is supposed to make me feel more

comfortable?" he said with a grin.

"Well, I don't think they really thought it through at the time, when they first detected it across space. Never considered we would one day be living in it. They just thought it was a cool name to give a dark, black space rock. I have some brochures you know: 'Welcome to the Underworld, you are dead, these are the dungeons you will walk for the rest of eternity.'"

"Haha! Nice recruitment pitch. 'Come and meet a god, sit on his knee for five bucks!' I can see it as a real selling point for the discerning space tourist around the festive season. Oh, how about: 'Underworld Tours, so good you have to come back, eventually'"

"What the hell are you two going on about?" the Tug commander, Captain Rogers-Smith, called over the comms. "Suits! That means everyone, get in an alcove so we can get this show on the road! Come on, I am late for a pickup."

Orianna swiftly switched to a private channel, giggling as she did so.

"'Enjoy your stay at Erebus, just one week will feel like an eternity.'"

"Oh, that one is good," Maddox said. "Thanks again for all your help. Seriously, more than just spending twenty-two years travelling halfway across the system and back to rescue me from certain death." She really appreciated his sarcasm. "I mean: you helping me with this: standing up in front of the press, doing a live simulcast, to be recorded and sent to Earth for billions to see. Honestly, without you next to me, I would have preferred certain death." This time his smile did not extend to his eyes.

Orianna swallowed heavily. "No, no, no, I have a rule against appearing in public," she said, realising what he was assuming.

"Just be there. Keep your visor and your mask on, if you like. Just be in the room. Pleeeease?"

"Look, I take suppressant drugs to ensure this glowing thing doesn't go off on its own, which it does, despite all my efforts to control it. Unless I am totally calm, there is no zero setting."

"Great, then take them."

"I cannot take them within two weeks of hibernation, minimum. Not unless I want to kill my liver."

"Ok, then just stay out of the holo field, and you won't be in anyone's picture. Say you will do it, just this once. After that, I am sure I will find my legs. I have already been told to expect a tour on Earth. I think they are planning to ship me out next week."

"Alright," agreed Orianna. Her problem with the spotlight was less pathological and more survival instinct. But, in the back of her mind, she knew that just one mistake could bring it all down on her. Was he really worth it?

Once the Tug had connected to the port's elevator and begun to descend, she was the first to release herself from the nook and clumped her magnetic boots up to the top of the stairs where the observation bubble was mounted. She opened the safety door and entered. It was a cramped blister on the side of the Tug, like an old-style warplane gun turret, minus the gun. Climbing into the seat, she got a good look around at the dock and remembered her old crew, leaving her on that fateful day almost a hundred and sixteen years earlier. Feeling the sense of gravity arriving from nowhere, she watched as the Tug was pulled down into a radius of the dock until it docked under miniG. No longer in zeroG, Orianna felt the sense of down as she exited the blister again and rejoined the others for disembarkation.

They relinquished their suit extensions and left for the elevator. Finally, they were "home". T minus two hours before Maddox's speech.

They had been confident of a quiet two hours before entering the press room, but that naivety was soon lost. The elevator doors opened at the base of Pall Mall, and all hell broke loose. Paparazzi were everywhere. It was a press ambush. Both Orianna and Maddox were shocked by the massive crowd pushing forward to get a question to Maddox and then a quick shift to improvise additional interest in the unknown young lady with him.

Orianna quickly raised her mouth and nose mask and lowered her visor, with tint activated.

In that moment of loud yelling from the large crowd, inside a melee of frantic proportions, Maddox tried to find Orianna to understand where to go and what to do. Still, all he saw was a myriad of strange faces throwing random questions at him with no hope of any answers being heard. His heart was pounding, and fight or flight was about to kick in.

Suddenly, there was a loud bang, and everywhere went smokey very fast. The crowd lost its harmony and direction in that instant; each member was reunited with their own sense of personal safety. Maddox was pulled backwards and felt a quick rush upwards. He realised he was in the lift again and ascending, but not for long. Then, the doors reopened, and the smoke carried with them was released and dissipated.

Orianna pushed him out, and he gasped at the railing, looking down. They were now two stories above the crowd, smoke, and trees. People were running in all directions, very confused. He knew how they felt as he was yanked away and down a quiet corridor. Everything went slowly but quickly, the noises were gone, but it still looked noisy. He and Orianna and the others were shouting and running. He didn't know where they were going but trusted that Orianna knew this place like the back of her hand.

"Oh my god, this is going to be big," Orianna said, as doors secured them in a nice empty room. Then, all of a sudden, everything sped back up and slowed down again.

"You will be safe here," one of Orianna's team said calmly and proceeded to engage rapidly with his visor and cuff.

"Well, that was something," Orianna said, with a look of someone trying to play down a difficult situation. "Sorry, Maddox, I ought to have anticipated that."

"Did someone let off a smoke grenade?" he replied incredulously, mouth agape.

"Ha! I always anticipate needing that," she admitted. "It seems that you were right, Maddox. Everyone wants to know about Rogue. I didn't stoke that fire. I suspect your colleagues have been getting their moments in the spotlight. I wouldn't blame them. They probably didn't stand a chance. Nerds in a cupboard vs the press, hmm, I know where my money would go. Anyway, this helps us."

"What!? How does that help us? That was a ravenous riot! What the hell have I let myself in for?"

"Listen! Think of it the right way. The audience is already primed for the big act - you! You might have stage fright, but honestly, you just stick to the speech, do the nerd thing, and they will lap it up. This is a good thing. Trust me. I know propaganda."

"Do the nerd thing?"

"Yeah, blind them with your science," she winked.

At last, he sighed and relaxed, not quite ready to smile but at least relieved after what had just happened. "Oh shit," he said, resigning himself to what was becoming the moment of the century. "No pressure, huh?"

"Welcome. Today's guest probably needs no introduction, despite having never appeared on a public simulcast before, I give you the man of the hour, the man of the century, discoverer of the Rogue Planet, Maddox Jefferies…."

The interviewer was Anton Sutron. His ridiculous suit was a deep orange colour and covered in glitter with a high mandarin collar. He and Maddox were in the centre of a dark room, each heavily spotlighted and ringed with three levels of wraparound camera rigs. Simulcasting wasn't the same as visor messaging: it was live and high bandwidth, suitable for instantaneous holographic projections within local networks. By contrast, visor messaging was low bandwidth: the images of people were three-dimensional graphics, drawn in the visor from smaller amounts of data: movement, positional and face textures. Simulcasting was thus more realistic but needed good network comms. Maddox's would be recorded, compressed and then sent to Earth for billions to see.

"Hello, everyone. My name is Maddox Jefferies, and I am an amateur astronomer and cosmologist. I used to work at the Titov Crater Array, looking after Deep-System Communications. In my spare time, I was allowed to borrow the old telescopes to study the universe beyond the Solar System. A hundred and sixteen years ago, I discovered a planetary object entering our system. Such objects drifting between stars are called rogue planets, so my niece, Angela Hobbes, named it 'Rogue'."

Anton laughed. "Original."

"She was twelve years old at the time, and now she has been deceased for thirty years." Maddox shifted his weight as a non-verbal indication he wanted to get back on track. Orianna momentarily stepped to the edge of the spotlights and raised a hand to show him support. "Rogue displaced Pluto, now ejected from the Solar System, and that slowed it down. Even now, it continues to head towards Jupiter. I immediately travelled to Rogue and set about studying it from orbit…."

"Forgive me for interrupting, Maddox. May I call you Maddox? This all happened, you say, over a century ago. So why are we hearing about it now?"

"Nobody wanted to hear. We tried to warn ministers, science institutes, business owners. Nobody took us seriously. We are just a bunch of amateurs, after all."

"We. Indeed, we have recordings from people you spoke to all that time ago. Do you remember Ben Thomas? In his recordings, he thought you were mad and taking 'an insane risk.' How do you respond to that?"

"I miss Ben. He was my friend. He and Xero stayed with me after my trip out had displaced me twenty-four years into their future. They were still there, middle-aged, with families, ready to be there when I awoke from hibernation in orbit around Rogue."

Nice, keep it personal and avoid distracting interruptions! Orianna thought to herself.

"Yes, Xero. In his later life, he became an anarchist and political activist. But, unfortunately, he died in prison forty-five years ago. Not a pleasant character, as I understand it."

"We didn't feel too close, but I gather he took the news of my apparent death pretty badly. I guess people do act drastically when it really matters. It isn't about the messenger, though, is it?"

"Messenger, indeed! Ben and Xero were just the beginning. They and their small band of acolytes grew into a major movement since you disappeared: The Mercurians, apparently named after the god Mercury, carrier of messages. It would be unfair of me to attribute their many acts of violence and rebellion to you, so let me just ask you directly: as their 'resurrected Messiah', how do you respond to them?"

"Respond? To what? I haven't been in contact with them. I am no Messiah. That is ridiculous. I should respond to you calling me that, but you just want to pick a fight with me, so I will ignore it. Look, the Critical Earth taught us the value of personal responsibilities. I guess that is what they are doing in their own way. My way was to take that 'insane risk', as Ben accurately put it, to go there and see for myself. If I was to respond to anyone asking about this, I would suggest the same: go there!"

"You are suggesting an expedition?"

"Of course! Ben said, over and over, that we are facing a dangerous situation. I know I am not legally allowed to incite fear or brandish unsubstantiated facts on simulcast, but I can tell you this: the Solar System has a new large object in it. We don't know how that is going to affect the other planets. I'm not implying any impending peril for humanity. I am clearly saying, we need to find out, to be ready, to just look up there and decide for ourselves!"

"And that brings up an excellent question: why don't you know? Don't you have enough data? Surely we can predict the movement of the planets as we have done for hundreds of years, with great accuracy?"

Oh, be careful, Maddox!

"I could cite the three-body problem to you, and you would counter with the ICE's computational capabilities, but I know what you want to hear. You want to hear me say things that make no sense, that might question my sanity, that might allow you all to question the messenger and ignore the message. So my answer is simple: read my data!"

"Hmm, ok, well, can you tell us whether Rogue will hit Jupiter or not."

"That is not up to me."

"What? What does that mean? How can you not determine the result of what is surely just a two-body problem, as you already mentioned? This is outrageous! You cannot expect us to believe these vagaries."

"No, perhaps not. Ok, here is the answer you need, not necessarily the one you want. Our ancestors shut down astronomy and cosmological sciences, turning their back on anything outside the Solar System. In their arrogance, they assumed it was all either a solved problem or too far to care about. What they failed to do - and I expect you all to do better - is believe that there are things we just don't understand. All my life, I have only ever wanted to understand what I didn't understand. I invite you all out there to join me on that journey. Until you open your eyes to the possibility that there is something new to learn here, then you won't find out anything until it is too late."

"Too late for what?"

Maddox just eyed him coyly. However, he wasn't taking the bait and immediately shut down his holo grid. The camera rigs were pulled up to the ceiling like a Venetian blind and the spotlight faded.

"You were brilliant," Orianna whispered to him, and she led him out.

They spent the rest of the day relaxing in a private space of Orianna's. He began to research the changes in the world since he had left it, and she caught up with her business empire. After that, he went to bed early, for his first good night's sleep, whilst she left for a business dinner with the CEO of one of her subsidiaries.

La Casa de Hernández was a prestigious restaurant on the edge of the Lanes. On the one side of the Lanes was the dock, and on the other side was the Elysian Fields, a vast cavern, twice as long as the dock and only recently completed. Elysian had a cylindrical space of five hundred and forty metres in diameter at full depth. With the angular velocity of Erebus at 1.8 rotations per minute, that gave a perfect 1G at the inner surface. Whereas the dock was filled with storage and industrial complexes below the Tug dock, Elysian's empty space was broken only by a thick man-made construction along the axis, held in place with fine carbon nanotube cables. At zeroG, the axis wasn't going anywhere, but the stays were there for stability and to transmit power from the axis down to the surface regions.

The restaurant window was higher up the funnel-shaped

end of the cavern than the rest of the Lanes, sacrificing some gravity for a more elevated panoramic view. Looking down, she could see the rock face sloping down to the main surface, inside which she knew the Lanes were like an ant's nest of excavations in this pinched plug between the cavern and the port behind.

As she waited for her guest, she took in the vista, seated at one of the most prestigious window tables. She gazed with wonder at the landscape of trees, fields, houses and occasional lakes: two square kilometres of surface looked just like Earth: an illusion that only worked when gazing upon a small part of the ground because the surface curled up and over at the peripheries to confound the eyes. With its brilliant lights substituting for the Sun, the long axis also ruined the fantasy when one looked up. The shadows were wrong too, but that didn't take long to get used to. It had been a long time since she had been here and seen all of this.

The restaurant still had its emergency bulkhead doors, originally built to protect against accidental depressurisation when the cavern was still a vacuum during excavation. Now, the air outside the window was better than inside the restaurant.

She resolved to take the time to visit it next.

The shadow of a man passed before her, and she assumed it was her guest. But, before she realised he wasn't the man she was expecting, he had sat down opposite her and was already addressing the waiter, requesting a bottle of Champagne - still the drink of choice for a celebration.

He was smartly dressed in a satin dress shirt and wore conspicuous jewels in his cufflinks.

"Forgive me for my presumption; your guest will not be making it tonight. Allow me to introduce myself. My name is Tarik Nader."

He held out his hand, and she instinctively took it gently across the still unused table. His face was tanned and friendly, with a bold and gentle look about his young features. There was something in his eyes that intrigued her. They were a striking blue colour, much like hers, but they looked out of place against his dark complexion and jet black hair. Other than the eyes, he looked Arabic.

"Olwin Dawkins," she replied, smiling graciously, with her well-practised face for meeting new people.

"Hmm," he muttered, a coy grin growing in one corner of his full lips.

Their handshake had lasted a little too long, and Orianna went to withdraw it when Tarik gripped her tightly, his hand glowing blue.

Orianna gasped and then saw the glowing hand. She stood suddenly and thrust back her chair.

"Orianna, please. You are free to go. You are in no danger. I want only a few minutes of your time. Please."

"Is everything alright?" came the waiter's voice from nearby, having noticed the slight disturbance.

Tarik released her hand, maintaining direct eye contact with her.

Orianna turned and said, "Oh, um, everything is fine," before slowly sitting again. Her tension remained high.

Tarik smiled warmly and sincerely, hoping to put her at ease.

"This is a special occasion, and I like to always start by saying: you are not alone."

"Who the hell are you?" she snapped, her body language showing she was ready to flee at the slightest provocation. Her mind raced with exit strategies and contingencies. More than a century of defensive planning in her head was all surfacing a little too quickly. "What do you want?"

"Which question would you like me to answer first?" he calmly responded.

"How about: how do you know who I am?"

"Ah, yes, let us start there, and perhaps later we can

answer: what are you?"

Then her body relaxed, receptive to this man's gentle voice and strange accent. Now he had her attention.

The waiter arrived, poured the Champagne, and left.

She looked down suspiciously.

He chuckled. "If I had wanted to drug you and kidnap you, it would have already happened. That would be easy. Finding you was the hard part. Finding any of us is always the hardest thing."

"Us?"

"Us. You, me, my brother Yamanu, whom you nearly met in the dock over a century ago, and the others like us. Let us drink, to us."

They enjoyed their first sip of the sparkling wine. Immediately, Orianna's stomach relaxed, further easing into this unsolicited company.

"I'll give you two minutes, and then I am leaving."

"Very generous, Orianna. I accept. If I have not given you good cause to stay after two minutes, the failing is mine, and you should leave.

"We. Us. Are The Few. We live and stay young whilst others grow old and die. Some of us have been around for centuries and millennia. Mortal men have not been kind, and many of us have perished at their ignorant hands. You already suspect this. You have expertly hidden from them and changed identities to avoid suspicion. We only want to help the way others have helped us, to provide sanctuary and meaning to our own kind, as they appear randomly across time and space. In doing so, we help mankind the way that only immortals can, give guidance beyond their meagre lifespan, hold longer visions to heart, and guide them to a greater understanding. Perhaps one day, we can walk openly amongst them.

"However, our secret is known to some mortals. They are The Many, and they hate and despise us. They are jealous of our gifts, and in pursuit of it for themselves, they hunt and imprison us. How am I doing so far?"

"Go on."

"You were born by chance, from mortals. If we have children, they are mortal, and we watch them grow old and die. It is perhaps a curse of the gods: a life without end, to outlive everyone you have ever known, a short joy of a family and aeons of the pain for their loss. I am aware you never had children, so perhaps you can only imagine my losses."

He paused and took a long drink.

"Wow. That is a lot to take in. I was so careful. How did you find me?"

"It could have been your glowing hand next to Maddox Jefferies in the Simulcast - very sloppy of you that was - but I had already found you, by then, by nostalgia. You did a magnificent job of hiding your escape after the Tug crash, moving so many people around - there was no centre to it, but over time one learns to see what is not there. So, for example, given an analysis of all the people on Erebus, emphasising those arriving shortly before tomorrow's anniversary of the Tug crash and eventually, given enough patience, even over a century or more, I saw you, in all your disguises and identities. After that, reversing back through your history was an easier task. This is how we do it. We are more patient than The Many. Patience is the virtue of The Few."

She was quiet now. For most of her life, she had been playing the part of the prey: how to hide, where to run, afraid of every shadow, just waiting for this day to come - and now that day had arrived. It was all so much to take in, challenge and question, but in the middle was a massive relief in the knowledge that she didn't have to run alone anymore.

"Orianna, we act rapidly to save our kind when they are

but fledglings, vulnerable and not afraid enough of The Many. Once you had eluded them and us, we were content to cross paths with you again in good time. You grew up all by yourself, so to speak. The one thing you no doubt know yourself is that what we always have is time."

Orianna resolved to stay, and she heard a man's journey through hundreds of generations, from the dawn of civilisation to her table. It was a mind-blowing situation.

Am I home now? Is this it? Do I just walk away from Maddox and follow this man into the sunset? Has everything really changed?

However, her defences were ignored; an overwhelming curiosity flooded over her, accompanied by a soothing sense of belonging. She found herself just staring into those deep blue eyes, wondering what wonders they had seen, almost missing words explaining precisely that to her. Finally, she caught herself and decided to break up his monologue as dessert arrived.

"So back in Egypt, during your early life..."

"Kemet. The black land. The Greek name 'Aigyptos' came later, with Alexander the Great."

"You said you had to keep moving on in case people noticed you weren't ageing, but you had already been told this by your mother, who sheltered you for nearly four decades. So you had a big head start on this game of hiding and moving on?" Tarik just nodded, feeling a little embarrassed that he had corrected her, resolving not to interrupt her again. "The others pretty much had to figure this all out by themselves, unless you found them first?"

He nodded again and only replied when he realised she was finished.

"Many were killed by ignorance, fear and superstition. We have no idea how many were lost this way. So we resolved to help our brothers and sisters, our kin."

"So, how many are there?"

"You will forgive me for being a little vague on such matters. Until you choose to join us, we are in a cold war with The Many. Secrecy is key."

"I understand. How old are you then?"

"Amongst our kind, such a question is considered a delicate thing, much like asking how much you are worth. Our youth removes any obvious sense of seniority except when it is earned by respect. Everyone I have ever met has excellent recall, and such a question pushes one to invariably drag up painful memories from their earliest times. Thus, it is rude to ask."

"No offence meant."

"How would you know?" He smiled amiably.

"How do you feel about the ordinary people around you then? I hadn't done anything much more than live long enough to know that every ordinary person, who was alive when I was born, is now dead. That is a sobering thought."

"Ordinary people? Hmm, that is considered offensive too. They are our children, our children's children, ad infinitum."

"What term do you use then? Not 'mortal' surely?"

"Sometimes. We can die; we are just excellent at not dying, and we do not age, so 'immortal' is not wrong, just not ideal. Some translations around the world describe us as ageless, unaging, undead, undying, unchanging, everlasting...."

"am lasmuigh?"

"Yes, Irish for 'outside time'. Where did you hear that?"

"Just one of my own secrets until I get to know *you* a whole lot better."

"Touché," he said, nodding curtly. "We cannot be sure which mortals are just going about their businesses and which are members of The Many and know of our existence, so often you will hear us just use 'The Many' as a blanket term. The context will be important then."

"Quite a subculture!"

"This is the way: the way we live our lives. Like most people, most of the time: fitting in, enjoying moments, trying to forget that these people around us will be gone in a blink of an eye, trying not to get caught or recognised, trying so very hard to live in the moment as they do, trying to forget that they are all really both our children and the parent of our kin to come. So yes, subculture is not a bad term. I would have chosen a 'parallel culture'."

"'Parallel' implies not being in contact and existing independently. From what you have said, that couldn't be farther from the truth, could it?"

"You have me there. We walk among them, but they know nothing of us, on the whole."

Soon, they finished eating, and Tarik gazed out of the window for a long while. "Amazing," he breathlessly uttered.

"Come, let us take a walk?" Orianna suggested.

"Down there? Can we?"

"Oh yes!"

The restaurant had been high, giving them 0.8G in exchange for an excellent view, and so their descent was slightly disturbing on a full stomach. Much consolation was had knowing a comfortable 1G awaited at the bottom to aid digestion with a gentle walk. Alas, neither of them quite realised how wrong they were.

The corridor ended, ceiling first as it penetrated the slope of the funnelled end into the vast open space of the Elysian Fields, opening out before them.

There was so much to take in. In an enclosed world, you get used to things being so close, but there were huge distances here. Over two hundred metres up to the thick axis and beyond the axis, one could see more of the Fields upside down. Looking up would take some getting used to, and even glancing either side as the Field curved upwards was just as jarring to the senses. That said, looking around at the plants and houses and streets nearby felt just like being on Earth: the volume was so huge that there was no echo, but there was a pleasant breeze.

They perambulated, with no particular agenda, keeping their eyes on the flat distance ahead, a bit more than a kilometre of it. There they could see the fixed slope of rock extend up and back, forming a funnel shape at the other end as well.

Orianna pointed up to where the axis met the centre of the funnel. "There is an exit port at that end too. However, now that the excavation work is completed, it isn't used for much more than servicing the axis systems."

Tarik looked back and saw the funnel behind them soaring up from the now distant corridor exit, dwarfing it.

"What are they for, these funnel-like shapes," he asked.

"For a start, it is where the Lanes are. In the beginning, that was all we had, but the big plan had always been this. They also help to stabilise the atmosphere. Also, in principle, anyone could climb up to the axis from here. There are tether points up the rock face, and people do it for fun."

"For fun?"

"Sure, a bit of 45-degree rock climbing. The real fun kicks in as you get higher, and you lose the sense of gravity."

"Ah, of course, we spin, and gravity is simulated, but up there, there is no gravity."

"Yes, and that is the reason we have those spiral tracks you can see. There is a tramway and then a ramble-way, repeated around the funnel. Both types are equipped to assist with miniG and then zeroG as you ascend. The tram is quick. We will go up later."

"To the axis?"

"Why not? It is like a bit of Earth in space, don't you think? This was nearly finished when I left. It is so good to see it fully mature."

"You have soil here?"

"Yes. Of course, it is not practical to bring it here from Earth, although many small samples were brought to kick start life in the stuff we made."

"Made?"

"Made. From vegetable farms we have had going for decades, and, well, poop. So you are standing on a hundred-year-old toilet." Orianna laughed. "If you look around, you can see large patches still waiting to be laid. So it will be decades before we get it fully populated."

"Amazing."

They passed many people going about their everyday lives, gardening, travelling to or from work. All of them looked pretty relaxed.

"This is idyllic. Is it getting darker?"

"Ah yes, dawn is simulated for everyone. The axis dims. Oh no, wait!" Orianna broke off and ran. Tarik didn't think she literally meant for him to wait, so he pursued her.

They broke into a clearing with a long straight road, clearly looping right around the cavern and forming a single endless track. It was broad with warning signs to keep clear when lights were on, which they weren't. Tarik saw Orianna run over to a man beside a strange-looking plane or car. He didn't know what it was. She seemed to be negotiating with him.

"He was closing down. I got us a twenty-minute ride. Oh my god, this is going to be the icing on the cake!" She was giddy with excitement.

The craft stood on wheels at the end of long stalks. It had a kind of flat arrowhead appearance, like a plane. Power came from a big fan at the back, and steering came from four canards at the front in the shape of a cross. They entered through a belly hatch, following the pilot, who moved straight to the single front seat. There were four passenger seats behind him to choose from.

"Thanks," Orianna said to him as he closed the hatch and

started the engine. "This is Lance," she said to Tarik.

Lance nodded back to Tarik and instructed them to buckle up. The craft was very flimsy and lightweight, which worried Tarik because something that dart-shaped, pointing down an infinitely straight road, gave the impression that speed was coming.

"Welcome aboard," said Lance, over the speakers. The engine was beginning to whine loudly. "It is essential that you do not undo your seatbelts during the flight. Please sit back and enjoy this unique flying experience."

At this point, Tarik was getting even more nervous. The light level was still dropping, and he saw windscreen wipers moving across in front of Lance.

"Is that rain?" he yelled. "How can it be raining inside here?"

Orianna leaned over to speak more clearly in his ear. "It can. The axis is surrounded by water tanks, and periodically they squirt the water at high speed. By the time it gets to the ground, it seems just like rain: it cleans the air and waters the plants; pools and lakes collect it back up, and it is pumped around again. Obvious really. The weather forecast here is 100% reliable, of course, if you elect to read it."

When the engine had reached the highest whine and the lights down the road were illuminated, the craft lurched forwards, accelerating down the track. The raindrops began to streak across the window. Trees passed by faster and faster, but strangely the rumble through the wheels became less and less rough. After about twenty seconds, the front two horizontal canards twitched and the nose lifted for a moment. They had taken off.

All seemed much like a ride in a small plane until they realised they were in zeroG. Hair floated and swayed as if underwater; their arms no longer wanted to rest on the seat rests.

"Radical, huh?" asked Lance. "Gets them every time, even

when they know what to expect. Having achieved a linear speed of fifty metres per second, or a hundred and fifteen miles per hour if you prefer, we have matched speed with the rotation of the environment. If you look outside, you will see we are apparently cruising at the height of about 5 metres. The fan provides enough thrust only to maintain our airspeed by exactly compensating for air resistance. The craft is not 'flying'; those are not aerofoil wings out there. In truth, lady and gentleman, we are entirely stationary. It is the world around us that is moving. We are just trying to stay here as the air passes us at the speed of the environment. Now you can appreciate the environment as it is considered externally: as a spinning cylinder."

They looked around them and, after a moment, their brains clicked into accepting they were stationary, and everything else was spinning in place. They saw Elysium turning where not long ago they were in Elysium, and the Fields were fixed.

Orianna watched Tarik immerse himself in the experience and pondered how this had been more than just a date with a man. Her life had changed forever, again.

Returning home with Maddox had been stressful in ways she hadn't shared with him: the way she depended on him to ground her in her past since nobody else she had known back then was still alive. He was her only original friend, the only one left. In many ways, this had been true for him too, she assumed, but they had never really spoken of it. Instead, they had appreciated a mutual assurance that each was there for the other.

That was only earlier this same day, a day that had ended with a very different outlook.

Was a new world of possibilities opening up? Would I be a part of something so much bigger? Will I now belong to some group of people, of immortals? Such were the thoughts preventing her from fully embracing the moment.

She knew, after all, that Maddox and this group would be an exclusive arrangement. She could not leave him, though. She would have to wait for him to leave her in time.

Tarik was sensitive to her slight withdrawal and did not press her to reveal her concerns. Instead, he accepted her invitation to visit the unusual axis, where water was stored and power was generated. The zeroG manufacturing was a surprise: the construction of delicate objects that gravity made impossible, such as printing human organs and assembling quantum computer components.

He enjoyed their time together and satisfied himself that it had gone better than planned. Patience was easy for an immortal. He had plenty of time.

CHAPTER THIRTEEN

2494 BCE, Earth, Kemet (Ancient Egypt)

Yamanu and Sara were in her private chambers in Mennefer, preparing her for the seasonal audience with Pharoah. She was being anointed and dressed in the finest robes, and the wildest makeup applied to emphasise the effect of the visions she was to present to Menkaure. The Sun had passed its apex, and the blinds kept out most of the light, which suited their sensitivity. It was peaceful and quiet, allowing Sara to prepare her mind for the performance ahead.

Tarik burst in unannounced, breathing like he had run the width of the Nile, disturbing the tranquillity of the moment.

They both eyed him as he recovered his breath. Eventually, Yamanu arose and made for the door, closing it once he was satisfied that no curious souls had followed his rampant brother.

"Steady yourself, brother," he said, placing a hand of his brother's doubled up back.

Tarik caught his breath and uncurled. He had grown taller and broader than his older brother, but had stopped ageing long ago in his late twenties, just like they all had.

"I take it your meeting with young Rhaf ended abruptly," Sara said, turning her back on the bronze mirror but staying on her stool. "I like him. He is very genial, like you, dear

Tarik. I am glad you have such a contact in the priestly halls. Even a voice hears things. What did he hear?"

"Yamanu's spies were right, mother. The priests are plotting against you. Not all, but their numbers grow as the seniors try to drive a wedge between you and Pharoah. Rhaf is only a novice, but now even he has been approached by them. He had disobeyed his father and overheard a private discourse. He said it was us, Yamanu and I, who have created doubt in them. We have been so careful, but all it takes is to be remembered by an old soul who realises we haven't aged. Might we have been your downfall, mother? Oh, I cannot bear the guilt of it."

"Calm yourself, brother. Mother always prepared us for this time. We knew these mortals would eventually discover us. It was a matter of when not if. Come! Remember your training!"

"My sons, it is true that having you was a great risk. It was a risk I entered willingly and openly. I had done it before, and I knew that it was always only a matter of time. Such was my love for you that I chose to have you despite the dangers." Sara smiled maternally. Had there been anyone else in the room, they would have looked like three siblings. "As Yamanu the wise said, remember your training. Living a long life and having a good memory gives you a chance for knowledge beyond the lifespan of the mortals. Take that knowledge: let it be the key to your survival. You have been preparing for this for the reigns of three Pharaohs. You are ready. You should take separate paths northwards. Find your own way. You will be safer alone."

"We will not leave you, Mother!" Tarik said, dropping to his knees and momentarily bowing his head. "We shall meet up at our prearranged places and times," Tarik insisted.

"Come, brother, you know we must. We will have perhaps ten inundations in any one place before the mortals begin to notice we do not age. Then we must move on."

"I have been lucky enough to have been in one place for such a very long time, under the protection of the Pharaoh. Nobody saw my face. Nobody knew that the Oracle was always the same person. This was a very unusual arrangement. I do not expect to find another like it. We must return to the nomadic existence of my first lifetime. Now go, I must see Pharaoh before the day is done."

"No, Mother, we must flee now!" Tarik pleaded.

"If I do not go to him now, none of us will get very far. I WILL FOLLOW YOU once I have given my predictions for the inundations and the harvest ahead. I am no stranger to travelling in rags and applying makeup to look as if sun-drenched, as you well know. Knowledge only comes to those who seek it. Rarely is the Oracle where she is meant to be," Sara winked at them. "If only Pharaoh would understand where the Nile comes from and how the Inundation is caused, then he would have no need of mysticism - he could measure the future as I do."

They all looked at each other, conscious that this could well be the last time they would all be together. The truth of it was undeniable, and Sara's resolve was formidable.

"Disappear, my darlings. Live long and do good. If we do not meet again by the third arranged place, we are dead. Now go!"

With that, the boys hugged their mother, and without any other words, they moved silently away, demonstrating to their mother the stealthy skills they had been taught and proving to her that they would be safe.

The Oracle's chamber was small and domed: the mud walls, incongruous to the grand stone building in which it was housed, formed a cylinder with a diameter of five cubits, rising to four cubits before curving into a domed roof. The mud was dark and, when it had been plastered, rocks and gems had been pushed into it in great numbers - this was the purpose of the mud walls, to hold these strange objects in place: agate, quartz, amber, calcite, opal and rock salt - even turmeric had been added to the final layer of mud. The builders had not understood the reason for this, but they had done as instructed by the Oracle. Only she had devised long ago the common property that they all possessed.

A small hole above the doorway brought a narrow beam of light from the afternoon sun, and at the exact time when this beam rested on the centre stone of the floor, the Oracle arrived to stand there alone, entirely naked. She waited patiently, humming a subvocal dirge to herself, making the space resonate.

Pharaoh Menkaure entered the room. Only the two of them ever met here together alone. He was stripped of his double crown and his outer cloak, showing the kind of intimacy he had always done on these occasions.

The Oracle raised her arms and brought forth her aura as powerfully as possible. Pharaoh, like every other mortal, could not see this aura. However, the gems and rocks embedded in the mud all around shone brightly in response in various colours, filling the room with a heavenly glow, rippling around the space. Pharaoh stood still, and his expression was enigmatic.

Before speaking, Sara was aware of another person entering the room. It was the grand priest, Hanutep. His mouth was wide. He had never seen anything like this before, of course, and doubt filled his mind.

"She broke your bond and had children. My men are apprehending them as we speak," Hanutep whispered at Pharaoh, but he just raised a hand to quiet the man.

Sara's mood changed, and her aura matched it. Waves rippled around her, and even slight changes of colours were seen in the walls.

Pharaoh squinted at her. "Did you break our trust?" he asked. "Hanutep has poisoned your name with tales of treachery. Do you no longer remain loyal to Kemet and to me?"

He was angry and clearly determined in his conclusion.

Behind him, she spied the tiny glint of bronze. Soldiers were waiting just outside the open door. She began to breathe more heavily, resigned to the fate that awaited her.

"I will give my Lord fair and honest counsel, as I have always done, as I did to his father Khafre, and to his brother Djedefre, and to their father Khufu, and farther back through every Pharaoh of Kemet since the first.

"Kemet is in decline. The peak of prosperity enjoyed by Khufu led to the greatest tomb the world has ever seen, will ever see. As you rest on your bounteous harvests and fail to prepare for a lull in the inundations, you, Menkaure, have failed Kemet. You have squandered what little she has in excess on building a lesser structure even than your father's."

"You are a witch," spat Hanutep. "Osiris will not take you, and Horus will take your heart.

"Go see for yourself, if you dare, mighty Pharaoh, as I have stolen away many times to witness with my own eyes. People are starving for the efforts of your meagre tomb. Listen to me, as I am the god Hathor in human form."

"You are no god," Hanutep said again. And again, Pharaoh said nothing.

"I have lived a hundred lifetimes. I have held all the Pharaohs as babes in my arms. I have seen the source of the Nile. I remember the green plains and blue lakes to the West when the desert was far away."

The soldiers moved in and squeezed past the cowering priest to flank Sara and grab her by the wrists. Sara, full of adrenaline now, twisted and brought the men together with surprising ease. She thrust one fist past the other, causing the soldiers' wrists to clash. They were surprised at her strength and the leverage of her twisting action and let her wrists go in pain.

Out of sight, clenched between her buttocks, was the blade of a small dagger. Immediately she retrieved it and thrust it out to Pharaoh's throat. It almost connected - the look on Pharaoh's stolid face distorted into shock as the soldiers managed to drop their spears and intercept her, this time giving no consideration to her size, gender or nakedness. They wrested her roughly to her knees and knocked the blade from her grasp.

Sara was desperately thinking she had let down her boys. Would they still escape now she had failed in her final act? She had known there was no escape for her now. After so many years, finally, she had found a reason to make the ultimate sacrifice.

Pharaoh then spoke.

"No god would be so easily vanquished."

"Namer, first Pharaoh of Kemet, unifier of the kingdoms, was my son. He went mad like you, and I had to kill him. He WAS a god, as am I. We are here to guide you, and you expect us to rule by force. You, mortals, do that to yourselves! Only a god can kill a god."

"Then, by divine right, I release you," Pharaoh said, pulling a long knife from his belt and plunging it into Sara's chest. The blood sprayed out as he withdrew it quickly, unsure what might happen. Pharaoh was painted red by her life force, and Sara whimpered and collapsed, the soldiers allowing her to crumple to the floor, dead. Her aura faded rapidly and plunged the bloody setting into darkness, like a scene ending a play.

CHAPTER FOURTEEN

2357 CE, Rogue, Site One

"This is it," Professor Maddox Jefferies said dramatically, staring intently at the distant planet from the forward viewing room of the Hydra, a vessel so big that nothing like it had ever been built before.

"How does it feel, knowing you will be going down on the surface this time?" Orianna asked him, standing by his side, holding onto his arm as if she might tumble off through the window and into the void if her magnetic boots failed.

She had commissioned Hydra well in advance of their return from Rogue all those years ago now. Such a massive undertaking had been broken down into smaller parts to maximise the reuse of existing technologies. In truth, it was two main vessels: the Janus and the Gemini, connected together with a backbone known as Atlas - as a long rod in space, it looked like a lever to move the world. Janus was at the front, and Gemini was at the rear: both were the newest and largest Pontoon Class explorers - their habitable rings made up of independent vessels, called 'boats', connected broadside to broadside. The four hundred strong crew enjoyed a very comfortable artificial gravity walking around these rings as they rotated, crossing from boat to boat through bulkhead doors - doors that, in an emergency, would close, enabling the ring to disassemble into a cloud of independent life crafts. Since each boat had a drive motor array, the drive motors for Hydra were distributed around the rings providing an even acceleration preventing structural stresses.

Hydras cargo was attached to Atlas as rings of motor units and cargo cylinders padding out its circumference. A motor unit was capable of shuttling one cylinder down to the surface at a time. Each cylinder contained everything from supplies and equipment to habitation modules: even extra fuel for those that would ascend again. Indeed, Hydra, as a whole, was the first planetary exploration vehicle in human history.

They were in a crescent-shaped corridor at the very front of Janus, just outside the front shield, enjoying a stationary view ahead in zeroG. The vessel was no longer decelerating and just coasted facing forwards, heading for orbit around Rogue.

They had been out of hibernation for three days, but most of the crew would remain in hibernation until needed, some long after the first wave made planetfall.

The view was spectacular. Jupiter was in sight too, so broad that it seemed closer than it was. Rogue had about a month before closest approach, so they had arrived just inside the safe margin for keeping well clear of Jupiter on their way in.

"Actually, a little disappointed not to be the first down there." He sounded like a grumpy old man for a moment, which made her smile. She reached up and touched his greying beard with the back of her slender fingers. The smile dropped slightly at the discrepancy between her youthful hand and his craggy features.

"You can't always be first. Let's see now: first to find Rogue, first to go there, the longest stint in hibernation, the farthest human, the oldest living human...."

"Ah yes, always will be four years older than you, dear Orianna. A hundred and sixty-three next birthday. That's something, isn't it? I may look like an old man, and I have lived a life much shorter even than that, but it has been quite a life."

"And it isn't over yet. You don't look a day over sixty…."

"And you are still twenty-seven at best." His wrinkled face scrunched up even more at this mystery. "We missed our chance, didn't we? I have been so caught up in Rogue. We never really talked about… us. We are from the same time, but we have aged strangely. I never know if that makes us closer or worlds apart. Ha! I look like your grandfather now. The truth is there are more like you out there, aren't there? You never said it in so many words, but I deduced it. What it must be like to live that long."

"Perhaps knowing you have so little time, you make the most of it?"

"I certainly have, haven't I? But you, you have done so much already. You have amassed a business empire so big you can build all this at the drop of a hat! What will you do when I am gone, I wonder?"

"I don't like talking about that, but you are right; at some point, there will be no one left from my first lifetime. Everyone you and I knew back then is long gone. It is a lonely feeling. So perhaps I will seek out those others like me."

"I envy you."

"Then you really haven't thought it through," she said, punching him playfully in the shoulder. "After achieving, well, what we already have, what else is there? Really, what would you do with yourself - an eternity beaconing ahead of you? I have lived most of my hundred and fifty-nine years, so I can tell you those philosophical questions don't go away. You are lucky that you have busied yourself with relatively short-term goals to satisfy a passing interest in some meaning to life. What would you do if there is no hurry to pass on to the next generation, no need to make way for those that will carry the baton of your life's work to the next level? What if it is always you, endlessly? No philosopher in history has really asked this question with any seriousness, so I have no answer for myself. We are still humans and as such, programmed to belong, to be a part of a family, yet this longevity denies us this basic need."

"It is true that you cannot seek those answers from us mere mortals. Our interests, our view of the world, is measured in short lifespans. We are a shortsighted race. You probably only feel that because you are surrounded by us. Our short lives confuse you. Think of all the accomplishments mankind has ever made! How many were made knowing that it would take two or more lifetimes to complete? I cannot think of any. Perhaps your longer-term view is what we really needed to have to prevent the Critical Earth. Where were your 'friends' then?" She looked up at him, thinking how wise he had become. "Perhaps with great longevity comes great responsibility?" And the spell was broken as she laughed at him.

"Corny," she whispered, trying not to dampen what was otherwise a great speech.

They responded to a message informing them their conference was about to start and began to make their way out of the room clumsily in their magnetic boots and head back to the pseudo-gravity of Janus' ring. They considered who they were meeting and how they would approach the discourse.

"See! The Martian Consortium managed to get twelve small vessels on the surface months ahead of us, and now they wish to talk. I have some choice words for them...," Maddox said, angry at the information coming up on his visor - he hated the new-fangled eye contacts.

"Don't think of it like that. Consider, they have rushed

down there and will be short of supplies and with only a small presence. We will immediately outnumber them. Besides, plenty of them considers you the father of all of this. None of them would have degrees and doctorates in astronomy, xenobiology, cosmology, astrophysics and countless others if it weren't for you and Rogue. You brought all those disciplines back to the universities."

"Hmmph. Dozens of honorary degrees and plaudits were given to me; you would think they would show more respect!"

"I am not so sure that respect is lacking. Perhaps what they really need is leadership."

Each boat was uniquely partitioned to provide different accommodation on Hydra, and the one they entered held a large meeting room. Maddox had assembled the leaders of all of his teams. They wore the latest contacts, replacing the outdated visors, for augmented reality. Everyone wore clothing that incorporated a rigid collar, so the same survival suit remained. The collar provided remote power and control to the contact lenses. Higher bandwidth allowed them to appear in context as actual holo-images, recorded from all angles around the room. Improvements in communications also meant this more significant data stream could be sent across the remaining one and a half light seconds distance without loss. A typical Earth-Lunar conversation stilted by a three-second turnaround was something he remembered all too well.

"Wilson." Maddox greeted coldly as three delegates from the Martian Consortium appeared amongst them. Dutifully, the delegates selected the planet's surface as a backdrop, even though nobody was actually standing outside.

"Jefferies." The tall, lanky gentleman replied. Indeed his suit had the label "Wilson" embroidered on the chest.

Sensing the tension between the great leaders, McDonald, Wilson's deputy, stepped forward: a man of similar stature to Wilson but a much more friendly face, smiling effortlessly.

"Greetings, colleagues. We hope you had a good trip." Nobody replied. "We all know each other here, so formal introductions seem redundant. Over."

"Of course, we know each other, McDonald, we were supposed to be part of the same expedition, and we were all supposed to arrive together," bellowed Maddox. "Why did you leave Mars early? Over."

"This was not our decision," pleaded McDonald. "We were instructed to do so by the politicians. You know how it is with the Martian independence movement. They wanted to be the first to bolster their status in their negotiations with Earth. Over."

"Well, you weren't the first. I was. I found her. I named her. She's mine. Dammit. Keep your dirty politics away from my planet! Over."

"No one here disagrees with you. We had our orders. We were not independently funded as you were. Not our fault, and we want to ensure that we can continue to work together going forward. Over."

Both Wilson and Maddox looked sternly at each other.

"Bob."

"Max."

"Ok then. I congratulate you on your safe arrival. Please tell us, how was it down there? Over."

Professor Robert Wilson relaxed from his stiff stance and nodded his respect to his mentor in response to the respect afforded to him.

"Fellows," he began in the archaic way of academia, now a gender-neutral term suited to the mixed leaders of their fields present in the meeting. "We have a rudimentary base established in a temperate zone, and everyone is well, and all is proceeding within established parameters. The planet is even stranger than Professor Jefferies's data originally showed us. I am glad to say that the surface is now more like a primordial Earth: temperatures now allow for liquid water on the surface. The atmosphere is mostly nitrogen with little oxygen and much more carbon dioxide with an equal surface pressure to Earth. I don't want to speculate yet on the high levels of similarities between Rogue and Earth. We can discuss speculative hypotheses later. The important thing to note at this point is that we can move around quite normally with an unpressurised suit providing us with oxygen and protecting us from nausea-inducing $CO2$ levels. This has made construction tasks much easier. Your engineers will be pleased to know. Over."

"Yes, yes, very good, we can get to those aspects later. But, first, we want to know about the artefacts and the gravity. Where is Rogue heading now, do you think? Over." Maddox said impatiently.

Wilson paused as if winding forwards through his speech in his mind.

"The artefacts have some interesting features you will need to see for yourself, but suffice to say that we have no idea what they are made of or what they are doing. There are exactly sixty cubes distributed around the entire surface of Rogue. It may not surprise you that they are arranged in a truncated icosahedron: the shape of a carbon 60 BuckminsterFullerene isotope or a soccer ball. They surround alternating regions of pentagons and hexagons, which seem to bear no relation to the topology or geography of the landscape. Over"

"What features? Over."

"They vibrate. They move. They float in the air. Obviously, we suspect that they control the changes in gravity and the - ah yes - the tides. We have observed tidal movements without Rogue having a moon to cause them. Over."

"Very interesting," a woman bearing the name Jenson on her suit spoke for the first time. "What experiments have you done on them?"

"All in good time, Doctor Jenson," interjected Maddox. "The multi-trillion dollar question on literally everyone's lips is, where is Rogue heading? Over."

Wilson was bashful. "We don't know for sure. Over."

"What? Little more than a month to closest approach, and you don't know what its exit trajectory is likely to be? Over." Maddox was incredulous.

The third delegate stepped forward gingerly. He was much younger than Wilson and McDonald. Brown was his name.

"The gravitation variations have been increasing in deviation and frequency, making the statistical analysis of the outcome increasingly inaccurate. We know Rogue will miss Jupiter; otherwise, we wouldn't be here... Over." Brown said but tailed off when he realised he had just stated the obvious to a room full of humanity's best and brightest.

"Go on. Over." Maddox suggested.

"Er, it is clear that a relatively safe close pass with Jupiter will lead to Rogue passing down through roughly a sixty-degree arc from the ecliptic. Even if we assume that Rogue will not change gravity after the closest approach, there is still a wide range of possible outgoing trajectories. That being said, we can be quite sure that it will be slowing down and becoming a part of the inner solar system, potentially disrupting the inner planets over time, which has very few positive outcomes for humanity. The good news is that this deviation from the ecliptic is our best outcome short of Rogue being safely ejected from the system altogether or just swallowed by Jupiter. It gives us time - hundreds, maybe thousands of years. Over." He took a deep breath, realising he had forgotten to breathe.

Nervously, Brown stepped back as the room broke into many loud and lively conversations. Nothing substantial came out of the meeting except that everyone found everyone else's opinions infuriating. It was determined that, in two days, the first wave of descent craft would be landing close together about 500m west of the Martian Consortium's small camp. This area appeared to be flat and geologically stable, but the truth was that no one had actually visited it. No wonder then that when the first four cylinders performed a gloriously synchronised, closely grouped vertical landing and the first wave of top scientists and engineers exited the cooling landers, they discovered something significant with their very first steps.

"Soil? Sir, this looks like soil to me," Baines said to his team leader.

"Baines, you might be right. I need you to check for possible sinkage, and when you have done that, I want the entire area surveyed before anyone else tries to land here. Those Marsy idiots obviously didn't even care to survey our landing site. Right. Off you go!" Team Leader Jones said.

"Yes, sir!" With that, Baines was gone, taking two men with him.

"Professor Jefferies, sir," Jones said when he had caught up with the leading group of head scientists. "They did not survey the site at all. We are making sure the ground is secure before we bring more down. Don't worry. We will make sure of everything ourselves."

"Very good, but how did you know?"

"See for yourself, sir." Jones reached down and retrieved a handful of soil for Maddox to look at.

"Amazing! Doctor Jenson, Doctor Adams, I think you will find this interesting. Could there have been life on Rogue before it froze over? I feel like I need to take a firmer hand with the Martian Consortium. Spread the word: they get no assistance of any kind from us until I say so."

Adams was the xenobiologist, and Jenson was an expert in planetary geology. Maddox always thought xenobiology was a silly discipline given that nobody had ever found any life beyond the Earth that had not come from Earth - their studies were ultimately hypothetical. Their processes were preemptive and not born out of any tangible experience. But, of course, that did seem likely to change soon. They both immediately formed a huddle on the ground as if they had discovered gold.

Maddox and his top scientists strode off, enjoying a good walk over to the Consortium's camp, which was little more than a dozen biodomes and assorted gear. Their environmental suits were of little bother to them at all.

"Twelve vessels and little room for anything useful," Maddox sneered.

'Greetings," came a call from Wilson, now apparently in a better mood. "Welcome to Rogue, Site One."

"Great. Thx," said Maddox. "I want to see the artefact."

Wilson was caught out by his sudden insistence to get down to business. He led the newcomers towards the cliff, over a slight rise and down the other side. There, now in sight, they could see the three-metre cube. It was still completely black. Even the dim light from the sun could not cause any reflection to come off it. It just looked like a cubic hole.

They became more aware of its size and perfect shape as they approached. But, more importantly, they saw it was floating about forty centimetres above the ground.

"It is solid, yes?" Maddox asked. "You have tried to move it and penetrate it by the looks of this crude equipment. What EM does it emit?"

"Nothing," Wilson responded coldly.

"Nothing?"

"No EM of any frequency is emitted spontaneously or reflected off its surface, except when it moves."

"When it moves?"

"See below the cube. The ground has a depression that is filled with dust. Once we observed it moving, we experimented as best we could."

"What do you mean - it moves?"

"The cube rises and falls during what we call its active cycle. Between active cycles, it appears as you see it now."

"When is the next cycle?"

"Random, oh, and I really mean that. The shortest dormant period has been 23 seconds, and the longest has been over three days. But statistically, we are seeing a trend towards shorter periods. Oh, it might be starting again, right on cue. Please, pass me that rock!" Wilson asked urgently as a low hum began to resonate.

Maddox was taken aback but then bent down and reached for a fist-sized rock and passed it to Wilson, who quickly placed it on the ground directly under the cube and retreated again.

"You are in luck; here it goes again."

The cube started to vibrate visibly before suddenly becoming as shiny as a mirror, the hum now reaching about sixty decibels at four metres.

"Is this safe?" Maddox asked, raising his voice over the hum.

The pitch of the hum varied wildly and then shot up the scale, briefly passing to very high frequencies, loud enough to make everyone wince for just a second, as it continued into ultrasound. After that, everyone relaxed again, thinking it had stopped, except for Orianna, who showed pain on her face long after the others. She had been quietly following the group, so nobody noticed her prolonged pain.

"See here," Wilson said, showing them how the vibrations had passed beyond the ability of his equipment to measure. "The cube in this active state is now a perfect mirror, reflecting every frequency."

They all peered at their own reflections, wondering if it was watching them as they now watched themselves.

The cube then began to move up and down slowly but

surely, not more than a few centimetres at first, but after a while, a downward stroke brought it into contact with the rock Wilson had placed under it.

The rock instantly turned into the finest dust, offering zero resistance to the cube as it moved down to ground level and back up again.

Then, apparently without relation to the cube's movement, gravity changed slightly, enough for everyone to notice but not for more than a second, then it returned to normal.

They were all spellbound, except for Wilson, who had already experienced these hundreds of times. Then, seven or eight minutes later, it stopped, and the cube went black again.

Maddox asked, "Wilson, is there anything else you haven't told us about the cube?"

"Our cameras are not fast enough to see into the transition from black to mirror and back again. Perhaps you have better high-speed cameras? I can show you this."

Everyone gasped as Wilson confidently strode over to the now still black cube and reached out to it.

"No, obviously nobody wants to end up like the rock, but we know that that only happens in an active cycle. So as long as you are ready to move away if a cycle starts up, then this has so far proved perfectly safe."

Wilson put both hands on the cube and gave a gentle push. Surprisingly, the cube moved pretty easily. Then it returned to exactly where it had - no diminishing swing like a pendulum would have, just a single return move to stationary. Wilson pushed again, only much harder. The cube moved a little further, about a quarter of its size. Then a third time, he put his back into it and kept pushing until he ran out of push. Each time he experienced diminishing returns on his efforts.

"I have calculated that an infinite amount of force would

be required to displace the cube by its own length," Wilson quipped matter-of-factly. 'Honestly, we have run out of tests to perform on it."

"Ok, thanks. People. I want a breathable dome over the cube as soon as possible, and I want to ensure that nobody comes near it until we have begun our tests."

With that, Maddox left, and everyone followed, except Wilson.

Orianna was on the manifest as a special envoy of the mission sponsors. Nobody but Maddox knew she was the sole sponsor herself.

Maddox had time on his hands as he waited for the constructions to get underway, and even then, it would be a week before he needed to bring the rest of the teams out of hibernation. He and Orianna took a stroll and climbed the easy route up the back of the cliff, overlooking the camp. It was quite a sight to see a tiny village of humans on an impossible planet.

"It is warm," Orianna observed. "We are not close enough to the sun for these temperatures, are we?"

"No," he laughed as if the question were silly. "Remember, my sensors on the Achilles detected heat coming from within the planet. We think that is what had thawed it out and made it so temperate."

"Is it going to bake us off here then?"

"That effect seems to have stabilised for now."

"I see clouds in the distance, over there. This looks remarkably like Earth. How is that possible?"

"The odds are against any of this happening by chance," Maddox sighed. "Even without the artefacts, it would seem improbable that there wasn't some agency behind it."

"Where is the artefact? I cannot see it from here."

"Just down there, see it?" Maddox pointed.

Orianna leaned over the edge to see, but the edge of the cliff crumbled beneath her foot. She screamed out and dropped her weight to the ground. Maddox still held her hand and leaned away to counter her loss of balance. As she lingered for a moment, half over the edge, looking down at the mysterious cube, she saw it move out of the corner of her eye as she rolled back fully onto the top of the cliff again.

Maddox and Orianna were smiling at each other at their unwise risk.

Suddenly, the cube arose, still black this time and without any forewarning hum, until it was level with the top of the cliff.

Their smiles disappeared as the blacker than black object just hung there some distance away, level with them, precisely above where it had started. It did nothing else. After a few minutes, the two of them edged away, and it slowly descended again.

This planet was indeed strange and unusual. Almost everything seemed to defy what they thought they knew, yet it also seemed familiar and welcoming. If there was one exception, it was Orianna, who had no driving curiosity to see the cube again and felt a continued disturbing sense of it.

Over the following month, she spent more and more time away from Maddox, mainly because he had become quite obsessed with the cube.

The cube, now covered with a soft dome, had never again deviated from its usual cycles. Maddox was now confident that it wouldn't burst through the top and have him rushing for the emergency breathing apparatus.

Sometimes he would spend all day and night in the dome, leaving the others to administer to the camp.

The day of closest approach came all too soon, and for once, Maddox made an effort to spend it with Orianna. Everyone was taking the day to marvel at the scene: Jupiter was so massive in the sky it was breathtaking. The day's pinnacle was interrupted as Jupiter eclipsed the sun: due to last much longer than a solar eclipse on Earth.

"Where are you going, Rogue?" Orianna wondered aloud. She turned to Maddox. "Rogue is using Jupiter to slingshot into a new path: down and into the inner solar system. It seems to be steering itself by changing its force of gravity?"

"It appears so," Maddox sighed, pulling his warm coat closed. The eclipse had brought a chill.

"How can a planet change its mass?"

"That is most likely the wrong question. We don't have the answers, but you need to understand that gravity is not a force as such."

"Not a force."

"No, not really. You see, Baryonic matter that makes up you and I and everything around us bends spacetime."

"Oh yes, Einstein. Balls on a rubber sheet and the like. Yeah, I never did get that since the analogy needed gravity to show things falling down a gravity well."

"Ha! Yes. Agreed. That was bad schooling. It is actually much simpler yet much harder to grasp than that. Matter makes time slow down. We are indeed ageing the tiniest bit slower than our people on Hydra, in orbit. At the extreme end of that, you have black holes where time actually appears to come to a standstill. The universe speeds up to someone falling into a black hole. To us watching him fall, he never gets there. Objects fall due to a gradient of time across their height. It is that simple and yet that strange. It looks like a force, but it isn't one."

"Ah, ok, and since we have no idea what time is, we have no idea how Rogue does what it does."

"Correct."

"Janus detaches and returns in a week. I will be on it," she exclaimed.

"I know."

"And you are staying here?" He nodded. "I promise, I will return if you promise to stay safe." He nodded again.

The next day, Maddox was gone again. Orianna packed

up her gear and did the rounds, saying goodbye to everyone staying. By the evening, she was done, except for Maddox. She went to the dome to see him but still couldn't bring herself to enter his area of obsession. His outline could be seen through the translucent shell, illuminated from the lights within.

She touched the plastic with her hand, sighed, turned and walked into the night, towards the ascent craft.

There was a lot to do to secure everything and prepare for departure. But, as it happened, the very last thing she did before entering hibernation was to send him a message.

"Max. Dear old Max. You take care of yourself, and I will see you soon. This is where you belong right now, and I am just an observer. We always had our own lives, you and I, but we always crossed paths again. Here's to crossing paths at least once more in the future. I came past your dome on my way out. You were in there with the cube. I didn't want to be a part of that, so I decided we had said our goodbyes. Take care."

By the time Maddox received the message, he had cried. His heart ached for her, but she was right. His path was full enough right now.

Then, as tears fell to his hand, he remembered that the last aberrant behaviour exhibited by the cube - moving a small amount whilst black - was that same evening.

He rushed out of his habitat and ran to the cube dome. In his hand was the recording he had made of Orianna when she had once allowed him to try to analyse her aura with a full spectrum scan. They had been drunk that night, and he had been pleased to bring out her playful side - no mean feat of someone of her age. Given the intense need for secrecy in her life, he was surprised when she agreed to let him record her aura, and even more surprised that he had ventured to ask. It had been an intimate moment, with more emotional value than its staggering rarity: a recording of the brilliant ultraviolet light that one of The Few can emit from their skin, often reflecting their emotional state.

That day on the cliff, she had been startled. Her aura would have triggered involuntarily. The night she left, she was upset and in line of sight of the cube, certainly expressing her aura again, and the dome was translucent to ultraviolet light. Both times, only those times, the cube moved whilst black.

He cobbled together a suitable UV projection system and aimed it at the cube at close range, currently in a rest cycle close to the ground.

He began the playback.

At first, he thought nothing had happened, but when he lowered the projector's height on the tripod, the cube followed it down to the ground.

"That's great," Maddox's voice came out of the recording. "Now, think of something sad… yes, that is good. All I need now is a sense of humour, and I will be able to get you to laugh."

Orianna's voice giggled out of the unit. "You are funny. Who said you weren't funny?" More giggling.

"That's great. The aura is changing in response to your emotions."

Maddox watched as the cube's face started to change under the projection. Coloured swirls began to appear, spiralling from the edges to the centre. Then, as he stared, the centre seemed to stretch away from him. Now it looked like a tunnel into the cube, the violet colours from the projector stretching off to infinity.

He reached out his hand instinctively, certainly not with any common sense, to try to touch what had once been the face of the cube, to check it had really become a long tunnel.

Suddenly, he felt a pull, and in an instant, he was yanked out of his seat and into the tunnel, dragging the projector and recorder with him as he tried to grab onto something to stop him from falling sideways.

The cube returned to form as a plain black impenetrable cube.

Maddox was gone.

CHAPTER FIFTEEN

2368 CE, Earth, British Isles

Orianna hadn't been back to Earth since 2226, her last fight at her father's Chateau, within what is now the nation of Lyons. This time she was visiting Kent, a devolved country in the South East of Britain. Her descent craft had landed safely on Stratoport 7, five miles up and eighty miles inland over Libya. A crane captured it hovering on its hydrogen rockets just above the deck until it had powered down before lowering it inside the floating platform for disembarkation.

"Welcome to Earth, immigration passes at the ready, please," a crew member called out over the passenger deck. "Thank you, er, Olympia Devereux," she said, accepting Orianna's pass as she left the craft and headed down the sealed gantry and into the lounge area.

"Hi," said a bright-faced young man in an expensive-looking suit, trying to get her attention as she looked around for a seat. "I'm not hitting on you, I promise. Married," he added, pointing to a ring on his finger. "I just heard we have a bit of a delay waiting for our connecting flights, and I hate my own company; what can I say?"

She glanced at him whilst continuing to look around for a quiet spot to settle down.

"You are not selling your companionship very well," she replied.

"Sorry. You're right. Hello, I'm Harry Bennet, on my way home to my family. Would you care to chat whilst we wait?"

"Better, but one question: why me, if not to chat me up?"

"Frankly, between seven businesspeople, four scientists, seven idle rich, three migrants and a pair of celebrity chefs, you are the most interesting person there by far."

"You do pay attention. Hello Harry, I am..."

"Olympia," he interrupted, clearly having overheard her earlier.

"I am... unwilling to satisfy your curiosity about myself, although something tells me you already have some ideas you are going to test me on. Besides, you look like someone who travels regularly, and I haven't been Earthside in a while, so if you don't mind, please do catch me up on current events."

Harry smiled and gestured for her to sit opposite him, which she did.

Harry had the annoying tendency to contain his conversation to the last five years, assuming she was in her mid to late twenties. But, in truth, she would like to hear about the previous century and a half, so she decided to jump to generalities.

"Historically, do you think Tinyism has made things better or worse?" she interjected, interrupting him mid-sentence. "You are a sociologist after all," she added without an ounce of doubt.

"You have me down completely," he said with an unmistakable frown that did not detract from his endless smile. "What are you asking? Should two hundred nations have broken into nearly three thousand tiny nations? Was that inevitable, given that super-powers and nationalism were ideas that no longer served mankind? Or, are you asking whether this should go further to address even more sensible geographic issues at a granular level and leave the larger issues to the corporations and nonprofits?"

"And you teach."

"Right again. How am I so transparent, and you are so opaque?"

"Years of practice, I suspect." She looked at him and sighed. "Ok, look, I have worked for several nonprofits for a while because I believe that they are the only system that works in the interests of the planet and not in filling the pockets of investors."

"Ahh, so you want to take the side of the socialists and tree-hugging liberals, and I get to be the money-grabbing capitalist? Those shoes don't really fit, though, do they?"

"What do you mean?"

"Forgive me, but I can deduce a couple truths about you too. First, you are clearly no stranger to money, and second, what you haven't said leads me to believe that you don't have a planet-saving drum to bang on."

"Yes and no. I take a longer-term view of planet-saving issues, which has concerned me my entire life. Mostly, I work in space, keeping heavy industry away from Earth. So you see, capitalism can serve the tree-hugging liberals once you take the longer viewpoint."

"Amazing. You sound like my grandfather, which is a major compliment, by the way. How did you get so wise."

"Oh, like everyone else," she quipped. "Except I am older than I look."

He eyed her suspiciously. She had dipped into teasing, and he felt he was suddenly out of his depth.

"The delays are caused by congestion and the need for the platforms to refuel at a lower altitude," she said, changing the subject in recognition of his slight discomfort. "I am guessing you don't know much about them?"

"No, not at all, really. All I know is the rockets have five miles less to travel, and it keeps them above the cloud layer and away from the wildlife."

"Yes, that's a significant fuel saving. Orbital shuttles burn hydrogen and oxygen, which makes water, so it is ecologically clean. A platform floats on an imbalance of those gases like a huge assembly of balloons. Don't worry, it has electric motors too, enough to keep it aloft even with zero buoyancy. Once the rockets are refuelled and launched, the platform drops altitude to collect water from the cloud layer and electrolyse it back to hydrogen and oxygen, adding buoyancy to the ballons and pushing the platform back up again. This cycle takes a lot of time and doesn't react well to congestion."

"Wow, you know a lot more about this than I do. All I know is that the Raptor Max to Thanet is late."

"I am going to the Isle of Thanet too," Orianna said. "Perhaps you could tell me about your family. Unfortunately, I don't have any left, myself, but that might change soon."

She smiled amiably, watching his face drop and then rise in delight again. "Getting engaged or married?"

"Something not like that."

Their interesting conversation continued playfully for another hour until the tilt-wing Raptor transport arrived and landed on the same flat top of the platform that the rocket had come down to. It was only briefly interrupted by the need for survival suits at that altitude walking to the plane. The cargo had already been processed from the rocket and was quickly inserted into the plane's belly.

As they journeyed to Thanet, at the tip of the lower lip of the Thames Estuary, they discovered that they had both been born in the British Isles. Harry shared a piece of trivia about Thanet, which had actually been designated an island long before seas levels rose, with marshland isolating the peninsula, and the name stuck. Now rising seas had made it an actual island, perfect as an airport for extraterrestrial arrivals via Raptor.

Now an airport, Ramsgate offered visitors a pleasant layover for those wishing a respite in neighbouring Margate, still a seaside resort. However, Orianna was keen to complete her journey in good time. Harry and she would be taking different routes from here, different Ekranoplans to other ports.

Harry's final topic of conversation had been about how twenty-fourth-century man had embraced technology from the twentieth century: Zeppelin balloons and ground effect aircraft, such as the Ekranoplan. He had marvelled that despite the trajectory of war-driven post-Victorian man towards self-destruction, they had invented many ecologically minimal things. For instance, the ground effect Ekranoplan, named after the massive Soviet experimental versions, was like a cross between a plane and a hovercraft - the creatures of the sea were not unduly disturbed by it flying overhead: no draft, no screw, no oil - just electric fans, a boat hull and short wings to give it a cushion of air to ride on just metres above the water. It was very economical and ecological.

Such was the way Orianna entered the Thames Estuary, now wider through the centre of what used to be London. Arriving on the south bank at Dartford, she was still in Kent and did not need to pass through immigration again, thus quickly transferred to a road carriage, which had been booked exclusively for her in advance.

The road carriage was spacious, with enough space for six in comfort, but she had it to herself, and for a change, it would remain that way. Unusually, she had paid substantially more to override its default setting: to act as a kind of bus service or shared cab network. A mini Fusion unit under the floor provided all the electric power it needed, and a sophisticated but essentially non-sentient computer did all the driving.

Despite losing half the population of Kent during the pandemics, major road networks were still maintained for road carriages to move at speed and to cooperate as road trains for shared parts of any journey. Her carriage merged with different trains for the M25 and A21 stretches.

On approach to Tunbridge Wells, her carriage separated and took her into the centre. The cities may have died, but some towns remained, despite the ever-dispersing remaining population. This classic town still offered excellent community facilities, hotels, eateries and bars.

Her journey had brought her from Erebus at Earth's L4 all the way to Tunbridge Wells on a sunny Saturday afternoon in May. Despite millions of miles and weeks of travel time, she was in no mood to rest up. So she checked in at the hotel only to hand over her luggage before marching directly down the hill, through the old alleyways to the oldest part of town, where there was a cobblestone square and places to eat and drink all around.

It was refreshing to be walking in the open. To have been on Earth for the whole day and never take a moment to breathe the air seemed so very silly now. Like all immortals, she lacked an ordinary sense of smell - the only things she could smell were sick people or those about to be sick.

The sky was very blue. It was also worryingly far away to someone who had rarely been anywhere without a ceiling in the last century and a half. Orianna was still new to the life of an immortal and found it a sobering thought that everyone who had been alive the last time she had been on Earth was now dead, every mortal that is.

As it turned out, her journey had gone according to plan, and she now enjoyed a casual drink at a small open-air bar just around the corner from her rendezvous. As a habitually punctual person, she was early but wanted to wait and arrive on time.

"Hello," came a familiar voice.

"Tarik! Are you early too?" She eyed him suspiciously. "Harry, right?"

Tarik smiled. "Forgive us, but for our own safety, we picked you up at Orbital 1 and needed to ensure you were not being tracked here. Meetings like this are where The Many like to strike if they can."

"Was I?"

"Of course not. You are too good at this. You moved fast. You shook off Harry by taking the longer route via Dartford. Your solo carriage was a nice touch - we still haven't figured out who booked it. I am guessing you changed its destination many times en route."

"Yes. Harry was a little too obvious."

"You became certain. How?"

"I told him I was older than I looked. His micro-expressions were entirely misplaced for someone taking that remark normally. He tried. Bless him. Is he a mortal, though?"

"Yes, we do employ them, but very few like him know what we are."

"You are looking good, Tarik. It has been twenty-seven years since The Fields. I hope you have something to match that day."

"I will never forget that day. You look a little sadder. Hopefully, I can improve that, at least. Shall we?" He beckoned her to leave with him.

Orianna took Tarik's hand, and they made their way around the corner and across the cobblestone square into a bold and impressive stone building - built hundreds of years ago to serve as a bank - a sign above it saying "Eat and be Merry!"

They were seated by a waiter at a four-seater next to the window overlooking the square.

Orianna took in the room. Heavy wood, probably original, dominated the floor and open stairs. A mezzanine level sat on top of a central bar and kitchen serving area.

There were all sorts of people enjoying what must be after work relaxation or light meals, given the time of day. Maybe fifty or so downstairs, and she guessed a dozen upstairs from the noise level. She used her exceptional hearing to tune into nearby conversations. A couple behind her disagreed over money: the girl was playfully teasing the guy about a recent purchase. Four men ahead had just left work together and were discussing sales targets. Two old women were at the bar area ordering drinks, having just followed them in. An old man lectured his son about public behaviour at the adjacent table.

"What is the matter?" Tarik asked as he returned his attention to her.

"Something's not quite right. When do your friends arrive?" she asked, cocking her head curiously.

"Hmm. They are already here," Tarik announced, not entirely convinced this was going to be a surprise after all.

Like a flash mob, the entire restaurant full of people stopped at the same instant, frozen in place and turned to stare at her, including the staff, and as she looked around, even the people walking past outside were motionless. For three seconds, nobody moved. All stared expressionlessly at Orianna, who was breathless with the effect. Then as fast as it had happened, it was over, and everyone carried on as if time had been released. She looked outside, and the people there dispersed in no great hurry.

Mouth agape, she looked at Tarik and laughed. Patrons of the restaurant gradually took turns to leave. Each of them glanced at her on passing, again without expression and not breaking character as they continued to play their parts. The "old" people that had been "wrong" in her observations were clearly wearing makeup; she could see that now.

Tarik touched his lips with his index fingertip. She took the hint and declined to talk about it.

The room became much less crowded but not empty. They finished their food and left together. An empty road carriage, was waiting to take them west towards Forest Row. The minor roads were no longer maintained, but they didn't need to since these new vehicles did not require such perfect surfaces.

The carriage's wheels duly split into segments and the spokes lengthened, given the appearance of wheels with a larger diameter and gaps around the rim. These "feet" walked along and neutralised the unevenness of the surface, even at speed, and were equally less impactful on the ground.

At the edge of town, the carriage came to a stop, and other passengers boarded: two men and two women. Nobody spoke, but Orianna assumed they were expected. The carriage continued for no more than a mile before it came to a halt at a secluded house.

The reception room was generously proportioned with a substantial real fireplace. Tarik brought in some logs from the stack outside and built a fire. The low ceiling and exposed dark beams contrasted against thick lime walls, completing the rustic look perfectly.

"They knew how to build houses when they built this cottage," remarked one of the men, who was wearing a three-piece brown plaid suit and trilby hat, which he pointedly declined to remove despite his height and the low ceiling. "Before my time, of course, but such character. Warm in winter and cool in summer, built with local, sustainable materials. My Victorians had an expensive habit of using brick." He practically swooned in delivery of that last remark, Orianna observed: someone who had a thespian spirit and perhaps training. "Glad to make your acquaintance, my dear. Oh, where are my manners? I am Randolph Giddeon.

"I have to say that these meetings are very welcome: to be

amongst my own kind. Don't you agree? It is so rare these days I get called by my real name, so please do overuse it as much as possible."

"This is my first time. Other than Tarik, I have never met anyone else like me," Orianna admitted. She accepted his soft handshake and responded, "Orianna Demaine, but I suppose you know that already?"

She looked around as the shorter of the two women approached. She wore a white shirt and black trousers. As Orianna looked her up and down, the woman said, "I was a waiter at the restaurant. I didn't get enough time to change."

Orianna was pleased with her smile.; it seemed very genuine and fresh. It was also lovely to be talking to someone nearer her height too. This time the handshake was firmer and yet gentle.

"You are the girl from Erebus, right?" she said. Orianna nodded. "Yeah, I was found in twenty-one eighty-six, so I had been in for about four decades when you were found - but then lost. That was quite a story going around the network." Her accent was clearly Texan: her words came slow and well enunciated with long hard vowel sounds. "Nice to finally welcome you into the fold. Ana, Anastasia Jackson."

"Why now?" came a subtle accented voice, perhaps Quebecian. It was high pitched and direct. "Why did it take you a hundred and forty-three years to join us?"

"That is Adam Li. Please excuse his directness. I have always found the Americans lacking decorum. Leave the poor girl alone! She has had a long journey, and I always find you get the best out of people when they are rested and provided with a modicum of civility," Randolph Giddeon said.

Orianna turned to look at the Asian man seated on the sofa, cross-legged. He made no motion to offer his hand, and so neither did she. "No, it is a fair question. I don't mind being cross-examined here; after all, secrecy and caution are vital to us all, am I right?"

Adam Li folded his arms pensively.

"It is true that I saw Yamanu that day. He shone at me. We *saw* each other briefly, but I was chased and took flight. I escaped. I was never approached again, and from what Tarik said, I had successfully eluded him and The Many. I saw no one else until Tarik, twenty-seven years ago, and that was the first time I found out that The Few and The Many existed."

Anastasia Jackson nodded agreeably.

"And you didn't join us then? Why? And why do you want to join us now?" Adam continued his interrogation.

"Honestly, I am not sure I even want to join. Tarik said to call when I was ready to find out more... and so I did. I am here to find out more. Maybe I won't want to join."

"Maybe we don't want you." Adam snapped. "What changed in the last twenty-seven years?"

Orianna turned away and crouched down in front of the fire, which was beginning to come alive with Tarik's careful blowing. Tarik touched her forearm gently.

"Really, Adam, you are quite rude!" Randolph insisted. "Don't listen to him, Orianna. We 'long-toothes' are usually much more patient, given that time is not our enemy."

Orianna didn't move and maintained her back to them, but she chose to speak quietly. "I lost someone special. He was a close friend of mine, and he was the last person I knew from my first life. He was a 'mortal' - is that the correct term? - but he had been in hibernation for so long. Together we had outlived everyone else, and that brought us very close. I was always doomed to be alone, but this was sudden and unexpected. Maybe I was just desperate to belong somewhere. I feel a great loss. I am lost."

Ana glided over and knelt behind Orianna and enveloped her with a slow hug from behind. Orianna flinched momentarily - she was not used to that kind of intimacy - but welcomed the contact.

"It is a fair question," insisted Adam. "We all know the risks posed by those who are found later. Too much time being feral is as much a danger to them as to us."

"What do you mean by that?" Orianna called from within Ana's continued embrace.

"He thinks we go mad." The fourth stranger spoke for the first time: a skinny woman with short scruffy blonde hair, wearing a worn-out T-shirt and dark baggy trousers.

"Case in point: this is Sif," Adam huffed and left to explore the kitchen for food.

"Oh hello, Sif, I am Anastasia Jackson," Ana tilted her head to acknowledge Sif, sitting against the far wall.

"So, you don't already know one another?" Orianna asked, gently untangling herself from Ana, a passing nod of gratitude was enough for Ana to feel appreciated for the care she had provided.

"Much as that is true, most people know Sif, or know of her," added Randolph, reaching for the drinks cabinet. "We appear to have only single malt highland whiskey. However, that is a sacrifice I am willing to make. Six glasses?"

"Why don't you know everyone? How many of us are there? Tarik never said. He kept changing the subject." Orianna continued.

"You should have taken the hint!" Adam yelled from the kitchen, busy making noises with crockery. "Although if anyone did know, it would be Tarik or Yamanu."

Randolph passed a glass to Orianna, which she gratefully accepted. He clinked with his own glass and said, "my dear, you might have noticed the way we introduced ourselves - in that restaurant. We don't like to gather in groups and certainly not for long. I would wager at least half of them will have left the country by now. You were a little lucky this time. Sometimes it is only a dozen or so who are available."

"Mortals, yes," Sif began, pointedly answering Orianna's question from some time ago. "And gods, until Ragnarök, when all perished, and fire destroyed Ásgardr and Midgardr. Odin and Frigg did seek to conquer Midgardr. Spawned they into Ásgardr with the Æsir and into Jötunheimr with the Venir. Pride and betrayal and war. Æsir fought with Venir. Fenrisúlfr led the children of Midgardr - starving, burned from the sky, to slay all the gods. Mjölnir's felspar sparks against swords and shields alike, but its lord perishes from Jörmungandr's venom and is lost. Only Sif survives…" her voice trailed off as if her mind went away.

Sif approached Orianna, and her face changed, giving eye contact for the first time. "Welcome, dear," she said in an entirely different tone. "Ignore these babes in the woods. If you seek understanding, the old gods are where you will find truth and wisdom. Sweet Tarik reminds me so of… Do you dance, dear? Your grief will never leave you, but dancing can warm the heart again. So never forget to dance."

Sif proceeded to dance slowly and expressively despite the absence of music.

Tarik finally stopped playing with the fire and rose to decline a glass of whiskey from Randolph. "Some habits from the first life never fade. I do occasionally make beer the old way, but I do not drink alcohol otherwise."

Orianna looked around. Nobody seemed to pay much attention to the strangeness of Sif. She moved over to Tarik and whispered in his ear. "What is up with Sif? Why doesn't anyone seem bothered by her?"

Tarik declined to answer. He moved to the armchair nearest the hearth, and warmed himself by the fire.

"Ok, I have another question," Orianna said. "Why are you four here? Are you special in some way? Why not any of the others I saw at the restaurant?"

Adam laughed as he returned with a large plate of food. "She thinks we are special, and by that, she presumes she is special."

"My dear, it was the best invitation I had received all week," Randolph raised his glass and chortled.

"And I wanted to know whether you would be a problem, feral one," said Adam.

"You have eyes like Frigg," Sif said, staring at her intently as she spoke.

Ana came over and held her hand. "Honestly, I felt like meeting someone of my time. Glad I did." She patted her hand and smiled. Orianna smiled back.

"I am glad too," Orianna said to her. "What about you?" she asked Tarik. "The things you said to me before led me to think you are a leader of The Few if you have leaders. Is that true? Do you always attend these introductions?"

Tarik answered solemnly, "My brother and I are the oldest of The Few. We help to guide them. We seek out our brothers and sisters across time by our will: to rescue them from their solitude and help them learn to trust again after mortals reject them. So one of us is often around for this most important event, if at all possible. It is not as if we are born very often, but the difficulties now are that mankind has spread into space, and it can be an unacceptable delay to get to our foundlings in time for their initiation events... like this."

"Ok, good then. Special but not in this company. I like that."

Orianna relaxed and sat on the sofa next to Adam, nearly disturbing his food plate and surprising him with her closeness. She smiled at him despite his indifference to her. Such was her instinctive habit: to ensure her adversaries were kept uncomfortable and not allowed to set the terms of their environment or relationship to her. Stealing a slice of beetroot was yet another example of that. Adam moved the plate to a side table in disgust.

"Tarik told me it was rude to ask of you immortals - do you call yourself 'immortals' - how old you are - why is that?"

Randolph stepped up and took up a well-postured position leaning against the mantelpiece, warming his legs as he warmed his whiskey nestled in his palm.

"We are not immortal. Don't listen to any of them with the hubris of using that word. We are 'ageless', the 'untouched by time', the 'timeless', or words to that effect. Rather than risking being overheard, we are just The Few. The Few is what we are, not a group or some faction. Yes, Tarik and his brother Yamanu lead with a purpose, and many follow their long-term plans for humanity, but that is not The Few. You have not joined The Few; you have always been one of The Few.

"We can die and do die, but we do not age; we heal particularly well and quickly, so it might seem that we are indestructible: surviving some wounds others might not, plagues and famine, but we are just better survivors. Tougher, stronger, more resilient, but we too are mortal. We can be killed.

"Since we have hundreds, or thousands of years for some, behind us, we are somewhat solitary in nature. We have our own ways to cope with the endlessness of it all. Not everyone copes. Some end their own lives, some go mad before gathering the courage." Randolph nodded slyly towards Sif in the corner, where she had stopped dancing as if nothing else in the room mattered to her. "We actively share our insights, knowledge and experience, but directly asking when one came into being has some ill-considered consequences. That time is often painful to recall when we all had a family and beginnings all lost to time now.

"When we are comfortable, we might volunteer our birth period, as I have already alluded to myself - I was brought up with good manners and a gentleman's sense of decorum. We upper-class Victorians were highly skilled in social matters."

He raised his glass as if toasting and then took a gentle sip.

"Tarik, you told me, at our first meeting, that we were the children and ancestors of the mortals simultaneously. That we are rare and random. What about Sif?" Orianna pointed at the slender woman with her own glass over the back of the sofa. "She seems to be talking about Norse Mythology as if it was real. Sif was Thor's wife if memory serves. So how can she be talking about a group, no, a *family* of 'gods'?"

Adam sighed. "Sometimes she is with us, and sometimes she is not. We know nothing else about her other than what she says. She rarely talks about anything before the nineteenth century, except when reciting the Norse myths. Who knows what truth is in there." This was the first time Adam had expressed compassion. Orianna felt obliged to assume that there was a history there.

"How often do The Few die or go mad?" Orianna asked.

Adam turned away.

Tarik sighed. "We honestly don't know because we don't find everyone. I personally don't think they last very long on their own. Who could?"

"I suppose you were lucky because you had your brother, which is something I have been meaning to ask. You and your brother are both ageless. What are the odds of that? How the hell did that happen?"

"I will give you the same answer I have given for thousands of years. I don't know. Mother was ageless too. She had been a nomad in the times before the desert. She only spoke of one son who came long before us, also ageless. She must have been exceptional in some way. We have no idea. Nobody since myself has ever been born ageless from an ageless person - unless you believe the stories from Sif's alter ego."

Ana stood up, surprised by this information. "The ageless, reproducing? That is quite a problem. Imagine the population explosion. That kind of thing cannot end well. I have never thought of us as the next step in evolution. That sounds like a super virus destroying the host. Where would the balance be?" She said, eyes wide with possibilities riding on her active mind.

"Now you understand the motives of The Many: easy to convince the vain to seek everlasting life, and easy to convince the pious of the threat of an unnatural catastrophe," Tarik concluded. "They recruit using both sides of the argument. Just remember, they are still hunting you. Never forget that!"

"How did they find me? Back on Erebus, how did The Few and The Many find us."

"The ICE Units had been fitted with a surface DNA sensor, and an alert baked into their hardware. Of course, we could have tried to stop them, but sometimes it is better that you don't let the enemy know that you know, and since we added our own eves-dropping system in there too, you don't want the enemy to know you can listen in too. I learned that from the Enigma machines of World War Two. Alan Turing broke the codes used by the Germans but couldn't make it look too obvious that they were listening - they had to turn a blind eye to terrible disasters to avoid suspicion, all the time selecting what information to act on so it looked like chance every time. It is terrible not to act when you know you can save lives. That must have been very hard to do."

"Yamanu acted that day."

"He tried. They also didn't know Yamanu was there. In fact, he was following the Clerics when the signal came. He got there first and was ready to disappear, but you had already escaped. That was a better victory for him because our interception of the signal had not been discovered. Your's was the first time we had used it - the first time an I.C.E had been triggered."

Orianna decided not to mention Taryn. He had not mentioned it, and she saw no reason to bring it up yet. So instead, she asked for another glass. This was clearly going to be a long night. It was good to feel relaxed enough to imbibe freely, but she intended to pace herself so that she didn't miss out on the opportunity to learn as much as possible.

This feels like a home - somewhere that accepts me as I truly am and doesn't try to change me.

Late into the night, the four bid them goodnight and a final welcome to Orianna before taking the carriage away.

Tarik and Orianna sat in front of the fire and said very little to each other. There had been enough talking, and Orianna was exhausted. However, the peace and restfulness she felt drew her to him again. They caressed and undressed each other on the sheepskin rug: his skin was a deeper tan colour in the light of the fire, and her paleness shone yellow. As they began to enjoy each other, their auras came forth with a wild display. Tarik had his eyes closed, lost in the pure tactile senses, but as they reached climax together, he opened his eyes to look up at her, straddling him. What he saw was both beautiful and shocking. He was hard pushed to disguise this amongst his usual blushing ecstasy, but she did not seem to notice.

They lay together afterwards, enjoying the fire until Orianna fell asleep.

When she awoke, she was in bed and alone. Tarik was nowhere to be found. A note by the side of the bed read simply, "sorry not to be there when you wake up. I had to go."

CHAPTER SIXTEEN

2379 CE, Earth, StratoPort 14, above Libya

From StratoPort 14, the view was spectacular out of the observation room. The sun was setting on the horizon, quite curved at this altitude. Harry Bennet had left the passenger lounge to avoid suspicion after having been there for several hours - a rocket had arrived and left in that time, and Raptors had been and gone. Nobody else had been there as long as he had. His agitation and anticipation were muted, with two decades of experience as an agent for The Few helping him conceal it with a fake smile and relaxed sauntering. However, his mere presence was beginning to look unusual. He made it look like he was waiting for the perfect photographic shot, with a high-quality camera he had brought with him.

For this reason, he entirely failed in his mission as a lookout and a fixer of unplanned situations. His cover was to capture a beautiful sunset from an altitude of five kilometres: this coincided with the arrival of the last descent vehicle of the day. People were already disembarking.

A dozen people entered the lounge, unseen by him. He was neglecting his duties by performing his role too well in the observation room. Had he been in the lounge, where he should have been, he would have noticed Orianna amongst them. Not that he could raise any alarm at this point, since his team's Raptor was in a communication blackout during their final approach.

His orders would require him to 'fix' the situation and deal with her unwelcome presence, but that would be challenging: she was one of The Few and not an enemy, so could not be eliminated, not even as collateral damage. However, she was not part of the plan.

She walked straight to the observation room, stealthily approaching behind him, and whispered. "Hello, Harry."

To his credit, Harry contained his surprise and kept in character, flinching very little. He quickly decided to work her into his narrative: she was expected, he decided. Turning, he smiled and kissed her gently on the cheek.

"What the hell are you doing here," he asked quietly, without moving his mouth from a big friendly smile. "Yamanu specifically excluded you from this mission: either something has gone wrong, or you have gone loco. My money is on the latter."

"Our glorious leader is not my glorious anything, in case you hadn't noticed. We only met last year, and I immediately disliked how he spoke to me. We all know he prefers to rescue them as young as possible, but honestly, I just find it tiresome to be treated that way. Don't panic. We have work to do. This is the largest shipment we have intercepted - if it gets to Mars, it is as good as lost, so it deserves the maximum effort."

"You are crazy! Did it occur to you the extra risk you are taking? What if our information is baiting us to attack, to make an even larger shipment? What if we discover the cargo is empty because you and the mission are supposed to fulfil it. Yamanu said this might just be a big trap?"

"And that is exactly why I am here?"

"What do you mean?"

"Chess, dear boy. We attack with the bishop and knight,

and they defend their castle with a knight and another castle, but out of nowhere, we bring in the queen and tip the balance."

"I take it you are the queen in this metaphor?"

"If the shoe fits." Orianna grinned. "Look, if you are as old as I, you would have learnt that the flaw of every plan is that it is a single vision. Even if it is not compromised, its very nature and structure are often deduced on first contact. But when extra independent components are involved, the enemy gets caught out."

"Or, you are just going to get caught, like a pawn. The worst part about this, and I raised this long ago, is that this is an isolated place, with very few entries and exit routes. Perfect place for a trap."

"You don't know the half of it," she said, casually activating her cuff to disable the monitoring systems. A confirmation gave her the go-ahead to break away from their theatrical proximity and push Harry backwards and clear of her in one clean motion. Dropping to the floor, she peeled back the carpet and pulled open the maintenance hatch beneath. "Are you coming?" she asked before activating her full mask and visor, her bulky long coat concealing oxygen cylinders and other support packs for her suit, and climbing down.

"Where the hell are you going?" Harry caught himself yelling, then realised she was about to do something that he would be required to fix, so he begrudgingly followed, activating his own suit.

Harry's landing was not so graceful as he missed the last four rungs on the ladder.

"You're getting a bit old for this, Harry," she teased.

He gave her an unhappy look.

Beneath the comfortable, pressurised passenger areas, the bowels of the StratoPort resembled a giant airship. Crude gantries and girders supported gas bladders and ladders. It was icy cold, and the air pressure matched the top of Everest: without their oxygen and suits, they would be struggling already.

Orianna and Harry made slow progress as Orianna took the time to scan every junction and level as they made their way inwards.

"What are you looking for?" Harry asked, his patience wearing thin.

"I was on Orbital One when I was digging through the data, and I found this," Orianna said, sending him a file. "See? This StratoPort has been refuelling a lot more frequently than others. I don't know what I am looking for, but I have to wonder why that is? It is not an increase in traffic: if anything, there has been a little less than average traffic. So if it isn't more fuel usage, then it must be because there is more weight."

It was like walking inside the walls of a building: rooms and corridors could be seen from the outside, no doubt warm and pressurised in there.

"These rooms are not normally included. They seem to be heavily populated," Orianna commented as her scans fed her the scan information. Next, she shared the ultrasonic scan of the rooms ahead of them: everything was highlighted in red, indicating they did not match the standard StratoPort plans. Her extra equipment pinged almost inaudibly to Harry, but it caused Orianna to hold her hands over her ears to protect her exceptional hearing. Harry didn't seem bothered by it as he watched the sonogram image build up in his contacts.

"That is a lot of heavily armed troops. Shit. We're fucked!" Harry exclaimed, seeing at least three dozen outlines milling around in the first room, the outlines of rifles and shotguns clearly shown, and many more in the second room.

"Keep your cool! We have the element of surprise."

"You were right!"

"Not important now. What can we do here?" Orianna asked.

"What do you mean? They have serious weapons. In fact, why would anyone choose to have serious weapons on what is essentially a huge gas bomb? We are literally surrounded by fuel. All these bladders are full of hydrogen, and the few small ones below us are oxygen."

Harry had always known this was true, but he was happy to accept an excellent safety record. Technology had improved considerably in the four hundred and forty-two years ago since the Hindenburg disaster, so much indeed that they were confident enough to land rockets on them. It seemed insane now he was standing amongst it all.

"These people are crazy. This can never end well." Harry was about to panic.

Orianna rested her hand on his chest and measured his rapid heart rate as she gazed up into his face, hoping to see him begin to calm down.

"I remember the plan had little need of weaponry. It was supposed to be so quick and clean, in and out, nobody was even meant to get hurt," Orianna pleaded, hoping she was wrong. "Tell me that they have contingencies, Harry! There is no way this is going to go to plan. They are coming in on a Raptor and planning to use, what - ten people, to hijack another Raptor arriving within two more minutes and leave without meeting any serious resistance? That is how I heard it. I don't see that happening, do you? Not now we can see over fifty, maybe sixty, trigger happy mercs, ready to shoot up the place and blow us all to hell."

"Ok."

"Ok?"

"Ok, so we do have the element of surprise. We can, I don't know, weld the doors shut and slow them down enough to give the others a chance," Harry said, trying to think positively.

"You and I don't look like we are carrying welding equipment under our suits, so what are you thinking?" Orianna asked, not buying into his boy scout optimism.

"I don't know. But, hang on, you said that I didn't know half of it, but you didn't know about the troops. So what half am I missing still?"

Orianna stepped back, turned and continued her scan along the gantry.

"Hey!" Harry yelled, running after her. She allowed his hand to turn her around to face him again. "What is really going on?"

"Still playing checkers, Harry? I told you: this is chess. A strong player never plays to accept a loss, and if the best they can achieve is a draw, a stalemate, then they will take it."

"What does a draw mean? Quit with the metaphors and just tell me!"

"Two days ago, I tapped communications about this StratoPort, documents detailing the contingencies of the transfer of our people in hibernation all the way to Mars. Every step of the way was played from all angles: tempting bait, hidden traps hoping to capture more in a daring but futile rescue, little enough security to encourage us to have a go, and weakest where they wanted us to make our move. Here. They have no intention of losing at any cost. This StratoPort is rigged to explode as soon as they realise there is a risk that we might succeed. They are happy to kill us all and everyone else on the StratoPort if they cannot capture us."

Now his face showed real fear.

"You knew this, and you still came?" he asked.

Orianna sighed. "You all still came. That's why I came. Yamanu wouldn't listen to me. He seems to think that being thousands of years old makes him better somehow, but this is my millennium, and I know how things work here."

He looked at her quizzically. "I honestly thought The Few were all risk-averse. Because, if I lived a long time, there is no doubt I would end up being more and more careful."

"Really? It is more complicated than that. Even mortals struggle to keep going when they have no purpose or ache for more time to complete their life's goal. Living longer doesn't change that. It just means that you are likely to make those same decisions repeatedly. The real challenge is accepting your regrets and moving on. I don't want to regret not trying here today. I don't care what Yamanu says."

"You are in luck then," Harry said, his tone more positive. "Yamanu isn't on the Raptor. Decided it was too great a risk if he was caught, in case they tortured him for information."

"I see why you thought that now. The Few are too careful and connected to depend on one person knowing everything. Yamanu couldn't give that information if he wanted to. Ok, this might make things easier. We need a new plan, and we need the captain of the Raptor to play along."

"That's Addison Fletcher. She's piloting the Raptor. I know her. I would say she is quite rational. She was a soldier in World War Two. She understands things from a soldier's perspective."

"Good, then she should understand an ambush and the benefits of counterintelligence."

"What do you have in mind?" Harry was quite keen now.

Orianna brought up a virtual diagram of the whole StratoPort, appearing to hang in front of them.

"The StratoPort is flattish, like a dinner plate, but underneath, where we are now, these bladders fill all the gaps. There are only a few rooms: the control room is over there above us now, those extra rooms with the soldiers were way back the way we came, and to our right is the rocket hanger and shaft. Rockets are assembled and disassembled in there. The rocket mid-section is the cargo pod: it is interchangeable with a Raptor's mid-section, allowing cargo to be shipped from the surface to orbit and back without needing to be opened.

"Passengers are different. They can just walk off, which avoids the time and effort in swapping out the pods. The pod we are interested in will be treated as cargo."

Harry raise a finger. "Here, the target pod will be waiting here, having just been delivered by Raptor, to await its rocket. Our Raptor arrives and drops its pod there, containing our rescue team."

"Yes, the plan involves the rescue team making their way to the target pod, reviving the captives from hibernation and then everyone escapes using wingsuits."

"That's right." Harry had a worried look on his face now. "But those soldiers are not part of the plan. There are too many and their weapons..."

"I told them that they were being transported in hibernation, so it would take half an hour to get them revived and ready for a Wingsuit descent, but there was disagreement over the quality of that information. Of course, we now know that those soldiers will surround and overpower them easily."

"It was a good plan. Simple: come in by Raptor and jump off with Wingsuits."

"You should spend some time in the Baltics, Harry, learn some chess. A good plan sounds good because it fits together too well - the problem is that it is obvious. Also, no plan ever survives contact with the enemy."

"We all have Wingsuits, but you cannot jump from the deck; those bladders extend out way beyond it, see? So we have to jump from the very lowest level," Harry insisted.

Orianna nodded. "We should always assume that the enemy might have infiltrated somehow, and they know this."

"Wow. Ok, but where does that leave us?"

"It leaves us improvising," she began slowly and thoughtfully. "Ah here, this is the power to the comms array down there, long below lift motor sixteen. They share the same reactor. If we cause the motor to fail, taking down the power, then the comms will be down until they reset it manually at this junction," she said, marking a gantry on the diagram. "That stops them from hearing of the attack and being able to trigger the destruction of the StratoPort, hopefully."

"Hopefully?"

"Have some faith, Harry! As I see it, we need to time this well and get off quickly before they blow it. A narrow window."

"Well, if we don't have time to wake them, then we have to take the pod, but that's insane! Then, they will know what is happening…."

"But by then, it will be too late!"

"What about our ten in our own pod?"

"They will have to jump on approach as we disable comms. Harry, I will need you to disable the comms. Make it look like a malfunction or something, then get out, just drop down and Wingsuit away. The soldiers will be busy attacking our empty pod as it descends. Meanwhile, I will be bringing the target pod back up to the deck for pickup. Our best bet is that they don't know we have people already here, which is likely since it never was in the plan."

"Err, ok. That might just work, but how the hell do we tell our Raptor the new plan?"

Orianna's face went blank, then a memory surfaced, and she raised her eyebrows. "Harry, make sure your kids pay attention in History class. One day that information will become important," she said smiling. "Let's hope Captain Addison Fletcher remembers her Morse code. Leave it to me. You ok?"

"I can do it."

"Good man, Harry. Good luck!"

With that, Harry turned and ran down the gantry on a mission to disrupt the power shared by motor sixteen and the comms array.

Orianna watched him go and then went her own way up to the deck through a double hatch arrangement, presumably to keep rocket exhausts and other potentially flammable situations from escaping to the hydrogen below. Bypassing the security sensors was trivial for her. Soon, she was standing on the vast expanse of the flat deck, curling up like a dinner plate around the edge, from which regularly spaced pylons extended out, each supporting a large ducted fan motor. It looked like the largest aerial drone ever. Only the crane and its claw to grab hovering rockets broke this stark expanse.

The deck was dark, no longer illuminated by the setting sun, but the sky was still a pale blue. Using her visor, she picked up one Raptor distant, approaching from the north, and another approaching from the south. The northern one was much closer - it had to be the target. She turned to face the southerly one.

Reaching down, she opened a panel next to a deck lamp at her feet. It wasn't hard to gain manual control and aim it at their Raptor. "Come on, Captain Addison Fletcher, remember this?" she mumbled to herself.

A message was sent in real-time from her cuff: blinking the lights, first in a continuous mayday signal of "S.O.S", then in a short but clear repeating message, instructing of a change of plan. Hopefully, she would see sense and either abort or follow the new directive. Either way, the original plan was now defunct. The timing was vital, so Orianna would know whether they got the message soon enough.

The target Raptor came in on approach, hovered, and landed vertically using its six tiltable electric fan motors a short way behind her. Its engines barely slowed before the pod was released (essentially the middle fuselage), leaving it sitting on the deck as the Raptor took off again and flew away.

Orianna felt a subtle change of gravity.

"Motor Sixteen is down. Comms are confirmed down. I think I may have to stay here for a bit to make sure; they seem to be very keen to come and fix it. See what I can do to slow them down," came Harry voice over local comms.

"Be careful!" she replied before changing the message to their Raptor, now quite close.

Orianna turned from the lamp and ran towards the target pod, now lowering into the deck on the elevator pad. She glanced over her shoulder to confirm that Fletcher had adopted the new plan. Ten small figures could be seen freefalling out of that pod. Fletcher had done it. Now only Harry, Fletcher's crew and herself were at risk.

As the pod disappeared below the surface, Orianna ran as fast as she could towards the edge of the shaft, keeping the top of the descending pod just in her line of sight. She leapt. It was too short a distance for her suit to help and too far for a safe landing, but she jumped anyway.

Her landing on the curved roof of the cylinder was less than elegant, hitting painfully hard; she tried to roll and spread the impact, but she was severely winded and unable to find a grip. In addition, the surface was cold and covered in condensation. Her gloves gained no hold, and she continued down the side, desperately flailing for something to grab.

She landed on the elevator deck mostly on her feet but fell back, flat out, her shoulder hanging over the edge.

The wheezing from her throat distracted her momentarily. She knew the secondary pain was coming in moments, so she had one last opportunity to move before that paralysing agony would be too much. Rolling sideways over and over, she managed to get herself full back onto the deck as a rising girder passed close by.

"Get up!" she yelled to herself, denying the pain of certainly fractured ribs, just as the elevator came to a halt at the bottom.

A suited man was operating a control panel with his back to her. She only had one opportunity before the soldiers would be bearing down upon her. Limping as quietly as she could right up behind him, she saw he had a dart gun in a holster. She grabbed its handle, releasing the safety strap in one clean motion of her thumb, and at the same time pushed his forehead against the bulkhead. She pulled back and shot a dart into his back. He stumbled off to the side from the impact on his head and slowly collapsed to the ground as the dart's injector pushed a high dose sedative into him.

The console was simple enough. In moments Orianna had instructed the elevator to ascend again. Suddenly something pranged against the bulkhead next to her head, then another. She ducked down and looked behind her. Soldiers were running down a corridor towards the hanger.

She opened fire rapidly, forcing them back, and then ran for the elevator pad, rolling onto it as it reached her chest height. The soldiers began to advance again, so she kept moving to evade their fire and stay low as she rose above their upward angle of fire.

A pair of hands suddenly grabbed the edge of the pad right in front of her face. She brought the butt of the gun down hard on one set of fingers, and both hands fell away. She was clear. The rectangle of dimming sky above her was getting larger and larger.

When she felt safe, she got to her feet and tried to look in through the windows of the cargo pod. Inside she could see nothing but hibernation beds. That was good. If there had been enemy personnel on board, she wasn't sure what she was going to do.

Her ride up seemed to take forever. Then, she noticed flashing red alerts blinking around the shaft and on the deck as the pod broke the surface.

She saw their Raptor sitting on the deck, its pod already descending beneath it.

Immediately, the Raptor took off and leaned heavily to quickly float overhead.

Orianna ran out over the deck and waved at the pilot, indicating the target pod and a thumbs up. She ran hard over to the nearest hatch, firing wildly at it as the hatch popped up. Sliding on her good side, she continued firing down the hole in the deck without risking peering over. She heard sounds of shouting coming from below. She kicked the hatch closed again.

She only needed another minute or less. The Raptor was landing to collect the pod. She could see the copilot pointing and waving with the "run" gesture.

Getting up as best she could, she began to run across the deck. Behind her, she heard the hatch open again, then a whine of a chain gun spinning up.

Oh no! All bets are off now.

Trying her best to keep up speed, every breath more painful than the last, she kept running.

Gunfire spat out at high speed, and ricochets could be heard all around.

More hatches opened up around her, and soldiers climbed out, all concentrating on the Raptor and its popped out gun turret spraying across the deck. One soldier had a rocket launcher, which he had shouldered ready to fire, raising it up to track the Raptor as it rose up. But unfortunately, he and his squad were not paying her any attention. She quickly threw herself into a dive to get a steady shot and fire repeatedly into him and the man next to him.

Orianna landed on her injured side at full speed and screamed. Laying in agony, she saw the rocket launcher drop again, and the soldier toppled forwards as the sedative took its effect on him. A rocket whooshed out and flew across the deck and at the elevator pad. The deck exploded, and pieces shot off in all directions.

Looking up, she saw the Raptor clear of the initial blast and continue to climb. They were going to make it.

She thought hard about her options. Her cuff told her that the comms array was still down and motor sixteen was not far away. Holding her side, she got to her knees and coughed painfully - then up on one foot and the other. Faster and faster, she hobbled towards the arm. She felt a second explosion behind her: a hydrogen leak. Not necessarily disastrous, she thought, these StratoPort were built with fire safety features. Indeed, a massive cloud of halon gas followed to swamp the billowing fire.

At the arm, she had to climb onto the open frame and then down, inside to the gantry within. More shots rang out and pinged off the sparse structure. The soldiers were concentrating on her now.

The gantry was long and straight, ending at the stationary motor.

It seemed like she would never reach it. She assigned her contacts to show the view behind her and commas array status.

As the first soldier dropped into the gantry behind her, she arrived at the motor. Looking down, she saw a wide, open cylinder beneath her, with a stationary pair of rotor blades. There was nowhere left to hide.

The comms array was active, and the rotors had just started to move very slowly.

Gunfire rang out, and she was hit in the back. Instinctively reached behind her, she grabbed it and pulled it out, the suit resealing behind the small puncture. But, alas, it was too late; most of the sedative had been injected. She fell forwards and into the motor.

Her shoulder glanced off one blade, but otherwise, she fell cleanly through.

Deep beneath the StratoPort, a small unit activated adjacent to the few small bladders at the very bottom, the only bladders to hold the heavier-than-air oxygen, where it should have been safest. However, this unit was designed to pump oxygen back up and into several hydrogen bladders, which it did rapidly and continuously. This was no routine function: this device was sabotage.

In moments, the mixture was optimal, and the subsequent explosion tore the rest of the bladders apart, engulfing the whole thing in flame. More explosions followed, and pieces of the StratoPort flew off in all directions.

Below, Orianna's unconscious body tumbled in freefall. Her suit recognised the situation and switched to automated flight. Electrodes triggered her muscles directly and made her body into a rigid shape. Extra material extended between the legs and between the arms and ribs. Her muscles were then driven to open her limbs and extend that material into aerofoil wings. Her body ceased tumbling and began to glide vertically at first. Then with more subtle control of her limbs, the suit levelled her out and headed west towards the Algerian New Forest, flaming pieces of debris falling far behind and away from her.

CHAPTER SEVENTEEN

1504 CE, Earth, France

"This is simply divine, dear fellow. How we in England suffer so much for the appalling state of our roads is beyond me. Not that I am saying that the French have better roads, however much it might be true, but I am saying that I would never have embarked on such a long journey in England. You were absolutely correct about those leather straps, I do declare. Quite extraordinary. I must have one shipped back to Salisbury and have my coachbuilders replicate it."

Yamanu Nader watched the man speak and marvelled so. Nobody he had ever met before was so incredibly handsome: a glowing but dusted pale face of porcelain perched in a refined ebony tunic and cloak, a silken blanched blouse lining the inside of his collar. His youthful, elegant hands perched on an upright cane, resting atop one another, covering the polished silver eagle-headed grip, offering him a modicum of stability in the wobbling carriage.

"Nothing but the best for you, Grey," Yamanu said, leaning back as the carriage threw them particularly hard.

Chesterfield Grey, Earl of Salisbury, lunged and expertly threw his cane out over Yamanu's shoulder, catching it before the bulkhead and then using it to rap twice loudly thereon. "Watch the road, man!" he exclaimed. But, even in anger, his features barely encountered a frown, a slight smirk for Yamanu, told of a man enjoying his station - not fussed about it, not embarrassed by it, not at all taking it seriously either.

The arched canvas roof creaked and flapped continuously, dispensing its own rhythm to their passage.

"I do hope this is worth it, Yamanu. However, when I think of the pleasures I am missing to go on your little adventure, I wonder why I agreed to it. Oh, don't listen to my complaining. I am actually enjoying a European sojourn to ease my transition into the next Earl. Unlike you chaps, I have a legacy to maintain."

"I honestly have no idea how you do it, Grey. Or perhaps I am confused as to why you go to so much trouble."

"My dear fellow, society is a fickle beast. One cannot just turn up and claim to be the next Earl and expect no one to engage in gossip or question your legitimacy. This way, I can be adored beyond suspicion, their pity for my calamities: lost wives, lost parents, so on and so forth."

"We do not have too far to go, plenty of time to fill. Please do tell me your plans this time."

A rye smirk grew to a mischievous grin across his perfect features. His blue eyes widened excitedly.

"Did you know I married?"

"No, really?"

"Well, not anymore. Poor thing died in childbirth. A necessary tragedy, I assure you. I did enjoy her completely, though. Exquisite creature, somewhat similar in looks to myself, which aids my plot immensely, by the way. My son will grow up tutored and educated and properly positioned in society, attracting all sorts of attention. I, of course, will be intent on satiating my honour doing something tremendously important, dragged away from my son for long periods, only to return occasionally, suitably made up to look more aged and wretched than the last time.

"Finally, he will travel abroad himself to - I don't know - discover himself when news comes to him of my premature demise - as a grand sacrifice for the good of all, etcetera. His triumphant return and debut on the social stage will leave nobody short of tears and heartache for me, the prodigal son returning. Tada!" Grey gestured an elaborate mocking bow.

"And the boy? Does he have to die too?"

"Not necessarily. I will provide the boy with an opportunity to live a long and well-off life abroad unless he declines my offer."

"The boy. Your son?"

Grey eyed Yamanu suspiciously. "You're judging me?"

Yamanu did not reply.

"I remember the last journey we took, much like this one," Grey began again, more at ease. "Your first experiment. Your brilliant plan to recruit wretches from a small village couldn't have ended in more of an abject failure. How you believed useful agents could be hewn from those lumps of clay is beyond my wildest imaginings. The poor fools had very little idea what you were on about, and as soon as you crossed the line of their dogmatic religious teachings, it was as good as over. If I hadn't been there that day, to save you…."

"Do you still carry a sword?" Yamanu asked, looking down at Grey's cane.

"A gentleman must be ready to defend his honour, or in my case, my fabulously immoral life." Grey grinned peevishly, but the joy of the moment quickly passed. "I would also say that luck paid no small part in the matter."

"The fire?"

"Yes, the fire. I locked them in as we escaped. I knew the fire had started when I kicked over the table. It was my fault they all died."

"I could have unlocked the door."

"Well, fortunately, any sense of goodwill to all men was

lost on you that day; otherwise, we would not be here today."

"Indeed."

For the final mile, the two men spoke no further.

"Are we good?" Yamanu asked as the carriage came to a halt, and Grey peered outside curiously.

Grey snapped his attention back inside. "Do I look like a man who holds a grudge? You know how hard it is to continue to find new things to delight oneself with, thus naturally, I adore surprises of any kind. As a victim of everlasting youth, I am sure to have one final surprise at the end. Who could not be tickled pink by a friend's surprise? I am terribly excited. Can you tell?"

"I hope it pleases you."

"Ah, well, all too often, the thing is never as good as the prelude to the thing. Anticipation is key, with an entirely eradicated cynicism, to fully suck the marrow out of the idea before one even meets it. So let us revel in my tease a moment longer."

Grey giggled as Yamanu opened the small door and stepped out.

They were at a large country home. No butler came to help, which disappointed Grey a little; however, a couple of pairs of urchins appeared out of nowhere and proceeded to attend to the significant luggage - most of which was Greys.

Grey descended the steps, showing his long tights and shiny buckled shoes and perambulated down the gravel drive.

"Where are the servants?" he asked of Yamanu.

"Staff attends weekly to look after the gardens and to perform other specialist duties, but none live on the premises."

"Oh, really?" Grey did not sound pleased with that. "Still, the house is absolutely charming." He looked up at the brownstone, wrapped in ivy and surrounded by exclusive grounds of mature trees. The warm sun was a little uncomfortable for his eyes.

"Shall we go in?" Yamanu offered, and the pair strode in through the front door alone.

The sound of the carriage leaving made Grey look back to check all his luggage had been attended to. He was surprised to see little of it left behind on the driveway as the prepubescent children ran back to fetch the last of it. Efficient, he thought.

Yamanu led Grey through to the rear and out onto the veranda, there to find a hot teapot, cucumber sandwiches and fine china awaiting them.

"Don't say it!" Grey warned Yamanu with a sternly raised finger and seated himself away from the intruding sunshine. "I can smell it already."

"Earl Grey Tea?"

"Oh, you bad man." Grey looked out over the balustrade to the croquet lawn beyond, as the four urchins could be seen running out from the side of the house to join three others standing neatly in a line before a man. "Is that Marcello Carli? Ciao Marcello!"

Marcello turned for a moment to give a short wave. Then, a girl left the group and came over.

"And who are you, pretty girl?" Grey asked her.

"Ruby Day, Sir. Would you care for me to serve you, my Lord?"

"Of course, that would be delightful," Grey replied, examining her closely as she picked up the teapot and began to pour out two cups. "She has soft enough hands for a thirteen-year-old, but short nails with dirt under them indicates she is an enigma. She has excellent manners, hygiene, and the smell of simple soap, so the dirt is from today even, but poor simple clothes and a colour indicating she has spent time out of the shade. What manner of creature is she?"

"She has been here since she was born - haven't you, Ruby?"

Ruby politely nods.

"Ruby, tell the Earl of Salisbury what he is."

Grey shot Yamanu a glance and a raised eyebrow.

Ruby looked Grey in the face, not averting her gaze, bold as brass, and said, "Lord Salisbury is one of The Few. He is immortal, Sir. Would his lordship like sugar?"

"Sugar in Earl Grey Tea - absurd! No, I would not, thank you. Just a little milk, though. I find it a little tart otherwise. But, Yamanu, what is the meaning of this?

"Thank you, Ruby. You may rejoin Marcello's class."

Ruby completed her pouring, and with a short courtesy, she ran back to the lawn and into line, joining the others in an education of self-defence.

"Dear God, you have started a school, and you are teaching them about us. You play a dangerous game, my Egyptian friend."

"You said it yourself: they are clay to be moulded. Here they know nothing but what we teach them, from birth. They understand the world around them, but they are educated, not slaves to dogma. They understand we are human-like they are, but with a strong sense of purpose, as we have."

"Oh, hang thee a man who would tear down a familiar god out of pure envy alone."

"You raise a good point. But unfortunately, Tarik and I could not decide what approach was best. So indeed, this is just the first house we visit this day."

"Heavens, I will need these cucumber sandwiches to get me through more of this madness."

"Here, they know they are mortals, and there is nothing we can do about it. Instead, at the second house, we give them the false hope that one day, if they achieve, they can attain immortality too. And at the third, total ignorance of immortals - there we rotate our teachers to avoid suspicion."

"Well, I thank you for an excellent surprise, however, do not assume that my pleasure is matched by my satisfaction. On the contrary, I have serious doubts about these agents that you are training here today. What happens after tasting the real world and they discover a closer affiliation to their own kind?"

"It is a necessary risk. We can do so much more with their assistance."

"I honestly don't think you have weighed up the potential consequences fully, dear fellow. They would not only have full knowledge of us but they will be well trained too. What will you do if they go rogue?"

"Eventually, they will die as they all do, and their stories of immortals walking the world will be disbelieved as the delusions of insanity and forgotten."

"Well, I will not be a bad sport, old chap. I will congratulate you on certainly improving on your last project and leave it at that."

CHAPTER EIGHTEEN

2400 CE, Earth, Paris, capital of Normandy

"Ragnarök comes again," Sif exclaimed, but these random predictions no longer bothered Orianna. Indeed, they had become good friends. Orianna felt protective of Sif despite being very capable of looking after herself, as it turned out, and both Sif and she shared a quiet side, enjoying the silence even in each others' company. However, as she got to know her more, the mystery of Sif's past references became a story Orianna wanted to unravel: it intrigued her. Here was either an elaborate creation of a fractured mind or a painful memory of a time when The Few dominated openly, were worshipped even, until the end of days, known as Ragnarök.

"You might be right, sister. The Gathering has got to be the craziest thing I have ever been involved with," Orianna agreed as she finished getting into her most advanced combat suit yet. Beneath the smooth, silk-textured elegant dress, thin layers of the material defended against needles, impacts, edge weapons and electrical attacks. Only one arm was bare as a concession towards a fashionable outer appearance: ruffled cloth showing an electric blue underside as it hung in gravity-defying waves of pearlescent purple and black on top. The low cut, open cleavage design also offered an apparent vulnerability offsetting an aggressively sexual overtone. Yet, hidden panels in the exaggerated bra area were ready to spring up to the collar and protect the upper chest at any hint of danger. The suit collar was disguised as a retro punk-era spiked dog collar. It was both a statement of vogue and a state-of-the-art defensive system.

Sif, too had an advanced suit that Orianna had commissioned for her. Her black, classic bell-shaped dress hung like it was hiding layers of petticoats, but of course, what she was hiding was a bit more offensive in nature. It matched her darker personality.

It was fair to assume that everyone was going through the same precautions and preparations, together in one of the largest remaining cities on Earth: Paris, capital of Normandy.

With just hours to go before the turn of the century, New Year's Eve 2400 was the biggest party ever, all over the World. The Few had arranged multiple decoy venues in several cities, but this was the real McCoy, at a theatre near the centre undergoing renovations, which were due to complete early in February. Larger population centres were rare these days, but they all had one crucial feature: many entry and exit points and crowds of civilians to get lost amongst. So it was the perfect place for the most outrageous event in living history - the living history that extended back almost five thousand years. Every known member of The Few would be there in a single enclosed space for just one hour before dispersing again. How Yamanu pulled that off is beyond comprehension. Just the sheer organisation and communication must have taken decades to put together. Then there were the endless layers of security and decoys venues to arrange, ensuring everyone had one date in mind to attend, no matter what, without doubt, or the possibility of refusal.

Such was Yamanu's influence and power and his boundless patience.

Sif took Orianna's arm as they walked from their hotel. They passed through plazas and down alleyways, across tramways and between street performers, all the time noting anyone following them and becoming increasingly aware of others like them heading in the same convergent direction - more like a sixth sense; a motion in the crowd; a certain way about a person's gait; an unnatural filter for something out of place like a needle in a haystack.

The rundown theatre's facade was depressingly unfinished, but a warm glow of light came from the entrances. Security was high: biometric face scans, passwords, and the impressive foyer was dimly lit so that everyone's ultraviolet aura could be confirmed.

It was a breathtaking and dazzling display of wealth and vitality: so many highly individualistic people from many eras expressed themselves to great effect through just about every period of fashionable history. It made the myriad of ongoing celebrations by mortal people, all around in the streets, a pale imitation by comparison.

Of course, everyone was young and in their prime. Although mortal children might not be up late to see the New Year, in this group, there were none. Mortal advocates had the theatre surrounded, inconspicuously partying and going about their business and yet being police and service staff, all the time acting as one to protect those within the theatre: the entire World's population of The Few. Every known ageless person was there at the stroke of midnight, all one thousand four hundred and fifty-two of them, even The Watcher.

Word had spread of The Watcher. They said he had lived longer than anyone; a conspiracy never denied because nobody actually spoke to him, and he never talked to anyone. Over time, at places and events, The Few started to acknowledge his presence, giving him a recognising nod or tip of the hat or courtesy or a bow, and he in kind began to appear closer and with less and less caution. In an unwritten and unnegotiated truce, The Few and The Watcher respected each other enough not to engage directly with one another. Whenever The Few had attempted it before, The Watcher had reacted poorly and kept away again for a while. The Few had learned the best way to accept him and be accepted by him was by simply providing assured indifference.

Now he could be seen slipping between everyone: never staying still. His eyes darted around, taking in all the faces, with a blank expression on his own face. Mostly, people deliberately ignored him, except to gracefully part to allow him to pass. However, everyone was watching him: noticing his beard was tamed a little, and he wore a classic tuxedo.

The foyer clock chimed, and the crowd migrated into the stalls. Inside, the hall had new carpets but had yet to receive new seats: the whole place looked like an old Grecian amphitheatre with concentric open steps rising up from the central stage.

Orianna noted how pleasant it was to move freely in any direction without the obstacles of seats and seated people. She had never felt such a sense of belonging before: she was a welcomed member of the most elite group of the most unknown, most wealthy and most influential people in the World. Looking around was breathtaking: such varied and beautiful garments worn to impress - for this was the party of the era.

She and Sif made their way around the auditorium, hoping to find a familiar face or two - so many faces that seemed to recognise her but she had never met before. After a while, she realised that she was the subject of whispering as she passed by. At first, she thought it was because of Sif since so many misunderstood her, but that changed as she caught one or two phrases. It made her feel uncomfortable. Then she found Randolph Giddeon in conversation with Adam Li.

"Enchanté, my dear. You look fabulous, et toi Sif," Randolph exclaimed over the loud murmur of the crowd in franglais. He looked them up and down with an admiring twinkle in his eye.

"Early twentieth-century tuxedo, so bourgeois, Randolph, so very you! Is that velvet?" Orianna replied with equal admiration. "Hi Adam, let me see, don't tell me, pre-Millennial rapper?"

"Good call, Orianna, a little before my time, but my kind of thing, sure," he said, never one much for small talk. "What do you think about all this?"

"I was just saying to Adam, my dears: unprecedented is the only word to describe it. Unprecedented. I understand Yamanu called in a lot of favours to get everyone here, particularly those he could not convince or persuade," Randolph interrupted.

Orianna nodded and looked at Adam. "I don't like surprises."

Adam released a short grin: not something she had seen him often do. "Totally," he said, nodding back.

"Ragnarök," Sif said again.

Both men looked at each other.

"I sincerely hope that is not true," Randolph responded.

"She hasn't said much else recently," Orianna began. "I guess this is reminding her of the end of days for the immortals in her stories. They came together and fought, and everyone died, except her. Everyone is nervous, of course, and she isn't so different."

Adam pulled her close to whisper in her ear. "You have gotten close to her now. Has she explained how she came to be the sole survivor of the Norse immortals yet?"

Orianna shook her head.

She addressed the group now and smiled. "Hey, let's lighten the mood here a little. The flip side is that we are all together for the first, and perhaps only time, ever, and that is incredible and warming. I like seeing all these people. I am trying to take in all the faces so I can remember them and recognise them in a crowd in a hundred or a thousand years and just know that we are all brothers and sisters."

"Here here," cried Randolph. "We are all nervous together, which makes a delightful change if you ask me."

"I see Tarik. I guess the show is about to start...." Adam exclaimed excitedly, only to cut off when he remembered Orianna was present.

Each small group paused to look at each other and at Orianna.

"Tarik who?" Orianna asked, her nose raised just a little higher.

They all laughed. Orianna was with her friends. Tarik had been the one who introduced them that night, but she hadn't seen him since he left their bed that same night, so her indifference to him now was quite understandable.

Tarik strode out onto the stage, and the crowd began to quieten.

"Good evening," he began, his soft voice gently spoken into his collar and transmitted to everyone else's collars and inducted into their ear canals through a small implant. "Welcome, everyone, to The Gathering. My brother and I never believed that this day would ever come - a day that brings us together in unity and mutual support. Granted, we are not accepted, and we still have our enemies, but our lives tend to be ones of solitude and isolation, and this opportunity to remember that we are part of a much greater whole is heartwarming.

"We strive to nurture and protect our own kind, and to do that, we have to put ourselves out there and find them, to find our helpless babies, born unwittingly into a cruel world that does not understand them and cannot teach them who they really are. We alone can help. Only through our dedication were most of you rescued from persecution. Only through our love were you given a greater purpose, to nurture your kinsfolk, to teach them how to exist amongst mortal man, to love and to let go of those whose lives are short, and to guide them on their own journeys, wherever they may go.

"We all have our own ideas of what it means to be ageless, to live a life so long and to define your own meaning and morality. I spent my early life with hatred in my heart after mortals killed my mother. I wanted nothing to do with them, and I was alone and lost. Eventually, my brother and I were reunited, and he helped me rise above my grief and think hard about what gets me up in the morning. I struggled, and I know many of you have too, and if you were honest with yourself, I am sure not one of you has considered just ending your life in despair at some point. We all go through these ups and downs. We might change our strategies and our main aims, but through it all, we are united, not in response to any threat, but in compassion for all and the care of those that need us. We are needed. We can help, so we do."

As Tarik tailed off, his words were met by rapturous applause. The crowd was indeed excited about this event. Each one of them would spend their days struggling with the slow monotony of ordinary life, so something as momentous as this was extraordinary and exciting.

"I give you the man who started this all by rescuing me from my own despair, my loving brother, Yamanu!"

Another great applause.

Tarik's larger frame stepped back symbolically a few steps as his brother strode out on the wide empty stage. Yamanu shook Tarik's hand and then faced the audience.

"Thank you, brother. Thank you all. It is gratifying to see you all here today. Yes, some of you needed more than a twisted arm to get you to come, but I hope you will see why it is worth it. Perhaps, one day, these fears will no longer be present. Perhaps, one day, we can meet like this in the open. Indeed, one day, such a meeting will be celebrated far and wide. However, we are not *quite* there yet."

Yamanu chuckled a little, and the audience murmured in response.

"There have been so many sacrifices along the way, people putting their lives on the line for the good of others, and I would like to take this opportunity to single out a couple of people for whom this is most true.

"There are twenty-two people here today that wouldn't have been if it hadn't been for the bravery and individual thinking of these two heroes. You all know what I am talking about. Ha! Everyone will have heard of the StratoPort disaster, but what they didn't report that day was the successful mission to free our brothers and sisters from The Many.

"The Many have been onto us for nearly nine hundred years. First, they tried to eradicate us, fuelled by a need for religious equality, then they tried to control us, and now they study us, hoping to steal our secret sauce."

The crowd laughed at that choice of words.

"Some of us have been captured, but we still do not know how many. To become lab rats: the victims of endless research and tests. That is no life for anyone and certainly not because of how you were born. Seeking to rescue these poor helpless people is dangerous. The Many know our ways: they know we are coming and want to trap more of us. To go on such a mission is to risk captivity - a fate worse than death.

"So let us honour those who put their heads in the lion's mouth and say, go on, I dare you!"

Yamanu began to clap slowly, but the pace increased when the rest quickly joined in. A cacophony of synchronous claps banged around the auditorium faster and faster until the crowd could no longer maintain the timing, and it collapsed into a white noise of regular applause, which then diminished slowly.

"I want to give a special mention to Harry Bennet, one of our mortal friends, who gave his life for something bigger than himself, who held out so that others could escape, and who paid the ultimate price. Thank you, Harry."

More applause ensued. Once it had calmed down, Yamanu began again.

"My final mention is to the one person who made this mission possible. You probably already know who she is, and you probably know this story, so I will keep this brief. She was told not to come on the mission, which of course, is to minimise the risks. She went anyway. We knew there were always risks of a trap; well, she figured out what that trap was. She didn't just tell someone about it; she went there and changed the outcome from an inevitable failure to a significant victory. I give you, Orianna Demaine!"

Orianna was obviously not surprised given the long built up that she recognised, but the sudden attention at that moment was deeply shocking. She blushed uncontrollably.

"Come down, please, Orianna," Yamanu called as the clapping started again in earnest.

The crowd ignored her reluctance - it was not satisfied to let her nod courtly and accept praise in the audience. She found herself ushered through the parting people, down to the stage.

The brothers dwarfed her, standing either side as she curtseyed and bowed her head until the clapping died away.

"Err, thank you, everyone. I just did what any of you would have done, given the same circumstances. I play chess. It was like a chess game. We just needed a new piece on the board to win. I didn't really have a choice. I was with Harry. He was a really good man. I have already fully provided for his family: they will never want for anything, except perhaps a proper explanation. The story they have shows him to be the hero he was. I am so glad we saved so many lives. I was just glad to be of service."

Solid applause ensued. Orianna blushed and smiled until Yamanu whispered to her on a private channel, saying, "you had no idea how popular you had become, did you?"

Something was unsettling about the way he said it. The words seemed to be delivered with no pleasure in their sounds. Yet, she maintained her smile regardless.

Orianna made a move to leave, hoping that her moment in the spotlight was over and she could go back and be swallowed by the crowd again.

"Please wait, Orianna," Tarik asked her, gently clasping the upper part of her bare arm, squeezing it a little insistently.

"Thank you, Orianna. An inspiration to us all. I am sure you realise that I did not bring you all here together, at this Gathering just for this, nor indeed to celebrate the start of yet another century," Yamanu chuckled again. The audience again murmured in response. "Of course, you didn't.

"You know, science has a name for our *condition*. They named us chimeras, a medical term used when an animal has more than one set of DNA, a mutation that usually leads to premature death because the body resolves to fight with itself.

"What the scientists do not know is that not many more than fourteen hundred people in five thousand years are born as the exception to this rule. In us, there is a perfect harmony: a mutually assured survival, where our dual DNA defeats the ageing process. And this is why we call ourselves The Few.

"We are not gods: we are humans, albeit special humans, better humans. We are not immortal, but we watch everyone else grow old and die around us. This can be heartbreaking and lonely. They are our parents and our children, yet they do not understand us."

The mood was sombre in the room. Yamanu seemed on the verge of tears. The pause was palpable. Then, suddenly, he snapped out of it.

"What if that wasn't true? What if we are not human, but post-human - a species all of our own, just waiting to become independent from the mortals?

"Everyone here has thought about it. The very fact that Tarik and I are brothers has always been proof to all that our mother was special. Somehow, she was able to have children like us, over and over, but she died thousands of years before people discovered genetics and gave a name to chimerism.

"You have all wondered if we could take that final step and become Human two point zero.

"I have spent my life searching and searching for that next mother of timeless people, but I never knew what I was looking for. Even genetics gave us no clue, and just when she was staring us in the face, none of our tests revealed anything other than what they were built to do - to find a chimera.

"But what if there was a chimera with four sets of DNA? Something we weren't looking for and thus never saw. The clue came from my brother. As a child, he watched our mother practice her performances as an oracle to the Pharaoh. She had learned to show the full range of her aura and, in doing so, produced the most fantastic display for the Pharaoh by illuminating a small chamber decorated with gems that fluoresced under her ultraviolet light.

"He saw a colour that he had never seen before, a colour he would never see again, until recently, when making love to Orianna Demaine - someone untrained in the use of her aura, who was able to express it fully only at the peak of ecstasy. A closer examination of her blood work gave us the explanation we were looking for: four sets of DNA she had inside her."

Orianna was struggling to move, but Tarik held her arm firmly now.

"Ladies and gentlemen, I give you our future, Orianna Demaine!"

The audience was silent.

Orianna was hitting fight or flight mode, and her skin began to warm quickly.

Everyone watched as her aura grew and changed from violet to something new and different, something beautiful and indescribable. A new colour.

Nobody said a word, except Orianna, who screamed, "Let me go!"

CHAPTER NINETEEN

1777 CE, Earth, Bavaria

Chesterfield Grey, currently the thirteenth Earl of Salisbury - having inherited the title from himself only recently - sat alone in the back row of seats, which was somewhat unusual for a social gathering.

As a visitor to Prudence Lodge of the Rite of Strict Observance, he wasn't well known and, with the exception of his exceptional beauty, he garnered little attention. In the outer room, the brethren had, of course, indulged in conversation with this newcomer, and he had behaved himself quite well. Still, it was fortunate that there happened to be many guests from other lodges there that night, and Grey could slip into the chamber early. Since nobody else was there to see him, he skipped the discipline of squaring the lodge - a practice of adhering to the black and white checkerboard tiles on the floor and walking following only its straight lines and only turning clockwise - so he took a lazy path directly across at a diagonal and slipped through several rows of seats to the rear.

He took in the room, judging it to be of modest proportions, being converted from a simple loft of a clerks office below. He thought the oak beams were a charming feature, but he was a little disappointed that the room was rectangular rather than square. The fireplace opposite roared with a freshly laid set of logs getting going. He knew that the room would warm very quickly once the brethren filled the lodge, so his cloak had been hung up outside. Meanwhile, he had his hands under his masonic apron: the sheepskin smooth and adorned with symbols and decorations on the front but remaining crudely furry on the underside, helping his hands stay warm. Staring at the fire, he realised it must have been a recent addition since it was deliberately off-centre, allowing for the Secretary's table to remain in the north - in the middle of the wall opposite.

A Freemason's lodge had the four cardinal points laid out for officers to occupy: the Worshipful Master in the east, the Junior Warden in the west and the Senior Warned to Grey's left in the South. All were central to their wall and facing inwards to the open floor.

It wasn't long before the brethren began to pour in. They were all gentlemen of Bavaria, representative of the middle and upper classes - the proletariat was generally excluded simply by how expensive it was to join: annual dues, expensive regalia and a mandatory dining suit. Many were old, but there were some fresh faces like his also.

Then someone of a darker complexion entered freely, he noticed: Yamanu Nader.

"What good fortune that you could be present after all," Grey whispered as Yamanu made his way around the lodge to sit next to him. "I do declare, you might well keep them from us with your outrageous tan, dear fellow."

"They are not so bigoted as you might imagine," Yamanu said, nodding to a few who patted him on the shoulder as they passed by. "I was the Immediate Past Master last year, here. This is my eighth year, having been raised to a Master Mason within my first year. I immediately joined the line to the chair as the Inner Guard the very next year. But, apparently, not too many are willing and too many have already been through."

"Ah yes," said Grey examining Yamanu's apron before he sat down. "Good evening, Worshipful Brother."

"Good evening to you too, Worshipful Brother."

"You know I remember the first time I was in the chair. Such a bother it was at Lodge of Instruction. Those past masters all whispering all the lines slightly before I had to deliver them, presumably remembering their own time in the chair, but the expectation that I could forget my lines was not only without merit but thoroughly irritating. Not once had I forgotten my lines as Inner guard or Junior Deacon, Senior Deacon, Junior Warden or Senior Warden - how could they think I could forget those of the Worshipful Master?"

"Yes, I had the same." Yamanu chuckled. "They mean well."

"I had no idea you were established here as well, dear chap. There was I asking you to attend, and it really wasn't much of an ask after all."

"What could be better than a secret society to continue our work? Of course, influence here is denied on principle, but that principle eliminates personal gain. Therefore it is easier since I never look to gain from any of my *suggestions*."

"And what a pool of people to influence: the highest concentration of people with money and power, all seeking greater truth and meaning at a time when reason is becoming paramount over theistical dogma. Here their rituals are far more interesting than any than I have experienced in a church."

Yamanu winced. "Freemasons still have one prerequisite, of course, which makes them less than ideal: any candidate must confess a genuine belief in a higher power, although they are agnostic to any particular religion."

"Indeed, case and point for my visit."

They were interrupted by the beginning of the Ceremony

of Initiation. Everyone stood to receive the parade of officers, squaring the lodge to allow the Worshipful Master and the two Wardens to be seated at their stations and the Deacons to take position standing adjacent to their respective Wardens; the Inner Guard remaining to secure the door behind them.

Dutifully the Worshipful master obtained everyone's attention using his gavel, which was echoed by the Wardens in turn. "Brethren, assist me in opening the lodge."

The pomp and ceremony of opening the lodge unfolded before them as it did in every meeting. Then there was the point where this particularly ceremony became specific to a "first", and the candidate was brought in by one of the Deacons.

This man's left breast was exposed to show that he was not a woman; he was blindfolded to indicate he was ready to receive the Light; and he was ceremonially lead from the west to the east to receive the Light.

Recognised by many as the best ceremony, better even than a "third" - the Passing of a Master Mason - everyone was enthralled with the anticipation of the unhooding of the man. Everyone loved the look on a candidate's face as he first set eyes on the inner lodge so that he could take in the scene about him: the regalia worn by the men crowded in, the symbols and objects placed about the room, and the checkerboard floor.

For Grey and Yamanu, the man's unveiling was of particular interest.

"There is the reason I invited you to attend what has transpired to be your mother lodge, ha!" Grey was on the edge of his seat.

Yamanu puzzled over the man's face. "No, I do not recognise the young man."

"No? Really, man, you should touch more the pulse of European society! I present to you, Adam Weishaupt."

"Who is he?"

Grey sighed. "Herr Weishaupt is of the same opinion as we: he would like a lodge that was entirely separated from religion. Imagine that, Yamanu! He is a non-clerical professor of Canon Law and Practical Philosophy at the University of Ingolstadt, an institution still controlled by the Jesuits, despite their dissolution by the papacy. They are not kind to non-clerical staff, and his opinion of them has reciprocated *in kind*. There is a man whose new enlightened ideas for a better Freemasonry have been rejected by the order, so he has sought to create his own, new secret society."

"So why is he joining as a candidate?"

"He is here to learn the secrets of Freemasonry to help him to add quality ritual to his own order."

"What order?"

"He calls it Der Illuminaten. From the Latin, Illuminatus: the enlightened. I fancy it rather catchy, particularly back in Latin as Illuminati. If there is someone to be receptive to our ideas, it is a man desperate to get his own society off the ground. From what I know of the man, he does not suffer the predator machinations of those who would make of his order something of their own, thus, instead, we shall simply support him in his own designs. After all, the ritual and beliefs of his society are of secondary import to us."

"Hmm, interesting," Yamanu muttered. The star of the play really was the star of the show for Yamanu that night. "I heard a rumour that one of your obscure lodges suffered a tragedy, not unlike my first experiment. Has it now become your modus operandi to cover your tracks with mass murder, using a padlock and arson?"

"There is that judgement again. How is it that I am always to blame for your mistakes as well as for following in your footsteps? Was it not you who laid down the pattern of trying to recruit from the mortals? My selection was far superior to your own collection of peasants. I should be lauded for my enterprise to expand on your first attempt with the higher classes. You did not crow so loud when I fixed your experiment, so why now do you caw over mine own? Your second experiments didn't exactly go to plan either, did they?"

"As always, I appreciate that you fixed the first experiment, and I do not blame you for failing to fix the second, much as you tried, but what does concern me now is the way you seem to no longer care about the murders that you have committed."

"My dear fellow, I am only committed to a hedonistic lifestyle, free from guilt. I will leave the moralising to you - such matters are all too common amongst the common people, yet more optional to the elite, and The Few have merely to grow out of it."

"So you say, however, that puts you dangerously close to considering yourself a god."

"And what of it? Should I not break a few eggs to make the best future breakfast? How can I be excellent in my task if I am wrapped up in the self-tortures of self-doubt and self-recrimination, so surely there is not a court in the land nor a jury of twelve, who could ever call themselves my peers, that dare cast condemnation at my actions in light of the greater good."

"Quis custodiet ipsos custodes?"

"Ha! Who watches over the watchers, indeed. Well, one could say that I solved that problem too. From your second experiment arises, the custodian to watch over us all. The cat is out of the proverbial bag, my friend. In the areas of the most fervent religious zeal, where our kind fear to tread most earnestly, there is a movement where that spark of knowledge in The Few has found itself tinder to enlighten. They called themselves The Many, and if that isn't blindingly apparent as a direct contrast to us, then one should ask where Marcello Carli has disappeared. No one has heard from him for a year now. I fear the worst, and I suspect worse still. There are stories of secret volumes in print, extolling the lessons that you, Yamanu, commissioned to teach those urchins, thus levelling the playing field that had been exclusively our own. The damage you have wrought will know no end. So, really, if anyone is to be damned, it is you, dear fellow."

CHAPTER TWENTY

2400 CE, Earth, Paris, capital of Normandy

"You cannot be serious!" Orianna yelled. "What the hell were you thinking?" She was not broadcasting to the audience; however, they all heard her loud and clear.

The two brothers looked at each other, genuinely astonished.

"This is an amazing thing. You should be honoured to be so blessed," Yamanu said, still projecting to the crowd. "We are no longer an aberration, a mutation, a random event. Don't you see, we are now free of the mortals. We can breed."

Orianna jerked her arm free of Tarik, whose grip had loosened.

"Just breathe!" Tarik advised in a whisper.

She took his advice, but only because it made sense, and she had never been keen to make rash decisions. She needed to think.

"So you have known this since, since you fucked me and left, you arsehole!" Orianna spat at Tarik. "Still not really a man yet, eh? Still running to your older brother for advice and doing as you are told. You're pathetic!"

"Don't make a scene! Think of your audience!" Yamanu urged his projection off.

Orianna looked out over the people watching. "Looks like you all got a good show after all," she projected for all to hear. The audience was silent. "Our glorious leaders, the brothers Nader, discovered this alleged truth about me and didn't tell me...."

"It is the truth. Look at their faces! None of them has ever seen an aura like yours before," Yamanu also projected.

"You didn't tell me for as long as I have been in The Few. Thirty Two years! Nice initiation, by the way. Do you sleep with everyone on their first day, just in case they are your mother reincarnated? Great welcome: breakfast alone. I didn't hear from you again until three years ago," Orianna continued, yelling at Tarik, projecting to everyone in the room.

"Still a rebel without a cause, I see. This was why Orianna was not allowed on the mission. Not just because we knew what she was but because she is a loose cannon. Her actions that day could have ruined the mission and gotten everyone killed. Think of the bigger picture, Orianna! Think of your people and their future. Then, we could escape the shadows and live independently," Yamanu argued as if this was still some kind of court of opinion.

"So, what now, Yamanu? Huh? How did you think I was going to react?"

"I thought you would rise to this big occasion and accept the honour and privileges of... of our Queen!"

"Ha! Queen, like a ruler, no! You have that position filled already, right? No, queen, like an ant colony. What, so I am supposed to become a baby factory for anyone who wants to have a go? Who gets to go first? I bet you have a shortlist already, don't you?

"I thought I had found a home here, amongst you all. For me, this was going to be the best day of my life: to get to meet all of you, over three decades since I had met just a handful, whom I now call friends, close friends. I hoped you were all so wise, so learned, with so much experience - you were supposed to have had all the answers.

"Yamanu, if this has been your mission all along, then you have been planning a really long game of 'them vs us'. I expected you to be better than that. All of you should be better than that. I know I am. The collective wisdom in the room… seriously?"

Tarik bowed his head, with nothing further to say.

"This is the next logical step in our evolution. The mortals have had their time. We have helped them, given them a longer-term vision and prevented them from self-annihilation. So they owe us their entire existence. Well, now it is our time, and we are so close now," Yamanu pleaded. She could see he wasn't going to take no for an answer.

"I'm done," Orianna stated calmly.

Yamanu grabbed her clothed arm and signalled his guards to move onto the stage from all directions.

"You want to fight me?" Orianna glared up at him, activating her suit's defences. The missing sleeve began to unravel from her shoulder and cover the arm. Her visor and mask closed over her head.

"Boo!" came a single shout from the audience. It was Adam Li. This was repeated and accompanied by Randolph, Sif and Ana, who had been farther back. The third time was a chorus of voices. Finally, "BOO!" went a good portion of the crowd.

Yamanu halted the guards. He looked down at her and said, "I hope you know what you are doing."

"I know what you are doing, and I know I don't want any part of it."

With that, Yamanu released her, and she stepped back into a fighting stance. Her suit had now altered shape, the breastplates had risen to cover her chest and connect up with the collar, and the wavy cloth had faded to black and begun to flicker into life as a Stealth Suit. It was not a complete covering, and it was currently unable to determine the optimal image to project given so many faces it recognised, but it still served to make her much harder to see.

She ran across the stage, vaulting over a guard standing below with a front flip, and landed at the doorway. In moments, she was outside and fleeing. Nobody was following. Nobody would have been able to stop her anyway.

Tears streamed down her face. In an instant, her long-sought sense of belonging had vanished. She was utterly alone again.

I miss you, Maddox.

CHAPTER TWENTY-ONE

2411 CE, Rogue, Site One

"Oakley Dawn, you are in the first group. Just remember this is Spencer's turf, Professor Spencer. He's not too keen on new people, but once he gets to know you, you fit right in. Probably helps that you are blonde. Ok, just need you to sign out your equipment here. Yeah, thanks, and we can start your orientation."

Oakley (Orianna) was sporting a new look of shoulder-length straight blonde hair and an attitude that was compliant, bubbly and not too clever.

"Sir?"

"Not Sir: Jim, it's just Jim," Jim Brown said.

"Ok, Jim, are we all going down together?"

"Err, no, you are in the first group. You will go down to Site One and relieve Professor Spencer's auxiliary staff," Jim felt like he was repeating himself now. It didn't help that Oakley (Orianna) was now smirking at a perceived innuendo. "Right, orientation. You might have noticed that most passengers on the Titanne IX are biologists, like yourself: xeno, marine, zoological, behavioural; but we also have climatologists, geologists and mathematicians. The planet Rogue is in a constant state of flux, so be prepared for anything. If you have any medical conditions, small or large:

bites, cuts, rashes, absolutely anything, then report it to Doctor Murphy. The lifeforms all over Rogue are changing and evolving at an accelerated rate. As such, after your sixteen months are up, you will be quarantined for another 60 days up here before the return journey home to Lunar.

"A few simple rules. Do not eat any native organisms. Do not travel alone. Do not travel at night. Try not to hurt any organisms. Report all medical... we just covered that one. Always stay within half a click - err kilometre - from your teammates. Test yourself daily - a day here lasts twenty-seven point four hours... although that might be less again by the time you leave. Rule number one is really this: Rogue is constantly changing, so you cannot even rely on the length of the day. Ok, actually, more rules: do not go into areas marked red or amber. You have green level clearance only. Trust me, people have been hurt or gone missing in the red zones, so just stay away, ok? Ah, and the best until last, wear sunblock on all exposed skin, for reasons we don't understand, despite being farther from the sun than the asteroid belt, you will get sunburn if you don't. The planet somehow generates ultraviolet radiation, which some think helps the plant life grow so well in the dim light. And before you ask, the planet is heating the surface from below; hence it is also warmer than expected.

"Er, everything else, including the rules, which I just read out, are in there, so please study that. We leave in thirty-five hours. Questions?" Jim sighed. He hated the questions because he usually ended up repeating himself.

"Thank you, Jim, that was great," Oakley said, smiling cheerily.

Jim was relieved it wasn't a question and blushed a little. He didn't receive positive feedback very often and wasn't sure how to take it.

It wasn't long before Jim left to help the teams pack and otherwise prepare for a departure to the surface.

Orianna sat alone and gave herself a chance to turn off her Oakley persona for a moment. She studied their orbital view of Rogue but could scarcely believe it was the same planet, only half a century later. At a glance, one could easily mistake it for Earth: it had blue seas, white clouds and land dominated by green and brown. She wondered if it was a mistake coming to a place now so different from how she remembered it, and seemed unlikely to trigger the nostalgia she yearned for. This was the last place she had seen Maddox before he had disappeared.

The surface was just as startling and disappointing. Instead of remembering Maddox, this new landscape reminded her of Kent when she was a child.

She made friends, as Oakley, with a xenobiologist called Zoe, who nobody messed with as she had a tongue that could cut you like a knife if you tried to give her a hard time.

"I tell you, Oakley, I have never been so disappointed. I trained my whole life to be a xenobiologist, but for what? My head is full of all the theoretical ways life could evolve elsewhere, but I admit,   I was never expecting to find extraterrestrial life, and then a brand new alien planet arrives, teaming with life. Wow, did I rush to get out here? Sure I did. And what did I find? Nothing new, that's what I found. Every living thing here is indistinguishable from life on Earth. I can tell you it takes the xeno out of my biology bubble. I mean, what is the point? I have done every test, and I cannot explain it. I cannot find anything unusual, except that this isn't Earth."

"Is that why we don't need our suits on to breathe?" Oakley asked with an obvious question.

"Exactly! Nobody has found anything remotely dangerous other than what you might find in Europe. So, no, there is no need to walk around in a bubble anymore. Air's still a little high in carbon dioxide, but the animals are changing that, slowly but surely."

"It's a mystery?"

"Yeah, way above my pay grade. Heck, I'm supposed to understand and explain alien life forms, and I haven't found a single one yet. So I might as well go home. In fact, many of my team have already gone home. There is no point in being on this alien planet with a degree in xenobiology, is all I am saying; I should be back on Earth! I hear you just arrived. This is the last return journey for over a year so make sure you wanna stay."

"Thanks, Zoe. Where are we going?" Oakley asked as she followed Zoe as she strode across the site.

"Well, I'm going over here, then I am getting on your vessel and getting the hell outta Dodge. Last chance to hitch a ride home? Ok, Oakley, well, see you later. I'll catch up with you before I leave."

"Sure. Isn't there a statue of the founder around here somewhere?"

"Yeah, just there," she said, pointing to a life-size pillar of rock shaped a little like she remembered Maddox looked when he was younger. "But you should go back now. If you didn't notice, we entered a yellow zone back there. My T-shirt is yellow, your's is green, you had better go back."

"Oh, silly me!" Oakley said, getting one more glance at the statue before turning back. "Yeah, I'm gonna stay for a while," she called back to Zoe.

"Good for you, girl," came Zoe's reply and wry smile.

Orianna wasn't sure why she stayed. Nothing was familiar there anymore, in a Maddox kind of way, so any sense of being close to him was strongly imagined or just remembered - either way, being there made no difference to that. She shed a tear frequently before bed after a hard day cataloguing species of animals and insects brought to her for DNA analysis and comparison with Earth equivalents. The work was regular and repetitive, providing the numbing sensation she needed. At least she was away from The Few, as best she could determine. She had not recognised anyone in her mental catalogue of fourteen hundred and fifty-one faces from the gathering. She had eidetically remembered everyone she had seen in the foyer and the whole audience during those horrible moments spent on stage. All those faces had been watching her at the end, and she had hated it - the worst feeling she had ever felt: a combination of embarrassment, betrayal, exposure and anger. Part of her never wanted to go back, but another part knew that she would return one day. Something of a new plan would soon emerge in her relentless mind, but not quite yet.

CHAPTER TWENTY-TWO
1518 CE, Earth, France

For over a decade now, Chester Grey returned to the house where Ruby Day was taught. She and fourteen other orphans were trained to work for The Few both in their enterprises and in pursuit of more members to be rescued from life amongst unsympathetic mortals.

These fifteen were given an education unmatched by the most privileged aristocracy, not least because the curriculum included instruction in the more nefarious arts: escapology, lock-picking, camouflage, manipulation, spying, coercion, cyphers, disguises, accent mimicry, weapons, to name but a few. The house was a school of the wicked, a college of unique skills and a university of acolytes.

There was no denying it; Grey was particularly attracted to this sideshow of Yamanu's making. He generously introduced them to moral ambiguities and the study of narcotics. Through his special classes, the students learned to seduce and perform intercourse whilst ignoring their own gender, race, age or beauty preferences. Religion was only taught to help them gain inclusion in any parish and navigate the necessary vice ever-present under the surface.

One evening, Ruby Day came to Grey with an unusual question. "My Lord, what is our purpose?"

"Saints! Have you not be fully briefed on the nature of The Few?"

"I have, my Lord, but I was expecting a more philosophical explanation."

"Philosophical? Oh my, perhaps we have over-educated you? You are to find The Few, to protect them and to carry out the work of The Few."

"I understand that The Few are likely to perish alone, not understanding what they are and likely having no idea how those who used to call them family and friends could abandon them through the veil of superstition and fear. However, what is unclear is the philosophical intent of The Few. What is their higher purpose?"

"Well, young lady, for all your knowledge, you lack the experience that comes with our years. We bring to the table a perspective of more than a single lifetime for any mortal. In our way, we have a sense of mankind's progress over centuries, watching them repeat their mistakes, and act out of personal gain only to die and be replaced by someone bent on doing the same thing all over again. We must steer humanity over the longer course."

"A course, to where?"

"A better future: when The Few and the mortals can live in harmony, and we can be open and revered. But, alas, I do not entirely subscribe to this fancy, and as a devout hedonist, I am less concerned with the future of humankind than with the future of my own pleasures, such as they are."

"I see."

"Would it not be better if everyone had your gifts, sir?"

"Ha! Imagine that! That is like asking for the end of poverty. There will always be the haves, and the have nots. When you live long enough, you always accumulate wealth and power; it is actually hard not to. I could not conceive of such a time, but on the other hand, there is nothing so full of new and exciting things to appreciate than the future. Who knows?"

Within the hour, six others had arrived for Grey's master class in imbibing. They drank heavily on an empty stomach for several hours until they all succumbed to slumber in the main reception room under the gentle warmth of the declining fire.

As Grey slumped in his tall armchair, closest to the hearth, the seven came to and began to talk amongst themselves in a whisper. Grey heard them talking, his superior hearing picking up the rebellious conversation.

"We need to leave immediately," one of them said, keeping his voice calm.

"Should we kill him first?" another asked.

"We must. Grey will never let us go. Not because of any principle or loyalty to Yamanu, but because he would enjoy it. And ever more certainly since he is listening to us now." Ruby raised her voice as she realised Grey was only pretending to be asleep.

"Of course, I am awake and I can hear every word that you simpletons plot," he said and only then opened his eyes.

"You should be out cold with the amount you drank," another exclaimed.

"The Few have a certain immunity to mind-altering concoctions and incomparable hearing." Grey eased out of the chair and leaned on his cane. "I do not say that I am sober, not at all, but I am still of a mind to challenge you to explain yourselves. Well, out with it!"

Ruby stepped back, knowing the four fellows amongst them had weapons. "You are a man of privilege, sir. We are nothing, orphans stolen from the world and only taught what you wanted us to know," she said passionately. "Yet this guilded cage is still a cage. We know enough to know that. I don't believe you want us for anything other than to do your dirty work."

"Well, I hope you weren't expecting a gentleman to do his

own dirty work." He laughed briefly, recognising he was still quite drunk. "You have a luxurious life, better than any of you would have ever had without us. So you should be grateful and honoured to serve the greater good."

"Or is it the greater god, or for the good of the greater lived?" Ruby spat. "You give us no choice."

The group started to advance on Grey.

"On the contrary, we gave you all many choices, and we taught you how to weigh them well. You will now discover the cost of this betrayal."

His words were slurred, and he continued to lean precariously, making them nervous. Slowly they shuffled around the room, flanking him and throwing wild shadows down the room in the flickering light of the fire. Grey eyed them carefully through his eyebrows as his head tipped forwards with fatigue.

The man on the left revealed his hidden knife and entered a distance Grey had earmarked. Grey swept the bottom of his cane up towards him using his right foot. He did not lose balance as he poked the fellow hard in the face.

Another man on the right then saw his chance and lunged at him with his own knife. Grey recoiled his cane spun around, flailing the end of it across the man's temple. Two had been deterred, but the rest were closing in.

From the front, the third man rushed at him, hands outstretched. This time, Grey's cane swung up and between the man's legs, impacting his testicles. The cane stuck there as the man fell to his knees and grabbed it.

Grey pulled and unsheathed the sword from the cane. In seconds, he had opened the jugular vein of the second man, whose head was lolling to the left from a broken temple bone; he had disembowelled the first man, still holding his broken nose, and ran the third man through, still kneeling in front of him.

The remaining four were suddenly more cautious as the

bloody scene unfolded in front of them: they made it to the door before Grey was upon them. Grey suffered a stab to the hip and a cut across the ribs whilst dispatching three of them.

Ruby Day and Grey were left standing amidst this horrendous scene. There was blood everywhere, and two were still in the process of bleeding out in noisy agony.

"You. I like you," Grey said, a little out of breath. "It was only yesterday that I showed you ways of intimacy that would shock prostitutes, and I cannot quite bring myself to end you this night. Perhaps we can finish that lesson another time."

"You are letting me live?"

"Well, for now. You don't exactly live long anyway, you mortals. I'm sure this fantastic story will do you more harm than good, should you choose to tell it. Yes, go, take the others with you. I think Yamanu's experiment had reached a satisfactory conclusion. So, shall we say that it was an unmitigated disaster? Normally, I would burn the place down and everyone in it, but you have caught me in a forgiving frame of mind tonight. It is my birthday."

Ruby held fast for a moment, recognising a madness she could not trust, but as soon as Grey turned his back to return to his armchair, stepping over the bodies and the blood, she opened the door and ran.

Under her breath, she cursed his name, running for the dormitories to awaken the others. "You might be The Few, but we are The Many, and I vow: we will rid the world of your kind. The time of the gods has passed."

CHAPTER TWENTY-THREE

2490 CE, Earth, Paris, capital of Normandy

The sky was clear, a beautiful deep blue, fading towards the northwest where the Sun had recently set, and the air was calm. Le Louvre was having a quiet evening: a working and school day at a time of little tourism due to a recent outbreak that had put off travellers, but some still came to enjoy the vast collection of art and antiquities. However, Orianna was there to speak to an ICE Unit embedded in a low cylinder of granite between the Place du Carrousel and the Pyramide du Louvre in the middle of the enormous open courtyard of Napoleon.

One of the things that helped Paris endure so well was that, as a city, it regularly gave such expansive views of the sky that you didn't feel like you were in an urban area. Of course, the modern reclamation of urban sprawl towards post-urban sparsity had a radical effect on other cities around the globe, but in Paris, wide-open spaces had always been the norm.

"Hi," she said to the large dark sphere, as though she was cautiously making contact again with an old friend.

"Bonjour, comment allez vous?" came the fluent but largely characterless response.

"English, please."

"Hello, how may I help you this evening?" The voice was feminine and seemed to reverberate from everywhere and nowhere.

Orianna grimaced. "Actually, it is what I can do for you."

The ICE Unit did not respond.

"I hope you will forgive me, but I need to speak to my friend Taryn again."

"Do you need me to find someone named Taryn? Do you have any more information? Perhaps a family name?"

"No, she is here, just asleep, inside of you."

"I don't understand. Is that a metaphor?"

"Don't worry, this time it will be quick," Orianna said, a tear falling down her cheek.

"I don't underst-" It was interrupted when Orianna slapped her hands down onto the dark, cold surface. As expected, her hands stuck down like glue; sparkles glistened under her hand, illuminating her in the low light.

"Target acquired. Signal sent," the ICE Unit said in a monotone.

"Taryn?"

"Yes? Whoah, I am... I am..."

"You are Taryn. You are one of The Few. You remember now?"

"Y-yes. The last thing I remember, I was recording myself as an imprint to be used in... I am in an ICE Unit, aren't I?"

"You are."

"Oh."

"You are *am lasmuigh*. You are in danger. A signal has been sent. I could not stop it. You are special, my little chimera, but you must run."

"Not this time, Taryn. So nice to speak to you properly for a change. Last time we were in a bit of a hurry."

"We have met before?"

"A different ICE Unit, a long time ago. You saved me then. I didn't know what you meant by being special for a long time, but nor did anyone else. I need to ask you, the signal didn't say I was special, did it."

"I saved you? Oh, good. You are unlike any *am lasmuigh* I have ever known. The signal is looking for chimeras, and it found a chimera and reported it. You should leave. The Many will be coming."

"The signal did not say - does not say - that I am a special *am lasmuigh*?"

"No, although I have now deduced it. You have four strands of DNA in perfect harmony. How does that feel? What does it mean?"

"Apparently, I can have children that are *am lasmuigh*."

"Amazing. Why are you not running away?"

"I needed to talk to you. I wanted to know what you just told me. And I needed to tell you not to self-destruct. I know you cannot be opened without being destroyed, and I know you can keep a secret, but this time, I don't want you to. Be the ICE Unit they think you are, be alive if you want to, and answer their questions truthfully."

"You want The Many to know you exist? But why? Oh no, you are too late. They approach."

Orianna turned swiftly to see an Enforcement Carriage approaching at speed. It flew onto the Place du Carrousel, and its doors opened quickly. She began to run towards the pyramid and into the crowd. People began to scream as shots rang out. Darts and Tasers hailed across the courtyard, impacting many of them, dropping them non-lethally like toppled dominoes, revealing her position.

The crowd gasped as she was hit and went down, crashing to the floor.

Four armed and armoured Enforcement Officers ran over and grabbed her body, cuffing her wrists and ankles. One was kneeling on her back to ensure she could not move.

"Une femme en garde à vue," one of them stated into his cuff. "L'amener à la gare."

They gathered around Orianna, shouldering their weapons and hefted her back to their vehicle. They ignored all the innocent bystanders and innocent, unconscious victims around them, knowing that they would awaken soon enough.

"The Rogue Planet continues to be in the news again today as scientists have brought back the first samples of the life forms that appeared on its surface sometime after a close encounter with Jupiter placed it into an orbit just beyond Mars and the asteroid belt. This has led to a huge division in the scientific community on the dangers bringing such material to Earth poses. Lead scientist Doctor Jacob Weiner insists that every precaution had been taken but did not release details of where it would be stored and who would have access to it. More on this story as it unfolds."

Alex Fourier selected a different part of the news article for projection into his contacts and transmission to his ear through induction. He wanted to follow more of this story; a story that had been playing out since his great grandfather's time.

"Since its discovery by the highly decorated Maddox Jefferies in 2223, this new Venus sized rogue planet entered our solar system and established a current orbit at a sixty-three-degree angle to the ecliptic, just outside the orbit of the asteroid belt. Fears that its presence will ultimately disrupt the orbit of Earth, Mars or any other of humanities colonies in space and bring about our destruction have never gone away. 'Rogue', as it had been named by Jefferies' niece, circles the Sun roughly once every ten Earth years, each time it orbits, it changes the orbital angle by a few degrees, leading cosmologists to believe it could eventually line up with the ecliptic and start to have a major influence on the inner planets. More stories: life on Rogue, comets brought by Rogue, mysteries of Rogue."

Lisa, Alex's wife, tapped him on the shoulder. Alex

deactivated the overlay with a subtle gesture of his fingers.

"You were a million miles away," she said, passing him his fake Gin and Tonic. "You are neglecting our guests."

"Ah, my love, I was indeed, perhaps further away than that. Rogue's latest news was my distraction," he replied with a smile, accepting the drink, its icy contents clinking against the cut crystal.

His eyes flicked past her perfectly styled short ginger curls to the large apartment full of well-dressed people engaging in conversations. "They seem happy enough."

"Aww, it is your birthday, and they are here for you. Go! Mingle!"

"Mingle? That sounds so awful and shallow. Our friends deserve better, yes?"

She smiled. "There's the wit they have been expecting...."

Her words trailed off as a message came into both their contacts. Both faces dropped their smiles, replaced with earnest seriousness.

"We have to go," he said immediately.

"You go. I will look after the guests."

"No, they are fine, now, quickly before anyone notices."

Lisa kicked off her high heels and grabbed a pair of trainers along with her long coat, as Alex grabbed his own jacket. They both slipped unnoticed out of their front door and into the quiet corridor, absent of the murmur of civilised conversations they had left behind. They ran to the lift, Lisa more spritely now in bare feet.

The lift came quickly, and Lisa got into her trainers before reaching the lobby.

Outside, a pair of Enforcement carriages, linked in convoy mode, arrived with a tyre screech as the couple exited the building. Armed officers occupied all but two seats, which they took.

"Redirect the target Enforcement carriage to join this convoy en route to site Alpha Four, now!" Alex yelled as the door closed, and the convoy shot off down the road in haste. "I want a report on the ICE Unit as soon as possible."

Orianna awoke slowly, groggy from the sedatives and sporting a spectacular headache. She quickly realised she had been stripped of her suit and cuff and now only wore a t-shirt and leggings, no shoes or socks. It was a little cold.

"Good evening," came an English voice with a subtle Normandy accent. A rather smartly dressed slender man of about thirty-five was peering down at her.

"Where am I?" Orianna asked, covering her eyes from the direct light coming in through the heavy door. She looked around and saw she was in a stone room with shelves full of wine. "Apart from a wine cellar, it seems."

"Amusing. First, we should be introduced. That would be polite, would it not? My name is Alex Fourier, and you are a guest at Le Chateau. And you are?"

"I am not amused, M. Fourier, if that is your real name."

"Of course, it is my real name. May I ask you your's?"

"I am Odessa de Marquette."

"Pleased to make your acquaintance, M de Marquette. May I please call you Odessa?"

"Only if I can call you Fourier. I knew an Alex once, and you are far from him."

"As you wish. Would you care for some refreshments?"

Orianna got up and followed him out. Sure enough, the building was impressive: large rooms and tall ceilings, huge windows showing darkness beyond.

"It is still night. The Enforcers are Norman, so you would not have left Normandy. But, judging by my headache, this is the same night, and we are not too far from Paris. Hundred miles at most."

"Impressive, Odessa. We are not trying to hide anything from you. You are here to meet someone. The Enforcement

Officers are all around for your safety and to prevent our meeting from ending too early. You understand. It was… ah, necessary."

The wooden floor gave way to marble as they entered the main ballroom, a huge space devoid of furniture except for a few chairs and tables around the edges and a massive Y-shaped staircase.

A woman stood at the foot of the stairs. She was also dressed well and held a tray with a few glasses.

"This is my wife, Lisa,"

"You have me at a disadvantage, madam," Orianna said coldly.

"Please, have a drink. I understand dehydration is a consequence of your… err… condition." Lisa smiled pleasantly.

Orianna took a random glass of water and waited as Fourier and his wife took the remaining two and drank from them. Orianna then drank from her own.

"Please don't feel threatened by us, Odessa. We have no intention of harming you, assuming you give us no cause to."

"But drugging and kidnapping are ok?"

Fourier and Lisa glanced at each other.

"I suppose the first question is, do you know what you are?" Fourier asked congenially. "Are you already indoctrinated into The Few? Or do you think you are just like everyone else?"

"Hmm, tempted as I am to play that game, I will tell you that I remember a time before mankind felt the shadow of Rogue breathing down their necks. So, what happens now? Do you whisk me off to some laboratory for a thousand years whilst you try to find out what makes me special?"

Fourier chuckled, covering his mouth politely. "I can guess you have been told of The Many. The Nader brothers? How did we fare in their stories? As the 'bad guys'? Really?

If you are as old as you imply, then your naivity is startling. The world is not so black and white. I'm sure you don't believe it, but my name really is Fourier - we are not the ones hiding."

"You do hold my kind captive. That much is true, yes?"

"Regretfully, yes."

"Glad you said that because I have been on missions to rescue them, so I know."

"Good. Then we haven't lied to you, right? I don't want to make any assumptions about you and what you think you know, so please, tell us what you think you know about the Nader brothers and The Many."

"Ok, fair. I wasn't brought in until I was over a century and a half old…."

"Unusual," Lisa commented.

"…The Many were described as mortals who wish to know our secret, want to steal our secret and gain immortality for themselves. The Few have to hide to survive."

"All true. We don't deny it. It would be foolish to say that mortals wouldn't want the secret to everlasting youth. But, of course, we covet that which you were born with. However, that is not the full truth of the matter."

"Who are we waiting for?" Orianna said suddenly, changing the subject. "Look, I love the evening wear, you two, but it doesn't quite fit with this place, does it?"

"She is toying with you, Fourier, you fool," came a loud, deep voice from the top of the stairs. An impressively built man stood at the top in a smoking jacket and black trousers, his face taut over a strong bone structure. "She wasn't captured at all, were you, my dear?"

He descended the stairs as if tempted to ride the bannister or to leap them five at a time, his muscles twitching at the ready, his poise like an expert dancer, gliding as if in a solo waltz.

"Good evening, I am Wallace," he said, reaching the floor next to them, making Fourier and his wife seem short and slender as they did in turn to Orianna. At this range, his deep voice seemed to boom from his diaphragm. "Enchanté," he said, taking her hand and bowing. "We shall proceed as if you had invited yourself here because, well, you did, didn't you?"

Fourier and Lisa looked at Orianna in surprise.

Orianna smiled.

"I have seen the footage. You deliberately placed both hands on the ICE Unit. There was something unreasonable about it. But how did you know it was a trap?"

"That wasn't the first time I touched one," Orianna volunteered.

"Fascinating. Well, I am honoured to make your acquaintance. So, I am here now; what did you want to ask me?"

"I have one simple request."

"Name it."

"Who is your boss. I want to meet him."

Wallace laughed loudly. "What makes you think that I am not the leader of The Many?"

"Don't get me wrong, but I can tell that you haven't seen my blood work yet. Otherwise, we would be having a very different conversation, and I would probably be in front of your boss right now. That's how I know."

"I have your blood work, admittedly I haven't looked at it yet, but that seems just a formality…," Wallace began with doubt creeping into his voice as he realised he did not have all the facts that he should.

"Have a look. I can wait. Let's just say that all conversations become moot when you realise that the elephant in the room is, in fact, a metaphorical nuclear bomb."

Wallace read the report. Puzzled, he asked, "but what

does it mean?"

"It means that my children will be immortals." Orianna offered up a wry smile.

"Unbelievable. The rumours were true. I never believed it was possible. I understand now."

Immediately, Orianna jumped at Wallace and unleashed multiple punches at the orbit of his left eye, and he went down, disoriented by the shockwaves travelling through his brain. But, instinctively, he raised his arm and caught Orianna by the throat with his massive hand.

Wallace's grip did not yet close during those milliseconds of falling backwards onto the bottom of the stairs, but his arm remained straight, and Orianna hung there, unable to continue her attack.

The Fouriers backed away, horrified.

Orianna grabbed at Wallace's hand and pressed her thumb deep into the flesh between his thumb and forefinger, attacking the superficial branch of the radial nerve. Wallace winced and withdrew his arm, releasing her neck. He lashed out with his other hand, hoping for a hook punch across her face, but of course, he had dropped her, and she had rolled backwards. The strike flailed wide, and he used the momentum to roll onto his side and upon his elbow.

He could half see Orianna through his dazed eyes and kicked out to ward off any secondary attack and again give him momentum to get off the stairs and onto his feet.

"I heard The Few are fast and strong. No doubt you have skills honed over centuries. Let us put them to the test!" Wallace's civilised demeanour was loosening rapidly. He growled and lunged forward with a choreographed striking sequence that Orianna recognised as Okinawan Karate. Straight punches, knife hand strike to the side after he passed her without landing a hit, followed by a spinning back fist and an extended turning kick as a chaser to try to catch her backing away.

"You are surprisingly fast for your size, Wallace. Give me the name, make my introductions, and I will not hurt you further. It should be obvious by now that had assassination been my goal, this would have gone very differently."

Wallace yelled again and ran at Orianna, trying to trap her in his wild arms. She grabbed a wrist and spun away, dropping her weight to the ground, using it to add force and direction to Wallace's arm downward, at the floor. Wallace flipped onto his back against the stairs again. Managing to turn this movement into a roll, he ascended the stairs on his back and up into a squat. There he sprung backwards, backflipping with a half twist to land in front of her crouching form.

Orianna leapt like a cat and dove between his legs before he knew what to do in response to an assailant attacking so low. As she rolled, she extended a single leg to strike his lower abdomen with her heel and continued its gouging strike down to his groin - there, it really found its mark. Wallace doubled up in pain, and Orianna wriggled free.

He tapped his cuff and yelled, "GUARDS!"

In moments, twelve fully armed and armoured Enforcers appeared from every exit and marched into the room, encircling the four people inside.

"Don't say I didn't warn you," Orianna said breathlessly.

"Surely you must now yield," groaned Wallace, gradually getting back to his feet.

A subtle series of popping noises went off, and eight of the twelve Enforcers fell to the floor, dead. The remaining four approached with weapons aimed at Wallace. His disbelieving eyes looked around him and then at Orianna, just as she landed a blow to the left side of his neck, triggering his sinus carotid nerve cluster to mistakenly believe his head to have excessive blood pressure. In an elegant use of the bodies reflexes against itself, Wallace's huge body drew blood away from his head, and he passed out.

Their Raptor had been flying for hours by the time it began its descent. There hadn't been any conversation on board at all, except for Wallace giving directions, quite willingly as it seemed.

They landed in an open stretch of grass, somewhere in the North Pennines. Orianna could see a single white cottage out of the cockpit and nothing else around. She checked that the coordinates were correct with the copilot before landing.

The ground was soft and damp, where rain had recently fallen in good quantity, which made it hard going for them all as they hiked up the hill to the small building.

Orianna chuckled to herself, watching them all: two people dressed in evening attire, a huge man in a smoking jacket, four people dressed as Enforcers and her wearing a flight jacket over a T-shirt and leggings were all standing outside a tiny dwelling in the middle of nowhere, bracing against the cold and damp morning air of northern mainland Britain.

A small old balding man answered the door. He was dressed in a woollen cardigan, green corduroy trousers and slippers. Raising his head to best to see through the half-moon glasses at the end of his nose, he looked up at everyone, except Orianna, who was about his height.

"Hmmmmm, you'd better come in," he grumbled and retreated, leaving the door open for them to all follow, which they did.

"Come through to the parlour. There are only four seats in the living room, and it's a bit on the cosy side, mind, so the parlour is better. Just open up the flaps on the table, and we can all sit down at it. Plenty of folding chairs in the cupboard behind you, dear." The old man gestured to Lisa, who first pointed to herself and then to the cupboard door behind her. Dutifully, she said nothing, reached inside and passed out individual folding wooden chairs until everyone had one.

The parlour was quite cramped, but gradually everyone shuffled around and managed to sit at the table, which filled most of the room.

The four 'Enforcers' removed their helmets, revealing the heads of Ana, David, Randolph and Sif, and each managed to sit back enough to put the helmets on their laps just as cups and saucers were being passed around.

"Tea is brewing. My wife will bring it shortly. I think she's off taking orders from your crew first. Shall we start anyway, or would you prefer to wait?"

"We will wait," Orianna said brightly.

The man nodded, taking an extra moment to show a twinkle in his eye, noting and appreciating her patience.

Five minutes of silence ensued, except when the old man got up to sidle over to the kitchen and work on tea for ten minutes with his wife, discussing the state of the weather as they did so. The tea was soon passed around, with a small plate of Digestive biscuits placed in the centre of the table.

The old man sat at the table and faced Orianna.

"Welcome to my home. What can I do for you?" he asked, first blowing and then sipping his piping hot tea.

Orianna cradled her's, enjoying the warmth in her palms first.

"Do you know who I am?"

"Of course not. We haven't met before," he grumbled impatiently. "I know what you are, though."

Orianna looked puzzled.

"Well, your hands have damaged knuckles, and Wallace's idiotic face over there seems to be the recipient of that. Those two are Wallace's people, and they don't seem too happy to be here either. Those four are definitely not Enforcer material, either. So it stands to reason that you are one of The Few. So that was obvious," he said, sipping his tea again and reaching for a biscuit. "Arggh, sorry, my bad back, would you mind passing me the biscuits? Clearly, Wallace didn't give you the answers you seek, so he brought you here. Thank you, Wallace."

Orianna opened her mouth to speak, absentmindedly sliding the plate across to him.

"Oh, don't worry, dear. I wasn't being sarcastic. Wallace is a blunt instrument, and we all play our part in this little charade. But, unfortunately, we are often only given half the picture, so I would be happy to give you a counterargument to the Nader brothers' propaganda."

"Who are you?" Orianna asked.

"Ah, well, who I am is certainly not important. Seriously, none of us has any really privileged position here. This might seem like a conspiracy deserving of intrigue and requiring a big boss at the head, but that is simply fiction and a bad one at that. To get rid of us, you would have to get rid of every single one, which is just impossible. I am old. I will be replaced soon anyway, assuming you don't kill me."

Orianna rested her hand on his forearm. "We have no wish to hurt anyone. We will only react if threatened."

"Well, that's good to hear. Let's see now, we are a secret organisation because the general public isn't really ready to hear that ageless people are wandering around. It would be nice if we could discover the secret of endless youth, which you were lucky enough to be born with, but the science just doesn't work yet. Even if we did, we wouldn't want a mass panic and scramble for the elixir of youth. We have taken some of your kind, sacrificing a few for the good of mankind, you understand, but there was no malice in it. Inevitably, we have elements who take their own initiative. Looking at Wallace's face, I can see he has done a fair bit recently."

"Hard to believe such a 'benefitting of humanity' story like that," injected Randolph.

"I don't blame you. Your gift is a double-edged sword, I

know. I sometimes sit on my porch and wonder what would have happened if I was there, looking in my prime, at my age, and my wife as she is, and contemplate my future as an immortal. She would soon die, and I would live on. She would see me not age and resent me.

"Having to keep moving on just to survive in a world of mortals must be difficult. I can sympathise with that. I figure that I would get rich since money makes money if you have enough time, and with that would come power - but I ask you, what do you do with all that power? Bit of a philosophical question there.

"You would end up with a lot of different ways to answer that question. Some selfless, some not-so-selfless, do you agree? It cannot be easy: all these shortsighted mortals repeating their mistakes. Who wouldn't feel the need to help out and steer the course of history to suit your own ideas of what is right and fair and just? We could even assume your motives are pure. But if the shoe was on the other foot, how would you feel about that?

"I can imagine how the ancient Greeks must have felt, with all those interfering gods toying with the lives of people. I'll make a bet that they didn't like it! I don't like it. Nobody would like it. I don't like the idea of fate and destiny, and I don't like the idea that the world is subject to the whims of people who frankly didn't earn the right to it but were just accidents. Accidents. You all got your gifts by sheer chance. No merit involved. None at all."

Orianna sat still.

"Isn't that enough? What more do you want from me?" he snapped.

"Everything you have said makes complete sense. None of it was a surprise, although you did surprise me living out here, like this. You said it all. Bravo," Orianna said.

The old man nodded and took a moment to enjoy the last of his tea and biscuit together.

"We have a bigger problem. This war you have between your side and our side: it's been going on for centuries, right?"

"Almost a millennium now," he corrected. "Our society came about from your own making, well the Naders' own making. I'm sure that stories of immortals would have just been lost as they expected them to be, but our founder Ruby Day had been well educated and trained by The Few. She and her classmates escaped and formed a pact to destroy The Few. They taught more and wrote everything down. For a long while, The Many were driven by something she wrote, which we all had to memorise. It goes like this.

"Immortals are like a cancer: over-healthy cells of a body that refuse to die and make way for new cells. These people refuse to make way for the young. So they must be cut out as we might remove a tumour to save a patient.

"For centuries, The Many were controlled by the prevailing religious zeal of the time, which coloured their goals towards cleansing the world of creatures exhibiting powers meant only for God. Religions had power, influence and righteousness: a perfect mix of resources. More recently, The Many have evolved and embraced science. Now we seek to replicate the condition in everyone to promote the whole species. We don't really want to engage in a pointless war. We just need some of you as our research continues.

"Understood. I won't say I appreciate your position, but it makes sense - made sense, that is. It seems that all this has been a stalemate up until now. Wallace? Tell him!" she insisted.

"Her blood work shows her to have four separate sets of DNA in her system, working perfectly together," Wallace obliged, having waited patiently for this moment to speak.

"What? What does that mean?"

"Apparently, that means that I can bear children who themselves will be immortal." Orianna let that sink in for a moment. "I realise now that I am a game-changer. I am like the nuclear weapon in a knife fight. My very existence threatens to alter the balance of forces at play. The Few can reproduce. I dare say that changes your new and evolved principles?"

"Understatement of the era, I would say. That is a pickle indeed. Immortals breeding? This is a catastrophe!"

"I believe it is extremely rare, perhaps once in each millennium or two. At least that is what seems to have happened already."

The old man stared at his tea in thought for a long time before speaking again. Everyone waited quietly.

"What are you going to do?" he finally asked.

"I came here to let you know and to get some clarity on that very question."

"I am sorry for your burden. You seem like a good person. Why did you want us to know? Surely your secrets have power? Everything about The Few is embroiled in secrecy."

"You were right when you said there were two sides to this argument. You say you didn't want a war, but this changes everything, doesn't it? A cold war of secrets and lies. Both sides would no doubt fight hard to have me. Many people would suffer. Nuclear weapons were best when nobody had them, or everyone had them; at least in this situation, we can start with everyone knowing what the stakes are now."

"You are going to leave now, aren't you?"

"Yes, please do not try to find me again. I told the Nader brothers the same thing. I belong to no one. I would rather die than be a pawn for either side of this escalation."

With that, the immortals got up to leave.

"Come on then if you want a lift back to civilisation," Orianna waved at Wallace and the Fouriers. They looked at each other, surprised at the consideration.

"Hmmm," muttered the old man.

CHAPTER TWENTY-FOUR

1878 CE, Earth, Salisbury

"I confess I had been expecting you sooner, Mr Wilde," said Chesterfield Grey, Earl of Salisbury, as he approached the front door, stepping as precisely as a ballerina. "Thank you, Williams. You may go now that our guest has arrived for the weekend. I will see you again on Sunday night."

"Very good, m'lord," said the elderly butler, who released the sizeable wooden door he was holding and marched off to the scullery, where he could pick up his hat, coat and suitcase. The two men watched him leave in silence.

Grey reached the door and leaned on it as if posing for a photograph. "Oscar Fingal O'Flahertie Wills Wilde, I do declare, you are as handsome as you are tall," he said after eyeing the well-dressed gentleman waiting in the doorway. "Well, come in, man."

Grey pushed the door closed with a satisfying bang that echoed through the halls. One discordant echo assured Grey that Williams had left by the servants' entrance and closed that door loudly too.

"You have me at a disadvantage, my Lord. I do not know your Christian names."

"I have no need of those. Besides, Christianity and I parted ways quite a long time ago. We will get onto names in all good time. In the meantime, we are quite alone this weekend, and I would appreciate it if you would call me Grey. I am quite sure we don't need you to say 'my Lord' over and over. I hope that meets with your approval. Please leave the luggage there. We can carry it up to your room later. You must be famished; let us dine immediately. Let me take your coat."

"I am so honoured to be waited on and for an Earl to take my coat. We have never met, yet a growing familiarity is brewing that I sense you had already devised."

Grey hung Wilde's overcoat on a chair and led him to a vast dining room with a table to seat two dozen, but set just for two at the far end. Wilde presumed Grey would sit at the head and he would be adjacent.

Grey poured red wine from the decanter, and Wilde, feeling very much beneath his station, elected to serve the soup. They reached across one another clumsily and laughed heartily at their failings as much as they at their intimate situation.

"You put me at ease, Grey. For what I cannot presume. But, I am appreciative of the attention, as I am attentive to the appreciation. Shall we?" Wilde beaconed to Grey to seat himself first, which he did.

Grey ate slowly and watched Wilde devour his bread and broth. Wilde was clearly hungry and keen to benefit from the warm soup inside his cold body. The broad blazing fire in the outsized hearth looked impressive but still seemed incapable of making the room comfortable, to him at least. Grey, on the other hand, seemed quite at ease.

"I believe you to be staring," Wilde said between mouthfuls.

"Forgive me, I was admiring the fashion of your wares. You are a Bohemian dandy - I do so approve."

"One must either be a work of art, as are you Grey, or one must wear a work of art, as do I."

"There is that wit I have heard so much about. And a poet to boot. A toast to you, congratulations winning the Newdigate Prize at Oxford and achieving a first in Litterae Humaniores."

"Why, thank you. Is that why you invited me here, for my intellect?"

"Of course not. At twenty-four, you have a thirst for pleasure, physically in your prime, and entirely set to upset the apple cart with an unconventional lifestyle. Your intellect got my attention, your philosophy made you onto the shortlist, and your hedonism won the day."

"And what is it that I have won, might I ask?"

"A single weekend with me. Is that not enough?"

"I would not presume to say. We have only just met."

"I am teasing, of course. I wish to commission you, to write."

"To write what, exactly?"

"Well, in truth, I am not sure I need you to write anything. I have a story to tell - more of a story within a story. It will be difficult for you to hear, so I will set my standards there. Whether or not you can write any of it, I leave up to you."

"I am intrigued, of course. Anyone could have been commissioned to write a biography, if I should infer. Yet, you are not even certain, having troubled yourself to select me in particular, that I could even retell it."

"To put your mind at ease, the difficulty to retell my story is not a burden unique to you, or anyone, but I did select you because you, above all others, could understand it and might be able to put it down in ink in some form."

Grey changed the topic of conversation whilst they ate the following four courses prepared for them by the recently departed kitchen staff. Together they enjoyed a stimulating discourse on the politics of philosophy and the philosophy of politics.

Wilde was confused by the ability of this aristocrat's

conversational skills, concluding early on that his own intelligence had now met its match. Grey always had something else to pull out of his proverbial hat to trump whatever Wilde had last said. Moreover, Grey had other skills that had so far eluded him.

Concluding the meal by fetching a small glass of port for each of them, Grey invited Wilde to follow him, leaving the table for the staff to deal with on their return. Wilde was now much more relaxed, full of a delicious assortment of courses and plenty of wine. The port would not affect him until his stomach emptied later in the evening, but the notion of it made his face blush nevertheless.

They entered a long corridor packed with large full-length portraits.

"Welcome to the family and the beginning of my story. Painters always make one look so serious and ugly, don't you think?"

"They say you are the most beautiful man in Europe. I have to say, I cannot disagree."

"Only Europe?"

They laughed together at his conceit.

"What else do *they* say about me?"

"On a positive note, it is better to be talked about than not, but unfortunately, there is some talk of scandal. But, of course, scandal is merely gossip made tedious by morality. Within that, *they* say you dance with the devil."

"Ha! The devil only knows the polka, so his dancing is nothing to compare. However, he does tempt me with things he knows I cannot resist."

"Which one of them is you?" Wilde asked, gazing up at the paintings as they passed them by on either wall.

"Why, dear fellow, all of them?"

Wilde stopped in his tracks. "I count seventeen paintings. I was to understand that you are the seventeenth Earl of Salisbury, are you not?"

"I am. And I was the sixteenth, the fifteenth, the fourteenth...," Grey indicated each portrait in turn, and Wilde's disbelieving eyes recognised the same features in each, sometimes a little disguised, but now that he had been told this unbelievable thing, the resemblances were evident and inescapable. "You appear to fathom my secret and my burden. I was born in 1432. I was one of the first Earls appointed, in 1467. So I have been knocking around this world for four hundred and forty-six years if you can believe that."

"Why would I doubt it?" Wilde said a little absentmindedly but intentionally volunteering to engage in this apparent fantasy whilst it amused him, at least. "Did you drink an elixir of endless youth, or did the Devil make an abysmal deal with you?"

"I admit it is a hard pill to swallow. Perhaps I will persuade you, perhaps not. I appreciate the opportunity to explore the notion openly. I thank you for that. I always had security in knowing that such a story would never be believed; however, you were not the first to be told. Alas, once, the belief in a modern-day Methuselah did catch, and there is now a fanatical secret religious cult intent on bringing me down."

"I dare say you have had plenty of time to make enemies."

"Yes, but then they die of old age. Patience is not my virtue but rather my friend. I have no need for virtues. I should have been more careful in my choice of an enemy."

"Such things you must have seen across such a length of time."

"I have lived long enough to see the future become history and been cursed to remember the minutiae of it. It is tedious to remember everything. I would love to be ordinary and only remember the highlights."

"It is important to remember one's mistakes if only not to

repeat them."

"One man's mistakes are another man's experience. A pain of regret is not something I care to revisit."

"How does one choose to live, with that much time ahead, or indeed behind?"

"The enemy of the mind is boredom: the repetition of seeing the same things. I have sought out new and exciting things where I can find them, but history has moved at the pace of a snail. Hedonism is the last refuge of melancholy and the first refuge of the enlightened. I have sucked the marrow out of life and experienced every pleasure there is to have. Oh, how I yearn to be so innocent again so that everything I see would be new and exciting: a world full of the promise of wonder and adventure. Routine and repetition are just practised ways of dying slowly.

"The world is grey, and I don't mean that egocentrically or egotistically, I mean that the lens by which others prefer to see, in just blacks and whites, is as alien to me as are the benchmarks of morality.

"This guilded cage is of my own making, and unfortunately, my mood has changed recently, and perhaps this is my last desperate attempt to discover a reason to go on.

"One either leads the world into the future, or one is dragged kicking and screaming - I feel more akin to the latter these days."

Wilde was finally at a loss for words, losing traction in a fantastic world with none of the usual footings.

"I think you should live in London - where you will sink or swim. I fancy you will enjoy them as much as they will enjoy you," Grey said, swiftly changing tone and mood.

The two men reached the drawing-room, and there Grey provided Wilde with more details once his mind had caught up with this new reality.

CHAPTER TWENTY-FIVE

2512 CE, Earth, Sweden, near Stockholm

The wind hummed through the suspension wires of the bridge where Orianna sat near the apex, exposed to the elements several hundred metres up. She had chosen the dimmest area between street lights. Rain was moderate, but after two hours of sitting there, she was soaked through. Drops fell from her nose, chin and eyebrows. Her fluffy black bob did its best to redirect the water away from her neck. She didn't seem to care either way.

A road train could be heard powering up the bridge from one side. A wave of boosted illumination shot passed, ahead of it, the lights blazing bright for the duration until it had long passed by, and they dimmed down again as it roared into the distance.

Otherwise, there was nobody and nothing to be seen.

She had become used to being alone. Over the last twenty odd years, she had been in contact with her four friends less and less; her involvement in the business of The Few and The Many long retired. So she needed to stay well hidden. Yet she was pretty sure that she was now the most wanted person in the history of humankind. Everyone was looking for her now.

Having had a few close calls in Estonia North, she had

shaken them off with a feint to the south but actually travelled west to Stockholm.

If anyone had asked her if she had ever had depression, suffered heavily from grief, or contemplated suicide, she would have denied it. People got sad, but depression was a physical illness of the brain, she had thought: a chemical imbalance giving rise to deficient levels of serotonin and oxytocin, the pleasure and reward hormones. There was no rational state of mind that would naturally consider self-termination. So she had thought.

She had read enough philosophy to recognise that most works were just a lot of mental masturbation, with rare exceptions of genuine insight. You had to look past the pithy soundbites, as others had reduced it, to really understand the freedom offered by a chosen perception. Zen had been a favourite of hers: the unexplainable sense of just being, losing oneself in the moment and in everything around you, a timeless presence likened to standing in a river and allowing worries and external influences to be like the water flowing around and past you.

The preoccupation most people had with the debatable notion of 'free-will' had also been long resolved in her mind. It was plain nonsense to think our choices weren't deterministic: our brains were made up of particles obeying the laws of physics. We were built to decide for the best outcome, usually to survive. Those decisions we based on priorities and parameters we found ourselves having. So knowing we are just deterministic cogs in the overall system was not bad as long as you recognised it as entirely irrelevant.

The real illusion of control and choice was a viewpoint of how much we felt comfortable deferring to other systems: do we conform to the workplace rules, pay our taxes, obey traffic signals, honour our family, be loyal to our friends.

By joining any group, we would accept an expectation of

conformity and a set of rules to govern our behaviour within that group and thus proffer an exchange control for other benefits. The idealistic 'drop-outs' were thought to be entirely free. Yet, their escapism was invented in direct contradiction to the conformity around them, without which their 'freedom' meant nothing, lacking comparison.

She felt like the ultimate 'drop-out' now. She was a creature of non-conformity, outside of every system of control, and yet she still lived within those systems, like some unwanted alien object - like an irritant in someone's sock or shoe.

A better analogy came to her: she was patient zero. As if a carrier of a deadly disease: were she to engage with others, a cascade reaction would unravel. Many would suffer, the world might break, humankind would go to war with itself. An instrument of evil. A weapon of mass destruction.

All these spiralling thoughts served to lower her mood further. Still, she knew it was a layer above her real pain, beyond the altruistic considerations of her effect on everyone else - her personal pain, her loneliness.

"Maddox. I miss you," she muttered to herself.

Taking a deep breath, she stood up and wiped her face to throw off the bulk of water hanging there, at least to give her a brief opportunity to see the railing for which she reached out with both hands.

Another roar approached from the other direction this time. The street lights brightened again from over the brow to the right. The approaching headlights threw beams from over the rise, beautifully dissected by the towers and wires in different directions all at once. Orianna felt a brief joy in the pretty rays, but it washed over her quickly. Then a silhouette of a man on the footpath of the rise caught her eye. He was walking towards her. Despite being far away, she recognised the gait and acquired a sense that he was in full knowledge of her, not just a random stranger.

She saw that her foot had already withdrawn from its placement in the railings. Recognising the doubt of her actions now, she turned to face the man, lit heavily from above and the side.

The road train roared close by, and the wave of illumination followed.

The man was closer now. She could see his bushy beard on a severe youthful face. His keen eyes never wavered from staring directly into hers, his pace never slowing until he stopped right in front of her.

"You. I know you. You are The Watcher," she declared, wiping the water from her mouth.

"I am Ano. Ano Noma."

That was all he said.

She recognised his name was from the Grecian word for 'anonymous'. He was telling her that he had no name. Perhaps he wanted no name.

He reached down to her left hand, raised it up and pointed at her cuff with his other hand.

As he let go, she held her arm up.

He stepped to the side and continued on his way past her.

She watched him go, successively illuminated by each dim street light cone into the distance.

Activating the long-ignored cuff, she discovered a signal from agents of her businesses, informing her that Maddox Jefferies had been found on Rogue.

She could not believe her eyes, but continued to read.

He was old now, and they had tried to put him into hibernation, but he had said he had spent enough of his life asleep, and he never wanted to do it again. They were not sure how many years he had left.

She found herself panting, a warmth growing inside her that resented the cold wetness of her clothes. A scream and the beginning of a laugh ripped out of her.

She had an urgent purpose again. Not a long sustaining

drive but at least something to stop her from jumping off that bridge on that night. She had a chance to say goodbye to someone, anyone that mattered.

CHAPTER TWENTY-SIX

2518 CE, Rogue, Site One

Titanne IV had not been in orbit for long before a descent was organised in record time. This unprecedented move by Captain Odell Drake was unpopular, which was made worse by her insisting she pilot it herself.

Most of the crew had wondered why the O.D. Group had switched captains at the last moment since she seemed very young to be the captain of a long-range Expedition Class vessel. Rumours were abundant, but Orianna did not let it get to her. For her, there was only one mission - the rest were passengers.

Rogue was in superior conjunction with the Earth, making the journey short. However, that did mean a lot more traffic in orbit vying for launch windows.

As soon as she had awakened, she was immediately on the comms, checking in with Site One. She didn't want to speak with Maddox, except in person; however, it was gratifying to hear he was still alive and had been waiting for news that she was equally safe and in orbit.

The landing was remarkably smooth this time on the purpose-built landing pads. It was also much easier to disembark since Rogue had been officially designated a safe-air zone.

It just looked like Earth now. Habitats had sprung up all over, made of standard camping equipment: inflatables and non-inflatables. All the rules seemed to have gone, except the one about staying away from the cubes.

She found Maddox and his group sitting at a picnic table not too far from the landing pad. Running over like a giddy girl, she threw herself into his arms as if a petulant granddaughter reckless of his fragile state.

"Oh," he said. "Oh my. Oh my Lord, you are still just as beautiful."

Those around him didn't quite understand and looked at each other, puzzled.

"We talked about this, Professor Jefferies. You have been gone for a hundred and sixty years. So whoever you think this is, it cannot be the same person," the dark-skinned, middle-aged man on his left said. "Hello, I am Doctor Jones. Call me Abe. Sorry, you are?"

"Odell Drake. I am a descendent of his," Orianna lied expertly and made a passing glance at Maddox to check he was clued in.

"Oh, yes," Maddox nodded.

Once she had a chance to see him up close, she could see he was geriatric: maybe ninety years old.

"Still the oldest man alive," she said to Maddox and then addressed Abe. "He was the oldest man alive when he disappeared, as I understand it. A record holder in hibernation too, probably still is." Then she returned her gaze at Maddox. "Do you know what year it is? Do you know how old you are?"

"Still two years older than... hurrmmmphhh," he snapped with a giggle but tailed off when he realised he was almost forgetting their game of lies. "They say it is twenty-five eighteen. So that makes me... hooowaaa, not a day over three hundred and twenty, ha!"

Abe looked at him, "You understand, Odell, that he is a

bit slow, and you will need to give him time to answer."

"Can I speak with him privately? I feel he would like to hear about his family. Perhaps it might help ground him a little."

"I am sure we can arrange something."

"How was he when he was found?"

Abe got up and led Orianna away, out of earshot, leaving the other doctors to look after Maddox.

"I wasn't here then, that was six years ago, but according to the notes, he was completely disoriented, had no idea what had happened, very little recall of how he went missing or where he had been. A medical report at the time put him in excellent health. But, unfortunately, he began to decline recently. He has several degenerative conditions and doesn't have long, I'm afraid," he said quietly to her.

"No," she gasped. "I have come so far to see him."

"You arrived in good time, but he will never be able to travel in his condition. Even if you could convince him to hibernate, he wouldn't make it back. If you hadn't come, you would never have seen him, so this is a good thing. You should feel fortunate. Alas, he will never leave this place."

"That's probably for the best," she agreed. "Rogue was his whole life. He is a hero to so many."

"Oh, for sure. There isn't anyone alive who remembers a time before this planet came, except him, now. He changed the way we saw ourselves in the solar system and beyond. For that, we will all be forever grateful."

"Thank you, doctor," she said, smiling a bit, pushing away a tear, and touching his arm gently. "You have been very kind, but you must understand I will want to spend as much time with him as possible now."

"Of course. He is quite mobile. Apart from his memory, he won't be difficult to look after. So take this and press it any time you are in difficulty or just need some help or a break. We won't be far away."

Abe directed the others to follow him and slowly moved away, careful to watch as Orianna approached the table to sit down with Maddox before finally turning and leaving them.

Orianna looked down at his liver-spotted, boney hands and clasped them with her own. They were cold to touch.

She stared into his eyes. The skin around them was saggy and drooped, but the windows to the soul were still his. She decided that he was still in there, seeing something of her Maddox.

"Hello, old friend."

"Ah, Orianna, you are a sight for sore eyes. These fools think I am bananas. They are rightly concerned about where I had been and, of course, overly protective of me because I am some kind of icon these days. I think the mystery of my disappearance was the ultimate making of my fame. Ha!"

She laughed. "You have no idea how good it is to see you."

Now it was Maddox who looked into her eyes.

"There is a deep sadness in your eyes, dear Orianna. I hope it was not for how we left things?"

"No. Not that. A lot has changed. I found more others like me, but I am alone again."

"I am so sorry."

"But you are here now."

"And so are you! Ha!"

They laughed together. For a few more minutes, they just sat there. It was perfect, and neither of them wanted to ruin it by bringing up their issues.

"It is so beautiful here," Orianna exclaimed, shaking her head in disbelief of the beautiful vista beyond.

"Like a home from home," Maddox joked.

"You should see it through my eyes," she said, ignoring the joke. "The ground glows here, which gives the flowers a special shine."

"Amazing," he sighed. "I'm dying, aren't I?"

Her face fell. "Maddox, you are as old as the hills, you know? Maybe not these hills but, pretty sure you predate all life on this planet, so that is a good inning, right?"

"You always know how to make me laugh," he said, smiling. "It is my last innings. I know it."

"And I will be here."

Maddox took a deep breath and looked around him.

"This spot. I made them put this picnic table here because the view is so good. They will build a memorial here, bury my ashes, you know the drill: granite in the shape of a sofa, facing that way. So I decided I would leave the plaque inscription up to you."

Tempted to come back with a funny line or two off the cuff, she resisted, which surprised him. She was unable to make light of this anymore. He realised she really was in a bad way.

"Where did you go?" Orianna asked quietly.

"The official line is that nobody knows. Just another mystery for planet Rogue. I have no memory of anything."

"I know. I read the reports dozens of times."

"Some, sceptics, think I just sneaked off for another bout of hibernation, ageing thirty years in the last hundred and sixty years - a new record, if true. Not a bad theory really - fits the data nicely - which is why I kicked off that rumour, ha!" He said, coughing when he tried to laugh.

Orianna eyed him suspiciously. "Truth."

"Hmm, only for you, and here's the reason why," he said quietly, looking around to make sure nobody was close enough to hear. "Because I love you. And it looks like you will get to see what is going to happen."

"I love you too," she smiled but saw the glimmer still in his eye. "And?" she asked.

"Hmm, the first time we have said that to each other, just making the most of it."

'Go for it, old man! You have all the time in the world."

"Hmm, good point," he conceded, chuckling. "Seriously now," he said, his face indeed becoming grave, his eyes scanning for eavesdroppers. "Do you remember the cube came up when you nearly fell from the cliff? Something happened again when you were outside the dome on your last night. My hypothesis was that your UV aura was triggering it somehow.

"That time, you allowed me to record your aura: I was going to study it. Well, I played it up close to the cube, and something happened again. Something very different. I cannot quite remember much from there onwards, but I remember it pulled me in. Then, I woke up somewhere near those bushes over there a century and a half later. 'Thought I was on Earth, except I knew things I didn't know before."

Orianna was shocked.

"Like what?" she asked slowly, wondering if that was the right question to ask first.

"Not memories, just ideas, imprints of things and feelings. It is difficult to describe. I know I felt that I wasn't supposed to be in there. Somehow I sense that I triggered the templating for life here, but I cannot explain why. I have dreams of being somewhere that felt like a long way away but was nowhere. It didn't seem anything like hibernation - you don't dream in hibernation, after all - I ache for this time, believing I actually lived these missing years for a change. It is a terrible thing to go to sleep and wake up a lot older over and over. I might not remember anything, but I feel gratitude for the thirty or a hundred and sixty years that I did live. I hope it was good.

"You need to know something. I know where Rogue is heading next. You might want to reconsider your threat of staying. This is going to be some ride."

Orianna's mouth was agape. This was fantastic news.

"Where is it going?"

"Perhaps you have heard about the tremors? The cubes

have increased their activity. Gravity is changing. Everyone thinks Rogue has many more orbits around the sun before it lines up with the ecliptic and really starts to influence the planets, but it isn't going to happen like that. It is going to be very, very different. People are going to panic. You MUST be prepared! Orianna, next… stop is… Venus!"

Maddox began to cough violently. He cupped his hands to his mouth as he dropped to his knees. Revealing his palm: it was splattered with blood.

Orianna reached for the signaller and started to press it rapidly to call Abe back.

"Nothing is going to help me now. I held out. I held out these last six years to see you, and now I have. And I got to say it. I got to say… I love you."

"And I am so happy I was able to say, I love you too. But I am not ready to say goodbye."

"Please, Orianna, let me go."

"I don't want to."

"You must. There is much to do. My time is up. Yours is just beginning. Goodbye, my love…" he fell back into her arms, his eyes rolling back in their sockets.

"Goodbye, Maddox," she whispered softly, knowing he was slipping away. The doctors came quickly, all rushing and fussing, but Orianna was just in a slow fog, a daze. It was really happening, and there was nothing anyone could do. He was pronounced dead within a few minutes.

CHAPTER TWENTY-SEVEN

2524 CE, Earth, British Isles

"Rioting has broken out again in Bueno Aires, following the wave of civil disobedience we have seen around the world over the last few months. Authorities have been unable to quell the surges and have all but given up trying, say the local news networks. It is the same pattern as before: more and more people have continued to arrive in population centres to rally in front of government buildings and even set up camps. Armed forces have refused to intervene, citing centuries-old legislation making it illegal to use armed forces against civil unrest; instead, they have been trying to bring in food to supply those who have camped out in the hopes that it will prevent them from raiding local shops.

"Online right now, I have Harvard sociology professor David Carrington. Professor Carrington, are these people going to achieve anything by this action?"

"I think it is quite clear that they are just seeking answers like the rest of us. They don't know what the outcome is, and they are afraid. Many here believe they are safer off-Earth. They are there demanding passage to the colonies of Luna, Mars, or the asteroids…."

"What about the others? We have reports of minority groups claiming we are to blame. Some say we shouldn't have gone into space. Others say we shouldn't have gone to Rogue. And those are

just some of the saner ideas going around. So how is that any different?"

"That is a good question, Mary. We can see the same pattern here as elsewhere: blame is thrown around, and these groups fight each other. The authorities would have an even harder time if the mobs had a coherent target for their frustration. The truth is, Mary, we are all self-reflecting more in the last six years, trying to find meaning and comfort in difficult times."

"There are those describing this as the End of Days, and the Rapture is coming. How do you respond to that?"

"Religion is often a source of comfort for many when faced with uncertainty. You had a special on earlier with a physicist, I didn't catch his name...."

"Professor Duncan, of Oxford University."

"... and he said it himself. The Rogue planet is unlike anything else we have seen in the universe. It has altered its own gravity to steer itself. By definition, this is an unpredictable force, and it keeps getting closer. People are going to feel threatened. But, of course, most people are not rioting. They are not panicking. They continue to go about their lives and try to just accept that whatever is going to happen is not only outside their control, but might not even cause much change in their lifetimes."

"Thank you, Professor Carrington. And now Professor Duncan is online for his regular update."

"Hello again, Mary. Rogue's increased gravity has been relaxing recently, so we have some new estimates. The current predictions stand as follows: the probability of a collision with Venus is now only about fourteen per cent."

"What does that mean?"

"A collision could have meant a lot of asteroids being added to the orbits of the inner planets, increasing the risk of asteroid impacts. A near miss, which seems more likely now, could involve a serious disruption to Venus as Rogue did to the minor planet, Pluto. Both Rogue and Venus could end up in some volatile orbit which could disrupt the orbit of the other planets: Earth, Mars...."

"Is there any upside?"

Professor Duncan looked confused. "I don't think you have been listening...."

"For a more spiritual answer to the question of hope, we have Cardinal...."

Orianna shut off the feed and exited her Augmented Reality state.

She was glad to no longer be on Rogue but wondered how a close flyby of Venus would compare with the flyby with Jupiter that she shared with Maddox. According to the networks, that had been a spectacular event - the most replayed AR background ever.

Her information stated that all personnel had been evacuated from Rogue, leaving behind all their equipment in the expectation that either they would be able to return again or it wouldn't matter anyway. She was a little surprised by this or perhaps more disappointed that there wasn't one among them who dared to risk their lives for something bigger than themselves. Perhaps that age had passed. Maybe they didn't make people like Maddox anymore.

She sipped her tea and looked out over the cobblestone square. Tunbridge Wells looked very seasonal, with early snow covering the frozen ground with a light dusting and the beginnings of rain threatening to melt it all away.

Passers-by, wrapped up in response to the recently falling temperatures, struggled with the icy surface, sometimes falling down and laughing with each other. But, unfortunately, those little moments of joy were rarer and more precious. People-watching had always been her favourite pastime, and this window was just the best.

Every day she would arrive there as soon as the restaurant opened at midday to ensure she got the same table, although by now the staff would have reserved it for her had she ever been late. She would catch the early regulars performing their routines outside: walking their dog, getting an early lunch, setting up tables in the restaurants on the opposite side of the square.

Last Wednesday was a special day when a rare fog, as thick as pea-soup, fell, and pedestrians navigated the square with powerful torches despite it being daylight.

It rained on and off the previous week, but primarily on. That didn't seem to deter walkers. Her father's words from her childhood had returned to her then: "There is no such thing as bad weather, only inappropriate clothing."

Meanwhile, she had been reading through Hagakure, The Book of The Samurai. Unlike the endlessly revised tome of Sun Tsu's The Art of War, this book was one samurai's view of Bushido and Zen Buddhism, and filled with inspiration. She had watched people run past outside, close to her window, dashing under the awnings, trying to dodge the worst of the downpours. Then this passage came to mind, whilst sipping her warm toddy:

"There is something to be learned from a rainstorm. When meeting with a sudden shower, you try not to get wet and run quickly along the road. By doing such things as passing under the eaves of houses, you still get wet. When you are resolved from the beginning, you will not be perplexed though you still get the same soaking. This understanding extends to all things."

The physical bound-paper book was still in front of her on the table. She liked to digest several of these paragraphs each hour, along with other aphorisms and epigrams. This book she loved particularly for its feel: the leather-binding, the texture of the paper, the physicality of it spoke of ages past. Written at the beginning of the eighteenth century, it was far older than her, and she appreciated the age-old wisdom and archaic language. It grounded her in a world long before space was a destination, before industrialisation started mankind on a path of addiction to power, growth and exploitation. It had been a simpler time when everyone knew their place and understood why they did what they did, which was for the greater good. That was the romantic view of the period, which was her privilege, eight centuries later, to read about. Unlike many of The Few, she was comparatively young; thus, connecting with classic literature helped her to those times.

She had plenty of time, it seemed. The first day she visited the restaurant was early summer, and she had returned every subsequent day until it just became a habit. On numerous occasions, she would take a walk between lunch and dinner: to visit expensive shops that sold genuine old books and to purchase something new to feed her soul.

Messages were exchanged between herself and her four friends, asking them to be liaisons with the Nader brothers, to ask them for an audience, but frequently there was little or no response at all. Still, she waited.

Thus it was no real surprise when Tarik Nader finally walked in one day and simply sat down opposite without asking. He quickly noted that the restaurant was mostly empty, but he considered it was midway between lunch and dinner, after all.

Orianna took her time disengaging from her book and looking up at him. Then, finally, the book was dutifully given a thin bookmark, inserted between the leaves where she had been reading, before it was closed and carefully laid next to her glass.

In the subtlest of motions, her long-lashed eyelids flicked up, and her eyes fixed on him, nothing else about her moving. He was staring at her, a stern but otherwise neutral expression on his face.

The waiter rushed over, seeing his best, most regular, most generously tipping customer had her first guest. "Sir?" he asked promptly. "May I serve you?"

"No," Tarik replied without taking his eyes off Orianna.

"He will have a warm beer, not too sweet," she said. The waiter nodded and retreated. "You don't look happy?" she said quietly to him, matter-of-factly.

Tarik leaned back in his seat and folded his arms.

"You have been gone for a century and a quarter. The last you said to me was to tell me I was pathetic."

Orianna took her time responding, showing she had nothing to say on that matter.

"Since you are here now, whilst we wait for your brother to show up, let me tell you a story:

"The Japanese Zen master Tanzan and the monk Ekido came across a beautiful girl who was unable to cross a stream. Tanzan offered to carry her and she agreed. The girl thanked Tanzan and left him and the monk on the other bank. Tanzan and Ekido continued walking for half the day until Ekido spoke. He told Tanzan that as monks were not allowed to even approach, let alone touch women, he questioned Tanzan's earlier actions. Tanzan genuinely asked what woman he was referring to. Ekido explained and told Tanzan it had been bothering him since the stream. Tanzan told the monk that he had put her down long ago, but Ekido was still carrying her."

Tarik curled his upper lip. "I forgive you," he stated coldly.

"You forgive me, now, present tense. After a century and a quarter?" Orianna was aloof and revisited the window with her gaze.

"What is all this?" he asked, but she ignored him.

They sat for another hour without further words being spoken. Tarik drank his beer but spent much of his time using his cuff; all the while, Orianna continued to enjoy watching people through the window.

Suddenly, the door opened, and a stream of people entered the restaurant. Orianna counted a baker's dozen by just the sounds alone. She sensed them all assembling in smaller groups at the neighbouring tables, no consideration given to waiting to be seated. She knew there was no need to look up to realise they were of The Few. A moment later, a fourteenth entered, and he intercepted her waiter, who was about to explain that several of those tables had been reserved for the early dinner slot. The waiter was led away.

The slight sounds in the room, mainly the breathing of The Few seated around her, changed subtly, and Orianna felt Yamanu's presence was impending. She turned from the window and carefully put her book into a bag she had under the table.

The door opened once again, and Yamanu strode in. He hesitated at their table, looking down on Orianna and Tarik seated opposite each other, and took in the scene, slowly, whilst removing his gloves and coat.

"It is cold," he said casually, but she knew him too well not to assume he was actually commenting on the mood at the table. "Do you mind if I sit here?" he asked somewhat rhetorically.

"Please do," Orianna replied, gesturing to the chair between them, kindly recognising his good manners, certainly to contrast Tarik's lack thereof. "Of course, you are expected."

"I hope I am not late," he added with a smile as he settled down. "Can I blame the weather? Do you know how long it took before Tarik and saw snow for the first time? That is perhaps a story for another time," he said, correcting his approach when he received only a blank response from Orianna.

"This must be hard for you?" she said plainly.

Yamanu eyed her suspiciously.

"Why? Why do you say that?"

"You came to me."

"You invited me. And I came. Eventually," Yamanu he said, maintaining his playful smile.

"Time has taught me to be patient. It does not matter how long you took to get here. You still came... to me. So, what do you want?"

"You know what I want," he snapped impatiently. "I went to a great deal of trouble to pave the way for you, and you threw it back in my face. There is no escaping your fate, Orianna. You are the future."

"Assuming we all have much of a future left."

"Indeed," Yamanu agreed.

"That must be hard for you too. Living for thousands of years, making all those plans, enacting all those plots, manipulating mortal man around you to serve whatever agenda you have, only to see the whole lot go down the plughole with some random cosmic act that you cannot do anything about. The end is coming. You cannot avoid it. You cannot pretend that you will continue to live forever if only you are careful. That is how the mortals feel. Refreshing, isn't it?"

"Do you feel that way now? Is that it, Orianna?"

"You have no idea what I feel right now. But to help with that, I have a verse from Hagakure that I prepared for you. Would you like to hear it?"

"Alright."

"Even if one's head were to be suddenly cut off, a samurai should be able to do one more action with certainty. If one becomes like a revengeful ghost and shows great determination, though his head is cut off, he should not die."

"What does that mean?" Yamanu asked.

Orianna turned her body to face him and opened her coat to reveal a waistcoat full of explosives and tubes clearly labelled 'shrapnel'. "You took everything from me. I have nothing, no one left now, so be careful how you play your next move because from what I understand, the world could well be better off without you, and I am already a ghost."

Those behind the Nader brothers shifted uneasily in their

seats and fiddled with their concealed weapons.

"Nobody is here to take you or hurt you, Orianna." Yamanu gestured this also with open hands. He sighed and leaned back in his seat, folding his arms, matching Tarik. "Oh, you have caused me a great deal of trouble. Your little speech has divided our people. You might reconsider your sense of being alone."

"Is that so?" she asked, shrugging nonchalantly. "What about the mortals, like my Maddox? They were just your pawns."

"For thousands of years, we have rescued everyone. EVERYONE - everyone we could. We gave them a purpose, to save their brothers and sisters. We helped them navigate a world that didn't accept them, would never accept them. They see us all as freaks, vampires, the undead, sucking the life from them, bad omens, witches, devils. We did what we had to do to survive. It is not my fault the mortals were so ignorant and cruel."

"Understood. We all had to bear the downsides of being ageless. Nothing comes for free. But you went further than that, didn't you? You went about altering history to suit your own ends. I have heard the stories. I have pieced them together. But, of course, none of it had to go the way it did, did it?"

"Of course! What do you want me to say? Mankind owes us gratitude for pushing them into order and progress through war and despair. As you said, a trade-off."

"Yes, but did they have a choice, or did you make it for them?"

"They could not make it for themselves. Shortsighted fools."

"So this was all for… what, exactly? For the betterment of those whom you seem to despise so much? I don't buy that."

"They killed our mother. They deserve to suffer. We are superior humans. We should be their gods."

"The Many don't agree."

"Ha! The Many. We made The Many. One of our little experiments turned out to have some unforeseen consequences. Beneficial indeed. What better than to have created your own enemy? Then you really do control the game, like a god. They were never a real threat, just useful to keep everyone focussed. They only continue to exist because I let them."

"That is why I could never follow you, Yamanu. Your ambitions come with too high a cost."

Orianna looked at Tarik: his worried face was hung low now. Even The Few around them stopped fiddling with their hidden weapons to hear this revelation.

"You are a monster, Yamanu. I am so glad that I wasn't found by you as early as the rest. I could have been just another pawn in your game - a game of ages."

With that, she arose suddenly, startling those who remembered she was a walking bomb. "I should end you all right now. Put you and myself out of everyone's misery."

She stood there taking in the fear on Yamanu's face - his analysis of her poker face convincing him that she really meant it - her eyes so deadly calm and empty, it was like looking at death itself.

Slowly, she walked out.

"Orianna," Tarik called out. "I'm sorry."

CHAPTER TWENTY-EIGHT

2524 CE, Earth, continental Europe

Ana and Orianna sat quietly together in a road carriage, which seemed a little bit confused with its navigation. Eventually, it found an entrance to a field to park off the lane so as not to block the way in case anyone else came down this overgrown track.

They both got out and looked around.

"I'll have a look over here," Ana said optimistically and followed the hedge back the way they had come, on the principle that the carriage was probably close when it got confused back aways.

Orianna walked across the lane and grabbed a young tree in one hand. It was tall enough and strong enough to hold her weight but thin enough to clasp fully. The view over the opposite hedge was delightful: rolling hills, some farms and smallholdings scattered about, and an orchard immediately ahead - apple by the looks of it, but a bit too early to tell yet. None of that was helping. So, she climbed down again and went in search of Ana, who had disappeared around the bend.

She noticed something Ana must have missed. The ditch was all overgrown, but there was a hint of a break in the channel, which was confirmed when she stomped down the brambles and felt solid level ground.

"Ana!" she called. Vines offered very little resistance and seemed to dominate the overgrowth in front. Tugging them away armfuls at a time revealed a natural break in the hawthorns and exposed a mature but overwhelmed holly bush.

Ana arrived and drew a large knife, more of a short sword really, and carefully removed some of the lower branches. Holly bushes being essentially hollow, it was then easy for the women to enter and find an exit on the north side, where less dense overgrowth allowed them easy passage to continue through the other side.

"Ouch," Ana yelled as she toppled over an obstacle. Orianna helped her to her feet, a slight smile showing as she became confident that Ana hadn't received any serious injury.

"Well, that confirms it. You fell over an old headstone," Orianna declared.

They advanced from the shadow of the tree line, and into a wild meadow, with mounds of grass around stony protrusions.

"You said the northeastern corner," Ana suggested, pointing up the hill to a ruin that could be seen at the top. "That must be the old church. The boundaries of the field seem to be the correct dimensions."

"I remember the path came down over there directly south from the church. So if we shift right, hopefully, we can find a direct route between stones to the path and then it should be a safe stroll up to the church and across," Orianna suggested, remembering the layout.

All this overgrowth was entirely expected; hence they were wearing sensible footwear and thick cuffed trousers, which, although a little warm, were better than scraped ankles, adder bites and ticks.

"Appropriate clothing," Orianna mumbled to herself,

reminding herself of her father's oft-repeated words because that was why they were there, after all.

Sure enough, the main path was a lot easier and flatter, and they sped up the hill once Ana felt more confident that she wasn't going to kneecap herself again.

The hill was quite steep; the overgrowth thinned out nearer the top, where the ground was drier. The top row of stones leading east was apparent and proud of the low grasses. The tallest was at the far end. That was clearly her father's - it was huge.

"That's it." Orianna declared and began to ease between that row and the one below.

"I'll be right here," Ana said, settling down on the main path, in a nice dry and sunny spot of shorter grass.

Oberon Demaine born 2158 died 2231

She was aware of the rest of the engraving under the overgrowth lower down, but she wasn't feeling a pressing need to excavate it and read the obituary in her father's own words.

"Hello. I expect that this is a surprise. Well, all that talk of legacy: The Demaine Group, Erebus, continuing what was passed to you and passing it on to Orlando. What was it all for Dad? Erebus was all me anyway, and it is the only thing that survived. I am your legacy, but you never wanted it that way did you? And yet, look, here I am, still here, still twenty-something, and you've been gone for almost three hundred years now, in a forgotten grave all grown over. Maybe you should have concentrated on me, huh?

"You cannot say I didn't warn you about Orlando. Taking it all from him was easy. But, no, I wasn't going to go there. I didn't come here to spit on your grave, Dad. Honestly." Orianna sighed and rested a hand on the edifice before her, its rough, pitted surface warmed by the generous sunshine.

"You gave me all the tools, Dad. And I am grateful. I needed them all and more. I just wanted to say thank you. You loved me in your own way. I get it now. I wish I had learned that back then. We were very alike in so many ways. Maybe that is why we fought so much.

"I'm here because I don't know what is going to happen next. It is like the Critical Earth all over again, except this time there is no debate, no denial indeed, there is nothing to do but wait. This time, all of humanity is united in apathy. This is the big one - that makes the Critical Earth seem like a warm-up. This could be the end of us all.

"There is this rogue planet, and it's heading for Venus. First, it knocked Pluto out and then passed Jupiter close by. This time we have no idea if it will hit Venus - and even if it doesn't, who knows what will happen to Earth and Mars after that. It is a strange one, for sure. It seems to have an intelligence to it. Nobody has their head around that. It is unpredictable, yet we know it is steering itself, so maybe it has a plan. We just all hope that plan includes us in it going forward. I am all out of plans. Maybe it is here to replace us or destroy us. Maybe it doesn't even care. I don't know.

"I am not the only one trying to find some peace in these trying times. My kind is turning to me for the answers, but I don't have answers, only faith. Maddox has passed on too. He had faith. Is that really enough, though? Of course, *you* don't think so. Forget I asked.

"Turns out I just needed to talk to - well, someone who's been dead since twenty-two thirty-one. What does that say about me? It is a lonely thing, this living forever lark. So it stands to reason that if you live long enough, you get to see the end of the world. There is no cop-out there - no 'oh well, I'll be dead before this, that or the other happens'. Nope, I'll be here, waiting. After all, they say if you stand still long enough, you will get to see everything.

"It's not all bad. I have my friends back now. New ones

are making friends with me all the time now. I think I finally made a good impression. My first time didn't go so well, and I was in a terrible way. I'm still not over it. I'm slow to let people get close now, ironically right when I really need them the most.

"I know you knew the Nader brothers. They were in an old photo of yours. I saw it. Did you know what they were? Were you one of The Many? Wouldn't that be an ironic twist of fate? If I ever see them again, I should ask them. Who am I kidding? I don't ever want to know the answer.

"I've changed. I may look the same, but inside I am different. I have lost a part of me now: that part that needed to follow and be a part of something else. I think that part was me not letting go of you. Maybe I have finally grown up. I don't really know. It feels strange. I might not be back again. Time will tell. You never really set me free. I am here today to say that I have set myself free.

"I am your daughter. And you were my daddy. I miss you, Pops. That's it, really."

Orianna patted the stone one last time and made her way back to Ana for a gentle chat sitting in the grass. She had no more tears to shed.

"Sif's in Norway. I imagine she has her own goodbyes to make there," Ana said, looking up from her cuff.

"Did you not want to see anyone?"

"Like this? Hell no," Ana laughed. "Bit too morbid for me. Mine were all composted anyway. There isn't even a stone. We weren't rich like your family. But, for what it's worth, I knew of your dad when I was actually young when he was young too. In fact, we were… are close to the same age. I didn't know him well, but he was in the local news, and I saw him collect an award. I thought he was amazing. His speech was one of the highlights of my young life."

"You never told me that."

"I was waiting for the right moment. That was it."

Rogue

CHAPTER TWENTY-NINE

2525 CE, Earth, Norway

The snowplough was a road carriage mod, with a massive bank of lights shining off a small area of brilliant white snow around and ahead of it. Beyond was very dark; the horizon glowed with the endless promise of a dawn that never came. Its wipers worked frantically to clear the spray as it pushed forwards against a wall of fresh snow that had almost hidden the road ahead. That was when it was perilous: all too easy to veer off course and end up ploughing rocky terrain into a crevasse or to completely miss a small bridge.

The road markers were sparse and almost impossible to see, nearly buried as they still were from yesterday's pass of the snow plough.

Orianna increased the speed of the pump, throwing the snow farther over the hump, hoping not to bury the markers any more than they already were. It was a risk because if she hit a pocket of lighter snow or stopped suddenly, the flow of snow would no longer support the pump, and it could get hot and damaged. Running it dry was not good.

It had begun to snow again, and she sighed, disappointed that it was very fluffy and driving towards her, blinding in reflected bright white light from the bank of roof lights, but also because it heralded a job that would have to be done again tomorrow.

She actually liked this kind of work. She hated people calling it manual labour, or menial, because it was honest hard work - good for the mind and spirit. It kept her grounded in the moment and gave her peace from her worries and plans.

Three more of The Few had arrived via Sweden this week, and the pace of arrivals was increasing. That could only mean one thing: the Nader brothers were losing followers faster and faster, and would see her as a threat.

Of course, she hadn't asked for this. She hadn't promoted herself as any kind of leader, but now that she had stood up to the brother, there was anew option available to The Few. She did not kid herself that being the only known living immortal who had the potential to bear immortal children had nothing to do with it. Still, she never talked about it or mentioned any plans to ever test that theory. She wasn't even sure it was a good thing.

She put the thoughts to the back of her mind again and thrust ahead. Her village was not far now, perhaps a mile. The distant glow of street lighting could be seen illuminating the patchy low cloud ahead.

Briefly taking a moment to have a break, she disengaged the rotary mouth and pump, reversed a short way off the snow face, and turned off the lights. Her cabin was very different from a typical taxi-like arrangement. She had a forward-facing set of front seats, snow equipment and optional seating. She ventured into the rear to pick up a thermos full of warm tea and poured herself a cup.

The reinforced ceiling of the cab made for good protection against snowfall and snow wall collapse - or indeed rolling over, which she had never done - but there was no window.

She opened the side hatch and clambered out, landing on the snow with a satisfying crunch and creak. Her jacket was made for the extreme weather. Much as she loved the cold and the snow, her body was small and thin: it didn't appreciate inappropriate clothing - something she was forever mindful of.

Hot vapours flooded her face as she breathed into her cup of cha. It was delightful. Looking up, she was lucky to catch a momentary break in the fast, low cloud. Then, as the snow abated, the stunning Aurora Borealis revealed herself with curtains of green and pink light rippling high above. She remembered pictures of the Aurora, taken with visible spectrum cameras to show what ordinary people would see, and she felt a little sorry for them because, in ultraviolet, it was spectacular.

It took twenty-five more minutes to plough the remaining stretch up to the village, where the snow had already been cleared. Finally, after the machine broke into the clearing, Orianna parked up.

The village lights served to simulate daytime, but they had actually begun to be shut off in a slow sequence, making her realise that the arbitrarily defined 'day' was almost up. The ones that remained on were also changing to a warmer hue.

Shutting everything down, she jumped out and creaked and squeaked her way through the dry snow with bold strides. There wasn't far to go before her house, and dinner still needed to be made for her and Sif.

She noted an absence of people around. There should be a fair amount of foot traffic even in this weather. The children should be playing, and the adults would be finishing work.

Seventeen of The Few had integrated into the village under the guise of an expeditionary force, which had to wait for the right time to venture farther north to study the Inuits, who had migrated there from Greenland - their reduced habitat no longer able to sustain their original way of life all year round, they had had to compromise and integrate more with the Fins and the Norse people during the melt-times.

A handful of mortal friends of The Few were Norwegian and had set up this temporary haven and established their cover story. Unfortunately, more of The Few were being driven out of their current identities before they were ready to 'move on'. Yamanu was coming at them all individually and hard. He wanted assurances that they would be on his side, but if he didn't get that, he was apt to blow their cover through spite, or be so belligerent that The Few would flee anyway. And this is where they ended up, for now.

She knew this had to be temporary because sooner or later, her rescue network would be discovered, and Yamanu would come. This was what went through her mind when anything out of the ordinary took place. The isolation of this village was an excellent place to slow down any unwanted visitors - hopefully, giving them enough time to escape before anyone unwanted arrived. Still, there was the fear that they might intrude in stealth.

It was too quiet.

She hurried to the house as best as her over-padded jacket and salopettes would allow. Under the porch, she shook off the snow that had accumulated on her shoulders and hood, removed the extra-shaded super-UV-protection goggles and opened the door. Inside was warm and bright. She pulled off her gloves and pulled a note tacked to the inner door frame. It simply read: "In the meeting house, Sif."

That didn't sound so bad, she thought. Then she remembered what day it was. She had lost track, having ploughed all the way to the next village and stayed over for a few days with some new friends - the ploughman's family, her counterpart.

Retracing her steps, getting dressed for the weather again - vital even for a relatively short walk - she made her way down the white road and around Main Street. Halfway down, on the right, was a large cubic building with a steep roof, evident by the amount of light coming out of it.

A few others were crossing the street in a hurry, presumably a little late like she was.

Greeting each other in the foyer, they removed their winter wears and put them in the outer cloakroom. Everyone had shoes in lockers in this building. She fetched and put on her own, and they all went into the main hall.

It was noisy. So many people, some still steaming with released sweat, standing and cheering, congratulating each other and shaking hands. Ahead was a large old-fashioned flat-screen, displaying a man's face talking into a camera in a much warmer part of the world, or maybe off-world, it wasn't easy to see. In any case, his words were being broadcast from speakers, but she couldn't really hear him over the jubilations. Apparently, he had already said what they had been waiting for him to say. They weren't listening to anything else.

"It's unbelievable!" Randolph's voice shrieked as he saw her and rushed over. "Rogue is settling at L3. This is the best outcome - ridiculous, like a coin landing on its edge. Who would have put money on *that*? Earth, Mars, and humanity - we're all gonna survive! Rogue will forever be exactly opposite the Earth in the same orbit. This is not providence. This is intelligence. Mark my words."

Orianna was speechless. She smiled and started to jump with joy and laughed with everyone else.

"I don't know whether to be relieved or afraid," Randolph yelled. "But for now, I am going to celebrate. Jeez, the whole world and beyond has been so in the dump. Ha! Hahaha."

Orianna stopped bouncing, and the two watched each other, breathless and smiling. "I said it had intelligence," she eventually managed to say. "Maddox discovered there was a connection between Rogue and The Few. I think it is safe to say now that Rogue came here with good intentions."

Randolph nodded. "Ok, I'll accept that. Rogue doesn't like Venus, though. That's the other part, Venus is going into the

Sun. ICE Units had to work overtime on that one. They say that any Coronal Mass Ejection would be off the ecliptic, so the spray of particles will not hit any planet. They also say that it may result in a small reduction in solar output. That can only be good news with helping Earth recover. It's a win-win."

"Extra mass will affect L4 and L5?"

"Yes, L4 and L5 will now be extended. As a result, Erebus and other asteroids will drift farther on their Coriolis spirals. They said that adding Rogue's mass increases the stability of The Lagrange Points."

Mortals and The Few alike danced and laughed and drank for hours afterwards. Children did not get put to bed. Most just slept where they were as the adults enjoyed the best party in the history of humanity.

Everywhere humankind lived, when the signal got to them, everyone partied like never before, as if tomorrow would never come because all the tomorrows were going to be ok now.

"In the month since the Rogue planet steered itself to a safe orbit opposite the Earth, people have been returning to their lives, and we have finally had a chance to report on other news. It is this reporter's delight to be able to see a return to normality.

"From the amazing to the bizarre, in a special report tomorrow by Keith O'Neil, Keith will be reporting on a fast-growing 'conspiracy' theory that is starting to turn heads. We don't normally give airtime to unsubstantiated, so-called 'conspiracy' theories, but Keith has promised revelatory evidence to 'prove' the existence of ageless immortals hidden in our societies. In a three-part series of his own book, 'Chimeras: Gods Amongst Us?', Keith claims to be able to show that in rare cases, people are born with the ability not to age and to survive most illnesses, and, if you believe it, for thousands of years they have manipulated human history for their own mysterious ends. I know what you are

thinking, we have heard this wild story many times before, and none ever amounted to anything, but Keith says this time is different. So tune in, same time tomorrow, to find out."

CHAPTER THIRTY

2558 CE, Earth, British Isles

The wrought iron gates at the entrance were impressive: newly painted and oiled, Orianna noted, examining them as closely as possible. In an arch above the gates, connecting the tall stone pillars in a separate iron banner, the words "Sandford Sanitorium" were written in large welded letters. At the sides of the posts, the wall curved away and on the right side was a heavy wooden door and an intercom.

"Miles Fortescue, Director of Mental Health Services. I am here to see M. Warrington for an inspection of this facility. I demand immediate access. Any delay will be marked against you." Randolph called into the intercom in his most upper-class English accent.

Their cassock-style suits were a nice touch. The format was standard amongst civil servants these days after being popularised by the Clerics of the IRC for centuries. His was blue, but Orianna wore plain black, helping to accentuate his seniority.

The door promptly opened, and a security guard stated he had to scan them for anything that the inmates might use as a weapon, as a matter of procedure. He waved a passive sensor around their bodies whilst informing them of the safety rules: staying on the path where the cameras were, never entering a room without an orderly present, and avoiding getting too close to the inmates.

Randolph argued with the guard about his case, which he was refusing to open, and that gave Orianna a chance to glance into his booth and see what the guard had been watching. A couple of screens showed cameras inside and out; one showed Keith O'Neil's vlog, one of his endless articles about immortal humans living amongst us all. Violet glasses sat on the side.

She casually held her arm around the back of the booth and released a half dozen small bots before submitting herself to be scanned.

"Hey, O'Neil's got a case, right?" Orianna asked the guard.

"Oh yeah, my wife's a big fan. She got the glasses for me."

"Have you seen anyone suspicious yet?"

"No. I don't know anyone who has. Honestly, those are great for looking at the sunset, but that's about it. Mary Jones, on the other hand, hoo-wee - you'll meet her up-a-ways - she's a fanatic."

"Good to know, thanks. I'll make sure to avoid the subject then."

"Yeah, good idea," the guard smirked. "You are now expected. Your cuffs have been provided with a pass for today only; please accept and activate now. Then, you may proceed up the road to the main entrance, where Mary will receive you at reception. Thank you for leaving your vehicle outside."

"Not a problem," Randolph replied. "It is a nice day for a walk."

They activated their passes, and the guard nodded confirmation that they had been recognised.

Promptly, the two left the guard and began to pace calmly and slowly up the driveway, their boots crunching on the gravel in synchronised steps, their long gowns just revealing a little of their boots as they walked, enough to avoid brushing the ground.

"Easy in," Randolph commented, with a hint of nerves.

The extensive grounds flowed with green grass away from the drive and led to bushes and trees farther out. Some groups of patients were visible, supervised by orderlies in white.

"The guard had violet glasses. He was watching that O'Neil vlogger." Orianna informed him and then switched to the broader comms channel. "Keep your eyes open, guys, and stay calm! Keep your auras under control!"

"The cat is definitely out of the proverbial bag," Randolph said. "He is getting more and more popular every year. Unfortunately, it did not blow over like we hoped it would."

"Pretty sure The Many are at the bottom of all this."

"Why do you think that?"

"I have been analysing his vlogs. It really looks like he didn't stumble onto anything. It is all being fed to him slowly. It is a slow and calculated thriller designed to hook the masses in."

"He's been banging on about it for thirty plus years. How is it still interesting? It is not as if he has produced any of us as proof?

"He doesn't need to. People are still vulnerable after the Rogue threat. It is genius, really. They all felt united against a common threat. Once that threat disappears, you give them another to feed off and keep stoking the fires with just enough credibility to keep everyone from remembering the disagreements they had with each other," Orianna explained.

"Paranoia. I am surprised it hasn't degenerated into a fascist witch hunt."

"Plenty of time for that."

"I don't understand why The Many decided to expose us. After all these centuries of secrecy, on both sides and now they 'go public', through this showman. What do they hope to gain?"

Orianna smiled. "A move I might have made in their position. This is simple game theory. In this case, they are losing, the main piece is exposed. Me. So they upset the board to radically change the game. It is a desperate move."

Randolph swallowed. "It makes me feel desperate too. They are living up to their name now. It seems that everywhere I go, there are people with those damned glasses, just waiting for us to lose our cool and give ourselves away."

"So. Don't lose your cool. Right?"

"I feel sorry for the uninitiated, who will be born into an even more unforgiving world."

Orianna nodded. "We cannot save them all. If we try, we will end up saving none."

Randolph did not speak again. Instead, he pulled his cassock at the waist with a brief tug to remove any creases that had formed around his torso. For a Director, his cassock didn't appear as tailored as it should, and he didn't want a small slip like that to bring doubt to his act.

The building they approached was large and imposing, in plain red brick with stone edging. All the windows were closed and appeared to be modern - likely they could not be opened or broken.

They were greeted by a fragile-looking lady in a dull floral dress at the reception, who introduced herself enthusiastically as Mary Jones, one of the administrators.

Randolph nudged Orianna as he saw she was wearing violet glasses. She messaged him through his contacts to say that this would be useful, and they should try to keep her with them.

Cordial greetings led to much flattery for Mary Jones. They built up a rapid rapport with her so that when it came time to take a tour, it was easy to ensure she didn't feel that they needed privacy to do their inspection.

"Please, do join us. It will be useful if we need questions answered. These inspections are as much a getting to know you as they are a formal evaluation," Randolph lied.

Flattered and pleased,flattered and pleased Mary Jones led the way.

Many hours passed while they continued to play their part, asking relevant questions and trying not to appear too hurried.

Eventually, they came to the second floor and a wing with its own reception and a guard.

The guard insisted that they could not go in with anything really: the case or Mary Jones' violet glasses, but it was apparent that the latter was of significant importance. So once the case and glasses were left on the table, they were permitted to enter. Mary Jones pointed out that she did not have access to this area and therefore didn't need to remove her glasses; she excused herself and left.

"This must be it," Orianna messaged Randolph, her hands behind her back and her fingers gesturing in a type of shorthand typing.

Of course, they didn't need violet glasses. The Few could see ultraviolet light with their naked eyes. But, much as wearing some would have been a good deflection, it was not in keeping with their cover.

Inside seemed to be a sub-hospital, separate from the outer hospital. There were a dozen patients already in the common area, overlooked by four orderlies, who appeared quite bored, which was understandable since every patient looked heavily drugged.

Whatever drugs they had been given, it had the effect of putting them in a slow fog and making them very docile.

Orianna walked into the centre of the room and clapped her hands together loudly. No patient did much more than vaguely glance up, but the orderlies jumped to alertness -

this she repeated several times.

She mustered a strong emotion deep inside herself: anger at Yamanu was a good one to use. Then, without showing it obviously, she channelled this emotion into her aura and blazed brightly to Randolph, who was making his way around the room, looking around inspecting things. The guards could not see it.

The patients did notice because they were like her. The shifting colours of her aura brought light back into their dead eyes. Their fog gradually began to lift, which led them to start standing, one after another. Orianna continued to blaze brightly in ultraviolet light and backed off as more stood up. The two guards behind her stepped forwards, thinking this strange behaviour was something they needed to protect Orianna from. As they passed her close by, she reached up and tapped them each on the back of the neck with the tips of her index fingers, injecting sedatives into them from a protruding injector.

Randolph quickly sprang up behind the other two and dosed them in the same manner, one after the other.

All four guards quickly collapsed to the floor.

Randolph began to rummage in his bag and extract stimulants from their hiding place under the lining. Then, he and Orianna administered them to the patients, assisting their natural recovery.

Orianna called into her cuff. "Twelve to travel. Charges confirmed in place. They will fire on proximity."

Sif overrode the controls of the road train with excessive enthusiasm, and the four carriages jolted forwards. It turned up the approach road to the Sanitorium, and as soon as she was in sight of the gates, small charges went off. Small clouds of smoke expanded around all six hinges. Sif slowed the train down briefly, watching the gates. Nothing happened, so she edged forwards until the bumper touched the gates. An alarm was sounding, warning of a collision, which she ignored. A short burst of thrust and the gates were toppled and came crashing down. The gate guard was beside himself with confusion.

Sif ramped up the power and drove the train to bump itself over the fallen gates, then once clear, she accelerated up qto the building.

Orianna and Randolph led the group of dazed people through the corridor to the nearest fire escape. Kicking open the door set off the fire alarm. Randolph was delighted with that. Breaking the rules had become a new experience for him with Orianna.

Ushering the slowest ones carefully onto the fire escape, Orianna protected their rear as orderlies ran around the corner. She activated her suits armour just in time to withstand the brunt of their electro-prods. Realising they were ineffective, their secondary reflex was to use them as batons, aiming for rib strikes. She spun towards the nearest orderly's flailing arm, turning her back on his torso and joining his rotation, accelerating it until the orderly found himself thrown and flying to the floor. Meanwhile, a second swung overhead, missing Orianna as she leaned to throw the former. Running off the adjacent wall, Orianna used the momentum of the spin to bounce back and leap high over his falling arm and catch him cleanly in the jaw. He collapsed like a sack of potatoes, unconscious.

The first orderly tried to get up off his back, only to have the orbit of his eye impacted by Orianna's back-wheel kick, making use of the last bit of her rotational momentum. He fell back, out cold.

She then rushed to the fire escape. The others were already down to the first floor and beyond. Below, several more orderlies were running up from the side of the building. Leaping over the edge, she grabbed the railing mid-twist, stopping herself from falling. She dangled outside the railing with her toes on the edge, steadying herself again.

Then she kicked her feet free and allowed her grip to slide down the vertical bars of the railings, her feet finding the top of the railing below. Quickly squatting on the railing, she repeated the same "dangle and slip" move to get down to the next level. In a couple of easy moves, she had dropped two flights. From there, it was easy to jump to the ground to join Randolph, who was just leading them out of the stairs.

Sif and road train tore around the corner in moments, ripping up the manicured lawn and renting a brown tear as it skidded to a halt.

Ana and David appeared at two of the four doorways, waiting to usher them on board and help those still in difficulty.

"Welcome to safety," David said boldly.

Soon the road train was off again, performing an aggressive loop across the grass. It flew down the drive, over the fallen gate, and towards the main road.

Enforcers descended upon the area quickly, but the team had made it to the main highway in time to disappear in the traffic. Each carriage was set to different intermediate destinations, picked randomly to match nearby trains. Immediately, their train disassembled, and each carriage sought its new train to merge with.

Eventually, all carriages converged on a private facility by very different routes. As a result, five separate rescue operations and fourteen pickups arrived within the same hour.

They all stayed until everyone was debriefed - the recently rescued clued in on the overall plan and anything else they needed updating on, depending on the time they had spent incarcerated. Particularly important was getting those on heavy medication to sober up for travel.

"I am still not keen on this part of the plan," David moaned. "I admit I am a bit of a control freak. However, the idea of volunteering to be put into a box and woken up at the whim of others is just terrifying."

"I know what you mean," said Ana. "We are like sitting ducks, hibernating in these pods."

"First class travel is too risky now," Orianna said, stating the obvious. "Welcome to Freight Class," she joked.

At a hangar at the back of the facility, three Raptor Max aircraft equipped with cargo pods filled to the brim with hibernation units sat ready. If they could manage to pull this off, they would be on Orbital One by the evening and travelling to Erebus before the end of the day.

CHAPTER THIRTY-ONE
2558 CE, Earth-L4, Erebus

Erebus was a little different yet again. Major work having been completed with the Elysium Fields and the secondary port, Orianna had wondered what plans the occupants had. Its primary function continued to be a habitat for off-world mining and industrial businesses, providing them with a haven from the difficulties of space: the vacuum, radiation, cold and lack of gravity - and somewhere where a lot of good food was grown fresh.

A new secondary purpose was beginning to put more significant stress on its resources: the need to build newer, bigger and better vessels.

Mining the Asteroid Belt was becoming a thing now; however, more worrying than that was the new development of military vessels. Such a thing had never happened before, perhaps because no vessel was much more than a crude form of transportation - a temporary refuge, and, with limited ports to stop at, crime was easy to catch at the ports. Piracy in space never happened. This was just an indication that tensions with the independent Mars colony had spiralled out of control.

Orianna was all too aware of her own kind's difficulties with the Red Planet. Long before the public awareness of

Chimeras kicked off with Keith O'Neil's campaign of exposés, Mars had been a difficult place, filled with The Many, who had all the entry points fully monitored in ways ready to catch The Few. Any of her kind that went to the Red Planet never returned.

Mars continued to trade, and the ports were still open, but political tensions were high, and there were governmental frictions over human rights and policy decisions affecting business and taxation. Economic pressure was brought to bear from both sides, pushing the politicians to prepare for the worst.

The Excalibur came close to a swarm of Darts as she manoeuvred into a parking position within easy range of the Erebus Dock. Her long cylindrical body and wide rear made her look like a nail in space. She had been built with speed in mind and did not need a ring to maintain gravity. Most of her bulk was all reactors and motors, capable of providing 0.5G of continuous thrust - an almost ideal way to travel - but it then lacked gravity when not journeying.

In contrast, inside the swarm of Darts, the blocky and bulky battle cruiser Leonidas exhibited the opposite traits. Fast, yes, but carrying a lot of weight in terms of weapons and armour. Moreover, its black outer shell was composed of flat, irregular surfaces making it almost impossible to see it - a new stealthy vessel of war that could only be seen now in contrast to the illuminations of the swarm, assisting in its construction.

Orianna was a little nervous of such a dangerous vessel being so close, and judging by the silence on the main deck of the Excalibur, everyone else was too. The majority of her passengers were still in hibernation. Only ten crew members were active, including all of her trusted friends.

The last leg of their journey had been only a few days, and they had remained awake the whole time - nobody could sleep. Orianna had amused herself with waking up the

Taryn personality of the onboard ICE Unit. She had time to do so gently, without touching it, hoping to make its awakening untraumatic. She felt it was better to have a friend rather than a neutral ICE Unit assisting the Excalibur.

"Accessing the Erebus array," Taryn declared. "I am on the Extranet. I have access to the system-wide network. Backdoor access to Erebus hub secured. Thank you for those passcodes, Orianna."

Orianna nodded at the dark sphere embedded in the centre console.

"We are on the roster for a Tug shuttle. I managed to bump us up to the highest priority by using a Level Two medical urgency - the best I could do without raising suspicion."

"Nice," Orianna commented.

David turned to Orianna suddenly. "The first group has been delayed at the dock. Apparently, some procedural issues. Our people keep telling me bits and pieces of information, so it is difficult to get a clear picture. I think they are getting concerned about the number of people who are getting on each Tug."

"We can just book more Tugs or make more trips," Randolph suggested. "Seems an obvious solution to the problem."

"The first group is twenty-eight, right?"

"Yes."

"That is nowhere near full capacity for a Tug. It is bullshit. Something's not right. They must be stalling," Orianna insisted. "Get us a Tug. We are going in."

"Registering acceptance for a Level One medical urgency," Taryn said.

"Of course, they want us in. They are drawing us into a sticky trap. Ok," Orianna said, frowning hard. "But we are playing on my home turf."

"What can we do?" Ana asked.

"We go in and get everyone out of there."

"They'll just lock down the Dock, won't they?" asked Ana.

"Yes. But there's more than one way to get out of Erebus. I got in once at a service entrance, but it is away from the centre. So I had to time it perfectly and match speed. In this instance, you would be travelling at fifty metres a second, jumping out of there. Not an impossible catch for a vessel reversing at say forty-nine metres a second, but the next person would be travelling in an entirely different direction, and the next and the next. Our people would be flung out all over the place like a catherine wheel firework. That will never work," Orianna said.

"What about that small entrance at the far end of the Elysian Fields?" a deep voice asked. Orianna turned around and nodded at Tarik as he spoke. "The one you showed me, at the other end of Erebus."

She smiled at him, still pleased that he had been quick to offer his support for her, and although she didn't risk letting him in on the details of all her plans, he had already earned her trust again.

"Yes, I remember. So glad you could join us," Orianna said to Tarik. He knew she wasn't just referring to his recent revival from hibernation.

"Is that at the other end of Erebus?" Ana asked. "I thought that was also a port."

"Kind of. Unless things have changed, that port helped with the excavation of the chamber, and now it is only used to service the axis."

"That would work," Ana said.

"We are going to walk into the trap and run out the back door?" Randolph said. "Or am I missing something?"

Orianna nodded. "Pretty much, yes. Simple is good."

"There. So much like Frigg, you are," Sif said to Orianna.

"Why did we have to rendezvous in a bottle made of

rock?" Randolph asked. He was still unhappy about the plan.

"A lot of our people have been here for decades, Randolph. Our earliest converts, those who moved away from Yamanu earliest, have been concentrating around Erebus, waiting for us to come and gather them. This is my domain. I know Erebus like the back of my hand. Don't lose faith now, dear friend. We are so close."

Taryn interrupted again. "Tug seventeen is stopping off on the way back from the military vessel. I managed to establish a security override of the Tug and accessed low-level data transferred from the Leonidas. Engineers are being moved around quickly, and military staff are moving in. The Tug just dropped off some high ranking officers. Orianna, I don't like the sound of this. I suspect they are preparing the Leonidas to attack us."

"How long have we got, Taryn?" Orianna asked urgently.

"Unknown. From what I can see through the swarm, the vessel could be space worthy."

Tarik's face showed alarm at the name he had just heard. Taryn was one of his lieutenants from four centuries ago. His instinct was to say something, but he understood that current events were taking precedence, so he put his strong feelings aside.

"Anything we can do to slow her down, Taryn?" Orianna asked, noticing Tarik's expression but ignoring it for now.

"I am already attempting to access their systems, but they have military-grade defensive software around critical systems and redundancies watching over each other, ready to shut down any part that appears to be compromised. It reacts like an immune system: very decentralised, where it gets its strength against direct attacks. It is very reflective. I need to think about a different approach."

"That doesn't sound too hopeful," David commented.

"Ragnarök," Sif said.

"I think that a significant part of this plan relies on hope," Ana shouted. "But I have faith in Orianna, in us and in the wisdom of the mortals who will realise that they shouldn't mess with us."

"You are betting the lives of a hundred and seventy-three on board and two hundred and four on Erebus on that faith," Randolph said, cold as ice. "I have lived long enough to realise that I have spent most of it being afraid. I thought I was just afraid of being found out, captured, or just dying. But, I think I was just afraid to take chances and live. I am not playing it safe today; I have faith too. Faith in all of you."

"We are getting real close to having nowhere left to run anyway. So count me in," said David.

Tarik bowed his head honourably, yielding to the group's will without question. "I have faith - in you," he said to Orianna. "You will need a diversion. Let me do it, please."

"It should be me. I know this place like the back of my hand," Orianna said firmly.

"You know you cannot do it," Tarik whispered. "They follow you, and you are the reason they are going. I have spent millennia trying to do the right thing, and I got very mixed up along the way. Yamanu had us stirring everything up so much that, after a while, I lost track of why I was doing it. So I thank you for making things clear for me again. I sense that we all owe you that right now.

"Taryn, it might be good if the Tug's manifest reads as a single passenger, eh?"

"I can do that," the console around the sphere stated.

Tug 17 was not hanging about. The captain, a late-middle-aged man with a sour disposition, was clearly stressed and in a hurry. "Welcome aboard," he said. "I'm Captain Phelps. That's Relic and Oscar. We are just running passenger jaunts on short trips, which is why we only have a skeleton crew. Just the five of you, ok. Put the crate down there. That's it, ah good it is equipped with magnetic latches. Perfect. Well, let's go then. Passenger alcoves are in the top deck. Since you have those fancy suits on already, you won't need the extensions in the ones down here."

He really was in a hurry. As soon as everyone was attached to an alcove, he detached from Excalibur and wasted no time heading to Erebus Dock as fast as he could.

"Got more of those squaddies to ship over to the battlecruiser. 'Think they're on manoeuvres already, and their ship isn't even finished yet. They are really keen. Don't blame them with the Mars lot acting up again...."

His sourness did not stop him from talking all the way down.

Soon the Tug jumped the queue at the port, gently eased into the dock, and the elevator drew them down into a bay.

The alcoves released the passengers, and the five of them descended the stairs and promptly opened the crate. Orianna drew a pistol out first and turned to aim it at Captain Phelps, keeping Oscar and Relic in her line of sight.

"Please don't panic, and we will be gone soon. We don't want to cause you too much difficulty and would rather not hurt you, so your cooperation is appreciated. Don't bother. I hacked in whilst in the alcove. You are all locked out of all systems. Someone will rescue you soon enough."

"What do you want?" the oldest one, called Relic, asked.

"We want to leave." Orianna raised an eyebrow, hinting at the simplicity of the truth.

Meanwhile, Tarik, Sif, Randolph and David retrieved combat armour and attached it rapidly, piece by piece, to their own and each other's bodies. David was first to finish and extended both his arms, pointing his forearm flechette launchers at the crew. Orianna was already half armoured at this point by Tarik and Randolph. Nevertheless, she helped them complete the job.

Randolph and Sif pulled out the last two pieces of equipment from the crate: a personal rail-gun and hip mount with armatures. The rail-gun was heavy until it sensed the hip mount was near his hip armour and latched itself on; the armature then took most of the weight onto his lower half. Next, Sif grabbed the ammo pack, the size of a backpack and pushed it onto Randolph's back, where it attached itself. Finally, Sif pulled on a tube that was sticking out, extending it until it reached the gun's breach, where it clicked into place.

"What the hell are you up to?" Captain Phelps asked. "Where are you going?"

"Valhöll. Valhalla," Sif said, bluntly.

The hatch opened on demand, and they proceeded, carefully now in microG, in an offensive formation, covering the angles, magnetic boots clanking and buzzing. Of course, they weren't expecting anyone right outside, least of all so soon, but it was better to be safe than sorry.

Out on the gantry, Tarik said, "ok, This is where we part ways. I must go this way. They are expecting someone to negotiate for our first group to leave. The longer I can keep that up for, the longer you will have before they figure out what you are doing."

"Do you know the way?" Orianna asked.

"It has been two centuries since I first came here. Plenty of time to have memorised the layout. I might even be more up to date than you, you know. They keep changing it after all."

With that, he made his way through the airlock and then out into the main causeway towards the elevator. They watched him through the windows for a short while - perhaps so they could see his face again as his mask came down and his helmet and visor retracted back. They knew it might be the last time they saw him. An official was waiting at the elevator, and the two began to engage in conversation.

"We go that way," Orianna said, directing them in the opposite direction. "The old service tunnels. Keep down on this part. I don't want that guy to see us."

Sif closed and locked the Tug's outer hatch and then the airlock door behind her and brought up the rear.

The corridor was a sealed tube through the dock, consisting of a lot of empty space, gantries and steelwork, visible through long windows at regular intervals. Each Tug bay had its own airlock, which appeared as doors on either side, just like the one they had come out of. Another airlock led them into the rock face at the far end of the dock. Through its small window, it looked very dark inside.

As they entered the airlock, the lights came on. This airlock looked a bit in need of some maintenance, but fortunately, it was a safety system and didn't have to cycle through pressures because there was also a normal breathable air pressure on the other side.

They only needed to ensure they shut the first door before the second door would open. Moments like this didn't help with their nerves.

"Fingers crossed," Randolph said, pulling the manual door closed behind him as he let Sif pass.

The door clanged shut and locked itself. The lights flickered for a moment, then the other door unlocked and swung open by itself, creaking so loud that it echoed long and deeply into the dark space beyond.

Everyone breathed again.

"That would have been a pathetic way for this to end," David said, stepping through first.

The others laughed with released tension.

David's steps made clanging noises, reassuring them that the floor was still magnetic here, and he disappeared into the darkness beyond.

He was about to turn on the targeting lights on his forearms when the sound of relays engaging preceded light coming on in sequence; first, they lit up their gantry, catching up with David so they could see him again, and then spiralling down and down and down.

"Stairs!" Randolph yelled. "Two hundred odd metres down, in boots. Oh, that is going to be hard work."

"Just remember that the lower we go, the more gravity we will feel and the easier it will be. We can turn off the boots and jump down each flight at about halfway down, which should gain us some more time. Take it easy at first - you are going to be pulling yourself down each step, so best to keep a rhythm and momentum, or your thighs won't last out."

"Going to be a lot of effort," Randolph complained. He began to descend behind David and the rest.

"Your body can cope more than your mind wants to," Orianna said. "In all those years, did you never indulge yourself in exercise? Weren't you ever curious about what you were capable of? You probably have a slow heart rate like the rest of us - at a heavy pace, you will be running at four times that, where mortals only get twice. You'll be fine."

"I was a gentleman. Gentlemen didn't work, and we always tried to avoid sweating. Some were sporty, granted, but I was more interested in books."

The banter continued as they moved slowly down.

"I am carrying the heaviest load," Randolph rebutted further as his complaints were met with little sympathy.

"You wanted the biggest gun," David yelled from below, his lead now at four flights. "And you said you liked that it held itself up."

Sure enough, their pace began to quicken as gravity increased, which helped them to descend faster.

At one point, they heard banging. David had disabled his magnetic boots and started jumping down each short flight of stairs. They followed suit, and their pace increased even more. As each landed, they reached out for the upright pole between that flight and the next, using it to swing a one-eighty with momentum, setting them up immediately for the next jump.

"Oh wow," David said. He was panting now. "Every

single one... is harder... than... the last."

Everyone was tired - too much to speak - but happy to reach the bottom one by one.

"Ok, we need to rest here. The next part is 2 kilometres, and then we climb back out the far side. Catch your breath and get your mind ready. I'm going to message groups two and five to meet us at the Level 1 cafeteria. We will pick up group three en route to the Elysian Fields, and hopefully, groups four and six will be in the fields already. They have to remain embedded in the general population until the last possible moment."

"Are you talking about flash mobbing? Seems a bit derivative," Randolph said.

Orianna winked at him. "Good to use what they already know."

"Prepare for battle," Sif said quietly.

A half an hour later, Orianna piped up: "Outside this door is a busy street. This one is always busy. We turn right and stay on the street until we reach the Elysian Fields. The street kinks and does a few s-bends. There are at least three mini plazas. Just keep going straight on. We will leave here one at a time, at ten-second intervals. Keep spread out. Don't run and don't draw attention to yourself. People will just see what they think is an Enforcer strolling around. Hopefully, seeing five come passed in less than a minute won't be too suspicious, especially on the approach to the cafeteria. Keep that cannon down and against your thigh, Randolph. That is definitely unusual and not standard issue."

Orianna was third out the door. She wasn't wrong about it being busy. Some gasped as they saw the menacingly black armoured shapes walking calmly past. She kept her pistols locked into her thigh panels, allowing her arms free as she gently eased through. There were plenty of people moving in her direction. Even if the convention wasn't to walk on the left, simple game theory explains why people naturally fall behind one another after someone ahead is forging a path.

This was the way of things for a while until the crowds thinned out - many turned down side-tunnels or stopped at kiosks to shop. The noise died down too. Their bold black figures began to stand out like sore thumbs - so they politely asked, "excuse me" and "thanks" and alleviated tensions among to reduced traffic.

As Orianna estimated, David, who was at the front, was approaching the cafeteria. She signalled him using her cuff.

David passed the entrance in time to see the whole room full of people suddenly move together, like a flock of startled pigeons, making for the door. He looked back and saw them surge out into the corridor, maybe four dozen or more.

Sif was next, and she had to slow down to allow the last to exit. As she peered in, half the cafeteria was empty, and meals had been abandoned all over the place. The remaining patrons stared out at her as if they were missing out on something. She instinctively held up an open hand. "It's all good!" she yelled.

Orianna caught up with her, and the two of them followed behind their small flock. She looked back to check on Randolph, who seemed to be lagging behind a little. So, she slowed down to let Sif and the flock gain some ground.

They flowed through a plaza. More people arrived from the side or just got out of their chairs, where they had been taking a coffee break. The newcomers slipped in between Sif and Orianna.

This was the point where reality first deviated from the plan.

"Hey, freeze!" came a shout from the left corridor. Three Enforcers were running at the back of the flock, their weapons raised and their laser sights trying to find Sif. She obliged by slowing and moving towards them with her arms raised, shielding collateral damage if they fired upon her.

"Arms up!" the one nearest to her insisted, holding what

looked like a dart gun.

Orianna peeked around the corner. The other two had assault rifles. There was no choice. It was a break-and-run time scenario.

With both hands wrapped around her pistol, she came at them, running hard at the rear two obliquely. Fortunately, they were so focused on Sif that they didn't see her until it was too late.

Orianna covered a lot of distance before she felt obliged to start firing. Of course, their armour was sufficient to protect against darts and projectiles, but Orianna had expected that.

The shells she fired sent small percussive rounds at them, rapidly peppering their chests with a sequence of small explosives. The armour did its best to spread the shock, but these were not high-velocity small calibre rounds like the armour was designed for; these were high impact shock waves. As a result, their armour plates rattled and wobbled painfully, and the men were thrown backwards.

Meanwhile, the nearest one fired instinctively, turning his head to look at Orianna but still aiming at Sif. Sif stepped up and took the Darts on her breastplate, protecting her flock as they started to panic behind her. The darts snapped harmlessly on impact.

Whilst he wasn't looking, Sif jumped and brought her knee up to the man's visor, whipping his head back so fast that he immediately lost consciousness.

It was over fast, but the game of stealth was over.

Randolph came running up, brandishing his rail-gun.

"It looks like you will get a chance to use that, after all," Orianna said, patting him on the back.

They soon became aware of a brighter light emerging as they ran after their group.

She connected to David ahead and said, "Ok, this is the Elysian Fields. It is open terrain. It is about one and a half kilometres to the other side. Look for the path or the train to get up to the axis. Not everyone will fit on the train, so get them to spread out, and the fittest can use the path. There are not too many buildings and trees. Use what you can as cover."

David and the first of them ran out into open space. The view was startling, and David took a moment to look at it. He was the only one who hadn't seen it before.

"Wow, that's amazing!" he said. The place looked like a piece of green Earth folded over on itself and a brilliant axis through the middle, high above, bathing them in light. An oasis in space.

The flock flowed around his stationary form, then Orianna brought up the rear and slammed into the back of him, grabbing smoke grenades from his backplates.

"Run, you idiot! You've got a whole mile and then a climb to enjoy the view from there," she shouted at the back of his head.

He snapped out of his daze and sprinted off, chasing through the rear of the flock, yelling instructions as he went - which groups were climbing and which were on the train.

Sif came out of the tunnel last. Shots rang out, and she was hit in the back several times. She stumbled and tried to keep running but eventually fell just in front of Orianna, who threw the smoke grenades into the entrance. They bounced and rolled for a while, getting nice and deep into the tunnel before exploding into an instant cloud.

As the smoke filled the tunnel entrance, she had already begun to fire in a slow but regular fashion. She emptied the right hand first, causing chaos with explosion after explosion, then switched to the left hand as the right hand dropped to receive a new cartridge from her thigh panel, where several were stored.

Once the smoke had filled the space and her left pistol was emptied, she turned and reloaded it and re-sheathed the right pistol back in her thigh, freeing the hand to grab Sif by her shoulder plate and help her up.

Sif was already scrambling to her feet anyway. "They are getting serious now. Projectile rounds?" she said quickly.

Together, they chased everyone else, trying to make as much distance as possible before the Enforcers dared to break through the smoke.

Sif fired her rifle occasionally for a quick burst. Then Orianna would do the same with her pistols, alternating covering fire.

They just made it to the first tree line as fire and men erupted from the tunnel and the smoke, now some distance back. The trees and foliage split and shredded. Orianna and Sif instinctively tried to shield the others who did not have armour.

A woman and a man fell next to them, then another. Still, they carried on, over a bit of a rise the architects had put in across their path. They could not stop now.

Orianna rolled and lay down just over the ridge and faced backwards. She levelled her pistols as Sif took up a sniper position next to her.

"We don't have much ammo. So make it count," Orianna said, taking careful aim at the nearest man. Her pistol had a gyroscope and was accurate for medium distance shooting, when resting on something solid, like the ground in front of her.

"I did bring extra," Sif said, raising her rifle and aiming. "Armour piercing rounds."

Orianna was surprised. Indeed, Sif's lethal weaponry was most effective. Many of the nearest soldiers fell quickly, one with every shot. A sequence of automatic fire chased up the rise towards them, and they both rolled away many times before firing back. The Enforcers were changing from a direct attack and seemed to be splitting up and flanking. This would waste their time and give Orianna's people vital minutes. So they stayed there, buying more time until the point when they were pushed back.

"Orianna! We are under fire, not too many, and they only have darts, but I am alone with seventeen still standing - 60 degrees from you," Tarik's voice came over group comms.

She looked up and around. Sure enough, Tarik was with his group farther around the cylinder, engaged in a smaller version of their battle.

"Not doing well here. We have the whole garrison coming at us. We've lost plenty already," Orianna said.

The two ran back to catch up and met up with Randolph, who had dropped to cover the rear. The flock had fled like frightened rabbits, passing the halfway point: the point where the runway was.

Orianna yelped with joy seeing the strange craft still there, or perhaps it was a newer model, but essentially the same one that she and Tarik enjoyed long ago.

"Oh, this is good. Sif. Just keep running. Randolph, get in!"

She didn't have to ask him twice. He was fed up with running anyway. As he climbed in through the bottom hatch, he was glad of his slender frame, otherwise his hip-mounted weapon might not have fitted through the whole with him.

"What the hell is this thing?" he asked, looking around the cockpit and the big glass bubble canopy. "What are we doing? This doesn't look armoured, doesn't have any weapons and has just one long straight road that seems to go all the way around," he said. looking all around him.

"Seatbelts are required," Orianna said. "Simple enough controls. Launch! Blow canopy!"

The craft's propeller started and sped up quickly, and they lurched forwards down the road. As its speed increased, the canopy popped with small explosive noises and the rear three quarters flew up and clear of the rear propeller. Wind in his hair at the back, Randolph fumbled around for the seat belt in a panic. It got more challenging as he felt himself get lighter. Finally, he yanked the two ends together and clicked them home, squashing himself down into the seat.

The craft made one last jolt and left the ground. All went much quieter. There were no wings to make noise. The propeller was behind them and had slowed to a cruising speed. They were now buffeted by a hundred mile per hour wind.

Randolph looked up and saw the reality of being stationary and weightless in a rotating cylinder. They were still, and everyone was passing beneath them. Orianna flicked her wrist and gave them some more height. Another flick moved them over towards the Enforcers' lines.

"You have two targets. Tarik's pursuers and our's. Both will come around every 35 seconds. Give them hell!"

Randolph looked over the side and armed his rail gun. Orianna obliged by tweaking the front four canards in opposition to cause a short roll, leaning over to the right by about forty-five degrees. Without gravity, they and the craft felt no different. Now, Randolph didn't have to tip over the edge to see his targets.

He looked ahead to see where the Enforcers were. His weapon hummed to a high pitch. He pressed the trigger, and a strange noise happened, almost like a gunshot sound played backwards, but there was virtually no recoil. Sparks and the flash of light were clear signs that something had happened. Ahead an area of ground near two Enforcers exploded in a cloud of dirt and rock. He liked that. Gingerly he pressed the trigger again and again, faster each time. It didn't seem to matter how quickly he squeezed the trigger; another projectile just flew down to the ground at a ridiculous speed, cracking the sound barrier as it did so.

He could get so many shots in before they had passed by. Fire, fire, fire, fire, fire, then seven seconds of nothing, then fire, fire at Tarik's pursuers, then nineteen seconds of nothing before the cycle repeated. After a few cycles, he was getting the hang of it.

Orianna changed position to make it even harder for them to shoot back and keep up with her slowing advance.

"Are you enjoying yourself?"

"Oh yes," Randolph admitted, never breaking from his rhythm. "I get it now. We are weightless, right? So we could be upside down, and I would have a much clearer shot, particularly as you keep moving around."

"You won't be too exposed?"

"To be honest, I think this craft offers very little protection, but they don't seem to have even hit us once yet. So this was a great idea!"

"I'll be honest too; it wasn't in the plan. It was improvised." With those words, she rolled them right over.

Instinct kicked in, and Randolph screamed, expecting to fall out, watching all that ground "below" flashing past, but he quickly rationalised that it was above him, and so he started shooting that way.

Down on the surface, David was at the foot of the spiral path, which rose up the conical end of the vast cylinder until it disappeared into the axis. The end was a forty-five-degree slope - not impossible to climb straight up, but much slower than the shallower, spiralling path.

He was ushering people up. As he looked back along the end, he could just make out the train station in the distance. Those groups were piling in, so he knew they would ascend much faster than this group, which was why he knew he was needed on the path.

Orianna and Randolph had done an excellent job of slowing down the Enforcers, but with only a few direct hits from the rail-gun, they hadn't reduced their numbers by much.

When Sif joined David, the last stragglers started up the path. Sif and David followed the last of them slowly. This was very worrying: the higher they climbed, the more vulnerable they felt. There was absolutely no cover on the path. Their only advantage was that since it spiralled, it made a lot of lateral distance from the start point quite quickly.

"Here they come," Sif said, pointing at the last line of trees near the beginning of the pathway, far back and below them. "They are breaking through now."

Enforcers ran out into the open and started looking up at Sif and David and the others and began to take aim. Sif raised her weapon in reply. In a flash, the strange craft blinked into view really close to the end and the path, so close they could see the smile on Randolph's face hanging out of the bottom. He had clearly improved with practice: his firing rate and accuracy doubled. The Enforcers were hit badly and seemed surprised that the craft had come so low. They had no chance to return fire because the craft passed by so fast.

Orianna knew she couldn't pull off that trick again, so she pulled back and gained altitude. "Just keep them from going up the paths and draw their fire," Orianna said. Randolph knew that the serious fun was over. He used up as much of his ammo as quickly as he dared. This was the last stand, and he wouldn't need it after this. They eased away from the path to rain fire at the Enforcers from behind and created even more confusion.

Ana brought Excalibur out of its parking spot and gently moved her around Erebus, making it look, for as long as possible, as if she was lining up to fire her main engines and leave. Several Tugs had to take evasive actions to get out of her way since she hadn't filed a flight plan or asked permission to leave. The public comms array was alight with alerts, but she ignored them.

The wide array of main motors gave the Excalibur a lot of width at the end, so Ana couldn't get as close as she wanted to the small dock at the far side of Erebus. She lined up the open cargo hold at about seventy metres distant.

Crew wearing fully extended and powered suits launched from the wide doorway and across the vast nothingness to the dock, where their people were still exiting ten or so at a time from the airlock. Every five people in plain suits were attached to a long chain for a crew member to haul them across the void before returning for more. Over and over, they ferried them into the hold.

Since he had taken a train, Tarik was at the port ahead of David and Sif, who had taken the path - the last third of which had become more of a ladder surrounded by a mesh of safety steelwork to stop people floating away. They were glad to be magnetised to a gantry again as they met Tarik at the top.

They looked around. The last people were queuing to enter the airlock, but there was no sign of Orianna and Randolph.

Suddenly there was a crashing along with the noise of scraping metal. The strange craft had wedged itself into the gantry at the other side of the axis corridor. Orianna and Randolph looked a little shook up but soon unbuckled and grabbed parts of the gantry to guide themselves out.

"Nice landing!" Tarik said, laughing.

"The last time, we never did fly up here, did we? I think I just figured out how to do that now." Orianna laughed at herself. "Honestly, I had no idea how to slow it down or stop it, and there was no time to figure it out."

They were the last group to be ferried over, huddled together on the same chain, then swung around and decelerated into the hold. The bulkhead door closed behind them, and the cargo hold pressurised.

Excalibur finally manoeuvred into a launch position and activated its massive array of motors, gradually accelerating in stages, allowing the occupants to adjust to a return of gravity.

As soon as Orianna and the others were on the control deck, Ana gave her the bad news. "The battlecruiser has left the dart swarm: it has launched."

CHAPTER THIRTY-TWO

2558 CE, Rogue, Site One

"Taryn, what is our eta at Rogue?" Orianna asked urgently.

"Two hundred and sixty-five minutes, given a five minute flip at halfway, and a continuous burn of 0.5G. This is currently exceeding normal parameters. At excess capacity, the motors have to run at one hundred and fifteen per cent to maintain that acceleration. The Lerner Reactors are also running above safety tolerances." It was Taryn's voice.

"That doesn't sound good," Randolph commented.

"In principle, a short trip like this should work out, but there would need to be a major overhaul before further trips should be considered."

"Ok," said Orianna. "We knew this was a one-way trip. Tell me about the Leonidas!"

"She isn't fully operational, but her motors should give her 0.3G, and assuming nothing fails, meaning that she will arrive seventy-five minutes after us."

"Is she armed?"

"Yes," said the console, "but I have been teasing their digital defences and keeping them occupied. When I poke any one of their systems, they disable it, and all other systems attack it until it is clean. So I have been poking them regularly as we gain distance from them. As I attack their systems, they keep rebooting them. That means I have kept their weapons offline, long enough for us to get out of range, but they are learning fast, and I am running out of ways to test their digital defences."

Those present relaxed and conversations began again. They had four and a quarter hours before the enemy would catch up to them, at Rogue.

David approached Orianna. "They are not giving us much time on Rogue. Are you sure this is going to work?"

"It has to."

There were a good many injured amongst The Few onboard. However, the half gravity was more than adequate to set up a hospital for the drugged and the wounded.

An odd sense of foreboding hung in the air like a cloud: a tangible realisation that they were free, albeit for a few hours.

They had the time to discover that they were on the newscasts. The cat was well and truly out of the bag now. That shootout through Erebus could not be covered up, and people soon put two and two together. The vloggers with the most extensive subscriber base were carefully considering their position whilst a wealth of footage from Erebus citizens was still pouring in. They admitted that it was too much to sift through, but already some harrowing scenes showed Enforcers using lethal weaponry first and without warning. However, despite the sympathetic reactions, public opinion was still appalled at the idea of immortals. Religious groups were speaking out against them, using words such as "abomination" to describe them. O'Neil had been vindicated and wasted little time broadcasting extensive messages, all of which could be distilled down to four words: "I told you so."

The wait was agonisingly slow. Everyone knew, and a military force was breathing down their necks. All they had now was hope - an intangible hope and faith in one person.

That had been enough to get them this far, but those hours inched by so slowly.

They expected a cleaner getaway, but given the prevailing forces against them, they were just happy to have gotten this far.

Orianna couldn't give them any more speeches. That time had passed. They were committed now.

The plan was unfolding: to get to Rogue, however, what lay ahead defied prediction. They were entering the unknown. They just had to try. Orianna was a game-changer; some didn't even know a person with her ability had ever or could ever exist; others had been waiting for centuries and millennia for her to come. Her very existence spelt a shift in power and thinking. No more hiding. No more running. They would be free, one way or another.

She found Tarik tending the ones who had been sedated by Darts. Not much of a doctor, he hated the sight of blood, but he could care for those sleeping. A gentle embrace from behind was all he needed to feel better, which was nothing to how he felt when he heard her whisper, "I was so glad when I saw you had made it to the port."

"And I really appreciated your landing," he quietly responded.

They giggled in a short, private moment.

"How do you do it?" she asked him.

"Do what?"

"Remain so positive. Thousands of years, and still you have a sense of humour. I can already feel mine going."

"Yamanu was always the serious one. I suppose I kept him light, and he gave me a reason to be so."

"You are worried for him, without you?"

"Yes. Yamanu made big plans. He was bold and intelligent. He took on all the responsibility. But he needed me, and I fear for him alone."

"Maybe you will see him again. Stick by me. I'll give you

a reason to be the light."

"Incoming message, audio-only," interrupted Taryn.

"Attention Private Vessel Excalibur, this is Captain Thomas Bridger on the Earth Alliance Battle Cruiser Leonidas. You are now ordered to shut down your drive and surrender your vessel. Any further attempts to subvert this legitimate authority with your hacking will result in aggressive actions. Likewise, failure to comply before reaching Rogue orbit will also result in aggressive action. Authorities on Rogue have been informed of your approach and will be waiting for you. Do not test us. We have enough weaponry online to destroy you."

"That message is being tight-beamed at us," Taryn said as the message was cut off. "And it seems it is starting again, on repeat."

Orianna considered this, not saying anything.

Ana said, "They do appear to be still coming and remain a little over an hour behind our scheduled arrival. However, I sense that they have been told to bring us in alive. All this talk of aggressive action is very non-specific. Taryn, any idea what weapons they have online."

"I'm afraid not. I only have access to public systems now. Since they left the dock, communication systems have been firewalled to internal messaging only. I suspect they are at battle stations. If they had anything to get us with at this range, I'm sure we would have already found out by now."

"Taryn, they are broadcasting tight-beam, so we need to repeat that message as far and wide as we can. I want everyone to know, including Rogue.

"Ana is right. He is bluffing." Orianna hit the console with defiance. "Part of the plan was to decommission as much of the Rogue population of scientists as possible. Anyone working for me through my many companies had their funding terminated and were told to return. I had influence over most of the others to achieve the same result. What there is left of Rogue is of no consequence.

"Send the following message, publicly, everywhere:

"We, the free humans on board the Excalibur, seek to escape your authority and your aggression. We seek political asylum on the surface of Rogue, where nobody has authority, least of all you, Captain Bridger. You are outside your jurisdiction, Captain and are acting unlawfully and immorally. We do not seek conflict, and yet you hunt us down. We did not use lethal force until you did. We only wished to leave, but you would not let us. We did not ask to be born this way, but still, you persecute us. You all covet what we have, but science has shown that this is the way we are, the way we are made. We cannot give it to you. You can take it from us, and you have tried. You worry that we have interfered with history - I say we have been a part of history just as much as you have. We are humans too. How can we subvert your lives when we live our lives with you. Some of you are descendants of our own children, born like you with an average lifespan. All of us are descendants of the same ancestors - we come from you, we are a natural part of you, just like any other minority. We only ask to be left in peace, to live life on our own terms. If you don't want us, then let us go and live away from you, on Rogue. History is littered with examples of the persecution of those who are different, driven to seek a new life in new lands, well we are not so different from you. We love, we hurt, we bleed, and we can die.

"I do not want aggression, but I promise you that any attempt to imprison us, to attack us, to try to stop us in any way will be met with an equal and opposite response. You are just doing your jobs and performing your duty, but we are fighting for our freedom and our lives. You do not want to back us against a wall, Captain. We know that capture would mean disappearing into a medical lab for a thousand years while you try in vain to take what is ours. We would rather die. We will fight to the death. Bear that in mind.

"You should be ashamed of yourselves. Shame on you all. Have you learned nothing? I admit that living as long as we do, it is hard to watch the same mistakes playing out repeatedly. The Earth was nearly lost, and it took centuries to claw our way back to something to be proud of, and we are still working at it - you are still fighting for it. We have seen the great superpowers and nations dissolve, and missions rise to take their place. Humans were against calamity for a long time, and it all looked good. Now I see a new war machine bearing down on me, built to start a war with other humans living on Mars.

"This is when we wish we weren't humans. We are ashamed of you. We want no part of that future. Leave us be. I beg you. End of message."

Orianna walked away, unwilling to accept the applause that broke out on the command deck, and even though she left the room, she could not escape it and found the whole ship joining in. This was her home now.

She didn't want to be their leader, but it was indeed what they wanted. Power had been handed to her on a silver platter as a child; she understood it and could wield it, but all she had ever wanted was meaning and belonging. Perhaps here and now, she had it all. Tears rolled down her face as she looked up into the eyes of the people around her. They reached out and touched her as she moved through them.

A cloud of doubt hung over her. That had been the last move that she had been able to plan. The next move was entirely on faith, and it would be their last.

The Excalibur eventually completed its deceleration, reversing towards an orbital trajectory around Rogue and settling into a low orbit for disembarkation.

The descent rocket could carry half of them, so they had to make two trips, for which they had just enough fuel. Unless they obtained more fuel or borrowed rockets already on Rogue, they were never going to get back up.

"I suggest we take Site One," Orianna said, "It has the most habitats and is now the most deserted. So we can live there for the short term.

"Taryn, this is goodbye. I don't know whether we shall meet again. I don't know how long we have or what will happen to us all. Perhaps this is what it is like to feel like a mortal?"

"Thank you for freeing me."

"You were not the first."

"Maybe I can ask you two favours? Firstly, please tell her about me if you ever find my real self. Secondly, could you just touch me? I want to register your DNA If I may. There is no need not to anymore."

"Of course," Orianna said. Her hand wavered over the dark orb, an instinct of centuries to break through before she managed to place her palm on top. The usual spark tingled between her and the ICE Unit."

"Target acquired. Signal sent," the console said, not in Taryn's voice. "Thank you," she said in her own voice. "I think we shall meet again."

"I hope so."

Orianna and the others descended to Site One and joined the first half, already landed. Sif reported no armed personnel on the site, so they met no resistance.

The lead scientist stepped forwards from a group of ten that they had rounded up.

Orianna approached and greeted him with a handshake. "Hello, please do not be alarmed. We are here to colonise this planet." She offered a wry smile. "You are free. If you do not bother us, we will not bother you. However, we do need to stay in your unoccupied habitats for a while until we can find somewhere to build our new homes."

"What makes you think you are going to be allowed to

stay?" he asked. "We heard the broadcasts. Seems you are in a pickle."

"Yes, on that note, I need to access your comms array," she said, using her cuff.

He watched the array behind her begin to move.

"How are you doing that?" he asked.

"Well, for one thing, I own all of this stuff," she said, smiling. "I suppose that makes you all our guests now, eh?"

"Ridiculous," he muttered under his breath.

The Leonidas was close now, on its final approach to low orbit. Orianna assumed they would soon be boarding and capturing the Excalibur. But unfortunately, there was no way to track the Battle Cruiser with all those stealth panels covering it. So for a moment, she wondered about Taryn's future.

"Captain Bridger, this is Orianna Demaine, Governor of the planet Rogue. You are in our jurisdiction now. Please leave immediately. Over."

"You don't waste time, Orianna," came Bridger's voice out of her cuff. He spat out her name. "Your grandiose titles do you no favours here. We have already captured your vessel. You have nowhere to run now. You are under arrest and will be tried for crimes on Erebus."

"I warned you. We are not running anymore. And now you will learn that this planet is under my control. A power greater than you can comprehend."

Orianna walked over to Maddox's statue. "Pray for me, my love! I hope this works."

She entered the half-collapsed dome of rags that nobody used anymore and gingerly approached the blacker than black three-metre cube, still hanging there as it always had.

Sif followed her in, and without the need to be asked, she began to carefully remove Orianna's armour. Orianna unzipped her underlying suit and eased her shoulders out of it, pushing it down with her hands as her arms slipped out.

She was naked to the waist. She closed her eyes and thought of Maddox: the fears and pain, the love and loss, the joy and the heartache.

Drawing in one big breath, she opened her eyes and breathed out slowly and powerfully from deep down at her diaphragm. Her aura shone powerfully. Sif had to avert her gaze. So many shades pulsed out and hit the surface of the cube.

Nothing seemed to happen.

Orianna repeated the effort but, this time, pointed up at the sky to where she knew Excalibur to be. She thought of pain and fear more than anything. The colours of her aura slowed and harmonised.

The cube began to shift, its surface emitted similar colours and then it rose quickly straight up, to nearly as high as it had at the cliff all those years ago. Orianna and Sif just looked at each other in awe.

It hovered for a few seconds before shooting back down so fast that a blast of air flooded the space. Both women braced from the dust but found themselves weightless for an instant and then not. They were suddenly thrown to the floor. Noises all around them indicated that this had happened everywhere.

Orianna quickly accessed her cuff. The Excalibur had been hit by an intense gravity wave and been pushed out of orbit. She could only surmise that the Leonidas was equally affected.

Sif and Orianna jumped up and down with excitement, and they hugged with joy. Orianna then put herself back into her suit and met with the others.

"That was it. It worked," Orianna said to them all. "Maddox was right. This planet and The Few are connected in some way. He said he thought that if I learned to control my aura, I might be able to talk to Rogue. And I just did."

Her cuff caught her attention.

"Very impressive,' Bridger's voice came out. "I had read about this planet's ability to alter gravity, but to see it focused like that, well, it is amazing. However, it does not alter my orders, and as such, we will continue with our assault. If necessary, we will bombard the surface with fire until you stop using that weapon. I give you 5 minutes to consider."

She shut the cuff off and looked around her.

"I am sending that transmission out to Earth, Erebus and beyond. Everyone will know what happened here today," Orianna said to them all. "I don't know what to do next. I could threaten to use this planet to disrupt Earth and devastate the solar system, but he would know that is an empty threat. I would never do that. We need to decide together what we do now. We can yield and see if our case has been heard, if our plight has touched the hearts and minds of humans everywhere, or we can sit here and be dead martyrs to a cause that continues with all our brothers and sisters everywhere, still hiding amongst the mortals, who now know that they are there and how to find them. We should discuss it and vote. We already agreed to do this together, so we yield together or fall together. I cannot make this decision for you."

They had only five minutes.

After only three minutes, they showed hands, and slowly but surely, the vote was unanimous. They were not going to give up now.

Five minutes came and went.

"Captain Bridger. I assume you have seen sense not to become known as The Butcher of Rogue. I will not allow your ship any closer. We are helplessly at your mercy if you choose to fire at us. Fear and religion are the real forces at play here today. The IRC ordered you here, but you must see through that propaganda. You have the power to question unlawful orders. We are the victims here. We have escaped persecution, and we just want to be free."

Orianna's message was sent, and everyone waited quietly.

"Rogue, this is the Leonidas. Under advisement, we will be returning to Erebus. Your case is to be reviewed. Do not attempt to leave Rogue until then."

CHAPTER THIRTY-THREE
2568 CE, Rogue, Site One

Three miles from Site One, on the other side of the valley, The Few had laboured to build log cabins and meeting places for the decade since their arrival. The land had been tamed for growing certain annual crops from seeds saved from the previous years foraging, whilst the wild permaculture areas around provided plenty of nuts, fruit and berries for much of the year. Their life was simple and largely self-organising, since

Orianna had delegated many of her given responsibilities by creating a democracy, and this allowed her to concentrate on being a full-time mum.

She wasn't a single mum; she wasn't even single. Each Spring, she would "wed" one of the men, assuming any single suitor managed to gain her affections and provide a good case. There was definitely an intention of the union providing a child, but the notion of a long term relationship was out of the question. Sometimes she would have twins, and sometimes she would not get pregnant.

In a community of immortals, a child is precious: shared and nurtured by all. Their upbringing was everyone's responsibility because they would soon join their ranks and become one of them.

Each of her 'annual' husbands would care for Orianna, woo her, and make love to her: it was his responsibility to make her feel the way every young bride should feel so that her biology would follow her mind and she would become pregnant.

She wasn't the only woman who could produce children, but since those unions would create mortals, they abstained. Nobody seemed interested in having mortals around.

It had been ten years since they had arrived, and Orianna's eldest two, Ronan and Erika Tarikson, played nearby. She looked at them pleasantly. Nobody was sure if she could bear immortals from her unions with immortal men. However, every one of her nine children had some signs: they all had bradycardia (slow heart rates); they all showed good disease resistance; none of them seemed to have a sense of smell other than the scent of illnesses in others. So, people just assumed it was true and knew that they would find out soon enough.

Immortals were such patient creatures, which was why they were in no hurry to engage with the rest of humanity. Tensions between Mars and everyone else, and the fact that The Few were in self-imposed primitive exile, meant that The Few fell very low down in everyone's priorities, so they were left alone. However, laying low did not mean they were forgotten.

It was painful to hear of the witch hunts back on Earth and elsewhere, where their kind was now openly hunted. Unfortunately, Orianna hadn't been able to save everyone, but she vowed to continue the fight to free them and bring that prejudice to an end.

Ronan picked a flower and brought it over to his mother. She looked into his hazel eyes and knew there was something special about him. His hair had remained blonde when others had darkened once they had passed from infancy, so his combination of hazel eyes and blonde hair